Radicle

Radicle

*fantasy stories
by debut authors*

Metaphorosis Library Collection

edited by
B. Morris Allen

ISBN: 978-1-64076-289-3 (e-book)
ISBN: 978-1-64076-290-9 (paperback)
ISBN: 978-1-64076-291-6 (hardcover)

from
Metaphorosis Publishing

Neskowin

Contents

From the Editor

The *Metaphorosis Library Collection* arose from a conversation with a Metaphorosis author who is also a librarian, and is initially intended to suit library needs. When a reader comes in and says, "Hey, do you have any SFF stories by this type of author?" here they are! But of course, the books are available to any reader.

A radicle is the embryonic root of a plant, the barest hint of what will eventually become a strong, well established support structure. Differently spelled, 'radical' can mean either 'relating to roots' or 'new, drastically different, or a little wild'. The stories in this volume fit all those definitions.

This volume collects fantasy stories by **debut** authors — writers for whom this is the first story they published, sold, sold at a semi-professional rate, or all three at once! As with any growing seedling, you're seeing these authors at the very start of their careers; they've just barely dug in, and we should all be watching for them to continue to grow and spread and provide shelter and fruit for all of us for years to come. For now, come and enjoy their very first sprouting!

B. Morris Allen
1 July 2024

A Wielder Does Not Know Regret

Katherine Karch

You are walking down a winter road that carves a gentle arc through a forest of hemlock and fir. Somewhere, a brook flows along icy banks, the soft murmur of its waters slipping between wide trunks and snow-bent branches. In your hand, a folded square of paper with the following:

A request for the services of a Wielder. Take the western road from the Citadel. Do not look ahead. Do not look behind. Do not lose yourself.

Quantum variations of the message's meaning swirl upon the paper, marking its authenticity. You fold it closed, hold it tightly in your hand.

From somewhere close to the road a songbird chirps a high, two-toned note. *Phee-bee.*

The sound elicits a smile. You stop walking, head tilted toward the tiny creature, and wield. The world bends around awareness, time slowing until it is like cool honey dripping from the comb of consciousness.

Pheeeeeeeeeeee —
beeeeeeeeeeee.

Eternity spirals outward, and in the endlessness of *now*, every possible variation of the bird's greeting is a joy. Delighted, you release the moment. Time flows freely once again.

A curtain of clouds is sliding into view over the treetops to the west. Their grey tones hint at snow. Barely visible behind them, the sun hangs upon a notably low zenith, and even as you hold your mind in stillness of now, nature's rhythms ebb and flow in the biology of your body. A gentle hunger tugs for attention.

It is midday.

Beside the road, a fallen pine lies blanketed in a powdery layer of snow that brushes cleanly from the rough corrugations of its bark. This is a good spot to sit and eat.

The pack you set between your feet is filled with items that invite speculation. With hunger as an anchor, though, it is safe to explore its contents. A blanket roll; wool shirt, pants, and socks. A hunting knife with a keen edge and a worn grip. A small measuring device of tarnished brass with the letters *L*, *R*, and *P* etched into one corner of the dull metal. You pull it from the pack, turn it over in your hands, set it aside.

In a folded square of linen you find several morel mushrooms. Their rich flavor sharpens the hunger in your belly, but a second folded square of linen yields a sizable cash of salted groundnuts.

There is a palm-sized book in the pack as well. Its leather cover is inscribed with the title, *Poems*. You glide your thumb along the soft and fuzzy edges of the book's pages. Words shape and stack themselves upon the paper, but you do not read them. Instead, you tuck the book back into the folds of the pack. It feels right to not spoil their undifferentiated state of totipotence.

The measuring device is cold now from lying on the ground. You use it to check the height of the sun's journey. Today, it says, is winter's solstice. The turning of the year.

With a fistful of snow, you chill the blade of the knife, draw it across your forearm alongside five matching scars. The pain anchors you, tethers you to the present, makes it possible to look beyond its boundaries, to see–if only briefly–how long it has been since you chose to become a Wielder.

Six years. There is a pinching in your chest that feels like sadness. Then, it is gone.

A strip of linen deftly tied is enough to pull the edges of the wound together and stop its bleeding. You roll down your sleeve, wipe blood from your blade, and set off again.

Evening is settling into the low places of the forest now, and a heaviness is building in your legs, a fatigue that implies a long day of walking.

Your left forearm aches.

Ahead, where the road curves and vanishes from sight, a figure stands silhouetted in the gloaming. The distance is too far to make out many details beyond the figure's stance, the wide and staggered placement of feet, the hunched uneven slant of shoulders.

"Hello," a man's voice calls out. "Are you coming from the Citadel?"

You shake your head. "I cannot look backward to answer that question."

The man tips his head like a squirrel at the sound of a snapping twig.

You are close enough now to see him clearly. He is dressed in layers of leather and fur to fend off the cold. His face is mostly hidden by a thick beard, but there is an urgency in the pull of his brows, the shape of his lips, the dark shadows beneath his eyes. He squints. Recognition haunts his features. His shoulders tense.

"It's you," he says.

A simple enough truth. "It's me."

"You are a Wielder, then."

"I am."

"I sent word to the Guild that I needed a Wielder, but..." his voice tapers into a stillness forming between you.

"Then it is good I am here." You hold up the paper in your hand, the words swirling in ever shifting fractals of meaning that only a Wielder can parse.

He tugs the back of his neck with a mittened hand, brow pinched as if in pain. "I didn't expect them to send you."

"Our Guild serves all who have need for our craft."

The light has all but left the world now. A quiet chill settles in as you regard one another — him wary and uncertain, you patient and eternal. Snowflakes begin to drift down through the evening air.

"Are you truly a Wielder?"

You smile at the wonder in his voice. "I am."

His mouth tightens as if to bite back something pressing for release. When he finally speaks, his words are stumbling. "You — I — My daughter. She's sick."

There is more, you are certain, but you accept what he tells you. "I am sorry to hear it."

"I've tried everything, but nothing's worked. I have food. A fire. A bed for the night. Will you help her?"

Such questions. You smile. "I cannot look ahead to see, but I am done walking for today."

●

His cabin is small but sturdily crafted, the close-set timbers deftly chinked. A season's worth of split wood is stacked beneath the roof's south-facing overhang. Smoke curls from a fieldstone chimney. The sight of it evokes a sense of comfort, of *home*. Inside, it is warm and softly lit, a single open room filled with a table, three chairs, and a wooden chest in one corner. Everything speaks of a hard but good life.

Wordless, you lean your pack by the door, then set to removing your many layers. When done, he gestures for you to sit at the small table and presents a bowl filled with something thick and steaming. It smells of carrots and onions and wild garlic scapes. Between each bite, you take in the smaller details of his home.

A copper pan and cookpot reflect the firelight like lanterns from where they hang on the wall. The wooden chest is a work of art, its edges embellished with decorative carvings that suggest a focused mind and a steady hand. Atop the chest sits a daguerreotype in an oval frame. In the image, the man stands beside a dark-haired woman in a white dress. They're both smiling, but you see whispers of doubt clinging to the edges of the woman's eyes.

"Who is she to you?" you ask.

He turns away and sets to washing the dinnerware. His voice is husky with sorrow when he answers.

"My wife."

Yes, of course.

You pull in a slow breath, noting the myriad scents filling the cabin. Sweat, wood smoke, vegetable stew simmering in the fireplace. Mink oil. Damp wool. A child's sickness, sour and sharp. There is a ladder leading to a narrow loft overhead.

The child is buried deep in a nest of old blankets. Her face glows with fever. Strands of dark hair cling to her sweat-sheened forehead. A necklace circles her throat. Six polished beads hang from its leather cord. The man comes to stand at the base of the ladder but says nothing.

"Let me see what can be done," you say.

Careful not to wake the child, you squeeze in beside her, find a comfortable position, take hold of this moment with your mind, and wield.

Reality stretches into an endless state. The child's life unfurls before you. Strings of possibility vibrate and shine in an iridescent rainbow of colors. Some tangle with your own, a tickling, pleasant sensation. No Wielder possesses the skill to touch infinity, but you can trace many of the girl's strings, heft their weight, gauge their strength and flexibility.

Time regains its linearity. The child's chest rises and falls in labored pants, and a sadness settles into your heart. You cannot resist reaching out to caress her feverish cheek.

Such a sweet young sparrow.

The thought bubbles up, unexpected, a temptation to look away from the present and lose yourself. Worse, lose the magic you possess now. Deep breath in. Slow breath out. The moment passes.

"The child's illness has taken hold deep in her lungs," you say as you climb down the ladder to the man below. "Many of her strings are collapsing."

He looks stricken, eyes shining in the firelight, brimming with tears. "There's nothing you can do, then? She's going to die?"

A silly question. Though the strings of every creature are unique, ever-shifting froths of potentiality diverging in beautiful and limitless arrays, they all share one commonality. With gentle sympathy you answer, "All threads end eventually."

"My little bird. Ever since..." He swallows hard, eyes fixed on the floor. "She's all I have left."

You should refuse. Reversing entropic decay requires perfect focus and an enormous transfer of energy. It is not without danger, even for a Master Wielder. You are only a Journeyman, but the sorrow in the man's voice is evidence of the truth in his words. It is settled, then.

"I can help you."

•

You settle in beside the child. Her pulse is rapid and weak beneath your fingers as you bring your thoughts to the focal point of the girl's origin. You set yourself like a fulcrum in the space between what is yet to come and what has passed, and *stretch*.

At the very center of the child, where infinite variations of a single life hum and swirl, the strings of reality are thin and fading. It is difficult work, gauging and assessing, finding threads that are both long and stable. Each transfer of energy from one potential life to another introduces uncertainty and invites a spontaneous collapse. Slowly, carefully, thread by thread, you wield. Fatigue is gnawing at your edges, so you release your attention from the girl. Time flows once again.

The angry flush of fever is withdrawing from the child's cheeks. Her pulse is settling, but her breaths sound wet as though her lungs are filled with water.

You activate your parasympathetic pathways. Rest. Recover. Wield. Thread by thread, you reshape the fabric of the child's existence. Rest. Recover. Wield. Again. Again. Again...

•

Daylight is easing back into the world now.

"The illness is not gone, but the girl has a wild, fierce little spirit," you tell the man. "Her possibilities are strong now."

"Thank you," he says and wraps you in a hug. There is a bed tucked beneath the cabin's loft. You accept his offer to rest, and sleep comes swiftly.

●

Long beams of sunlight catch in motes of dust that drift and settle across an oval portrait atop a wooden chest. A bed of glowing coals pops in the hearth. The thick aroma of molasses and peppered yams permeates the warm cabin as a man sitting by the fire lifts the lid of a cast iron pot and stirs the contents.

You stretch, rise to dress. From the loft overhead comes the sound of a small body shifting.

"Stay for dinner," the man by the hearth says.

His face gives no sign of threat, though there is a certain familiarity to his features and his voice. As a Wielder, the intuitive sense of knowing this man cannot be examined, only acknowledged.

"Thank you. I am hungry."

His smile falters, but he nods, then turns back to tend the pot above the fire. You slide into one of the three chairs at the table and watch in silence while he retrieves a pan from the wall. The pan sizzles, and the smell of grease and frying chicory root is a delight.

"What's it like?" he asks with his back to you. "The Citadel, I mean."

Your pulse quickens. There are rules that must be followed when speaking with a Wielder, and you are certain that this man knows he is breaking them.

"Why do you ask a question I cannot answer?"

"I'm sorry. It's just... it's good to see you again." He turns to set the food on the table, catching your gaze furtively.

A series of creaks and shifts from above draw your attention upward. The face of a young girl is peeking down from the loft. She is pale, thin, brown hair tangled and dirty, but her eyes are bright and curious. For several moments, long even without your magic stretching the world, the two of you regard one another. She does not speak. Instead, she regards you with an openness and a calmness befitting a member of your Guild.

"Hello, little bird," you say, then look at the man. He's gone still and is staring.

With a startling ferocity, he begins to weep. His broad shoulders sag inward. His head sinks toward his chest, and he collapses into his chair.

"You really don't remember, do you?" he cries.

"To remember is to forget. A Wielder —"

"But you weren't *always* a Wielder. You had a family. You had a *life*."

"Do I not have a life now?"

He shakes his head in frustration. "Please don't leave. You can stay here. You can stay with *us*, Lena."

That name in his voice plucks hard upon a single string, sets it vibrating with a force that bends your awareness towards it. Strings resonate, harmonize, phase with one another. A probability begins to manifest as a memory.

You stand, leave dinner untouched upon the table, retrieve your pack from beside the door. "I must go."

The man's eyes fill with anguish. "It's been six years, Lena."

He is hurting, but this hurt is a thing you cannot heal, a weight you dare not carry, a test. The strings of your reality continue to orient into parallel states, with fewer and fewer degrees of freedom. Your breath grows shallow.

"I am a Wielder. I look neither forward nor back. I am here, now, always. There is nothing to miss."

His grief overbalances, tips into anger. "That's a lie. There *is*! You had a life, a family who loved you! The Guild showed up, and —"

"Stop!"

Without conscious thought or intent, driven by the biology of your panicked body, you wield. Time slows, stops, stretches, expands, elongates, ceases.

There is only *now*.

From the loft above, the girl continues to watch, her eyes calm and without judgment. You smile up at her. She is beautiful in all her various possibilities.

Be well, little bird, you think.

Cold bites at your cheeks as you close the door on the warmth of the space within the cabin and let time flow once more.

The sun is sliding slowly downward on its journey toward the end of day. In your hand, a folded square of paper with the following:

The Citadel welcomes you, Master Wielder. Take the eastward road. Do not look ahead. Do not look behind. Do not lose yourself.

Quantum variations of the message swirl upon the paper, thus marking its authenticity. You fold it closed, hold it tightly in your hand.

As the shadows lengthen, a grey bird hops from branch to branch in a nearby tree. A smile touches your lips at the sight of a pink underbelly as it fluffs itself against the cold, black eyes curious and bright.

Phee-bee, it calls, and your whole existence catches on the sound. The center of awareness shifts, the strings of reality harmonize into the memory of a child's name and of a choice made. The world shivers, tightens, threatens to collapse into something singular.

You draw a slow, deep breath in and hold it. The moment passes, and you remain.

Katherine Karch's story "A Wielder Does Not Know Regret" was originally published in Metaphorosis on Friday, 4 August 2023. See magazine.metaphorosis.com

About the author

Katherine Karch is a science teacher and speculative fiction author living with her family on the North Shore of Massachusetts. She made her authorial debut in Metaphorosis with her first published story, "A Wielder Does Not Know Regret." In it, she blends concepts of quantum reality and the power of mindfulness. The story also honors the bittersweet bravery involved in a woman choosing to honor herself and live the life she wants rather than a life others would try to limit her to.

Since her debut in *Metaphorosis*, Katherine's work has appeared in *Metastellar, Radon Journal,* and *Uncharted Magazine.* She claims to be mostly harmless, probably human, and 100% nerd. Find her chatting about reading, writing, family, and various other things on Instagram (@katherinekarchwrites), Mastodon (@karchwrites@wandering.shop), BlueSky (@karchwrites.bsky.social), or on her website (www.katherinekarch.com).

The Guardian of Werifest Park

Carly Racklin

The train car reeked of cigarettes and rumbled like a storm. Loud enough to drown out the voice of every passenger crammed inside it, but still Inez's heartbeat rattled between her ears. It had started when she stuffed her backpack with clothes in the dark, and only boomed louder as she'd slipped out past her mother's wheezy, sleeping form on the couch, thirty-six or so hours earlier.

It had followed her through the cracked streets, then onto the bus, and all five trains after that. Or was it six, now? She hadn't slept a wink since the drumming started. She'd begun to think nothing would ever be quiet again.

The bruise on her cheek had faded enough now to be mistaken for a shadow on dusky skin, though it throbbed faintly in time with her pulse. No one had even spared her a passing glance when she boarded the train.

Inez had wedged herself into a far, windowless crevice of a seat, clutched her backpack hard against her chest, and waited for the dread to loosen its grip.

No luck yet. So onward it was.

Once her current train clanked into the station, she shuffled onto the platform and took a deep breath, only to taste even more bitterness in it. She reached into her pocket and drew out less than a dollar in change.

"Shit."

Strangers shoved past her and onto their trains. The longer she stood staring at those coins, the louder the dread rumbled in her skull. She needed to keep moving.

She drifted across the sprawl of washed-out tile, out of the paths of others who searched the flickering TV screens beseechingly. Everyone she passed was going in the opposite direction from her.

Inez stepped out into the stale summer air and walked. She walked until the afternoon bled into dusk and the day wasted away under the heels of her second-hand sneakers. She wove through gray streets flanked by gray buildings wearing more gray smoke like scarves. The hollow chill thickened in her gut with each step against the hard sidewalk, but she slogged on.

There had to be *something*. Something, not anything. No shelters — she wasn't a stray. A church could work. Hell, she'd take a bench at this point. Anything would do, so long as it wasn't that house.

Unlike her mother, Inez knew when to quit. When to give a place over to the vermin wasting it. The situation turned out to be comically simple, really. In the end, it all boiled down to a choice. Get out, or get wiped out.

Inez kept walking. Her stomach kept roaring, and her heart drummed on and on and on.

Then, the trees.

So many trees, all soft edges and swaying and green. An ocean of trees stretched to the sky and down the block and farther, farther than bleary eyes could measure. The first real trees she'd seen in days, wearing a collar of what was probably the sorriest excuse for a fence in the entire world. Inez jogged across the street and approached a large, slightly crooked sign.

TRESPASSERS WILL BE PROSECUTED.

The words were printed in bold black type and hung against a background that at some point must have been white.

PARK HOURS: 7AM-7PM.

The last dregs of sunset fell yellow and molten over the skin of her neck and the heavy padlock on the gate. Inez glanced over her shoulder to the city. Just looking at it made her itch to take a puff of her inhaler she knew she couldn't spare. No telling when she'd be able to refill her prescription again.

Despite the heat, Inez shivered, and a whisper from somewhere deep and dark in her chest asked, *What were you thinking?*

Behind her, the street was miraculously clear of cars. For one floating, dream-still moment, the only things breathing were her and those trees. Rustling, watching. Waiting to see what she would do.

She ignored the voice and climbed the fence.

Her feet hit the earth with a soft thud. She tore off her shoes and stuffed them into her backpack, sighing as grass eased the concrete's ache from her soles. Another sign accosted her a few strides in, this one so eroded it seemed ancient, hanging around the trunk of a tree like an amulet: a thirty-one point list of the park's prohibited activities. Vines and moss skirted its edges, entwined in the gaps of the chain that held it aloft.

No smoking, no hunting, no trapping, no littering, no fishing in the pond, no carving the trees, no, no, no. They would have saved a lot of paint if they'd just written KEEP YOUR DAMN HANDS TO YOURSELF. Inez wondered if there were security cameras in the park, but that would involve breaking about four of their own rules.

She ambled on until the fence disappeared from view. There weren't even any real footpaths, just vague stretches of faded grass, mostly concealed by the shells of parched leaves. *No digging. No vehicles.* Sounds of the city beyond waned with every step until they were barely memories. The dulcet crooning of unseen birds replaced the din of construction, of razing machinery. No sign of the skyscrapers, no sign of a single gray thing.

Huckleberries dotted the dark brush. Inez plucked them up in clusters as she walked, barely chewing, her relief turning even the most unripe clumps nectarous and intoxicating.

The path curved, and around the bend stood an enormous weeping willow. Under it: a bench. For the first time in weeks, maybe months, Inez laughed.

She sat down, shucked off her backpack, and took deep, even breaths. The air tasted sweeter than the berries.

But her clothes still smelled of her mother's cigarettes. So did the backpack, and the short dark coils of her hair. Now, though, in this park, the bitter smell seemed to have dissipated a little. Like the fresh air was washing her clean from the inside out.

Dusk elapsed in minutes; night draped the trees in obsidian. With the dark and stillness and her newly full stomach came syrupy fatigue. It colored everything — even the dingy bench was transformed into the softest and warmest bed she had known in years. For a long time, the only thing she did was breathe, letting herself sink further into the summer air, and it into her.

With every inhale, she imagined it purifying the black secondhand-smoke stains in her lungs, then sneaking into her veins and her brain, erasing every ugly thing that lived there, every memory molding in every dark corner and inside every wall.

Yes, she was alone in a city she didn't know the name of, broke and bedding down on a park bench. And there was a stubborn weight in her chest that she couldn't ignore, and bruises still clinging to her skin. But there were wild berries too, and trees tall enough to blot out the sky, and she didn't have to think of her mother ever again. For now, that would have to be enough.

The willow leaves rustled loudly above her, though the air was still. Inez couldn't bring herself to open her eyes again once they fell closed. So she just listened, and after a while, the rustling ceased.

She couldn't remember the last time she'd slept in air this clean, or the last time she'd lain in the night without listening to her mother slinking in the door with her latest fix. It was a different world entirely, a world made only of crisp, bright things. Balmy green things her mother's smoke could never spoil.

Inez slept like the dead, and dreamt of nothing at all. Until a sharp rattling cut through the gloom and jolted her awake into a dry early dawn.

For a moment the world reeled and her head spun, full of dizzy white flickers. She was stuck between spinning and floating, half numb still from the previous day's exhaustion. The rattling continued, and Inez jerked up from the bench when she recognized it as the sound of the metal fence.

The sun had just barely begun to light the park, like the first translucent strokes of an underpainting. What could it be, six in the morning? No way anyone was opening that gate right now.

But she hadn't needed to open the gate to get in.

The heavy crunch of footsteps sounded from nearby.

"Shit!" Inez hissed, and in a frantic blur, snatched up her backpack and dove for cover behind the thick trunk of the willow tree.

The footsteps lurched slowly nearer, down the same path she'd taken to the bench, and on. When they passed the tree, Inez held her breath, and leaned just slightly out into the open to regard her fellow trespasser.

Square shoulders, baggy jeans, dusty combat boots. The man plodding past couldn't have been much older than her, judging by his height and clothes. He stomped listlessly through the grass, clutching an aluminum can. Drunk.

He stopped walking a few feet past the bench. A lit cigarette teetered between the fingers of his free hand. He took a swig from the can, then a puff from the cigarette. The cloud of gray smoke he breathed into the air caused a queasy flutter in Inez's chest. Moments later, the scent hit her, and despite how hard she tried to fight it off, she couldn't breathe.

She hadn't smelled such strong cigarettes since her mother last lit one. That night could have been a lifetime ago, for how far away it felt. Ever since she was a little girl, any fresh whiff of that bitter smoke, and she was gasping, looking for fire, looking for ruin. She'd woken from nightmares of her mother turned to nothing but a heap of char on that ratty couch too many times to count.

When she was fourteen, the doctor had diagnosed her with asthma and recommended nicotine gum to her mother. And every night since for three whole years, Inez had slept with her window open and door shut.

Just when she thought she'd found the one place on earth where that smell couldn't follow her.

The man took another drag, his head lolling back with the inhale. Then he flicked the cigarette away, and it fell to the earth. The ashy end of it sputtered against the brittle foliage. Inez knew what came next, but when the orange flickers caught and burst outwards, she gasped as if she were the one burned.

The stranger whirled about. His glazed-over eyes met hers. Inez trembled and flinched, dropping back from her haunches into the dirt. Smoke drifted up from the ground in a thin curl.

A splitting thrum cut through the air. It sent a stabbing pain through the base of her skull, so loud it could have been coming from inside the bone. Like the whole forest had just trembled with her.

The willow tree above her shook violently again, without even a whisper of a breeze. The drunk man was not looking at her anymore, but up at the tree.

She followed his gaze to the branches. They weren't where she remembered them being.

The boughs bent to the ground, splayed apart wide like fingers. Inez took a breath that froze in her throat. Then the trunk of the willow tree uprooted from the earth.

It was much quieter than she would have ever guessed — to hear a tree tear itself out of the ground. For a moment, there was only a hum. Then a sharp crackle rippled through the stillness, and the trunk split in two. The halves met the ground, looking like the lean brown legs of a Titan. On either side of the tree, the remaining branches twisted into coils. Green vines dangled in a tight, roundish cluster at the willow's crest: a faceless head glistening with dew.

Inez had barely heaved in a new breath when the tree-thing angled its colossal semblance of a body toward the drunk man. At his feet, the cigarette still sputtered, glowing like a shrunken sun but giving no life. It would drain the green from anything it touched.

A yowl, like the groaning of a twig right before it snaps, sounded from the bundle of leaves atop the tree. It stuck in Inez's ears, in her teeth, in her ribs. It clashed with the piercing blare that the lit cigarette had conjured and for all she knew they were the same thing. Maybe that was what everything sounded like when you were going to die.

Inez's body moved separate from her mind. She crawled toward the cigarette on her hands and knees, and the willow moved too, overtaking her in one heaving stride. The drunk man had already started to run.

The whole world was rattling and that cigarette was still burning in the grass, like her mother, poisoning everything, and she couldn't breathe. She had to make it stop. In her peripheral vision the tree creature continued to move, its gnarled limbs cleaving through the air.

Inez mirrored it, throwing out her arm and smothering the cigarette against her hand. Ahead of her the creature halted, one of its branches seizing up mid-swing. The man disappeared into the brush and out of sight. When the metal fence jangled sharply in the distance not long after, the creature lowered its arm.

Inez's vision blurred. Panic pounded in her skull, almost loud enough to drown out the giant's gait as it turned back and thumped toward her.

Her chest burned with emptiness. She fumbled in her pocket for her inhaler. Blackness choked every thought in her head except the ones steering her hands.

Nothing left to exhale. *Click. Hiss.* Breathe in — hold — breathe out.

It took three puffs for the vise around her lungs to loosen. The world came slowly back into focus with every heave, centering on an ugly red burn glaring up from the center of her palm.

A tall shadow crashed over her. Inez looked up, breath thin again.

The creature had no eyes to meet but its stare still pierced. It stood rigid, a monument of bristled greenery. Tears welled up in Inez's eyes. Either from fear or pain, she wasn't sure. It didn't really matter, because she was going to die any second now. The creature craned its verdant body downward as if in confirmation.

Inez snapped her head down, closed her eyes, and waited to be crushed. Waited like she had those nights ago, back pressed to her bedroom door as it rattled with the force of her mother's fists, the air bloated with cigarette smoke and a voice screaming out for her blood.

She'd thought her mother was still sleeping off her latest bender when she flushed the pills. But her hands just wouldn't stop shaking, and everything had clattered to the floor, and she'd only gotten a few handfuls down the pipes when fingers had twisted into her hair and wrenched her back. A hand had crashed against her cheekbone, knocking her into the wall. Her ears rang and her mother had slipped on the tile, so Inez ran. She'd locked herself in her room and wept until long after her mother had given up on threatening to strangle her.

She'd made her decision before the latch even clicked. The next time she ran would be the last.

Curled in on herself in the dirt, Inez let the tears fall. Choked whimpers leaked through her teeth, clenched tight against the smoke. It could have been her mother there, all smoldering ash. Geared to snuff her out like an ember into a cracked tray.

Inez waited to die.

And waited. And waited.

Something soft brushed down her cheek. She gasped and the aroma of damp foliage flooded her mouth.

Rustling surrounded her. A faint creaking joined it, lurking just beneath the steady hum of leaves. Alike in timbre to what had sounded in the chaos, but with none of the venom — the same voice, a different tone. She blinked the tears out of her eyes. The green mop of vines hung just a few inches from her face, the rest of the creature bent in an awkward, jointless attempt at kneeling.

It didn't crush her. Instead, it raised one of the branches from its side and took her gingerly by the wrist of her burned hand. The long sprigs of leaves drew open her fist. This time, the noise that rose from the creature's unseen mouth was nearly a chirp, the pitch of it leaping, like a question. Shrill with curiosity, maybe even concern.

Before she could dwell on how pathetic that thought was, the giant punctuated its remark with a tilt of its massive leafy head, and sparks stirred in Inez's skull.

It was *talking* to her.

She searched for any hint of eyes behind those vines. "I . . . um, I don't understand," she muttered, unsteady with the new weight of this wonder. But it was true: she was still alive, and a beast dressed in forestry had really just materialized because someone burned the grass.

She looked to the gray smudge between the two of them, where the extinguished cigarette lay, then at her palm, cradled by the willow's wispy fingers. "It burned you too."

The vines around her hand drew upwards a fraction, and a thin stream of clear water trickled out from a fissure in the branch and washed over her ash-dotted palm. She flinched and hissed at the sting.

The willow made a cooing noise that sounded an awful lot like the calming hums other people's mothers made to their fussy children. Had it learned that from observation? Or did nature have its own language of tenderness?

"Thank you," Inez said, brushing her fingers over the bark.

Again that rustling echoed around them, and the giant let her go. It rose with a chorus of creaks and trod heavily back toward the patch of ragged earth behind the bench.

Sunlight broke through the canopy and gilded the grass so fiercely Inez had to squint. Soundlessly, the earth began to knit itself back together once the rooted feet of the willow settled into the hollow they'd created. Time seemed to move in reverse as its limbs unwound and stretched to their original shape. By the time she blinked the brightness away, the bench and willow tree stood perfectly undisturbed, the burn in her palm the only indicator that any of it had ever happened.

Inez pushed herself up on two wobbly legs and teetered over to the tree, a small grin fighting its way across her face. She hitched her toppled backpack onto her shoulder; it weighed practically nothing now. One errant breeze and she might just float away like a petal, sheer and light enough to never touch the ground again.

That didn't sound so bad.

When she was just a little girl, 'never' had been the scariest word in the world. A cage that would suffocate her if she got too close. But now, 'never' was more secure than anywhere. Not a cage, but armor. She could lie down inside it and it would keep her safe.

Never was a survivor's word.

She'd whispered it in the din of every train, to the dread each time it returned and choked the breath from her chest — *never, never, never*. She was never going back.

And the dread was quieter now, like she'd finally gone far enough.

Inez rubbed her fingertips gratefully over the knobs and valleys in the willow's bark.

Someone would be opening that gate soon. If she were careful, she could get out before anyone knew she'd entered at all. She would be anonymous again.

Anonymous, but not free. Not free of the dread, or the smoke, or the exhaustion of searching for hope in a colorless city.

At least this place had rules. Rules meant care, and she'd seen precious little of that for a long, long time.

Inez pressed her ear to the willow. She didn't know what she expected to hear, but when it was silent, she couldn't stop her heart from sinking.

"Hello?" she mumbled, and rapped against the wood lightly with her knuckles. "Are you still there? I, um, didn't realize this park was already occupied." Her chuckle came out crumpled like the leaves dappling the undergrowth. No reaction. Maybe it was sleeping. Maybe it just wanted her to shut up and leave it alone. Or maybe it didn't care about her at all, so long as she didn't break any of the rules.

Leaving it be seemed like the safest bet. She didn't want to test the limits of its hospitality, not after what she'd just witnessed.

Feeling childish and yet vaguely like she was being watched, Inez started off in a new direction, away from the pseudo-footpath she'd first followed and into the brush. The noisy layers of expired leaves crackled like tinder with each stride.

By late morning, the air swelled with heat. She downed one of the water bottles she'd had the good sense to buy during her train-hopping, and had half-stuffed the empty plastic shell into her backpack when the sound of real running water hit her, muffled a little by distance. She followed it until her bare feet pushed through a hedge and slipped into blessedly cool mud.

A thin stream wound through the clearing. On its bank, hundreds of yellow flowers gleamed from spray cast off the rocks. Inez propped her backpack up against a tree, sat down on the edge of the brook and dipped her legs into the cool, glossy water. She splashed a handful over her face and scrubbed the scum of the last few days away.

Sighing, she shut her eyes and lay back against the bed of flowers. Her fingers carded through their velvety leaves, tight and tangled like her own curls. Her head went woozy with the blossoms' sweet scent.

She listened for any sounds of the city, knowing it lurked on all sides of the park. Still nothing. If the skyscrapers were teeth, then this forest sat in the middle of a wide-open jaw, surrounded on all sides but never devoured.

Something was different here — she'd noticed it before, but not realized how deep the sensation ran. It wasn't just the air, or the trees, or the ground. It was everything.

Her thoughts drifted again to that list of rules. It hung in her mind in the same looming way it hung on its tree, fixed in place even by the foliage. Different from everything else, but not unwelcome.

Inez opened her eyes, and swallowed a yelp. A figure hovered over her, though that was all she could really call it. Its vaguely human-shaped body was comprised entirely of clustered leaves and budded flowers. It seemed to watch her, though the closest thing to eyes it possessed were two blossoms just slightly larger than the rest, fixed at the middle of its lumpy crown.

She sat up and turned around to face the thing. Its maybe-head followed her. It looked like some kind of artsy hedge trimming from a magazine. Like someone had tried to haphazardly sculpt a person out of foliage, someone who didn't know for sure, or didn't care to know, exactly what people looked like.

"Oh, there are more of you," Inez blurted, heart still racing. Rustling filled her head. She held up her burnt hand and gave a short wave.

The leaves on the creature shook slightly, back and forth.

Inez worked her bottom lip between her teeth. "No? You're . . . just one?" She gestured over her shoulder back toward the general direction of the willow.

Another hum, then all the flower buds on the creature's body bloomed into striking tiny suns. The blossoms skirting the stream repeated the display, petals flaring out in a long wave. Warmth so far from the summer's unflinching aridity saturated the air; she breathed in and felt it in her chest, searching for soil to take root in.

Inez smiled, and caressed the leaves below her again. The little red dot glared up from her palm beneath the vegetation, a reminder of the damage already done, how they'd both been burned. A handful of soft gestures wouldn't erase that.

But it was better than nothing. Or so she hoped.

Inez watched the creature watching her, and wondered if it felt her touch like it had felt the cigarette. Maybe it felt everything the forest did, every inch of every acre. Like veins, connecting each life to the next, tying blade of grass to sprawling tree to sunning flower, each to each to each. A system, and its heart. What a thing to share a wound with.

"Those rules back there are yours, aren't they? They were written for you," she said.

Thirty-one rules was nothing compared to all the ways a thing could be hurt. All the ways a life could be snuffed out. No death too small to grieve. Like it ignored no offense, no wrong. Carrying a memory as old as earth.

Inez saw it all again: the cigarette, and the man, and the creature's arm raised knifelike in the air. A threat, and a response. She'd only seen it respond like that once, but judging by that sign, she guessed it had happened before, and often, who knew how long ago. How many small wars had the creature waged before someone had taken pity on it and written the restrictions that hung over the place?

Too many, of course. It was always too many.

The sun retreated and plunged the bank into shadow. She looked up, but found her vision swimming. The creature was closer now, an unreadable blur of gold and green. Inez shuddered under its unyielding stare. Her smile grew heavy on her face, and fell away without a sound.

She peeled her limbs away from the flowerbed and stood. Papery yellow petals came away with her, stuck with sweat to her skin. The moments of her life from before then unspooled behind her eyes, faded by time but still clinging like old stains to the fabric of her memory. She didn't want them.

Her heart pounded. "Do you want me to leave?" Inez asked in a small voice.

The creature gave no response. The warmth in her chest turned sour.

"Do you?" she said, louder now, though a shameful crack in her voice split the word. Dread wormed a cold trail through her. She didn't need an answer to know it was true, but the miserable reality of it hollowed out her chest. She swallowed down a sob.

The creature's form shrank back at the accusation, all of its flowers returned to buds.

It wouldn't have been the first thing to want her gone. Wouldn't have been the first place better off without her.

Inez knew pity when she saw it. It looked just like disdain, but with a prettier face.

She stumbled back a step, then another, until the hedge she'd first emerged from brushed her ankles.

She really hadn't learned anything, had she?

"I'm sorry," she mumbled. Her feet scrabbled for purchase on uneven ground. "I just wanted — I just —"

Inez turned and ran. The tears finally fell as she lurched through the bushes, over brittle grass and twigs that jabbed like needles. Each one another twist of the knife, a reminder of what she had known before ever climbing that fence but had refused to admit.

She didn't belong here.

But it was worse than that, and she knew it. She didn't belong anywhere.

A root smacked her ankle, and Inez tumbled into the dirt with a weak yelp of pain. Every heaving of her breath scorched like swallowing a red-hot sword. She pushed herself up on limp arms. Stinging outside and in, she clambered backwards until she hit a tree's gnarled trunk, decked in winding dark leaves. Then she hugged her knees to her chest and wept into her hands.

She wished the earth would just swallow her up. If she could just bury all her deluded fantasies and dissolve into the soil, maybe something good and useful would finally grow out of her, something that deserved to be there in that fence, a part of that system.

Loved. Or worth loving, anyway.

And that was just it.

The nameless weight beneath Inez's ribs swelled and flooded her chest with a gloom blacker than her mother's lungs.

She couldn't breathe, again. She fished out her inhaler from her pocket and took a puff, barely able hold it steady. The last time she'd triggered an attack from crying had been the night she flushed the drugs. She could almost smell the smoke again. Could still feel the grain of her bedroom door grate against her shuddering back.

Her breath returned in gasps, a thousand aches with it.

Just barely, on the edge of the forest's din, Inez heard rustling. The foliage beneath her shook.

A whorl of vines crept away from trunk and curled around her, covered in enormous scarlet roses. The mass encircled her in moments, overflowing with the balmy scent of petals. She gasped, and a rose-dappled vine reached out and swept over her bruised cheek, wiping away the last tear still inching down through the grime.

Something had grabbed hold of her lungs again, and her heart too, and held them with such puzzling fortitude and tenderness that Inez thought she would weep again.

The mass of vines and roses embraced her. Softly and resolutely. Tenderly and fiercely. The way her mother used to, before everything went wrong. She'd forgotten what it felt like.

She exhaled and sank into the creature's arms. Links of thornless blooming vine cradled her, stroking her hair in the same smooth motions her hands had used in the patch of flowers back by the stream.

"Why are you doing this?" she whispered. "I'm just the same as them."

A low hum reverberated from deep in the petals, but Inez couldn't decipher its meaning. The creature only held her tighter when she made no reply.

Inez breathed until the pain in her throat subsided to a faint prickling numbness. She wanted to lie down until she remembered nothing of her mother or the gray-stained house she'd run from. But the memories clung to her bones like weeds. She wondered if she would ever be able to uproot them without also uprooting herself. If she would ever be as green and blooming and free as the things that held her inside the fence.

Hesitantly, Inez reached into the leaves and returned the embrace.

The creature's silken-edged form stiffened, then recoiled. The climbing roses and vines receded, slumping limp against the trunk.

By the time she'd gasped and called out brokenly after it, the creature was already gone. Inez stood. Confusion struck her first, then cold terror. Something was wrong. Goosebumps mottled her bare arms and legs. She stared hollowly into the horizon for a long time.

When a breeze blew, she tasted smoke on it.

Not the bitter tobacco, lung-rotting stuff. Worse. The kind that swallowed houses and skin. The kind that cooked.

Inez went rigid. All the green around her swayed as one vast wall, revealing almost nothing. No more than a few slivers of sky to search, and no sign of the stench's source.

"Move, just *move*," she spat at her quaking knees. "Where are you?" she cried up at the trees.

No answer.

Then, voices. Men's voices, the words turned garbled and staticky by distance. The murmurs became yelling, and by the time Inez had turned in their direction, three men careened out of the trunks' thick barricade.

They nearly barreled into her, but the one leading the charge skidded to a stop just inches in front of Inez. His scuffed combat boots kicked up a small cloud of dirt.

A flock of birds scattered noisily from the treetops.

"Holy shit," he whispered. Inez flinched at the rancid booze on his breath. "It's you."

Two others crowded at his back. They could have been triplets, for their shared tawny hair and pasty white faces. A lopsided tattoo of a tiger stared directly at her from one's bare shoulder.

Inez blinked, unable to call any words to her tongue.

"I told you someone else was there," Combat Boots said over his shoulder with a laugh. He stepped toward her, and she stumbled back in turn. Her pulse boomed in her ears.

"Who cares, dude? Let's get the hell out of here," interjected one of the others, grasping his friend by the shoulder and giving it a good shake. Shaggy hair obscured most of his face, except for a lip ring that glinted in the sun.

Combat Boots laughed louder. His right hand clutched an open lighter, the flame thrashing.

All the warmth drained out of Inez.

"I was right. All along — about everything, I was right. What do you think of that, assholes?" he howled, turning on his heels. Inez barely ducked out of the lighter's arc.

Tiger Tattoo stepped aside. "You're out of your damn mind!" he scoffed. "I'm not about to die here."

The smell of the smoke was stronger now. Past the undulating trees, Inez thought she glimpsed a smudge of gray. "What did you do?" she muttered, slack-jawed.

She took another step back, but Combat Boots swung around and seized her wrist. She yelped; his bony fingers held deceptively strong.

"Let go of me." She tugged hard, but he clamped down harder. "*Ow* — stop! Let *go*!"

A tremor traveled up her legs from the ground.

Lip Ring and Tiger Tattoo glanced at each other, then broke out running, following their original course into the treeline.

Another tremor, then another. Softly, in the back of her skull, a familiar hum sounded.

"You know I'm right. You were right there with me," Combat Boots ranted, pressing his pale, pocked face in close.

Inez had readied a leg to kick him where it would hurt, when thundering footsteps broke in. The air smelled like death.

The treeline shattered open.

Inez barely recognized the willow. Swirling fire engulfed its extremities, each wispy vine a wick. Dark billows rose thickly from its upper half. It looked hasty, incomplete, the trunk barely divided enough for movement. It limped forward, and each ungainly step filled the air with a cacophony of dreadful cracks. Behind it, a trail of red and black cut into the park as far as Inez could see.

The air was kindling.

She wanted to scream, but her lips formed useless shapes around nothing and made no sound. Combat Boots' grin melted away. He released her arm and ran.

The willow screeched, heaving after him. One leg splintered apart as soon as it met earth, and the whole creature teetered, then came crumpling thunderously down. Breathless, she couldn't call out for it.

Embers flew, swallowing the brittle foliage in a flood of char. The willow craned the blackened remains of its head down and made a high, broken sound, then collapsed in a tide of cinders.

Tears and smoke burned Inez's eyes. She whipped around and around, but couldn't find the trees, or the sky, or the creature. Ash coated her tongue and crept down her throat no matter how she coughed. She fell to her knees and wheezed helplessly.

Everything was falling apart again.

Nowhere to run. The air was red, her sweat was red, her thoughts were red.

There was a choice, a choice. What was it?

Inez reached for her inhaler.

Get out —

But it was gone.

— or get wiped out.

Darkness descended. It swallowed her whole and washed away the scorched clearing. A rough and solid slab slipped under her legs and hoisted her up, and up, and up from the ground. She scrabbled for balance, gasping weakly. Her fingertips scraped bark.

Cracks of light revealed the mass shielding her: a thick canopy of leaves.

Inez reached out to touch them, and her inhaler fell into her palm with a muted thump. She took two doses. On her first good breath she tasted foliage, then hacked out black dust.

The tree lurched into motion. The branch beneath her shifted and nestled her against the upper part of the trunk. She heard the distant crackle of fire, and vaguely smelled the smoke. More than anything she felt the rocking of the tree, of the giant as it walked, cradling her against its bulk.

Lost for words, she took deep, grateful breaths of the mossy bark. Tears streamed through the dust on her face, over her cracked lips, and onto the tree.

She was alive.

Seconds or minutes or hours passed before the creature creaked to a halt, and Inez's forehead lightly smacked its rough flesh. The limb that held her curled up and drew her away from the trunk.

Air crashed over her. The shield of leaves unraveled and bared her to the sunlight. She blinked, and saw the chugging smoke leaking from the center of the park, how glowing fire split the trees with crimson light. For a moment she soared, weightless, against the bleeding sky. Then the branch that bore her stretched and tilted. She slipped from bark to concrete.

Sidewalk chilled her feet. A shape heaved through the air and smacked the pavement: her backpack.

The creature pulled away, back toward the burning forest.

Inez howled with every last shard of herself, "*No!*" She shot forward, fingers grasping the rusted fence.

The creature's limbs groaned as it withdrew, unheeding. Fear thundered in her skull. She hauled herself halfway up the fence in an instant, until the tree turned back to her in a creaking blur. Bark met her shoulders, leaves pried her fingers open. Together they pushed her, struggling, back down to the pavement.

Sirens resounded from the verging streets.

"Don't go back in there." she rasped, fresh tears stinging in her eyes.

This couldn't be happening. It couldn't save her just to disappear again. She was so tired of being left, of being alone.

"It's too late. You'll burn."

The creature replied something just as broken. Still, it pushed her to the sidewalk.

"Don't, please. Stay with me," she cried, clutching the branch and tugging it closer. Leaves caressed her face.

The giant murmured quietly and pressed itself into her hands for just a moment, then pulled away. Behind the fence, the creature turned and stomped back into the forest as fire engines pulled up on the street, and Inez wept, drowned out by the sirens.

When figures began to pour from the trucks, she scrambled across the street and deposited herself on a bench beside a dried-up fountain. Flocks of chattering onlookers crowded at the fence as the minutes drew on and smoke stole the color from the sky. None spoke to her, and she didn't speak to them.

Once she turned her back to the park, and the fire, and all the clamor of the scene, she didn't look back. She wouldn't.

It was what she'd done when she left her mother. She made her choice and knew not to turn around, but not because she'd go back if she did. She couldn't look back and move forward at the same time. She had to choose. So she chose running. She chose a future, just like she'd done before.

Dread and shame roiled together in her chest. She'd had no right to beg a guardian to abandon its duty, its home, for her. She was nobody.

She'd been so naïve, thinking that running away was the same as escaping. The same as healing. But distance had nothing to do with it. There was no escaping the past, just learning to carry it.

Her mother, that house, they were just memories. Soon the park would be too. There were so many hollow places in her now; she had more than enough room to keep them safe. She could carry them forever.

Inez sat quietly for a long time. Then she put on her shoes and walked to the train station.

Inside, the building was even colder than before, with polished floors that squeaked with every footfall. She passed at least ten TVs, their screens all flashing red, alternating headlines reading, FIRE IN OLD LANDMARK WERIFEST PARK. AUTHORITIES RESPONDING TO REPORTS OF UNIDENTIFIED FIGURE SEEN WITHIN.

Groups huddled beneath the television sets, their eyes squinted, gesturing emphatically at the footage of the fire, but Inez was too far away to see what captivated them. They paid no mind to her or her ash-caked clothes.

She washed herself clean in a bleached white bathroom. The soap smelled harsh and fruity, and it erased the must of scorched earth from her skin. When at last she scrubbed at the tracks her tears had left in the dirt on her face, the door squealed across the tile, and a woman walked in.

Contorted over the sink, Inez froze, and the stranger did too. She was blonde, with ivory skin, and wore a red pantsuit. Her eyes examined Inez with scalpel sharpness for only a second, then softened to glimmering amber.

Droplets of lukewarm water ran down Inez's chin and puddled on the floor. The woman's hands flexed around the handle of her purse. In a saccharine voice that could only belong to a teacher of small children, she asked, "Are you all right, dear?"

"Yeah," Inez said.

"Are you sure?"

She wiped her chin. "Yeah."

The woman's lipstick was the color of freshly bloomed roses. "Do you . . . need anything? Is there anything I can do for you?"

"Yeah."

The woman bought her a ticket for the train. When asked where she wanted to go, all Inez could think to say was, "Somewhere green, with no fences." No more skyscrapers, no more smoke, and no more living things in cages. She was sick of suffocating.

They stood together on the platform afterward, and Inez thanked her, clutching her ticket. The woman just smiled, nodded, and pressed her hand on Inez's shoulder briefly. She watched the slight jerk of the woman's eyes as they flickered between her face and the news still playing on the TV behind her.

She expected some kind of warning. A *"be careful out there"* or, *"take care of yourself."* But all she said was, "The world is a very big place, you know. It's easy to get lost in."

But it's not, Inez wanted to say. It's not. It's very small. And everything burns just the same everywhere. Burns again, and again, and again. The only thing that changes is who gets blamed.

No words came. The woman smiled blankly, then turned and left, and so did Inez.

Practically deserted, the train started off with a metallic screech the moment Inez sat down. She let her backpack slide off her shoulders. A tunnel swallowed the car in darkness, and sleep stole her away before the light returned.

When she woke, the train was still moving, but the city was long gone. The woman had slipped her some extra cash before leaving, which she'd spent on a ridiculously expensive sandwich at the nearest food cart to her track. She scarfed the whole thing down in huge, graceless bites. Her stomach soured and ached after that, so she pulled her knees to her chest and stared out the long, scuffed window at the landscape whistling by.

The train passed sun-bleached hills dotted with sparse, squat houses, though for the most part, the land was sprawling and desolate. The weights in her chest shifted and settled and scratched at her like a bundle of needles. The train car was gray and the upholstery smelled just faintly of cigarettes.

Inez put her head into her hands. A soft rustling sound stirred between her ears.

She jerked up, and found bright flickers dancing in her peripheral vision. She turned to the window.

A swarm of golden petals floated astride the train, undulating like a murmuration. Inez gasped, then keened, and pressed her burnt palm to the glass.

A cluster of petals pressed back, vaguely in the shape of a hand.

Carly Racklin's story "The Guardian of Werifest Park" was originally published in Metaphorosis on Friday, 27 September 2019. See magazine.metaphorosis.com

About the author

Carly Racklin is a writer, editor, and vulture enthusiast with a passion for the fantastical and visceral. Her work has appeared in *The NoSleep Podcast*, *Haven Spec Magazine*, *Frozen Wavelets*, and more. She can be found at carlyracklin.com and on most socials @willowylungs.

Pyrrha

Antony Paschos

I open my eyes and see a rifle pointing at me. Well, not at me exactly. At me and Sister. Or just at Sister, I'm not sure, because the barrel is dancing in circles and zigzags. Sister's heavy breathing rumbles, *hur, hur, hur,* lulling me. Her snoring shakes her chest, which, in turn, shakes my head, as it's tucked under her tit. I elbow her hard.

"Sis," I whisper.

She grunts, tightens her arms around me. Then she spots the gun barrel and jumps up.

I can make out only one comrade's face in the candlelight; I think he's called Yiannis. A lot of people are called Yiannis, not just comrades. Some switched to Yoan or Yanko, because that's what the Bulgarians told them to do. Some refused but when the Bulgarians killed them, their relatives went and carved their new names on their graves.

Sister doesn't talk for a while. I don't know why, maybe because from time to time comrades point their rifles at each other for no apparent reason. Sometimes they even shoot each other, and then the last man standing says that the dead one was an agent. An agent means a bad comrade.

"What do you want?" says Sister.

"Get up, let's go. You, and the girl."

"We're not going anywhere."

"Comrade..."

"I said no! We've discussed this already. We agreed. Perhaps your ears got full of wax and you went deaf, but we've made a deal with the Secretary. So, stick the rifle up your ass and let us sleep."

Yiannis raises his hand to his ear, but stops halfway; he gets hold of the rifle again. "My ears are clean..."

Crackling, the candlewick burns out. Darkness, footsteps, rustling. "Find a match, you asshole, don't you have any matches?" Commotion. I can help. Here. Now everyone can see. My finger is like a vigil lamp, except that the flame is the shape of a dove, quietly perched on my index finger, illuminating the rough walls of the cave, Sister's books, the two logs we have for chairs, the little table with the crooked legs; there's a beach pebble underneath one of them so it doesn't wobble too much.

Clang. Yiannis picks the rifle up from the floor. The barrel is shaking. The comrades take a few steps back, as if they're scared of my little dove. I don't know whether they're really afraid of it, but, truth be told, my doves are often followed by silence. Just like now.

"Shall we?" It's me who asks.

●

We go down the slope. I wrap my coat around me. The moonlight falls on trails that look like rivers, on pine needle hills that look like giant hedgehogs, on oak trees that look like... I don't know what. Sister would know. Sister always knows; she comes up with the best similes. Not the most pleasing, but the most peculiar. Now, she's holding my hand. Two comrades walk ahead of us, one behind us, Yiannis, with his rifle.

"Are we going to an assembly?" I ask Sister.

"To what?"

"To an assembly."

She extends her hand and touches my shoulder. "My little Pyrrha."

My name is not Pyrrha. I had a different name, once. But Sister gave me this name because, she says, I've got red hair. Same as the comrades change their names, more or less; but Sister says that I'm too young to be a comrade.

Now she squeezes my shoulder.

"I don't want any tricks, comrade," Yiannis with the rifle says from behind.

"Shut up," Sister tells him. "If we were to play any tricks we'd have already burned you alive."

"You want me to burn them, Sis?" I ask. This is a game; I don't mean it. We play this whenever Sister says that we'll burn this and we'll burn that. I don't mind, even though after every game I remind her that I don't want to burn a person ever again. She always says she knows, but I remind her anyway.

"Hmm, maybe later," she replies.

Silence again.

"Sister?" I whisper.

"Yes?"

"Will they give us molasses where we're going?"

"Where did that come from, love?"

"I'd like some molasses now."

"That's what you meant to ask me?"

Sister can tell when I lie.

I pull her sleeve and whisper in her ear: "You remember that I don't want to burn anyone ever again, right, Sis?"

●

Four more comrades wait for us in the vineyard. I know they're comrades because I recognize one of them. He has all kinds of names, Captain this and Captain that. Some call him Secretary. He wears a pair of pretty riding boots, made of leather, and he's round, with puffed-up cheeks hidden under his beard. Almost all comrades have a beard, but his is thick and frizzy and its hairs look like black thorns.

The Secretary approaches me and squats. He fumbles in his pocket and fishes out something small and wrinkled.

"I don't like gum," I say. I'd ask for some molasses but I dare not. Not yet.

He laughs. "All right, little comrade. Will you show me your magic tricks? And I'll give you whatever you want."

"I'm not a comrade yet," I reply, squeezing Sister's hand.

"You think this is a freak show?" she asks the Secretary.

"Comrade," the Secretary says, gets up and shoves the gum back in his pocket. "If she's going to be a part of this Revolution..."

"She shouldn't! She's a fucking child!"

"Yet if what they say she can do is true..."

"It doesn't matter if it's true! Even if you make her do it, have you thought of what will happen afterwards? What will the Bulgarians do in retaliation? They'll lay waste to the entire countryside."

"Let them lay waste to it, then. If that's what it takes for the people to wake up, let them do it. These lazy-ass yokels put up with anything the Bulgarians do to them; they won't take to the mountains, if no blood is spilled."

"We're not talking about a little blood. There will be a bloodbath." Sister looks ready to catch fire, same as I can set anything I want alight.

"Comrade, we made a decision in the assembly. Do you dissent from the assembly's decision?"

"The decision didn't involve her, did it?"

I don't want them to fight. As Sister would've said, I've had enough.

I light up five little doves, one for every finger. Wings of fire come to life, making the smallest of sounds, *phoop, phoop, phoop, phoop, phoop.* Suddenly, I hear proper fluttering: something jerks up from the vineyard and flies into the sky. I wish it were a dove too, but it's probably an owl, and an owl is never a good omen.

Yiannis with the rifle brings his hand to his chest and makes a quick gesture as if he's crossing himself. The Secretary shoots an angry look at him and Yiannis squeezes his hand into a fist, brings it to his mouth and coughs. It's not that it's forbidden to make the sign of the cross, but the comrades never do that.

Meanwhile, five doves burn quietly on my fingers and Sister has taken her hand from mine and has placed it on her forehead. She mumbles something I can't hear, but I know her and I can read her lips under the light of my little fires. "Fuck, no," that's what she said. I guess I did something stupid. I put the doves out. No one speaks for a while.

"All right," the Secretary says in the end. "But do these damn birds work, or is it just a trick?"

"They do, they do!" I say.

"Oh, they do, huh? And can you do it from afar, little comrade?"

"She can do nothing!" Sister screams. "She's a child, she's not a part of this bullshit!"

"Comrade," the Secretary says. "It's the only way and you know it."

"You mean to tell me that this bullshit plan of yours depends on some rumors about a magic child? Didn't we have an inside man at the power plant? Why do you need her?"

The Secretary shuts his eyes and snorts. His breath smells of onions. He opens his eyes. "They caught our inside man in the power plant yesterday. His replacement supports the Bulgarian Exarchate. Meanwhile, everyone up on the mountain is waiting for the power to go out. We don't have any other options left, comrade. You have to choose, you and the girl both. You're either with the Revolution, or you're against it."

Sister looks at the comrades; at their faces, at their hands, at their rifles. She doesn't answer.

"So," the Secretary says. "Let's go."

●

The moon has climbed up and the night is now a heavier grey. We walk on unseeded fields. Sister and the seven comrades have swallowed their tongues, as if the animals lurking in the wilderness would overhear their secrets. In the silence, I hear the *hroop-hroop* of their combat boots.

Speaking of boots, the shoes I'm wearing are too big and I've tucked crumpled newspapers at the tips. They're not mine; Sister got them and my coat from a short agent. I asked her whether she'd stolen them, but she said that when we take something from the dead we don't call it stealing. We call it looting. I asked why we call it that and what it has to do with playing the lute and she explained to me that it might be a very old simile, so good that, in the end, it was forgotten and ended up being a word of its own. I'd love it if something like this happened to one of my similes; to be so old that it finally becomes a word. Even though I think that if something like that happened, it would happen to one of Sister's similes. They're very good. Not always kind to the ears, but peculiar.

I walk carefully because my looted shoes sink in the ground, which is dry on top but plump underneath. There's my chance to chat with Sister.

"The ground is like frozen snow," I tell her.

She smiles. She's thinking. Now she's going to say a simile and it's going to be way better than mine.

"Yes, that's pretty much on the spot," she finally says. She couldn't find a good one. "Or like fresh bread, hard on the outside but soft on the inside." She found one, after all.

"Why the long face? You didn't like the simile?"

"It's not that."

"What is it, then?"

"Are we going to start a revolution now?"

"We're going to do shit now."

Sometimes, Sister swears.

I hear someone from behind: "Comrade, what happened to your high morale?"

"Shove it up your ass, asshole."

Sometimes, Sister swears too much. Now the comrades are whispering to each other.

"Comrade, we have to inform the child." A hoarse voice. The Secretary.

"I'll inform her," Sister replies. Inform is a more difficult word to say tell. The comrades use difficult words from time to time, especially when there are many of them around. I've been at an assembly once. I didn't understand a thing, that's how many difficult words they spat out.

Sister informs me. She tells me I must burn the power plant from afar.

"Yes, but I don't want to burn people, OK?" I don't want to burn people ever again. When my doves burn people, they scream.

"You won't burn anyone, my love, don't worry."

"You swear?"

"I swear."

"Do you want me to burn the power plant?"

Sister keeps her eyes shut for a while. She sighs and opens them. Just like the Secretary did earlier on, only that she looks sad and not angry.

"I do. I do."

"And there won't be a bud...a blood..."

"A bloodbath?" Sister asks.

"Yes."

"We don't know that. The Secretary was right. There are times when you have to choose, even if you don't know what."

"All right, then. But, when it's finished, will you find us some molasses?"

"I will. I'll find us some molasses."

I hear a *psst* from behind. A hand stretches towards Sister, holding a small jar without a cap. It's Yiannis. "For the little one," he whispers. Sister looks at him; then, she looks at me. She takes it and gives it to me.

I can't see in the dark, but I can tell from the smell. It's molasses.

●

The power plant is close to the river and the train station, but you can hear neither the gurgling waters nor the trains. You can hear nothing; not even the comrades breathing. It's a huge building made of bricks. The bricks don't look red under the moonlight — everything looks dark blue under the moonlight — but I know they're reddish-brown; all bricks are reddish-brown.

An owl. It's bad luck when an owl comes to your house. That's why I never light up owls. Also because I don't like them. I like doves. I wish I could make real ones, not just flames shaped like doves.

I lick my lips. My mouth still sticks from the molasses.

A thud. Not close to us, but a couple of Yiannises jump.

"What is it?" I whisper. A second thud.

"It's coming from the trees," Sister says. "Over there, you see?"

She points towards the trees at the train station. Behind them there is an array of train cars and another building, with a roughcast exterior and a round clock on top. A few meters away there's a train car, collapsed to the side, gutted.

I'm not surprised by the thuds; the trees make all kinds of noises. Especially at night, if you're in the woods.

"The aspens stretch their limbs," Sister says. "It's as if they're yawning."

"The aspens are like a fence," I answer and Sister smiles.

"So," the Secretary says — he must be obsessed with the word —"Come on, hurry up."

"What's wrong? Is the Party in a hurry?"

"Comrade, I remind you that when everything is finished I'll have to write a report."

"Who gives a shit?"

The Secretary clears his throat. He speaks to Sis: "Comrade, I'm afraid you haven't chosen a side."

"Of course I have. I just chose the wrong side. The idiots' side."

A comrade makes a move towards Sister — it's not Yiannis, the one who gave me molasses. He holds his rifle with both hands, as if it's a bat. The Secretary places his hand against his chest and stops him.

Sister grants them a glance; then she kneels down and grabs my shoulders. She always has something important to tell me when she does this. Like now. She explains to me what I need to do.

●

"Do you understand?"

"I do."

"All right," she says and caresses my hair. She knows I like it when she caresses my hair. She likes it too — even though it's cut like a boy's — because it's ginger and soft.

"And then we'll ask the comrade where he found the molasses and we'll go get some more," she says.

"All right," I say and softly push her with my elbow. I hear whispers. I don't light up my doves yet.

"What happened?"

I turn and look at her. "Are there people in the power plant?"

"No."

"And how does it work, then?"

"It's automated, my little Pyrrha."

"What's automated?"

"When something is automated, it means that it runs on its own."

I'd ask her if we're all automated, but, "Hurry up!" the Secretary's yelling through clenched jaws. "Shut up!" says Sister.

"And what are those whispers, then?"

"The comrades, my love." The tone of her voice is the same as before, when she talked about the whole automated thing; flat.

"Sis... You remember that I don't want to burn anyone, right?"

"I remember, love." Here, the same tone again.

"All right." I wait a bit. The owl has stopped crying. Now, I can hear the wind blowing, like a trowel smoothening mortar. This is Sister's simile.

I hear more things, apart from the wind. Whispers: "She's a pain in the ass. Let's just toss a grenade." "The grenade's not enough, you idiot. The machines are inside. Even ten grenades wouldn't be enough." You could say that the whispers too were like a trowel smoothening mortar. "And what's this bitch telling her?" "She's her sister, you asshole." Lies. "Bullshit." Oh, he knows. "Isn't she?" "No, you fucker, the little shit's an orphan." I'm not a little shit, just an orphan. Long story. But Sister said that now she's my sister.

"Love?" Sister's voice; same tone, same tone.

"Yes," I say. And I do what I have to, in order for the trowel to stop smoothening the mortar. That is, to make the whispers stop. Not the wind. Even though, in a short while, I'll make the wind hush too. It happens when you cause a ruckus; softer noises disappear.

I light up ten doves, one for every finger. I feel the air through their fiery claws. It's a nice, night wind, just a bit moist from the stream, but not too much. It swirls around my fingers and tickles my skin where the fingers join.

"Is that it?" someone asks.

A little dove flexes its wings. Another one picks the feathers under its armpit. Or wingpits. Whatever doves have.

Someone spits. "We shouldn't have come. The kid's a fraud."

"Sssh."

Two doves flap their wings and hover above my hands. Another one coos silently. Well, not exactly silently, it makes a subtle *fthup*.

"We'll have to barge in, I'm telling you. And how will we get out?"

"Shut the fuck up!"

"Shut up? With all this bullshit and the damned birds they'll sniff us out. And then…"

My doves take flight. They lift themselves up, more like butterflies and less like real birds, leaving glimmering sparkles as they go — a small flock of flames — and then they enter the power plant through a window on the ground floor.

●

The fire rises with a gust of wind, *foup*.

"Look," I say to Sister and point at the ground floor windows. "The fire is like a beaded curtain." I look at her, but she's not smiling.

Indeed, orange ribbons dance like paper curtains blown by the wind. My doves are flying inside the building, their wings brushing against wooden beams, chairs, tables, floors, ceilings. I can't see my birds, but the windows, one after another, gain their own ribbons, while a yellow, blinding light pours out of the first ones, the kind of light you can't look directly at because it'll hurt your eyes. The crackling of the fire sounds like a lullaby and still no Bulgarian is on to us. My doves must be sowing fire in the upper floor now, while grey snakes of smoke lash out of a ground floor window, shapes I can't control, with bodies that swell more and more and turn into trees with fiery blossoms. The power plant's burning pretty much as regular houses burn, and as I'm thinking that, over the crackling of the wood and the furniture crashing and the beams falling apart, I hear something. It happens sometimes, to hear something not as loud as the rest of the commotion, maybe because what you pick up is strange or unexpected. Now, for example, this something sounds like fluttering, like an owl's wings, and my heart clenches.

"What's this, asshole?"

"What?"

"Up there."

"Where?"

"There. Top floor, at the window."

For a moment, my heart feels lighter at the thought that the living dove that takes flight might be one of my creations. The next moment I notice its wings burning; it's like the ones I make or, rather, like a firefly — would Sister like this simile? I don't know, I just hear her breathing cut short, and it's strange, my hearing must be excellent to be able to hear her breathing and the bird's fluttering as it manages to fly away. The wind that ruffles its feathers slowly puts the fire out; the bird will make it. It flies off into the night sky. Behind it I hear a hissing sound, something weak and weird that I recognize too. A chick appears on the same window sill. It's tiny and it's frantically looking around and one of its tiny wings is on fire. A small fire springs up behind it; no, it's one of my doves, and I immediately put it out with a small explosion which scares the chick; it hops delicately on the windowsill, slips and jumps off, and I hope it follows the other bird that got away, but no, the chick falls, then flutters and manages to gain some height, only a little, so little. And then I hear the soft thud on the ground.

A hand squeezes my shoulder. It's Sister's. I said that I didn't want to burn anyone; and when I said anyone I meant any people. Sometimes you have to think of every little detail before you say what you want to say.

My doves have faded, the power plant's on fire, but the city remains silent, just like the comrades. Something is moving at the window, perhaps there's a third bird or the flames may be playing tricks, now they look like... I forget what they look like. I hear the scream.

●

It's a human scream. It comes from inside the building and breaks down into shorter screams, sharp and loud and desperate. A ground floor door collapses and a human shadow appears at the frame in front of an orange, blazing background. It's probably a man. I see him in a blur, because tears have welled up in my eyes since the chick fell.

"The guard."

"Sister," I whisper and feel her moving. Her hand flies off my shoulder. She elbows the comrade next to her. "What are you doing?" he says.

"Don't just look at him, you asshole! Shoot him!"

"Sister…"

"They'll hear us."

And at that moment, they do. Not us, but the power plant, out of which comes a deafening bang that swallows the man's screams. The man runs and falls and gets up again; runs, falls and gets back up. The flames on his body almost fade whenever he stumbles, just like with the birds earlier, but every time he gets up they rekindle, and I don't want to say it, but they do look like wings.

"Can't she put him out?"

The one asking is Yiannis, the comrade who had woken us up, the one who gave me the molasses.

"No, she can't," Sister says. "And now they definitely heard us. So, stop wasting time. Finish him."

Yiannis puts the butt of the rifle on his shoulder.

"Fuck him," the Secretary says. "He's Bulgarian."

"Sister…"

"What is it, love?"

"Sister." I smother a sob. The bang from the explosion has left a constant *iiing* and a buzzing in my ears, as if from a truck engine. "I told you I don't want to kill anyone…"

"Yes, my love, but…"

A shot and Sister collapses in my arms. I step back and her hands fall off my shoulders, they slide down half-clenched, they scratch my clothes and end up on her throat as she crouches on my feet. A spring of blood gushes from her neck, painting her hands, her fingers, the skin between them. A truck's engine. More shots. Voices in Bulgarian. The guard's screams. Yiannis, who gave me molasses, falls down, pretty much like Sister. The Secretary kneels above her. Shakes her. "Tell her! Tell her to save us! To burn them!"

Sister opens her mouth, but says nothing. Shots, fire crackling, explosions, screams. Yiannis moans, injured. The Secretary grabs the rifle.

I drop next to him, on top of Sister, her blood sticks on my fingers, like the molasses on my lips. Her eyelashes flutter. The Secretary aims across the field and shoots —

the sound is deafening. Then, a shot from afar, the Secretary jerks away, drops the rifle and falls on his side too. He clutches his shoulder and groans. He grabs my arm with his other hand. His fingers are trembling, his nails dig into my clothes, so I stop shaking Sister.

"Wake up," I tell her, "you swore to me..." I don't want to blame her for swearing to me that I wouldn't have to burn people. Her face is still, her eyes are still, white, like landscapes. "Wake up and I don't care how many of them I burn!"

"Leave her," the Secretary says. "She's gone. Dead."

Sister's blood gathers in a pool around my coat and knees. It's warm and my skirt floats on it, like a water lily. She would love this simile. But she'll never hear another, neither will she come up with one. Perhaps, if I repeat her good similes again and again, then they'll too become words, like "loot" has?

The shots from the comrades are sparse now, but I can hear some far away, from where the truck engine was coming, scattered, then three in a row, three more, two, silence, one, silence. Silence, by which I mean fire crackling and comrades groaning. The guard has fallen silent. Yiannis has fallen silent. Footsteps are approaching, voices in Bulgarian. Shadows in the dark, I can see them moving; they're coming.

"Burn them," the Secretary says, now barely standing on his feet. He's panting, like a hound. "Burn them, they're Bulgarian. Didn't you just say to your Sister you don't care? Burn them, perhaps she's only wounded... Perhaps we can save her, perhaps..."

"Shut the fuck up," I tell him and his mouth drops. It's like an O now. "I'm not stupid and I don't burn people, you asshole." I sound like Sis. I push his hand off my arm. The blood in the pool is now lukewarm against my knees. My skirt is soaked.

"I — I know you're not stupid..." he stutters. "But... But if you don't burn them, they'll kill you."

The Bulgarians are close. Under the dead moonlight I notice helmets, rifles. One of them shouts, but I don't understand a word he says. I don't speak Bulgarian. He must be yelling something at the Secretary.

"So, you have to choose," he says, as if he's talking to himself. Now he's not panting as much. "You're either with the Revolution or against it." And then he gets ready to shoot, but the shooting comes from the Bulgarians. Not one

shot; four. The Secretary collapses next to me. There's a
hole above his ear, black blood is pouring out. His round
belly doesn't seem as swollen now, perhaps because he's
lying face down. A black pond forms underneath him,
smaller than the one that swallowed my knees, my skirt, the
edges of my coat. A small stream of it comes towards me,
warm blood mixes with cold.

The Bulgarians are here. They have the butts of their
rifles on their shoulders and they tilt their heads to take
aim. They say something and they lower their guns. They
hang their rifles on their shoulders. One of them takes a
pistol out of a leather holder and leans over the comrades.
He shoots them on the head. Every bang sounds deafening,
but I don't jerk any more, I'm used to it now. In the end,
you get used to anything.

I shut my eyes. The shots continue, once in a while,
steadily. Bam. Silence. Bam. Silence. I open my eyes. The
hand with the pistol is near me. The soldier is skinny and
hunched and he smells of garlic and unwashed clothes. His
eyes are sad. "Sŭzhalyavam, momiche," he says and I think
he says he's sorry. Sister's face seems silver under the
moonlight.

The soldier's pistol aims at her head.

I light up ten doves and the soldier steps back. Scared
voices, rustling. Rifles pointing at me. A dove lifts its tiny leg
from my finger, another one stretches its wings. Silence.

The Secretary said I have to choose. Sister had
promised that I wouldn't burn any people. But I did.
Sometimes you have to choose yourself. Sometimes,
choosing is a total mess.

Every gun barrel is on me. Rifles and the pistol that
was aiming at Sister point at me. I wish Sister would wake
up and speak to them; if she woke up she'd find a way to
save us. But her face is still silver and her blood cold and
sometimes you have to choose yourself what to do.

The doves have stretched their wings, ready. But a
fluttering that comes from the power plant is quicker. I turn
to see and I hear the shot and then something burns my
throat and my chest fills with something wet and warm, like
Sister's blood around my knees. I see the tops of the aspen
trees, far at the train station, the power plant on fire. I don't
see my doves, but up there, in the sky, among the stars that
blink behind the blurry ribbons of smoke, a bird is
fluttering and flies up high; I don't know why, but I'm sure
it's the chick that fell off before. My arms and legs are

heavy; I can't help it, and I fall like a marionette with its strings cut.

●

Antony Paschos's story "Pyrrha" was originally published in Metaphorosis on Friday, 7 February 2020. See magazine.metaphorosis.com

About the author

Antony Paschos was born in 1979 and lives in Athens, Greece. He is a member of the Science Fiction Club of Athens. He has worked as a Paintball field operator, a delivery boy, and an air taxi pilot. He currently works as an airline pilot.

Heart of Stone

Chris Cornetto

Light filtered through the debris, igniting a spark in his crystalline heart.

Bending all his will to the effort, the little golem opened his eyes. Pink, hazy dawn — or perhaps twilight? — filtered through a cloud of dust motes. It was barely light at all, yet it set his body thrumming, energy tingling through silicon veins. The light soaked into his heart and filled it with life.

He tried to move his arms, his legs, but he was too weak. He tried to check if he still had limbs, but he couldn't lift his head. Even his thoughts trickled like tar.

How long had his core been dim? Where was he?

From above came scraping and grunting. A rustle of debris, as pebbles tumbled down. More light squeezed through the gap, and the gears of his mind began to turn.

Grand, he thought. *My name is Grand.* He was a Clay, a Stonesinger, a servant of the Lord of Earth. And he had failed his Master.

Somehow, Grand had to make his way home. He wondered if the Master would be surprised to see him after so many centuries — how many had it been? Perhaps the Master would be pleased, if only the smallest bit, to see his wayward Clay return?

It was a queer thought, Grand knew. Emotion was a defect of logic. The Master had no defect.

It was not the first queer thought to have crossed Grand's mind, in his ages in the dark. But now there was light. Unlooked for, unhoped for, undreamed of *light*.

●

Grand was not his name. The golem had no name, only a designation: GR-A90.

He had taken the name "Grand" on a whim; to pass the years in the dark, he had imagined himself part of the city above his tomb. Through the stone he had felt the vibration of a thousand voices, a thousand souls. He had dreamed that he walked among them, sharing their joys and cares and woes. When they spoke, he spoke back, though none could hear him. His favorite voices became dear friends, and he ached when they were silent.

Grand knew it was mad affectation to play at being a flesh-thing, that he was damaged in ways he could not comprehend. It was his guilty secret and his only joy. It had been a way to pass the centuries.

Then the city vanished, all voices silenced but his own.

He spent another age gently humming to the stones of his prison — a waste of energy, but also a comfort. It was the task for which he was made. He knew the song of every mineral, and with a bare touch could set them singing in purest tones. At his full strength, he could shake mountains.

But sealed away from light, Grand had no strength. He, master of stone, became its slave. It had been a mercy when his core went dim.

●

The stone above shifted and the pink glow welled through the gap, fainter now. So, it was twilight after all.

From above came a gasp of excitement. A gaunt face peered into the breach, eyes wide with wonder. It belonged to the most ill-fed, ill-favored seraph Grand had ever seen. Even stunted, it towered over him, at least thrice his size.

A seraph. He had never shown a seraph mercy, and had no right to expect any. After untold ages of waiting, his rescue would be his death. The irony stung him.

The seraph shouted in a language Grand could not comprehend, some distant kin of the tongues he remembered. Had the world changed so much in his sleep?

The seraph called out again, turning his back to Grand. No wings. Not a seraph. So what was this flesh-thing?

The golem dredged his recollection, mind sluggish with sleep. Even now, the dim light fading from the sky, his brain threatened to shut back down. He was designed to never forget, but how much damage had he suffered when the city fell atop him?

A human. That's what the flesh-thing was.

Grand had warred with many races, the creations of pretender gods, but humans he barely recalled. They were an aberration, an error, sprung from the dirt with no god to claim them. They had been beneath the Master's notice, and so were beneath his.

A second human appeared, this one bearded, older. Just as gaunt. He eyed Grand skeptically and prodded him with an iron rod, clinking it against his chest.

Grand tried to reach for the bar, but his arms would not obey. He lay in the pit, as still as the rock around him. All he could move was his eyes.

The men jabbered in their strange tongue, until the young one persuaded the elder to help him dig. They pried at the rubble, levering away fragments of broken wall. And, with each stone moved, more debris cascaded down.

The pit grew choked with sand and stone. Grand's small world closed in until it reached no further than his body, more claustrophobic than ever. Panic welled within him. Were they burying him? His thoughts swam with nightmares of eternity beneath the dirt, alone and forgotten.

Anything but that, his mind screamed. Grand prayed feverishly to a Master who could not hear. Let the flesh-things kill him if they must — only, let them do it above the ground, beneath the boundless sky. Outside of this tomb.

Grand fixated on the scrape of iron on stone, the sound of salvation. He *had* to get out. The fear of darkness without end weighed on him physically, crushing him like the very rock that pressed down from above. So close to freedom, it was too much to endure.

Time passed. Grand flickered in and out of consciousness, his power ebbing. Though intoxicating after an age in darkness, his sip of twilight had been scant. Straining to hear the blessed scraping, his thoughts ground to a halt.

●

Moonlight. Two men in headscarves inspected him, one holding a shovel. They chattered in their nonsense tongue, disagreeing. One enthusiastic, the other annoyed.

Sand and broken stone stretched to the horizon in every direction. The city was gone. He had known it would be, but seeing was different from knowing. It was ironic how he ached for its loss — he who had tried, and failed, to destroy it.

A man placed him gently into a sack, not quite empty. It drew shut, and the darkness returned.

●

Grand woke to lamplight. He found himself lying on a bench or table. Something made of wood.

Even had he the strength to move, Grand had no power over wood. Its structure was messy and random compared to the beautiful order of stone.

Voices argued. Grand tried to look around, but couldn't. He was sprawled amidst knickknacks and rubbish. He heard the men who had found him bickering with a third.

No, not bickering. Haggling. Haggling over the junk on the table, with which he had shared a sack. They haggled over a brooch, a buckle, an ivory comb. A granite face chiseled off some capital or lintel. The hilt of a long-rusted sword, and so on. All sorts of rubbish.

The men who found Grand were scavengers, which made *him* salvage. He, a Clay, mightiest of the Master's tools, was now junk, pulled from the refuse heap of history.

The shame stung him. An eternity in the dark hadn't extinguished his pride.

Grand lay and he listened, having no other option. Though most of the haul was rubbish, some pieces caught his interest — the gears and springs and tubes of forgotten machines. There were even two small piezo-crystals, which the elder scavenger presented reverently.

The buyer placed a lens on his eye to inspect them. He turned them over in his hand, clucking his tongue as he studied them carefully, facet by facet.

At first Grand thought the collector was checking for damage, but soon realized the man simply enjoyed the sparkle — as if the crystals were nothing more than shiny baubles. He was amazed. How far had civilization fallen? Humans were infants, ignorants. Barely more than beasts.

Grand itched to explain their error, but held his tongue. Even had they shared a common speech, he wouldn't have spoken. With creeping discomfort, he realized that he *feared* the flesh-things. Did they see what he was? Did they know what he had done?

Would they destroy him if they knew he lived?

Perhaps not, but Grand would take no chance.

Once they had settled terms on the rest of the detritus, the younger scavenger hoisted Grand, his large hands wrapped around the golem's trunk. He chattered excitedly about the prize of the collection.

It was an honor to be saved for last, the finest garbage. He was the Lord of Junk.

At least, held upright, Grand could finally look around the room. The walls were lined with cabinets where trash and treasure mingled freely, the shiniest bits of debris given places of honor. Weapons and potsherds and mechanical parts were sorted loosely by theme, but with several wrong guesses. Other bits were unidentifiable even to Grand.

The centerpiece of the whole collection was a golem power core, shimmering and dead. It was too large to belong to a Clay, large even for a Stone. A fissure ran halfway through, rendering it inert.

It was the crystal heart of a living thing. It should have been brought home, to be repaired and born again in a new body. To display it like a sparkly trophy was beyond cruel. It was barbaric.

Grand pictured them prying him like an oyster for the shiny bits inside, and the thought filled him with horror. He strained to draw in light, willing his body to absorb it, but he had no strength to fight. He couldn't even move. He was nothing but a helpless stone doll, who waited centuries in the dark for nothing.

The collector, a stooped man in a gold-threaded kaftan, leaned toward him. He looked weary from the endless dickering, and clearly bored. He rolled his eyes and made an offer.

The young man replied with disgust; the sum had been paltry. The other scavenger gave a derisive grunt, universal to all language. It said, "I told you so."

So Grand was worthless after all. Not even the Lord of Junk. Merely junk.

But then realization set in. The flesh-things were, indeed, clueless. They didn't know what he was, didn't know his danger or his worth. Their ignorance was his salvation. To them, he *was* a stone doll, and nothing more.

Relief washed him like a wave, more refreshing than light itself. He would be a doll until he had his strength back. After that, let it be their turn to fear.

The scavengers finished their business, took their money, and left grumbling under their breath. They brought Grand with them, perhaps hoping for a better price elsewhere. He'd never been so pleased to be stuffed into a sack.

●

Grand had traded one prison for another, but at least this one had light. Precious light.

His new prison had walls of mud brick and stucco, with windows open to the sky. Outside was a neighborhood of similar houses — whitewashed, flat-roofed, two stories tall. They ran in neat rows along a terraced hillside, beneath an endless blue sky.

The scavengers left Grand in the downstairs room — a living area with a kitchen to one side. A doorway peeked into an adjacent workshop, while stairs led upwards, disappearing into mystery.

Though the living room was spacious, the furnishings were sparse. The scavengers' home felt hollowed-out, full of empty places where things should be. What remained was a table and chairs, some sackcloth bedding, shelves of crockery, resentment, and the lingering embers of faded hope.

The ragged scavengers were father and son. The son had a ragged wife, and together they had a ragged little girl. On the mantle, behind a votive candle, sat a painted wooden soldier, but there was no ragged boy to play with it.

From his perch on the shelf, Grand watched the drama of their lives unfold. Their words meant nothing to him, but their tones, their expressions, told him everything.

Though the old man walked and breathed, he was already dead. He spent his time in the workshop, puttering over junk as if he could restore its lost worth. He avoided his family, even slept in the workshop.

The son was a disappointment to both father and wife, and, by the way he hung his head around them, he knew it. He was a dreamer, always hoping the next haul would restore them to better times. His wife kept him grounded with her scowls.

As for the woman, she was proud and bitter. Though her dress was a rag, the bangles on her wrists were pure silver — Grand could tell by the way they clinked and chimed. She found labor distasteful, and had no words but sharp ones. Sometimes, while the others slept at night, she cried.

And then there was the little girl, skinny and precocious. They called her Farah, and, if there were any smiles in that house, they were for her. Even the old man warmed when she spied upon his work, though he pretended not to see her. Mostly, though, they ignored her.

For want of an audience, she often spoke to Grand, chattering words of longing and wonder, whispering secrets he couldn't comprehend. She showed him her treasures — a ragdoll, a top, some colored glass beads. She had a piece of granite, glittery with mica, that he rather liked.

One time, she draped a garland of wildflowers around his shoulders. Though Grand couldn't fathom the purpose of the dead vegetation, it was the first gift he'd ever received. He wore it with confused and wary gratitude.

Of course, the girl also spoke to the toy soldier, but nervously, and only when no one was looking. Grand wondered if she wasn't a touch daft.

Regardless, she was the closest thing to a spark of light in that dismal house.

●

After a week of milling about, the scavengers left on another expedition. At last, Grand had a chance to explore the house.

He had prepared for this day by flexing his limbs and testing his joints in his few unwatched moments. Though still feeble from centuries of light deprivation, his body functioned. It was a minor miracle, and he did not take it for granted. In his crystal heart, Grand praised the Master for the genius of his craftsmanship.

Even with the men gone, there remained some difficulties, but Grand had already planned for them. He would make his way down the wall by gently deforming the plaster, gouging a series of handholds. He would do this at night, after the woman retired to her chamber upstairs. He worried that, in the dark, he'd find himself too weak to climb back up, but he'd spent several days basking in the sunlight that trickled through the window. It would have to be enough.

Grand's one obstacle was the little girl. Her bed was a mat beneath the window — one of two mats, actually, though none used the other — where the cool breeze wafted away the heat of the day. Most nights she slept soundly. Yet, if she woke, he would have to...

Grand didn't want to think about it. While it was his duty to return to the Master, his right to kill anything that interfered, he wasn't eager to kill Farah. Her randomness intrigued him. Though she had no Master, she flitted about with enigmatic purpose. She raised questions he hadn't thought to ask.

But, for now, Grand put his questions and worries aside. He scaled the wall, hands and feet boring into pliant stone. He worked slowly, but if caution delayed his homecoming, delayed his punishment, so be it. Perhaps a delay wasn't so bad.

He prayed to the Master that the girl would not wake.

●

Grand explored the house each night, digesting a room at a time.

First he searched the kitchen, but its barren cupboards held no wonders. He climbed a short way up the chimney until it grew too narrow. He clambered back down and shook off the soot.

Next he chanced the staircase, but only far enough to peer into the room above. Nothing interesting there, either, save a crack in the wall that whistled with each gusty draft. He reached into the plaster and repaired it.

He told himself he was merely testing his powers, that he was irked by the disorder of ill-crafted stonework, and a dozen other lies. The quiet voice inside knew better. He hungered for purpose.

Grand touched the wall, feeling for the Master's gentle pull. Nothing. Perhaps, in his weakness, the straw-laced bricks confused his senses?

The second night, he sneaked outside. Behind the house was a small garden, with a stone corral that ran up the hillside. Though there was room for perhaps a dozen beasts, Grand found only a pair of floppy-eared goats. He patched the walls of their pen, adjusting the stones into a sturdier, more aesthetic configuration. Strength and beauty were inseparable; all that served its purpose well was beautiful.

The open air reminded Grand of escape, of his duty to the Master. At least outside he had solid earth beneath his feet, with no straw to muffle the song of the stones. He pressed his hands to the ground, straining to hear the familiar drone of the Master's voice. Besides the restless shuffling of the village, he found only silence.

Grand pushed harder, flaring energy recklessly. He reached deep into the world around him — and found it shifted, wrong. Barren desert, where rampant jungle once thrived. Mountains thrust up from the ground to twice their old height. The very geography was changed, as if cracked and split and reformed from its parts.

And the voices had changed, too. There were too few, and too many were *human*. Where had the old races gone? Where were *his* people?

Shaken, Grand made his way back to the shelf. Without the Master to guide him, how would he find his way home? What if he *never* did?

It was a lonely thought, but also a relief.

When Grand had failed the Master, he ceased to be useful. He had earned his destruction — it was right that he should be broken down, his parts recycled. Still, if he was centuries late, what mattered another delay?

By the third night, Grand's sense of urgency waned. He would still escape, of course, but in his own good time. In the meanwhile, there was exploring to do.

Mostly, the house was empty and dull, but Grand had saved the best room for last. The workshop was filled with the cast-off fruits of the scavengers' excavations — some neatly shelved, others sorted into piles. He was amazed to find that some of the pieces weren't junk at all, but lovingly restored relics, the tools and toys of a bygone age. There was a signal glass, a mechanical gauntlet, a clockwork beetle, a light-drill, and much more. He studied them with reverence, savoring connection with the world he had lost.

Some of the objects were nearly whole, nearly repaired, with hand-machined parts replacing those missing. Others *were* fixed, and lacked only a power source. The old man was a genius. If only he hadn't sold the piezo-crystals, who knew how many of the devices could have been brought back to life?

On a hunch, Grand searched the room thoroughly. It took an hour to find what he was looking for. In a hidden drawer beneath the workbench, he found two gold coins and a single tarnished crystal.

It was chipped and beyond use to the old man, but not to Grand. The particles wanted to align, to fuse and be whole again. They just needed a nudge.

He worked until dawn to mend it.

All through the next day, Grand bubbled over with impatience. Centuries of waiting, and somehow a single day was torture. But wait he did, and dreamed of the workshop, that temple to the past that was his world.

As always, the woman retreated to her chamber shortly after sundown. Grand pressed a hand to the wall and felt her moving around, oddly busy, but he didn't care. Once upstairs, the woman never came down before sunrise.

The little girl's eyelids fluttered shut, and he was off the shelf in an instant.

Grand scuttled across the floor, as noiselessly as his stony frame allowed. He made a beeline for the workshop, head full of possibilities. All of the tools called to him, but the one little crystal — bathed in a day's worth of sunlight on the windowsill — would have precious little charge for experiments.

He tried not to think how his heart would break if none of them worked.

After a minute's deliberation, Grand settled on the practical choice. Of all the relics, the light-drill would be most useful. With it, there would be no need to blast through the straw-laced bricks — while he could, it would be sloppy, noisy work that might bring down the house. With the drill, he could carve silently through the door when he was ready to escape. When he was ready to go home, and face deconstruction.

As Grand reached for the crystal, he felt the gentle rumble of a key turning in a lock. He froze. The house door creaked open.

In strolled a man with oil in his beard and a swagger in his step. Though Grand had never seen him before, he crossed the house as if he owned it, and climbed the stairs to the private chambers. From above came swift footsteps and a gleeful squeal.

Grand looked around. Nobody had noticed him or thought to look for his absence. The girl was still on her pallet, hopefully asleep despite the noise from above.

There was no telling how long the man would be occupied. Grand crawled back along the floor, inch by painful inch, torn between terror of being caught and missing his chance for escape. What if the scavengers came back tomorrow? What if they found his crystal?

The crystal. It was still on the windowsill. He had to go back for it.

Panic got the better of reason. Grand turned and ran, clay feet clunking across the floor.

He remembered Farah, and skidded to a halt.

Grand peeked at the girl; she rolled over but did not wake. Cursing his stupidity, he scurried briskly through the shadows — not pausing until the precious crystal was tucked safely in the secret drawer. From there he made his way back to the other room, this time with caution, achingly slow.

Upstairs, the animal grunts and moans gave way to silence. Grand felt for his subtle handholds and scaled the wall. He crawled across the shelf and climbed to his feet, resuming his usual position.

Below Grand stood the little girl, peering up at him with wide, curious eyes. She stood on her toes and stretched toward him.

He was discovered, doomed. It was her life or his. Kill her and flee. Reach into the stone and bring the whole house down around them. He would be buried all over again, but he would be safe.

Safe in a tomb.

Grand's mind raced in frantic circles, goaded by fears of death and imprisonment. He was paralyzed.

The little girl poked him and giggled.

●

For several more days the scavengers did not return, though oily-beard arrived nightly. Farah used the opportunity to make Grand her plaything.

It had been a near thing when she dragged him from the shelf — he wasn't so much lowered as dropped, and had almost crushed her beneath his stony bulk. Though he only reached her waist, he was nearly her match for weight. Next she had lugged him outside and, with more strength than he expected, hoisted him into a little two-wheeled barrow. With it, she hauled him across the little village and beyond, jabbering to him the entire way.

Grand understood not a word, but the sunlight was glorious.

Day after day they came to the same spot, a meadow with a trickling stream on the shady side of the hill. The little village was blocked from view by a spur, but Grand could feel its vibrations, the sounds of life, through the soles of his feet. Aside from the sheep milling in the distance, they had the hillside to themselves.

Along the stream was a profusion of life, a stark shock of color that stood out from the dry grass and, beyond, the dusty countryside. Though Grand himself never knew thirst, he could see the ground was thirsty.

Farah liked to pick the flowers, to talk to Grand and show him her finds. She had a strange ritual of holding the flower first to her face, inhaling, and then to his. By the dozenth-or-so time he remembered that flesh-things could detect chemicals in the air, and he wondered what the experience was like.

After that he played along, and pretended to inhale, too.

By the third day he felt more comfortable around the girl, and no one else was in sight. When she talked, he spoke back. Neither could understand the other, but it made for companionable noise. When she hunted flowers, he searched for stones. They showed each other their prizes, and sometimes they traded.

On the fifth day Grand found a lovely red jasper, which he smoothed with his hands until it gleamed. It didn't serve any function, but he liked it all the same. As he played with it, catching the sun, an odd idea struck him. He could *give* it purpose. Finally, he understood the riddle of the flower garland.

Grand traded Farah the jasper for a little violet flower — not because he liked the plant, but to make a gift of the stone. A gift was its own purpose.

On their way home that day, Grand realized that the violet flower was the only one he had seen. It might have been the only one in the whole meadow. He placed it in his mouth for safekeeping.

Farah watched him and giggled. He grinned back.

Life continued in this way for another week. Grand let himself dream that the old world really was gone — the wars, the enemies, even the Master. Though brimming with energy from days of sunshine, he invented new excuses to postpone his escape.

So what if he had become a plaything? Was that any worse than a weapon?

●

One morning, after Grand stopped counting the days, the scavengers came home. The woman embraced them both, her smile tight and manner nervous. Farah, on the other hand, met them with kisses and unabashed glee. The old man picked her up and whirled her about.

The young scavenger displayed a string of glittering coins. His face glowed with pride. It had been a good haul.

The woman's eyes grew wide, and for a moment she forgot her unease. She kissed him on the cheek, took some coins, and left toward the market.

The old man walked over to Grand, who stood now on the floor. He eyed Farah with a frown. He asked her a sharp question, his manner stern.

Farah lowered her eyes. She nodded and gave a shy reply, pointing out the door. She took a flower from her hair and gave it to him, a token of apology.

The old man's frown cracked, hints of a smile crinkling around his eyes. He patted Farah's head and shooed her away. With the girl gone off to play, he picked up Grand and took him to the workshop.

The old man looked Grand over with a critical eye. He spoke, but Grand knew the man spoke only to himself. He unrolled a bundle of new tools onto the table.

Grand craned his neck ever so slightly, hoping to steal a glance. He saw tiny brushes, picks, chisels, and a delicate hammer.

What was the man going to do to him?

Old panic welled back up. The man would shatter him, pry out his heart. He would make a trophy of it. He would sell it to the collector. The chisel reached for Grand's face...

...and softly tapped his cheek, the kiss of a feather. It shifted slightly and tapped again, twice more.

Then the old man brushed him off, and scuffed his cheek with a calloused thumb.

Grand held statue-still, struggling to rein in his fear, his whirling thoughts. What was the man doing? He looked again at the tools, and this time he understood.

They were sculptor's tools. He should have known. Every artifact in the room had been repaired, invested with time and care. With love. The man was a healer of machines.

The old man placed a magnifying lens over one eye, and Grand saw himself in the distorted reflection. He saw what the man was fixing.

Half of Grand's face was a shattered ruin.

●

The old man labored all through the day and into the evening, stopping only when the woman brought him supper. It was better fare than their usual, and a more generous portion, but the man barely touched it. He was consumed with his work.

In the glass reflection, Grand watched his new face take form. Tender, skilled hands shaped and smoothed his visage into something new — different, but beautiful in its own way.

With his cheeks scraped down until they were even, his new face could not help but look gaunt. But the old man was an artist. With a gentle cast around the eyes and a little twist of smile curling the edge of his stone lips, Grand thought his face looked kinder than before. In a way, he now resembled a human child.

He looked like Farah, if she were a boy.

The old man finished his work, curled up on his cot, and wept.

●

That night, the young man and his wife stayed up chatting in the kitchen — amicably, for the first time Grand had seen.

Once everyone thought her asleep, Farah crept off her pallet and tiptoed over to the workshop. She peered inside to wave goodnight to Grand, a ritual he had come to enjoy.

The girl saw him and gasped. She ran to the shelf, snatched the toy soldier, and hurried back to the workshop. She tried to press the toy into his hands; when he would not move to take it, she rested it reverently at his feet. Eyes watering, she kissed his forehead. She skipped around the room, making a circuitous route back to her bed.

The moment she lay down there came a knock at the door. It would be the man with the oily beard. Farah didn't like him, so neither did Grand.

The conversation in the kitchen ceased. The man was perplexed, the woman terrified. He rose to answer the door. She dragged at him, pleaded with him, but he shook himself free.

Before the man could reach the door, it opened on its own. In strode oily-beard, tucking a key into his pocket.

The young man's shock gave way to fury. His face turned red, then ugly purple. He pushed his wife away, and the other man laughed at him. They traded angry words.

The young man moved to strike the other, who was much bigger than him. His wife hung from his arm, shrieking.

Oily-beard didn't hesitate. He bowled the young man to the ground and began punching, punching. Blood flew from his knuckles and flecked the floor.

The woman shouted and tore her hair. The old man rose and watched from the doorway, hands shaking. But little Farah charged.

It was insanity. There was nothing the girl could do to hurt a man that size, and yet she screamed defiance and pummeled with her useless little fists. She leapt on his back, biting and clawing like a wild thing.

Oily-beard grabbed a fistful of Farah's hair and dragged her off him. He tossed her roughly, and she tumbled across the floor.

The girl climbed to her feet, heedless of her hurts, and again she charged.

This time the man was ready for her. He stopped her with a backhand that sent her sprawling. He stalked over and kicked her.

The woman screamed. Farah rolled on the ground, clutching her belly.

Grand's stony flesh tingled, his hands trembling like a human's. His crystal heart flared with an unpleasant new sensation. He had never felt it before, but he knew its name.

Rage.

Not caring if he was seen, Grand swung off the edge of the desk, dangling by one hand. He yanked the hidden drawer so hard that it broke loose. The coins tumbled past, but he snatched the crystal before it could fall.

With one arm he hurled himself back onto the desk, rolling to his feet. He brushed away tools, junk, and priceless relics, searching frantically. And then he found it.

Grand slammed the crystal into the light-drill. He wheeled around and pulled the trigger.

As the big man aimed another kick, a searing beam raked his chest, charring clothes and flesh. He looked down in wide-eyed astonishment, sank to his knees, and fell. Curling black smoke rose from the wound.

The woman and old man both rushed to Farah, cradling her protectively. The young man, nose smashed and lips split, struggled to sit up. He spat a bloody spray at the corpse.

Farah curled, whimpering, against the old man. The woman looked at him, eyebrows arched. The old man shrugged and pointed at the workshop.

The woman picked up a candle and walked cautiously to the workshop door. She held the light inside and peered around the corner.

Guiltily, Grand dropped the light-drill, drawing the woman's gaze.

She saw the toy soldier, and then she saw his face. Her knees buckled and her eyes rolled back into her head. She dropped, limp as the dead man.

●

They buried the corpse in the goat field, and did not speak of it again.

The next day the woman refused to look at Grand, refused to remain in the house with him. She screamed and shrieked and wailed, casting an accusing finger at him. Nothing would console her. Nothing would satisfy her, except for him to be gone.

Reluctantly, against Farah's tears and protests, the young man returned Grand to the sack in which he'd arrived. The old man frowned, but did not object. They took Grand back to the collector and sold him. They bartered eagerly and settled for a poor sum, despite the beauty of his new face.

After they left, the collector smiled to himself, pleased with his acquisition. He placed Grand in a box and sealed the lid.

●

Alone in the dark, Grand sulked.

Again he had failed. He had thrown away his chance at escape, risked his own survival, all to save a flesh-thing. He, who had toppled their cities, cracked the very earth to kill them by the thousands.

What had changed?

For centuries, the Master's truth had been Grand's truth. Utility was value, and the flesh-things served no function. They were as random as lichen growing on rock, with no purpose but to exist and to spread. Their rampant variation was an affront to the blessed uniformity of stone.

So why had he chosen Farah over himself?

Maybe Grand was broken, delusional. Maybe, in the Master's silence, he had finally heard his own thoughts.

Or maybe he simply preferred Farah's truths to his own.

To Farah, uniqueness wasn't error. It was beauty, something to be treasured. It was the only purple flower in a field. And though she had no Master to guide her, to give her life meaning, she still had purpose. Grand understood this now.

Like the garland, like the jasper, she was a gift — something brought into the world to make it a little brighter. A gift was its own purpose.

It was a dangerous thought, this idea of purpose without a Master, but it resonated with Grand like song to a stone. It was a thought rich with possibilities, and he had ample time to ponder them.

Grand reached into his mouth for a violet flower that had already begun to wilt. He clutched it and settled in to wait.

Chris Cornetto's story "Heart of Stone" was originally published in Metaphorosis on Friday, 14 February 2020. See magazine.metaphorosis.com

About the author

Chris Cornetto is a physics teacher by day and writer by night, time and coffee permitting. He likes exploring ethical questions through fantasy settings, and enjoys long walks with small dogs. In addition to *Metaphorosis*, his stories have appeared in magazines such as *Wyldblood*, *Hypnos*, and *DreamForge*, and his "Shadow and Full Dark" was a finalist for the Baen Fantasy Adventure Award. His novella, *The Door in the Mountain*, is available through Of Metal & Magic Press.

He can be found online at cjcornetto.wordpress.com and cjcornetto.bsky.social.

Wytchen Wood

Lori J. Fitzgerald

A decade of shavings covered the floor of Lewys's carpentry shop. He didn't bother sweeping any more, although he probably should — wood without magic produces a drab dust that desiccates the throat, shrivels the lungs. He coughed and gulped from his flask, stepping back from his work. Carving the finishing scrollwork on yet another hope chest for the latest bride-to-be in town did nothing to fill his own hollowness.

"Wait for me," she had whispered in the wytchen grove so many years ago, her berry-scented breath caressing his cheek, "I will come back to you." She'd taken magic with her, in the wytchen dust glinting in her sunlit hair as she waved goodbye from the newly-carved wagon. She took his heart as well, but left hope in its place.

Over the years, hope had drained into loneliness, empty and aching, present in the sound of his saw's jagged edge, the taste of his own cough-strained, stale breath, the starkness of his bedroom above the shop. No chance of a bride now, for him, in this small town where he had spurned all coy glances sent his way, waiting for his true love to return.

He wished he hadn't waited.

Still coughing, Lewys threw open the window shutters. He gulped fresh air. Delighted cries of children entered with the breeze.

A pageant wagon creaked into the town square outside his shop, horseless, shedding curls of magic onto the cobblestones from its warped wytchen beams. Children dropped coins into a box attached to the wagon's carriage and scrambled for seats. Eyes widening in shock, Lewys unconsciously dug his fingernails into the windowsill. The wagon's wood was peeling, its stage floor crooked, but it was still the same one. The only one.

As the threadbare curtain opened, more wood peels and sparkling dust showered the stage from the covered wagon's rafters, a natural emission of the enchanted wood, once cut and carved. A princess puppet slumped against a painted forest backdrop. She wore a gown the deep blush of sunset, the falling wytchen dust creating a net of crystals in her golden hair. With the clack of wooden joints, she began a light, graceful dance. A troll, lumbering in from stage right, tore a gasp from the children.

Lewys saw what the audience did not know to look for: The shadow of the puppet master's hands weaving along the stage floor. These puppets had no strings. The wytchen wood itself conjured the play, the magic within the wagon and the carved puppets animating them, their movements directed from above by the puppet master's hands.

After the princess outsmarted the troll, she befriended a dragon, its velvet tongue unfurling like a panting dog. Adults and children alike cheered when she saved a village from a witch.

The curtain closed; the crowd dispersed.

Lewys grabbed his jerkin and dashed outside.

The wagon's damage looked even worse up close. Red rope secured the corners, but it was a temporary bandage for the cracked joints which exposed the wood's inner pith.

The old puppet master emerged from behind the curtain. "Master Lewys, look how well your craft weathered the years. Although, I must admit, some repairs are needed."

"Master Rhodri, you take me for my father," Lewys replied. "He is gone these last ten years. I have his carpentry business as well as his name now."

Hobbling towards him on gnarled joints as the stage boards shifted and groaned, the old man squinted at Lewys. "Aye, I remember you," Rhodri said, beckoning the carpenter to follow him into the narrow living space behind the stage backdrop.

"Is your daughter here?" His lips were dry; his heart constricted with a bare remembrance of hope.

A slow smile deepened the lines on the old man's face. "You remember Roselyn?"

●

The first time Lewys had seen Roselyn, she was sitting on a stump in the wytchen grove, her hair a curtain over her face and lap. He was passing through on his way further into the forest, hatchet slung over his shoulder. "My lady?" he said, approaching carefully, as he would a hare in a thicket, "Are you well?"

She looked up then, and instead of a face smudged with tears as he expected, he saw one smudged with ink from the parchment and quill in her hands. Her eyes were startled, as blue as an open sky. The sun blinked through the branches and transformed her hair into spun gold.

Lewys caught his breath.

"Indeed, I am very well," she replied. "Do you like stories?"

"What? Uh...yes. Doesn't everyone?" he stammered.

"Good!" She jumped off the stump and pocketed an inkwell that had been lying in the grass. "This one is finished. You can be our practice audience." She grabbed Lewys by the wrist and he let go of his hatchet in surprise, dropping it behind him. He spluttered a weak protest — he was supposed to meet his father for work — but the girl tugged him away, into the stand of birch trees that bordered the road into town.

"Audience for what? You don't even know me!"

"Of course I do. Father!" She shouted as they came upon an old wagon pulled into the grass on the side of the road. "The carpenter's son has agreed to see the new play!"

Lewys recognized the man sitting in the grass in front of a small fire, stirring the contents of a pot hanging from a tripod. He was an itinerant toymaker; every girl in the village had at least one of his wood and cloth dolls. Lewys himself had a painted jester on a stand, cleverly rigged to somersault when a button was pressed. It was still on a shelf above his bed, even though he was too old to play with it now.

Master Rhodri looked from his daughter to Lewys and back again. "Roselyn, are you sure..."

She pulled her father to his feet and thrust the parchment into his hands. "Look, I finished! It's the perfect story for the new puppets! Oh, be careful, it's still wet."

"All right, then," Rhodri said, pulling a handkerchief out of his vest pocket to wipe his fingers, "but only if the young man does not mind."

Lewys did not. Roselyn showed him where to sit in the grass beneath a tree, the gentle push of her hand through his shirt sending thrills along his skin. She was a flurry of activity, her bright hair and patched dress swinging to and fro as she fetched the puppets and whispered to her father as he studied the parchment. The puppets were exquisitely carved, like all the dolls Rhodri made, but these had moveable joints and strings, each attached to a cross of wood. Their hair was tangled yarn and their clothes multi-colored swatches of fabric.

Roselyn and her father climbed into the wagon and lowered the puppets into the grass below. The wooden figures clacked as they began to move, and within minutes Lewys forgot about the strings connected to the pair in the wagon above, their hands moving the crosses gracefully. A curtain lifted in his mind.

The story unfolded, wordless but spoken through the puppets' movements. Within Lewys's eyes, the wagon turned to mountain ranges, the grass to a river ford, so real that he could feel the cold wind in the high cliffs and hear the rush of the river. He was immersed in the hardships the brothers faced as they searched for each other. His heart leapt at their final happy reunion. When the puppets bowed, the story's spell over Lewys's mind broke, and he returned with a jolt to his seat in the grass, cooled by the shade of the tree. Roselyn's pleased face smiled down at him from the wagon. He broke into spontaneous applause.

"That was well done," a voice called from further back in the trees. Lewys turned and sprang to his feet. His father approached with his two apprentices. "No wonder my son has shirked his duty for the day." He held out the hatchet. Lewys took it as his father said more quietly, "I was afraid something happened to you, lad." Lewys's face reddened.

"It's my fault," Roselyn said, as she gathered the puppets up. "I did not give him much choice. Please do not be angry with him."

Rhodri came down from the wagon. The carpenter shook his hand, then looked up at the girl, his eyes squinting against the high sun. "Well," the Master Carpenter said, then turned sharply to Lewys, whose color deepened to scarlet. "I can see the appeal of such a play." The apprentices, a few years older than Lewys, grinned and elbowed each other.

"The puppets," he turned back to the toymaker, "are they a new crafting?"

"Yes. My first two. My daughter has great plans for me to make others. She wants a dragon and a witch in particular. And a girl puppet, of course."

The elder Lewys rubbed his chin, dark with beard. "There was something about that play, something quite powerful. I forgot where I was for a while. And I realize that I am long overdue for letters to my own siblings."

"My daughter wrote the story," Rhodri said proudly. "First I had the puppets in mind as another toy, but it was Roselyn's idea to perform plays with them. Do you truly think others will enjoy such entertainment?"

"Truly, but you need a proper stage — a pageant wagon, perhaps, so you can still travel as you do." The carpenter hesitated, glancing at his apprentices, then looked up at Roselyn again. He seemed to make up his mind, and continued, "There is a special wood that I use only for certain projects. I would like to build a pageant wagon for you with this wood. I never take payment for wytchen," he added quickly, when Rhodri blanched. "As I said, it is only for special creations. And I believe this project, and your work, is worthy of it."

Lewys looked at his father in shock. He vaguely remembered the wizened man, passing through town, who had shown his father how to cut wood from the strange trees that no axe could fell before, how to craft an object — for him, it was a staff — with tools and words.

His father had used the wytchen only one other time, as far as Lewys knew, to build a cradle for their neighbor's infant born two months too soon. It was a gift that his father carved in haste, neither eating nor sleeping, in order to finish it by dawn the day after the birth. Within hours after a peaceful nap in the cradle, the child stopped struggling to nurse, and thrived thereafter.

"Come with your daughter to my workshop tomorrow," the master carpenter continued, waving away Rhodri's stammering gratitude. "I'll draw up the plans and we can talk about them over supper." He gestured to Lewys as he turned, a slight smile on his lips. "Let's go. Enough stories for today. Back to chopping wood, lad."

●

The aged puppet master did not answer Lewys's question, but he did not have to. There was no sign of his daughter among the clutter of tools, wood, parchment, and ink pots on the table. Clothes spilled out of a trunk, child's dresses with snippets removed. A torn blanket lay rumpled on the floor. Lewys's heart sank.

How foolish he had been to wait.

The puppet princess was sitting upright in a cabinet with the troll, dragon, and witch on a shelf beneath her. A pile of bedraggled puppets lay at the bottom.

"I'd like to commission you for repairs."

Lewys looked at the rafters and walls, sunlight spearing through the gaps. Rhodri added, "I have the coin to pay you, whatever the cost."

"It's not that, sir." He tried to control his tone, but anger still sharpened his words even after all these years. "There are no wytchen trees left." One of the apprentices, addled with mead in the tavern, had broken his oath and spilled the secret of the grove; news that the master carpenter could release the trees' magic had spread like fire afterwards. The townspeople turned on his father when he refused their foolish requests for wedding rings, pendants, furniture, even an entire house made from wytchen. But the final demand, a flagship, had come from the duke himself in his manor on the coast, delivered with a subtle threat on the carpenter's son's life.

The entire grove was consumed. His father had fallen ill during the ship's crafting and died soon after it was completed.

"But surely you can repair the existing wood?"

Lewys regarded the puppet master, with his bent back and knotted bones, and said kindly, "All due respect, Master Rhodri, but perhaps a warm hearth in a home without wheels would serve you better now."

The old man nodded. "It probably would. But," he gestured to the puppets in the cabinet, "I must continue to tell her stories."

The puppet princess was as finely crafted as porcelain, the warm scent of beeswax polish lingering on her milk-white skin of peeled wytchen wood. Lewys slipped his fingers along the gold cascade of her hair, a silken balm over his callused skin. He had touched Roselyn's hair this way, shyly, so many years ago in the wytchen grove, as his father cut and shaped the wood for the pageant wagon. The elder Lewys murmured words under his breath as he worked, words that he whispered in Rhodri's ear when he handed him small blocks of wytchen.

Coaxed by his daughter, Master Rhodri had fashioned them both toy swords out of plain oak. Lewys and Roselyn pretended they were heroes, fighting trolls and witches, befriending dragons, crafting their own fairy tales from shadows at the forest's edge. Lewys was awkward and reluctant at first, feeling as if he were too old for this play, but Roselyn's earnest imagination captivated him. And it was worth the teases of the other apprentices just to sit close to Roselyn afterwards, their heads touching, as she penned their play into stories for the puppets.

Her lips were always stained blush from the wytchen berries they were not supposed to eat, the red berries marked with stars that she hid in her dress pocket. When the pageant wagon was completed, oiled and shining like the moon, Lewys watched as it rolled away from the grove without need of a horse, Roselyn blowing kisses as she peeked out from behind the curtain. When it was gone, he ate the berry she had slipped into his hand with a whispered promise.

It had flooded his mouth with bitterness, the taste surprising him after a her sweetly-scented breath.

Lewys finally asked the question he had been dreading. "Roselyn is happily married, then?" He tried not to sound bitter, but her name was no longer sweet in his mouth either.

"No. She is not. I wish..." Rhodri took a deep, shaky breath. "Her heart just...stopped." The words were a hammer blow to Lewys, leaving him cold and numb, his mouth drier than bone. His fingers, still caressing the puppet's hair, froze. "One minute she was reading aloud her new story and the next.... It was soon after we left the grove. I don't know what happened."

The old man paused, wiping his eyes with a grimy handkerchief from his pocket. "My wife had died when Roselyn was an infant. My daughter was all I had. My heart lies in that grave with her. To keep living, to keep going...." His voice cracked, and he cleared his throat. "I wanted to save her, to bring her back to life. Impossible I know, but a father will do anything for his child...at least, like this, she can live on in her stories. The stories that she loved, that she lived to write. Her legacy." He reached out and touched the puppet's hair also. "Roselyn and her mother had the same color hair. It is beautiful, isn't it?"

Lewys snapped his hand away, stumbling over the puppet detritus spilling out from the cabinet's bottom.

"You must understand — I could not let her go! But she grew so cold...her hair was the only thing unchanged. It was the only thing still her." The old man twisted his hands, choking back a sob. "Everything I did, all my carving, was for my daughter. *She* was the meaning behind my life's work. She still is. And I have to give her what life I can."

Master Rhodri's struggle to contain his grief echoed in Lewys's own hollow chest. After a moment, he said, "I do understand."

Slowly Lewys collected the puppets from the floor, a mess of small swords and fractured oak limbs. All princes. "Can I fix these for you?" he asked.

Composing himself, shaking his head, the puppet master replied, "They were my gifts, to commemorate her birthdays." He cleared his throat again. "She never got the chance to create a story of true love. I thought perhaps I could write one for her. But the words never came, and the princes never worked right. And I'd find them damaged the next day. If they were made of wytchen, perhaps it would be different, but I used all the blocks your father gave me. Nevertheless, I keep trying, every year."

Lewys was silent for a while, his hands cradling the broken princes. Wytchen dust drifted down from the wagon's ceiling, glittering bright as a promise that had not been broken after all.

I will come back to you.

"I will do something for you, Master Rhodri. And for her."

Back in his room he packed a satchel with a flask of water and food from his meager pantry, then secured a hatchet to his belt. Walking through the bare patch that had once been the grove, he glanced behind him, making sure he was alone before entering the thick forest beyond. He had released the apprentices after the flagship was completed; his destination was a secret only he knew, now.

After an hour, the woodland sloped upwards as the pine trees thinned. He came to a ledge where a single tree grew, slanted trunk and low, leafy branches thriving against the crisp sky: The wytchen sapling that Lewys and his dying father had transplanted here, hidden from human greed. It was larger now, although not as thick and full as the ancient ones in the grove had been. Another sapling, perhaps a year or two old, grew in a sunny spot near its parent. Lewys swallowed the sudden lump in his throat.

He poured water on the roots as an offering, giving some to the sapling as well, and tied a red ribbon around a thick branch as he had seen his father do. Then he sat, the trunk pressing into his jerkin, thinking of what could have been, while the sun painted the sky the color of the princess's gown, of Roselyn's lips, which had never touched his. As the sun descended into the dark forest below him, he hefted his hatchet and spoke his request to the tree.

He hoped he was worthy.

When Lewys came back to the wagon Rhodri was snoring in a corner, blanket wrapped around him and tucked under his grizzled chin. He used the old man's tools, peeling and smoothing the small branch the wytchen had granted him, carving a face, body, and limbs, whispering his father's words to the wood for the first and last time. Rummaging through the trunk, he found the remnants of a white shawl which he cut with a pair of silver scissors to make a doll-size tunic and pants, needle and red thread moving as deftly as when he sewed patches into his own clothing. He painted the eyes and mouth.

Lewys took the puppet princess down from her shelf, arranging her carefully on the work table next to the newly carved prince, staring at her for a long time. He touched her hair again. Leaning close, his lips almost touching her cheek, he breathed deeply. As his lungs filled with her wytchen wood scent, his heart returned, brimming with magic and love as when they had been younger. "Roselyn," he murmured, "I kept my promise too. I waited."

With the scissors he cut his own hair off, and stitched the dark locks to a small felt cap. Uncorking a bottle of pine resin, he brushed the thick glue on the cap and attached it to the puppet prince's head.

Wooden hands twitched, clacked against each other.

Lewys's joints buckled and he flopped to the floor.

●

His name, whispered against his cheek. A whiff of familiar berry.

Lewys opened his eyes. He was sitting in the old wytchen grove under one of the trees, crisscrossing branches spread out above him, and for one disorienting moment he thought the branches were the rafters of the pageant wagon.

Someone was sitting next to him. He turned, and Roselyn's smiling face filled his vision. Reaching out, tentatively, to touch her cheek, he whispered, "Are you real?" His fingers felt strange, stiff.

She laughed. "As real as you," she replied, standing. A pile of berries cascaded from her billowing silk skirts. She pulled him to his feet, and his joints cracked loudly. Lewys pushed the aches in his body aside — Roselyn was here, in front of him, alive and looking more beautiful in a sunset-colored gown than he had ever beheld. Her hair was a curtain of golden strands over her shoulders, a net of crystals holding the strands away from her perfect face.

"I am glad you are finally here, with me, my love," Roselyn whispered, standing so close to him, her eyes sparkling. Lewys folded her into his arms, his heart overflowing, seeking out her lips with his own.

"Not yet," she said, placing her fingers over his mouth. A loud roar sounded from the depths of the forest. Roselyn broke from his grasp. "Father wrote us a story. I don't know all the details, but I know it has a happy ending. We have to work to get there, of course." She gestured to the sword buckled at his hip and, when he stared at it dumbfounded, unsheathed it for him and put it in his hand. The blade was etched with runes. "You're a prince, Lewys."

She pulled a matching sword from a concealed fold in her gown. "I found this one hidden in a wytchen trunk before you came."

Another roar, closer this time, shook the leaves of the trees. Both sword blades began to glow.

"An enchantment! But do you know why?" Prince Lewys asked.

"No," Princess Roselyn said excitedly. "I suppose we will have to figure it out! Remember that friendly dragon? Things aren't always what they seem. We must be clever as well as brave." She smiled up at Lewys, and he had never known such happiness, such excitement.

"We have a new life ahead of us, my love," Roselyn said, and Lewys ached to kiss her. "Are you ready for adventure?"

Magic fell in curls and crystals from the wytchen wood above them. Strange shadows began to move beneath their feet. Lewys took his true love's hand, and together they turned to face the beginning of their story.

●

Lori J. Torone's story "Wytchen Wood" was originally published in Metaphorosis on Friday, 15 December 2017. See magazine.metaphorosis.com

About the author

Lori J. Torone is an adjunct Speech and English professor at her alma mater, St. Joseph's University in Brooklyn. She lives in New York (both upstate and downstate) with her two teenagers and a small, bossy (but lucky she's cute) dog. "Wytchen Wood" was her first semi-pro rate paid story, an audio version of which can be found in Podcastle. She has continued on to publish stories in *Crow & Cross Keys,* the anthology *Museum Piece*, and 99 *Fleeting Fantasies*, and has some independently published work on Amazon under Lori J. Fitzgerald. She is a member of SFWA and is currently writing a mythic fantasy novel. Lori can be found on Twitter/X @MedievalLit and Instagram @whiteraven829.

Hope on the Vine

R.E. Dukalsky

It was early August and hope was withering on the vine.

It had withered every year so far for the last eleven, so Nima was disappointed rather than surprised. Disappointed, frustrated, demoralized. She really thought she'd gotten the balance right this time.

She knelt in front of the raised mound of earth that should have been nourishing the hope vine's roots, her dirty boots poking out behind her and the sun glinting gently off her greying curls. By this point in the season, the vine should be about three feet tall, with multiple spurs twining eight to ten feet in every direction. Heavy buds the size of the first knuckle of her thumb should be swelling between pairs of reniform leaves gleaming a lustrous dark jade. She should be out here looking eagerly for the first open blossom, a rich yellow stellate flower the size of her hand, shading to the orange of glowing embers in the center. She hadn't seen one for many years.

Instead, she stared disconsolately at a meager vine supporting a few anemic yellow-green spurs. The remaining leaves, with two notable exceptions, were the same undernourished shade, their ribs showing more starkly every day, while their edges turned brown and flaked away. Only one spur, the one that twisted around the rail of the fence, showed any semblance of health, and Nima was as baffled by its continued vitality as she was by the parent vine suddenly giving up on life. It had seemed to be growing on schedule — perhaps a little undersized but a good color

— but instead of progressing to the next stage of growth and putting out buds, it had drooped, retreated, withered. Just like its ten predecessors — those that had even bothered to sprout.

Eleven long years on this struggling piece of earth, trying to tease a hope vine from seed to fruit. So far, this was the closest she had come to success. One fruit was all one could expect from such a young vine, but one was all she needed: proof she could send to her Arbiter that this vine would thrive. Then, at last, she could move on. On to the next impoverished, war-scarred town and the next desiccated, abandoned farm, where the potential for hope or fortitude or patience lay dormant under years of neglect and acres of weeds.

The next, and the next, and the next. One by one until the tired land put the years of war and sorrow behind it for good and all.

But there wouldn't be a next and a next if she couldn't bring this vine back to life. Nima doubted she'd live to see the land restored, but leaving here would be its own reward. She dreaded another roasting summer and dreary winter in the small blue house behind her. Another year of being ignored by her neighbors, loathing them in return, and never forgetting no one wanted her here.

Maybe she hadn't fertilized enough? But no; she'd been side-dressing the vine with the recommended half-cup of the special expensive blend that came from the Wizard's Herbarium, and she marked each application on her calendar so she knew she hadn't missed any. Was the mix itself wrong? They said it was guaranteed, but you never knew what that meant with the wizards you got these days. In her time, guarantees had come with blood, not a letter under shiny gilt seal.

If the mix was good, was water the issue? Possible, but hope vines were notoriously flexible in their water needs. In theory, they could take root and grow anywhere, with minimal tending. That was why they, along with fortitude trees and hedges of patience, were among the first recommended plants for war restoration project sites. Even someone who'd never set finger to a garden should be able to grow one — and once a hope vine established itself, every living thing in the area would flourish as well.

Probably she hadn't figured out the right tending regimen. This was where hope vines could be tricky, according to both her own vague memories and the instructions she received each year with the new seed. Fortitude trees could be watered with either sweat or blood (both of which she had in abundance, particularly in the summer). A hedge of patience would grow well with tears, sighs or, in a pinch, prayers. Hope vines demanded fiddly, intangible things: dreams recounted, promises exchanged, plans laid. But wizards didn't dream, she had no one to make promises to, and under the circumstances plans were not hers to lay. She'd tried making promises to the old farmhouse, to the wasted land around it, to the rickety fence and the empty road, but she wasn't sure they counted. If she were honest, the only promise she meant to keep was the one about leaving.

She'd walk out the gate now and never come back if she hadn't given her word, and not with some fancy seal, but in the old way, with consequences for breaking her oath. She'd promised to stay until she could prove she'd restored local resilience to an acceptable baseline — in plainspeak, until the hope vine was able (or willing?) to reproduce. No one back in the capital knew, or really cared, how long it took or what it asked of the grower. The point was to have wizards scattered across the land, repairing the scars of war where everyone could see them doing it. So here she was until she could cultivate her release.

Nima stroked a finger across one of the limp leaves. "If you stay alive, I leave and you never have to see me again. So save us both some pain and just *grow*," she whispered, putting all the force of her will into it. No effect, of course, except a dull burn up her right arm to complement her aching knees.

"What's wrong with your plant?"

The voice was high-pitched and unfamiliar. Nima looked up to see a girl of about twelve years draped across the fence near the gate ten feet away. Just about where the questing ends of the vine ought to be right now, Nima thought sourly. She'd never seen the girl before, though she had the look of a local: a short, wide body, tawny skin, a blunt nose, and straight, thick black hair cut short above her shoulders. Her eyes were close-set, small, and twinkling with curiosity.

"It isn't growing," Nima said shortly. She was sick to death of these suspicious locals. "Did you need something?"

"I'm Yun," the girl said, completely ignoring the pointed question. "Did you forget to water it?"

"No," Nima replied, trying to rein in her temper. It wouldn't improve her relationship with the locals if she started yelling at children. On the other hand, she didn't care that much about having a relationship with the locals. She turned back to the hope vine, scratching gently in the dirt around the main stalk to see if there was something preying on its roots.

"What about fertilizing? Did you feed it?" Yun asked.

"Yes," Nima said without looking up.

"Did you put it in the right kind of soil?"

"*Yes.*"

"Does it get enough sun?"

Exasperated, Nima gestured at the open sky. Her back twinged, and she looked up with an even more unfriendly expression than she'd intended.

"Hm. Maybe it's getting *too* much sun," Yun mused, unfazed. "Or maybe this isn't a good place for it to grow."

Nima clenched her jaw and bent back down. Maybe the irritating child would get bored and wander away. After a few seconds she heard soft footsteps against the dust and dared to hope. But no luck.

"But I don't know," Yun said, from much nearer, almost right in front of Nima. "It *feels* like it wants to grow here." A brown hand appeared at the corner of Nima's vision, stroking the leaves of the one remaining spur.

Nima looked up sharply. "Don't touch it," she snapped.

Yun whipped her hand away and looked, for the first time, as if she were picking up on Nima's unwelcoming demeanor. "Why not?"

"Because it's *my* vine," Nima replied, hearing how ridiculous she sounded even as the words came out of her mouth. "What I mean is, it's fragile and it isn't polite to touch other people's crops."

This was evidently a new concept to Yun. "I help Aunt Lio with her beans all the time and she says —"

But Nima was done with this conversation she hadn't wanted in the first place. She didn't want what passed for local agricultural expertise, especially from a child, and needed peace and quiet to think about what to try next. "Then I'm sure she would appreciate your help now," she interrupted, then stood up and stalked away, pushing through the stiffness in her knees. "Don't touch my plants," she called over her shoulder without looking back.

●

Working on a half-baked theory that her bad mood was somehow hampering the vine's growth, Nima stayed away from it for the next few days. She kept a sharp eye on the fence, but the girl had vanished back to whatever ramshackle farmhouse she'd come from. Nima saw her traipsing by once on the road, but the girl showed no inclination to stop or pester the vine.

After a week, Nima woke up having slept well, and decided she'd waited enough time to test her theory. If her mood did somehow affect the vine, she'd given it time to recover and should be able to see the effects. She filled her big watering can, sprinkled in the special water-soluble fertilizer and lugged it out to the fence.

The vine looked exactly the same: anemic stalk and spurs, withered yellow leaves slowly crumbling off their ribs... and one perfectly healthy spur climbing slowly around the fence rail along the road. The good spur had even put out another two leaves while the rest of the plant died.

"What...?" Nima stood there, hands hanging down open at her sides. She had learned to grow things; the profusely healthy vegetable garden behind the house attested to that. She glared at the vine, disregarding the theory she'd been testing. "What do you *want* from me?" There was no reason this should be so hard, no reason this spur should thrive while the parent plant died, no reason the one plant that mattered should wither while the rest of the garden flourished.

A sharp trill pierced her despair. Yun was tromping down the road in heavy boots several sizes too big for her, swinging two empty beaten metal buckets, whistling like the cloudy morning had been made for her alone. There was something odd about the buckets; they were the wrong shape somehow, too rounded on the bottom, with asymmetric sides. Nima squinted at them and realized they were infantry helmets, inexpertly beaten into a slightly more bucket-like shape by a *very* amateur blacksmith.

"Did you figure out how to fix your plant?" Yun asked. She must have taken Nima's attempt to parse the helmets-turned-buckets as an invitation to stop and chat.

"No," Nima said, trying to think of a task that would take her away from the fence but allow her to keep an eye on the girl.

"It looks better, though," Yun said, waving one of the buckets at the flourishing spur. At least she wasn't trying to touch it. She wrinkled her nose. "That part, at least."

Nima picked up her watering can and began dribbling the water gently around the roots of the vine. Yun didn't take the hint. She tromped a few steps closer, set the buckets down with a dusty *thump*, and squatted on her haunches in front of the vine. "I think it's happier on this side of the fence."

"Plants don't feel happy or sad," Nima said repressively. She saw Yun shrug out of the corner of her eye.

"Aunt Lio says they do." Aunt Lio was evidently the arbiter of reality. She leaned closer. "What kind of plant is this anyway?"

"A hope vine," Nima said shortly, then surprised herself by continuing, "at least, it's supposed to be."

"I never saw one of those before," Yun said, scrunching up her nose and peering at the plant with renewed interest.

"They aren't very common after the war," Nima found herself explaining.

"Ah," Yun said sagely, although she wasn't old enough to remember even the final years of the war and couldn't possibly understand what lay behind the disappearance of the country's native resilient vegetation. "What's it for?"

For giving you and all your ungrateful kin a future worth growing into, Nima thought but did not say. The last thing she wanted was this girl's irate aunt descending to put the wizard in her place. "If it grows," she said, biting off each word, "it will reinforce the local ecosystem — that means the soil, the water, other plants, the animals that eat those plants, and people who rely on the plants and animals," she added, confident that the local school, if one even existed, did not cover the ecology of resilience.

"We have been having some problems," Yun agreed thoughtfully, just as if she were a grizzled veteran farmer. She leaned even closer to the vine, body rolling at such an angle that Nima feared she would pitch face first into the plant — and the railing.

"Be careful," she said, more harshly than she had intended.

Yun straightened up, but didn't look abashed. "I think maybe this part of the plant isn't bothered by something that's messing with the rest of it," she said. "Or maybe it just likes that I talk to it."

Yun's comment niggled at the back of Nima's brain. Maybe there *was* something affecting the roots or the leaves on the parent vine that hadn't spread to the healthy spur yet — or maybe the spur had some kind of natural resistance...

"I have to go restake the beans," Yun was saying in the background, but Nima was no longer paying attention. She didn't even notice the girl stretching out a stealthy hand to give the new leaves a friendly tap. "I'll be back tomorrow."

●

Yun kept turning up after that. Sometimes for an hour, sometimes for ten minutes, sometimes carrying her ridiculous repurposed buckets, sometimes hauling a feed sack on a little wagon, frequently with her arms full of hollow reeds as wide as her wrist and as tall as she was. She never seemed to be in a hurry or fear that whoever sent her on these tasks would be impatient at her dawdling.

Aunt Lio either ran a slipshod operation or didn't particularly care what this niece was up to. Yun never mentioned her parents, so maybe she was a war orphan dumped on her only known relative. Maybe Lio had so much help on her farm that one lolly-gagging child made no difference. Or maybe they were just relieved to get a break from her questions.

"Do they have hope vines where you come from?" she asked one time.

"No," Nima said.

"Then how do you know how to grow one?"

I don't, Nima thought. "Resilient plants need the same things as any other plants —"

"Where *do* you come from anyway?" Yun interrupted.

"Not here," Nima said, picking up her rake and walking away.

●

"I know this isn't your farm," Yun said another time.

Nima was pruning back the dead leaves on the spurs closest to the healthy one, in case the problem was some kind of spore or mildew. Her shears jumped and nearly clipped a healthy leaf. "What is that supposed to mean?" she demanded.

"Everyone knows you aren't from here, even though you've lived here forever," Yun said with a limber shrug. "When are the people who belong to this farm coming back?"

"They aren't," Nima snapped.

"Maybe this would grow better if they did," Yun said, bumping the vine with grimy knuckles.

"Don't touch," Nima said, but she'd long since given up on the idea that Yun would listen.

"Don't worry, *I'm* not going away," Yun said, more to the vine than to Nima. "Hey look, there's a new grabby bit here!"

●

"How does a hope vine help the... ecosystem?" Yun asked after she'd been coming by regularly for almost a month.

"Different ways," Nima said distractedly, her words punctuated by the *thonk-crunch* of her trowel. She was digging some small trenches to drain excess water away from the hope vine's mound just in case the roots were becoming waterlogged. "Other things... grow better... near a hope vine. Fewer diseases... more abundant production. Roots... stop erosion and make dead soil fertile again. You can live... off a single fruit... for a long time. Healing tea or tincture from the leaves. And just being around the flowers..." she sat back on her heels and wiped her forehead, "I really can't explain what that feels like, you have to experience it for yourself."

"We could really use one of those," Yun said. "Aunt Lio says the beans need a miracle."

"Hope vines aren't miracles, they're applied magic," Nima said sternly. "And you shouldn't expect either to do your work for you."

"I am doing the work," Yun said, but without heat. "But there's a bug that came and it eats the buds before they can bloom." She reached a finger out toward the vine, then pulled it back again.

●

"What's it like?" Yun asked on one unreasonably hot day.

"What's what like?" Nima replied, only half listening as she teased a tendril gently through a gap in the climbing frame.

"Being a bad wizard."

Nima froze with the tendril balanced on one finger. "What do you mean by that?" she asked carefully. Sweat trickled between her shoulder blades.

"Everyone knows," Yun said without noticeable concern. "You're a bad wizard who made all the bad stuff happen in the war."

Nima snatched her hand away from the vine so she wouldn't transmit her feelings through the tender shoots. "That's a gross exaggeration."

"Also, I saw your thing," Yun pointed at Nima's right arm, where the geas runes constraining Nima's magic and her free movement crawled with slow abandon. She'd probably spotted it the first time they met, but Nima found herself tugging her sleeve down anyway, angry at her own shame. She hated any reminder that she was permanently separated from her magic, even though she'd accepted the geas binding to avoid lifetime imprisonment.

"Aunt Lio says getting a nice farm to run isn't a real punishment," Yun persisted. She reached out and casually flicked the vine. Nima winced, but the vine held firm. In fact, it flexed a tendril toward the sun.

Nima picked up her trowel, hefted it, set it down. She didn't like the idea of Yun and her aunt discussing her sentence as if were just moderately interesting village gossip. "Your Aunt Lio doesn't know everything. It's not a punishment. It's a collective obligation."

"Hah!" Nima wasn't sure whether Yun's hard, fierce laugh was meant to dismiss the possibility that Aunt Lio could be wrong or the official line that felt flat even to the wizard herself. "Then why do you have that?" Yun jabbed a finger at the geas runes.

"Yes, fine, technically it's a punishment," Nima said sharply, "but I *cooperated*. I *agreed* to community service. I could have just done my time, but I entered the program voluntarily to try to make amends for what happened. Nobody forced me to wear this." She shook her right arm at the girl. "Nobody forced me to be here."

"Then why don't you leave?" Yun asked in genuine curiosity.

In all the years she'd endured in this place, no one had ever asked Nima what she thought about her situation. It was humiliating to be grateful for a child's fickle attention, but her life was nothing but humiliations now.

"Because what the wizards did was wrong," Nima said, striving for patience. Not native to this farm and not native to her either. "We had the right — we had good intentions. But we did things that had consequences far beyond what we intended, beyond what we could have imagined when we started."

"What were you trying to do?" Yun asked. "Aunt Lio says all you wizards just wanted to keep your power and when the war happened you decided to burn the country down instead of sharing even one good thing with regular people."

There had been a time where Nima would have drowned in their own sweat anyone who dared speak so harshly, so honestly. "How fortunate that a bean farmer knows the absolute truth!" she snapped, then reined herself in. "Look, the war was complicated and you're too young to understand most of what happened."

Yun crossed her arms, stubborn. "Aunt Lio says the wizards hoarded all the best food and medicine and magic in their towers," she persisted. "She says the headwomen of all the villages went to the towers and asked for the wizards to share, but the wizards said they had nothing valuable to trade. So the villages stopped sending tithes to the towers and then the wizards came out of their towers and ruined everything. And Tonji says the wizards never loved anything but themselves and that's why they could do what they did to the land and the rivers and everything."

Nima had no idea who Tonji was and she didn't like their assessment of the war. "That's not an accurate picture," she said stiffly, although it was, if boiled down to its essence and told through the eyes of the victors. "There was... more to it." In the back of her mind she heard, was always hearing, the soul-shattering crack of her tower's foundations.

"Like what?" Yun asked pugnaciously.

Nima thought of her tower, its dimensions aligned precisely with the planes and angles of her interior self. Like a phantom limb, she could feel vast power seeping from the land into her tower's stones, and from its stones into her. Power that extended the reach of her hand as far as thought could take it, that honed her vision, peering keen-edged with magic into any secret she desired. When her tower stood, she was the secret composer of the song beneath everything... and then they had pulled her tower down and she was nothing. Keeper of a withered garden in a mutilated land. Bitterness welled up in her.

"I couldn't possibly explain it to you in a way you could comprehend," she said, aiming for austere, but coming no higher than cruel.

Yun gave her a very straight look then shrugged deliberately. "Well, it's not like you know the first thing about growing beans," she replied.

It toppled Nima like she was a tower herself. Yun hadn't spoken in pettiness, but rather with the world-weary familiarity of someone who often had to defend her own worth. Maybe she'd heard her aunt use the line and seen the seed of truth it held. Yun didn't know what it was like to wield power that could make and unmake the world. Nima didn't know how to grow beans. Once, the difference between them would have been too vast to comprehend. Now, it meant that between the two of them, Nima was merely the less capable subsistence farmer.

Nima was used to wrapping prickly defensiveness around herself like armor, but she suddenly couldn't reach it. They just sat there looking at each other, black eyes to brown. "I never had any reason to grow beans before," Nima said, conceding.

The silence stretched for several more minutes while Nima pretended to rearrange the dirt at the base of the vine's main stalk. "Wizards cared for the land a long time," she continued at last. "People couldn't see what we did. For generations we kept the soil fertile, managed the weather, sustained the forests...we didn't intend to destroy so much, not when the rebellion started and not after. We were just desperate to make the war stop."

Yun tilted her head skeptically. "If you wanted the war to stop, you could have just given the headwomen what they asked for. You didn't have to do all that bad stuff," she said.

Nima had used a lot of noble sentences and fine words to get her through the dark nights of doubt, but none of them volunteered to stand up against that unflinching logic. "You're right," she said, after a long minute. "But we did do it. I. I did it. All I can do now is try to repair what I can."

Yun glanced away as if the subject had never really been that interesting in the first place. "So why is this vine so important?"

Nima scrubbed her hands over her face. "This land, one of the things it has — had —" she paused. Started again. "A long time ago, wizards found a way to cultivate resilience. *Yes, wizards,*" she snarled at the skeptical look on Yun's face. "They taught seeds to grow hope, patience, and fortitude. They infused rivers with trust and stocked lakes with solidarity. They showed the land how to produce the things that would sustain it, no matter what came." She pressed her lips together and bit down hard on the sour feeling twisting her belly. "But the hope vines and trees of fortitude and all the rest of it didn't survive the war."

"Because of you," Yun interrupted. "You wizards, I mean. Right?"

"It wasn't just —" But it was. They had stretched out their hands and stripped the land of everything their forebears had grafted into it. She was out here trying to make amends for her role in that enormous crime, so what was the point of spinning a sweeter-sounding version of the truth to this child who wasn't buying it anyway? "Yes. Wizards weren't responsible for all the bad things that happened in the war, but they — we — did destroy the resiliency ecosystem. We did that."

"Why?" Yun asked.

A simple, deadly question. Nima had answers she'd given herself, answers she'd given her colleagues who doubted their course of action, answers she'd given the court that sentenced her.

Only we have the knowledge and experience to guide this country to its better future. Our better future requires peace and peace requires order, and order can only come when the villages bow to our authority.

These rebel armies are destroying the land — perhaps if they see harsh consequences they will surrender before we have to kill them all.

Some of the Wizard's Consortium chose to cross that final line and the rest of us let ourselves get pulled across.

So many answers. But none of them sufficient, in the end, to justify stripping the land of everything that held it together and helped it thrive. Not when you boiled it down to a young girl and an old wizard crouched on opposite sides of a fence in a dusty nowhere trying to understand why nothing good could grow.

"Because we forgot that wizards first built towers to serve and protect the land," she said at last. She suddenly became aware of how stiff and heavy her legs had become. "We thought of the land as something under our rule, not under our care. So when the rebels — when the war came, it was easy to use the land as a weapon."

Nima remembered standing atop her tower filled with grim righteousness as she stretched out her hands and drained the Ko River into the bedrock. She remembered the sense of urgency that filled her heart when she walked in the fortitude groves, blighting the ancient trees to strip the rebels of their will to fight. She remembered having those feelings, but she couldn't reproduce them. Now, all she could feel was shame and despair at the enormity of what they had done. How could she ever have thought that growing one stupid hope vine would mean anything in the face of their atrocities? Even if she lived to be the oldest wizard in history and grew a new vine or tree every year, it would be a pitiful drop in the desert their crimes had created.

"And now wizards must undo what wizards did," Yun chanted the first line of the decree that doomed all surviving wizards to a lifetime of penal restitution — out here in the backlands, it was probably the only part of the decree she'd ever heard. She bopped one of the withered leaves unceremoniously. "You're not very good at it, huh?"

Nima lurched forward to cup the leaf, jerked herself back, then stared at it as it seemed to stretch out luxuriously. Was a deeper green flushing outward from the central rib, or were her eyes lying to her? "This work is much harder than I expected," she admitted.

Yun nodded sagely. "I bet it's hard to make this place hopeful when you aren't." Then her head shot up as if hearing a voice calling her. "Whoops, gotta go," she said. She hopped to her feet, scooped up her buckets, and took off at a steady trot down the road.

Nima watched her go, rolling her last words around and around. *It's hard to make this place hopeful when you aren't.* That could be the problem. Perhaps the hope vine couldn't grow if its tender had no hope of her own to share.

But then — Nima leaned over the leaf Yun had bopped, without touching it herself. It was noticeably greener and drooped less. And then — she peered down where Yun had been flicking her careless fingers, and there was one, no two! new tendrils peeking out. Nima thought about all the times she'd scolded Yun for touching the vine. Was it a coincidence that the healthy spur was the one closest to the road, the easiest one for Yun to reach? Was the vine nourishing itself off her innate hope for the future, a future Yun expected to be part of in exactly the way Nima didn't?

Nima brooded on it all night.

●

Yun came back the next day, and the next, chattering about the problem with Aunt Lio's bean crop. Nima made noncommittal noises or gave answers she forgot even as they came out of her mouth. The beans weren't her problem. She was watching Yun and the vine, trying to learn the secret of how she made it grow.

The girl didn't appear to be doing anything special. She didn't even seem to be paying attention to the vine most of the time, although she always crouched by it when she stopped, even though it meant she had to perch in the ditch on the side of the road. She would bump or stroke or tap the leaves or tendrils to emphasize a point or sometimes as if it were agreeing with her, but she might have done the same thing with her buckets or the wagon. She certainly didn't treat the vine with the care or deference that Nima herself did. Nima couldn't see any one thing that set Yun's interactions with the hope vine above her own — except, of course, that the vine grew where Yun touched it and withered everywhere she did not.

And 'grow' was a bit of an understatement. On Nima's side of the fence, the other spurs had desiccated into dry, spindly stalks, their leaves long since crumbled into the dirt. On Yun's side, seven feet of rich jade green sprouted leaves the size of Nima's palm, twisted tendrils around every surface of the climbing frame and the fence rails, and were sending out new spurs in two places. There was even one tiny green nub that, given time, would become a bud.

Nima never, ever touched the healthy spur. She even stood on the dead side of the plant to water and dress it, hoping not to poison it with indirect contact. She didn't encourage Yun to touch it either, superstitiously worried that the vine would pick up on her desperation and stop responding to Yun's presence. She just held herself in nervous stasis, waiting for the bloom.

●

Maybe it was the empty rattling of the sledge that drew Nima's attention, or maybe it was how Yun's feet dragged in the dusty road as she approached. Whatever it was, Nima looked up one day to see a new expression on Yun's face: despair.

The girl squatted in her usual place on the other side of the fence, her hands flopped over her knees and her black hair sticking to her sweaty temples. She didn't touch the vine.

"What's wrong with you?" Nima said, more harshly than she'd intended. But then, she'd never been a gentle person.

"The bean crop failed," Yun said, looking burdened in a way Nima had never seen her. "Aunt Lio says there's no way to save it now, even though we built reed irrigation all the way from the river and I pick off all the bugs I can find."

"I guess you'll have to eat something other than beans this winter," Nima said, trying to remember if beans had some sort of local cultural significance. "Variety is good for you."

Yun looked at her like Nima had just suggested they try to eat the sun. "We don't eat beans, we sell them," she said. Then, in a cadence that sounded like something she'd heard from someone else many times, "No beans, no money. No money, no winter stores, no shoes, no seeds for spring."

"Oh," Nima said. Of course Yun's entire livelihood hung on those stupid beans. "That's...bad."

Yun sighed heavily and gave the swollen bud close to her face the gentlest of caresses. Nima sucked in her breath, but Yun didn't notice and the vine didn't show any immediate negative effects. "Do you know any way to fix the beans?" she asked suddenly, looking a little nervous for the first time Nima could remember. "I mean...I know you said we shouldn't expect magic to fix our problems, but you also said wizards used to take care of the land..."

"Not with this," Nima said, jerking her right arm in a sharp motion so the geas runes caught the light.

"Oh, right," Yun said, subsiding back despondently. She sighed again. "We sure could use one of these hope vines right now." Nima suddenly recognized the line as something she'd heard Yun saying a lot lately.

That night, Nima found herself thinking of Yun's beans instead of the hope vine. There wasn't any reason to be thinking about either one — all she could do for the vine was what she'd done, and Yun was someone else's problem — but she kept coming back to it like a piece of food stuck between her molars. It wasn't just the girl's despair; Nima hadn't spent a century as a powerful wizard with a tower of her own because she was susceptible to sad peasant children. But what if the bean crop's failure forced Yun and her family to leave the farm? What if they starved? What would happen to the hope vine if Yun suddenly stopped coming by, telling her cheerful stories and helping pass the long weary days with impertinent questions?

And more than that — Yun's intervention, however unintentional, had resuscitated Nima's own hope of escaping this pastoral prison. Which, in a way, put her in Yun's debt.

And that was the nub of the problem, Nima realized as she dried her dinner dishes. She felt indebted to Yun, who had helped her while enduring Nima's constant unwelcoming attitude. And there was a way to repay her. But it would cost Nima the one thing she valued: the opportunity to leave.

On the other hand, if she didn't pay this debt, Nima would be proving Aunt Lio and Tonji right: that wizards would rather let the land and everyone who depended on it suffer than share even one good thing. And even more than she hated being in debt, more than she hated being here, Nima found she hated the idea that Lio and her ilk could be right about her after all. If they were, then Yun would keep believing they were right about the war, would keep thinking wizards were bad people who embraced destruction to feed their own selfishness.

"Damn and damn!" she swore, looking down to discover she'd worried her washing cloth into threads.

She couldn't repair the land. She couldn't undo the systemic destruction they'd wrought, not even in a wizard's lifetime.

She could save one bean farm. She could persuade one girl — maybe one family — that wizards could help as well as harm. Not just for show, or to win release, but because she wanted Yun to welcome a future with wizards in it as enthusiastically as she welcomed everything else. It would cost at least a year of her life; there was no guarantee that this hope vine would fruit two years in a row. But after eleven years of loneliness and failure, was one more really such a sacrifice?

"Yes it *is*," Nima snarled to the empty room, to herself. "But wizards must undo what wizards did." Then she picked up her lamp and stomped out of the house.

Hope vines thrived on promises, after all.

●

Nima waited with characteristic impatience for Yun to arrive the next morning, but the girl didn't appear until mid-afternoon, trudging along in her too-big boots and carrying her mangled helmet buckets. She flashed Nima a wan smile as she crouched down by the vine, petting it as if seeking comfort from the silky leaves.

"How are the beans?" Nima asked awkwardly after a minute. She hadn't thought about this part, not once she'd made her decision. And, she realized, she'd never started one of their conversations before today. It was always Yun, interrupting her work with a question or observation.

"Still bad," Yun said. "Aunt Lio says we'll be lucky to get a quarter of the crop."

"Well, look," Nima said, her eyes fixed on the hope vine while her hands fiddled anxiously in the dirt. "This thing is about to flower. If it fruits, I could — you could have it. You could plant it near your beans. I'm sure it would grow for you."

Yun looked up, her eyes shining in a way Nima had never seen. It was like all the dust had washed right out of her world. "You mean it? We could have a hope vine of our own?"

"It won't make your bean plants come back," Nima warned. "Probably."

"But it means they'll grow good next year!" Yun said with an enormous grin. "That's right, isn't it? Everything grows better where a hope vine grows?"

"That's the theory," Nima agreed. She felt surprisingly guilty giving the girl hope when she wasn't sure the vine was capable of producing a fruit this late in the season. But then, hope was all she had to offer, from beginning to end.

"But... wait." Yun crinkled up her face around her nose. "Don't you have to send that fruit to your Arbiter? So they send you on to your next place?"

"There will be another fruit, in another year," Nima said with forced calm, giving the vine an affectionate little stroke with the back of her hand. And to her utter astonishment, a tiny bright green tendril unfurled from beneath her knuckles.

●

The vine bloomed four days later, opening like a star and drawing the eye from anywhere in the garden. Nima found herself staring at it for uncounted time, just tracing its silky depths with her eyes. She could see, if she looked closely in the way wizards were trained to do, runes tracing and retracing themselves deep within the flower's genetic structure. But mostly she just stood beside the vine, falling into its radiance.

Two days after the bloom, Nima came out early to gaze at the flower. It was a habit she'd fallen into immediately, getting in close to the luminous petals, tracing the dew that beaded gently on their surface, filling her lungs with the flower's scent before facing the tasks of the day. It made the whole day seem more bearable; no, it made tomorrow seem so promising it was worth today's labor.

At the cottage door she gasped in horror; even from that distance she could see the blossom was withered, almost completely gone after only two days. What would she tell Yun? How had she killed the flower so quickly even when everything seemed to be going well?

But when she drew close, crouching down and parting the leaves with trembling hands, she saw the flower had died a purely natural death. Hope blossomed fleetingly, it seemed, or perhaps her decision had hurried it along. There, glowing greeny-golden as a brand-new promise, a small orb poked up from the heart of the crumpled petals.

The vine's first fruit.

R.E. Dukalsky's story "Hope on the Vine" was originally published in Metaphorosis on Friday, 4 March 2022. See magazine.metaphorosis.com

About the author

R.E. Dukalsky writes speculative fiction about memory, change, conflict and what happens afterward. She has been told that she has School House Rock charm and that she would make an excellent rebel leader, among other dubious accolades. Since debuting in *Metaphorosis,* her stories have appeared in *Beneath Ceaseless Skies, The Fabulist, Medusa Tales,* and elsewhere.

The Conch Shell

Elizabeth Raphael

Mira sat on the couch, clutching the conch shell tightly in her hands. Her back had gone stiff and her legs were sweating against the soft leather of the couch, but she dared not move — not yet. If she stayed there just a little longer, she told herself, surely she would remember why she was holding the shell. Despite everything, she still had faith in the power of her mind. All she needed to do was focus, and with a bit of time, it all would fall into place. She took several slow breaths, the kind she had learned in the yoga class that Thalia insisted she take, and waited for the moment to return to her. It did not.

Mira let out a breath in a huff, the loops of her ever-present pearl necklace clinking softly against each other with the motion. She had never been one to wallow in self-pity, but she could feel it now, coiling itself around her body and threatening to pull her down. Her late husband had once told her that her ability to find the smallest sliver of positivity in any situation was a big part of what made him fall for her, but at the moment, she felt far removed from that version of herself. She could see no silver lining to dementia. She was being stolen away, piece by piece, and there was nothing she could do about it. Logically, she knew it was an indiscriminate condition, but the raw emotional side of her still wanted to throw herself to the ground like a toddler having a tantrum and wail about the unfairness of it all. She had done everything right, everything that was supposed to ensure that she aged as gracefully as possible.

She had eaten a balanced diet, enjoying her food but not overindulging — or, rather, over-indulging only on special occasions. She had stayed physically active, swimming a daily mile until her early sixties, when arthritis seized her shoulders and she was forced to switch to walking. She had never been as graceful on land as in the water, but she had taken to walking regardless. As long as she was up and active, she was happy.

The cruelest bit of all, or so it felt to her, was that she had been just as diligent with her cognitive health. In addition to her daily crossword, she periodically took up disparate hobbies so she'd gain diverse skills — everything from archery to rangoli. She had walked through life with a tenacious optimism that everything would turn out OK, and it hadn't.

Fighting off a wave of despair, Mira tightened her grip on the shell. She knew it was risky to stay in this pose. That new helper of hers — Kylee, Mira recalled after only a brief hesitation, Kylee with a double 'e' at the end — was due any minute now. If Kylee came in and saw Mira frozen like this, she would immediately call Thalia to let her know that her mother was having another episode. Thalia would then leave work straight away and drive the nearly 100 miles that separated them, likely using that time to work on a new pitch for persuading Mira to move into a retirement home.

Mira's mouth twisted at the thought. Thalia was too young to fully understand the situation. To her, it was simple: Mira's dementia was progressing — a fact that Mira herself could not deny — and therefore, she shouldn't live alone. Why not be part of a community full of people who were going through the same sort of thing, cared for by workers trained for that very purpose? Mira shook her head. How easy it was for Thalia to come to such conclusions when it wasn't her being forced to leave the home she had lived in for nearly 60 years. It wasn't her being expected to leave behind the living room where her child had taken her first steps, the library full of her carefully curated books, swimming trophies, and assorted treasures, the bedroom that she had shared with her husband for 54 wonderful, too-short years. No, it certainly wasn't Thalia's freedom and privacy being stripped bare. It wasn't her world being compressed down into one personality-devoid room.

Mira's pulse thrummed an angry staccato inside of her, each beat a warning. She had to stop getting angry like this, she chastised herself. It wasn't good for her, and it wasn't fair to Thalia. Thalia's single-mindedness could be frustrating, true, but she was a good woman and a good daughter. She was just a worrier, as her father had been. There was no ill intent behind this retirement home crusade of hers, Mira knew; there was only love. Thalia had harbored concerns about Mira living alone after her father's passing, and Mira's short-lived disappearance six months back had unfortunately given meat to those fears. If Thalia didn't have to travel so often for work, she undoubtedly would have cleared out a bedroom in her condo and convinced Mira to move in long ago. As matters stood, this was her way of trying to keep Mira safe.

A cell phone trilled loudly from the coffee table, interrupting Mira's line of thought. Prying a hand from the shell, she slid her turquoise reading glasses down in place from the top of her head and leaned over, squinting at the name flashing across the small screen. It was Thalia. A smile quirked Mira's mouth. It was almost as if Thalia had sensed Mira's train of thought and waited until she meandered into a more positive frame of mind to call. Thalia had always been an intuitive child.

Mira picked up the phone with her free hand. "Hello, dear," she said, her back popping as she leaned back against the couch. "I was just thinking about you."

"Hey, hey. How's my favorite mother today?" There was a faintly echoey quality to Thalia's voice, which told Mira that she was on speaker phone. That was not unusual. Thalia was usually doing at least ten things at once. At the beginning of her daughter's career, Mira had been surprised by how busy the life of a marine biologist was, but she was well used to it at this point.

"Your favorite mother is fine." Mira supposed that was a partial truth. Her eyes flicked towards the mahogany grandfather clock that stood solemnly in the corner. "It's early for a call from you. Late lunch?"

Thalia clicked her tongue, a nervous gesture that had started when she was around eight. Nowadays, it indicated that Thalia was particularly worried about Mira's health. "No, Mom," Thalia began carefully. "I'm leaving on my trip to Mexico today. We got the grant to go to Lake Xochimilco and study the axolotls. I'll be gone for a month."

Mira muttered several choice curses inside her head — phrases that Thalia would have been shocked to hear, had they actually slipped out of her mother's mouth. "I know all of that, Thalia," she lied. "I just thought you left tomorrow."

There was a brief, weighted pause. "Oh. Yeah. This trip has been such a long time in the making, it is hard to believe it's finally here." A horn honked faintly in the background. "Ugh — this traffic." Thalia tsked. "I thought by leaving early, I'd get ahead of it all."

"It's tourist season. Rush hour is every hour."

Thalia snorted. "That's true. So" — her voice took on a tone of practiced ease —"how are you doing today?"

"You already asked that, love."

"I know, I'm just..." Thalia clicked her tongue. "I applied for this grant before everything happened, and it's such a long trip. I don't know. Maybe it's not the right time."

"Thalia —" Mira tried to interject, but Thalia seemed not to hear her.

"I'd like to be there to get things going, so I could always go and then leave after a week or two. Dr. Slater is more than qualified to handle everything on his own. Well, on his own with all of the research assistants. He'd be fine. I'm superfluous, really."

"THALIA," Mira's voice was loud and firm. "You are not now, nor have you ever been superfluous. This trip has been your dream since you were a child, and it's your hard work that made it happen. You will go on this trip, all four weeks of it, and you won't think of me at all while you're there. That's final."

"Oh, Mom." Mira could hear the smile in Thalia's voice. "How could I not think of you? If it weren't for you, I wouldn't be a marine biologist. You taught me everything I know."

"Ohh, pshh," Mira said dismissively, just as her cheeks flushed with pleasure. "I think your professors probably did that."

"Not really. You knew that the Greenland shark was the oldest vertebrate over the bowhead whale before that research was even published. That bit really impressed my 'Intro to Marine Bio' class. I think Professor Gruber thought I was a witch," Thalia laughed. "Though witchcraft is as good of an explanation as any. Your knowledge of the ocean has always bordered on the supernatural."

"I read a lot of books, love. That's hardly supernatural."

"True, but that doesn't fully explain —"

"So," Mira interrupted, pivoting the conversation. There was an explanation, she knew, but of course she couldn't remember what it was. Thalia didn't need to know that, though. "You mentioned that a Dr. Slater will be on this trip. Is he that handsome British fellow we ran into at that Cuban restaurant?"

"He is," Thalia answered suspiciously.

"He's the one with the wife and three daughters, right?"

"Hmm — no, Dr. Slater is single. I'm not sure who you're thinking of," Thalia said before picking up on her mother's comfortingly familiar matchmaking attempt. "Oh, wait. I see what you did there. I tripped right into that one."

Mira smiled. "Your old mother still has a few tricks. I know you'll be busy on this trip, but hey, there's a lot of hours in the day."

"Duly noted." Thalia clicked her tongue. "So you're really all right? Really? I worry about you all alone."

"I won't be alone. I have Kylee, I have that yoga class — I'll be fine."

"But you seemed fine before your disappearance." Thalia took a deep breath. "You know, Coastal Gardens is really more of an apartment complex than a retirement home. You'd have your own space —"

"I'll be fine. That's not going to happen again," Mira said, willing her voice to sound more assured than she felt.

Thalia clicked her tongue. "OK, mom. I'll still have my cell. So you can call me, and I'll call you, of course. Let's see..." Thalia drummed her fingers on the steering wheel. "My itinerary is on your fridge, but I'll text it to Kylee so she has it, too." She clicked her tongue. "I guess that's everything."

"Have a good trip, love."

"Bye, mom. I'm only a phone call away if you need me for anything. I love you."

"Love you, too."

The smile slowly faded from Mira's face as she set her cell back down and wrapped her freed hand back around the shell. Her disappearance. It always came back to that. It was a specter that she could never escape from, one determined to wreck her past and present. There had been mental lapses before then, but that blasted episode was when it really became a problem. Cruelest of all, the events of that day remained a mystery.

Familiar feelings of frustration and fear rose in Mira as she once again tried to remember what had happened the day of her disappearance. She had eaten her usual breakfast — soft-boiled egg on a piece of wheat toast — then dressed in her exercise clothes and set out for her daily walk. After that, she recalled nothing. Nothing until nearly two days later, when she was found on a beach nearly 65 miles away by a group of early morning surfers, soaking wet but otherwise fine.

Shades of that day occasionally came to her. They bore no true form but gave an overall feeling of peace. However she had gotten there and whatever she had been doing, she had not been afraid. The fear had come later, when she was being subjected to every test possible in the hospital. On the beach, she had felt safe.

Mira sat up straight, scooting to the edge of the couch. The beach. That day. That's when she had gotten the conch shell, wasn't it? Yes, she realized with sudden clarity, excitement buzzing through her. She had argued with the EMTs — they hadn't wanted her to bring it in the ambulance — but Mira had refused to get in without it. She kept insisting she had found it, it was important, and she wasn't going to give it up.

But no, that wasn't quite right, was it? Mira's nails drummed against the rough exterior of the shell as she thought. That was what she had told the EMTs, but she had already started to forget by then, hadn't she? Forget that she had not found it; it had been given to her. Yes, that was it! It had been given to her by someone she knew, someone she loved, someone she had not seen in a long time. Mira's right leg bounced in time to the drumming of her fingers as the moment solidified further. She could almost picture their face, but the image was distorted, as if viewed through a warped mirror.

The front door burst open in a flurry of noise and motion. Mira reflexively leapt to her feet, nearly dropping the shell in the process. A small blonde woman — Kylee — stepped through the entranceway a few seconds after.

"Sorry, sorry!" Kylee said, bowing her head in apology. "That wind is nuts! The storm must be coming sooner than they said." She shut the door behind her with visible effort. "That door got away from me."

"So it would seem!" Mira's voice was faint, her heart still pounding from the surprise.

Kylee quickly finger-combed her windblown tresses and pulled the hair back into a low ponytail, securing it with a black scrunchie that she slid off of her wrist. "Your doorbell is broken, by the way. I was out there ringing it for, like, five minutes."

Mira chose to avoid the obvious question as to why Kylee didn't just knock on the door. Instead, she tsked in sympathy.

"I told Thalia I didn't need one of those camera bells. The more fancy parts an item has, the more likely they are to break."

Kylee slung her purse down on the coffee table. "No biggie — I'll just give that handyman of yours a call. Hopefully he'll be able to come out soon and do some troubleshooting. Is his card still on the fridge?"

"Should be." Mira settled herself back down on the couch.

"Good. I'll put on a pot of coffee while I'm in there. After being tossed about in that wind, I could use a warming up. Want a cup?"

"Mmm — add a splash of chocolate milk to mine."

Kylee raised her brows. "Oh, that sounds good! I'll have to try it, too." She gestured towards Mira's lap. "Cool shell, by the way! Doing some dusting?"

"Oh!" Mira looked down. She had forgotten that she had been holding the conch. "I was...admiring it." That was right, wasn't it?

"I can see why. It's a beauty!" Kylee reached out and stroked the smooth inner curve of the shell. "Look at those colors — just like a sunrise! When I was 10, my aunt went deep-sea fishing off the coast of the Florida Keys and brought me back one of these. She ate the conch, and I got the shell. I thought it was the prettiest thing in the world — almost as pretty as yours. Anyway, it broke during a move just two years after I got it. Military life, you know? I was crushed. It was the star of my shell collection." The corners of Kylee's mouth turned down ever so slightly, an odd sight on her normally impossibly cheerful face.

A pang of sympathy struck Mira. She knew that to most, Kylee's story would seem inconsequential. But as a woman with more than one collection, she knew it to be quite serious, indeed.

Mira patted Kylee's hand. "I'm sorry about that, dear." Mira took care to make sure that her tone sounded serious and respectful.

Kylee met Mira's eyes and flashed a grateful smile. "Thanks. You know what's silly? Every night before bed — when I still had the shell, obviously — I used to hold it up to my ear so I could hear the ocean. I'd sit there like that for at least five minutes." She chuckled. "That's funny — I haven't thought about that in forever. I was an odd kid. Memories..."

Kylee shook her head, amused with herself, then disappeared into the kitchen.

"Memories," Mira echoed in a voice barely loud enough to even be considered a whisper.

Mira waited until she heard the coffee pot start bubbling and the murmur of Kylee chatting with the handyman before she began. Supporting the shell with both hands, she raised it up with a slow reverence and placed it carefully against her ear.

Mira gasped. At the sound of the soft woosh from inside the shell, it all came back — who she really was, where she'd really come from. She remembered her whole life, which had begun beneath the waves. Warm and weightless, she would ride the currents and tides, powered by the undulation of her tail.

Oh, her tail! It had been beautiful, a glistening gradient of blue and green scales that melded seamlessly with the soft, pliable skin at her waist. Her family all had the same colors on their tails, though arranged in different patterns.

Oh! She had a family down there — a large family! Parents, six sisters, and four times as many aunts, uncles, and cousins. She had loved them fiercely, and they had loved her in return. It had broken her heart to leave them behind, but she had known then, deep in the marrow of her bones, that part of her destiny lay on the land. As with the other mermaids who had made the choice before her, she had been granted the opportunity to leave the water with the understanding that when her human form was nearing its end, she would return it and her soul to the sea. Far from being an unwelcome caveat, she had taken comfort in the knowledge that some day, she would return.

Mira gasped yet again as it all connected. That day, her disappearance — she had not had an episode. She had been called to that beach! One of her sisters — Adria, beautiful Adria with the long black hair that curled like no one else's in their family — had been waiting there in the waters for her. She had aged at approximately one quarter of the rate that Mira had on land, but it was the kindness radiating from Adria that truly made her beautiful. Mira would have been content just to gaze upon her sister again, but Adria had called her there to give her an important gift — the shell. Not just an object of beauty, it was a talisman designed to help bring Mira back to herself.

Tears pooled in the corner of Mira's mouth as they streamed down her face, their salty taste carrying with it the echoes of the sea. Her heart bloomed with a joy beyond words. She had lost much over the years, and she knew that even this moment might soon slip away from her.

But right now, she remembered.

Elizabeth Raphael's story "The Conch Shell" was originally published in Metaphorosis on Friday, 12 May 2023. See magazine.metaphorosis.com

About the author

Elizabeth Raphael enjoys arranging letters in pleasing patterns. She is most at peace in libraries and bookstores, where she whittles away many moments gazing wordlessly uponst ink on pages. In writing as in reading she dabbles in many genres, but speculative fiction has her heart.

ElizabethRaphael.com

The Bagel Shop Owner's Nephew

J. Tynan Burke

Last night, Murray called with another bunch of prophecies, so Yonatan Kaplan hasn't slept yet. He stayed up preparing dossiers on some doomed socialites instead. Now it's a little after dawn, Friday morning, and he's standing in line outside Fox's Bagels with a thermos and a tote bag. He's shaky from too much caffeine and too little sleep, but he doesn't regret it. The socialites will die this weekend, according to Murray, and Murray's got a good track record. When they do die, the obituary writers will call the Morgue — The Pre-Morgue Clipping Service, Yonatan's business — to buy the dossiers, expecting the usual thoughtfulness and prescience. So it had been best to begin the work immediately.

The line shortens when a gaggle of tourists leaves Fox's. Yonatan steps forward, fills his thermos lid with hot tea, and covers a yawn with the hand still holding the thermos. He thinks back to Murray's sneering tone when he 'apologized' for calling so late, his fake sadness that Yonatan would stay up all night working. It doesn't matter if Murray made a lucky guess or if it was knowledge from Murray's divine gift — either way, it's *rude* to mock a man for doing his job. Yonatan takes a big drink of tea and frowns. *Fucking prophets.* They're nothing like what you read about.

The line shortens again and it's Yonatan's turn to enter the shop. The woman in front of him holds the door, and he nods to her as he steps inside.

Yonatan is welcomed by a burst of humidity, which carries the smell of fresh onions and the accumulated yeast of three generations. He's also welcomed by a new cashier, a young man of maybe twenty who shares the owner Shay's big ears and too-skinny frame. The hunger in Yonatan's gut is replaced with a rarely-felt electricity, once debilitating, though he has learned to weather it. For him the closest analogy is the shock of a new and severe crush settling in, but he's not gay, trust him, he's checked.

This young man, whose name tag reads 'Stephen,' is perhaps a Tzadik Nistar.

"Morning," Yonatan manages, stepping to the counter. "One of everything, please."

Stephen raises an eyebrow over a baggy eye. "Like, one everything bagel, or..."

Yonatan cringes and tries to twist it into a smile. "Sorry. Bad joke I have with Shay. One of each kind of bagel, please."

Stephen counts off on his fingers. "So one plain, one poppy, one sesame, one onion..."

"And one everything," Yonatan finishes.

Stephen collects and bags the bagels. "I don't get it."

Yonatan shrugs. "I said it was a bad joke. Is it even a joke? Who knows how these things start." Yonatan knows. He tried making a pun five or six years ago after a long night of drinking. "Shay might remember. Do you know Shay, uh..." He points at the name tag like he just noticed it. "Stephen?"

"Uncle Shay? I sure do. It's Steve, though. That'll be fifteen dollars." Steve beeps some buttons on the register.

"You know what, Steve, why don't you add another poppy."

Steve wraps the extra bagel while Yonatan observes. No piercings or ink that he can see. That's good, it's one of the rules Adonai actually cares about any more.

The register beeps again. Steve says, "Eighteen dollars."

Yonatan hands him a twenty and puts the bagels in his tote. "Nice to meet you, Steve. Tell Shay Yonatan says hi."

Out front, Yonatan leans against the wall and takes two deep breaths while his gut settles. It turns to growling, sour with too much tea and too little food. Much better, easy to address. He returns to the Morgue and goes straight to the computer, where he opens a password-protected document and types an addition to a long list of names, in a column headed 'CANDIDATES': *Stephen 'Steve' Fox, ~20, Lower East Side, NYC.* And then, at long last, it is bagel time. Poppy, toasted, with leftover veggie cream cheese.

Later he's on the office couch, taking a little break and reading a space opera, when the landline rings. It's barely audible over the Norwegian black metal he put on to stay awake. His watch says eight-thirty, but he decides to take it anyway — it can't be any less interesting than the exposition dump he's at in the book, or the *Page Six* profiles he's avoiding. Off goes the music and in goes a bookmark. The bookmark has an Emerson quote he likes. He can read part of it sticking out: *Time and space are but physiological colors which the eye makes, but.*

While he crosses the Morgue, he steps over a spilled pile of clippings, and growls. Always more work, dossiers to build, Tzadikim to chronicle, things to file. Sleep, somewhere in there. And the phone keeps ringing, and he almost yells something passive-aggressive at it, but no, that's more something his father would do. With a silent glance back at the clippings he walks the rest of the way.

"Pre-Morgue Clipping Service, this is Yonatan."

"Thank you for answering, Yonatan. I hope it is not too early." A woman, British? Her voice seems far away, like a long-distance call in some old movie.

Her comment reminds Yonatan that he stayed up all night, and he stifles a yawn. "It's no trouble at all, Ms..."

"How rude of me. My name is Ariel."

Like the mermaid? Yonatan thinks. He can't help himself — he's never met a woman with that name before. He gets a stupid grin at the idea of talking to a cryptid.

"How can I help you, Ariel?"

"I am looking for somebody, of course."

Yonatan clears his throat and recites a spiel. This happens. "I'm sorry, Ariel, but this isn't that kind of place. We do collect information on people, but we don't release it until they're deceased. I can refer you to several good private investigators."

A pause, then Ariel continues. "Yes, of course, how silly of me — he *is* deceased. Or that's what I've heard. I was hoping you could tell me, and then if... I am looking for his remains."

Yonatan bites his lip. This feels like the sort of thing that will involve lawyers, maybe family drama. He should have let it go to voice mail. "Why don't you tell me who you're looking for, and leave me your contact information, and I'll get back to you," he says, a little too quick, to get her off the line. He wonders if the machine that records his calls is still working. He hasn't had to check in a while.

"I'm sorry, have I said something wrong?" She sounds sweet, like she doesn't know.

And maybe she doesn't, maybe there's a language barrier or Yonatan is maybe cranky. A saying of his mom's pops into his head, *Make sure to offer somebody an offramp before they drive too far down stupid street,* so he does. "Did you mean to say you're looking for his *grave,* instead of his *remains?*"

Another pause. "That is probably the better word. We wish to pay our respects."

"Alright." He explains the fee structure, and takes down a credit card number and the name of the man in question: John Miller, possibly died 'quite recently', near San Francisco. It startles him — that's the name of a Tzadik Nistar. And about a million other people, of course. Anyway, last he checked, John the Tzadik was alive and living in San Diego. Still, something feels off about Ariel, so after he hangs up, Yonatan decides to download the call from the recorder. He finds the device inside a junction box by the front door, warm and smelling like hour-old tar. It's fried. His assistant Sarah comes in a minute later while he's digging in the wiring with a flashlight between his teeth. He turns and asks for help, and accidentally blinds her.

While they extract the recorder together, he brings her up to speed on the socialites' dossiers. Could she pick up where he left off, and also run to the gadget store for a new recorder? There're fresh bagels in the kitchenette. He grabs his space opera and goes home without telling her about

Ariel's call. She doesn't need to know, she isn't a Searcher. From the privacy of his apartment, he sends an email to the Searcher who follows Miller, checking in. Finally he goes to bed.

Asleep, he dreams — who doesn't? Sometimes he has one of the dreams everybody gets, like having a test he forgot to study for even though grad school was six years ago. Once he had an entire month of dreams where every day was Saturday and he had to follow his dad's Shabbat rules, which he never had to in real life. His dad didn't go all Haredi — instead of 'Haredi' you can say 'ultra-orthodox,' if you want to piss his dad off — until after the terrorist attacks really started to ramp up in America, around when Yonatan was starting college.

This morning's dream is about a maple tree. He's squatting on a crook in the branches, up where the trunk first splits, with a magnifying glass and a clipboard. The clipboard holds a chart, the scientific names of bugs on the left and numbers on the right. He's a scientist doing a population survey. He counts tiny black ants through the magnifying glass, writes the number next to their species name. The name's in Latin, and he wishes he knew how to pronounce —

Of course he knows how it's pronounced, he's been studying liturgical languages for years. This is a dream. He straightens out his back and stretches. Even here, it hurts from all the time he spends at his desk. He should really get a better chair.

"What are you doing? Don't just squat there if you aren't going to work."

Yonatan looks down. The source of the voice is a park ranger in iridescent green, like a beetle with a chip on its shoulder, gender indeterminate. While the ranger glares, Yonatan inspects some leaves. Aphids are munching on the cellulose while lady-bird beetles munch on the aphids. He's too distracted to count them, so he hops onto the grass and brushes crumbled bark off his shirt.

"I guess it's time to go, then," he says, pocketing his magnifying glass.

"I guess so," says the ranger.

"What'd I do wrong?"

"I just don't like people climbing in my tree when they don't have a good reason." The ranger puts their fists on their hips, a superhero pose.

"Just this tree?"

The ranger spreads their arms. "There aren't any other trees."

Yonatan sees he's in a field, wild grasses stretching to the horizon. He looks up at the maple appreciatively. It's well-pruned and healthy. "You must be very dedicated to your work," he says.

"We all do what we must." The ranger rolls their eyes and bows. "But seriously though, thanks for your part. Now get going."

Yonatan nods, climbs into the Ford Explorer he hasn't owned for ten years, and drives off to the lab.

He wakes and showers, and by the time he's finished, the sun has set and it's Shabbat, the Jewish day of rest. Many in his neighborhood, inside the old borders of the Manhattan *eruv,* observe it; a quick glance out his apartment's paint-flecked window confirms their absence on the streets. Yonatan rarely observes; he's usually busy with Searcher work, and today is no exception. The only concession he makes is accessing the office remotely, which is not really a concession at all. He looks back at his laptop, at an email from Sarah. Executive summary: she finished the socialites' dossiers and got a new call recorder set up. The old one only broke that morning, so they have Murray's call, but nothing after.

Yonatan goes to make a cup of tea and heat up some leftover beef *pad see ew.* The tea is black and steeps in his favorite mug, also black, to match his jeans and hoodie — *even your favorite **tea** is black,* his dad jokes. Text on the mug reads *The Chosen Son.* It's half-blasphemous, a birthday present from his mom a few years ago. *Shh, don't tell your father,* she said with a wink. They're still together. He'll never understand it. Carrying his dinner back to his computer, he stubs his toe, and narrowly avoids saying "God damn it," choosing instead the more respectful "Fuck!"

There's a reply in his inbox with bad news about John Miller. During a business trip to San Francisco this week, Miller was beaten into a coma. He died of his injuries just this morning. Yonatan blinks twice. He hopes that Ariel wasn't asking about *that* John Miller, but can't really convince himself it's a coincidence. Then he reminds himself that people usually call right after a death — it's the Morgue's whole business model. Difference is, nobody ever asked him about one of the Tzadikim before.

To still the dread creeping over his scalp, he plugs his phone into his sound system and resumes the Norwegian metal playlist. The part of him that isn't freaking out hopes it annoys the upstairs neighbors. They're always clomping around at four in the morning. What are they, meth heads?

He sets a couch cushion on the floor and sits, closing his eyes and counting breaths. He wishes there were a Searcher manual to consult, but theirs is an oral tradition, a secrecy born from the historical necessity to hide. The next best thing would be to ask Leonard, his old mentor and thesis advisor, but Leonard's been dead almost a year. Upon reflection, Yonatan knows Leonard would just repeat the fundamental rule about Searching: *If somebody asks for information about a Tzadik Nistar, you must provide it.*

Yonatan's no good at following rules he doesn't grok the need for, but the rationale behind the rule is obvious, to somebody who knows the history. His thoughts go to his first real Searcher meeting. It was in a faculty bar that the university had shoved into a basement.

"So you've passed the hard part of the test," Leonard had said. "Now for the oral portion. Explain, in your own words, the Tzadikim Nistarim."

Yonatan nodded. "An old Talmudic legend. Thirty-six righteous people who are so great, they keep God from trashing this place. If some day only thirty-five people held that honor, God would wipe us out."

Leonard tut-tutted. "Please, use one of the other names, around me at least."

"Does... Adonai actually care?" The word felt funny in Yonatan's mouth.

"There are things Adonai cares more and less about. The work I do with the Tzadikim, securing the life of creation — it's more important than, say, Shabbat, if you need it to be. But Adonai's name is a matter of basic respect."

Yonatan glanced at his vodka tonic. "Sorry, Leonard. I'll work on it."

"Thank you. So these Tzadikim Nistarim, they're special?"

"One could even be the Messiah," Yonatan said. "A Tzadik Nistar doesn't know they're a Tzadik Nistar. Some say it's a metaphor to encourage you to behave well — you never know when you might turn out to be one."

Leonard waved his hand. "But..."

"But you say they're real."

"I don't say, Yonatan, I know. And I know you can feel it — you picked one out of a full lecture hall."

Yonatan grunted. Both men sipped their vodkas. Leonard put a hand on the table. "Eschatology aside, the archive is still a brilliant career opportunity, you know. I'm old, and I need an apprentice. And — this is just a personal observation — I don't see academia in your future."

Yonatan snorted and then agreed. So began his life with the Searchers, who identify and chronicle these Tzadikim, and provide information about them whenever it's requested. Yonatan jokes that it's in case Adonai ever loses his phone book. And they have a simple principle: *always provide the information.* After all, you never know who might be asking.

Well, as Leonard liked to remind him, one has principles so one can follow them in uncertain situations. Thinking about the present, Yonatan adds, *But that doesn't mean one has to like it.* This situation is uncertain as fuck. Miller was *murdered.* Why is Ariel drawing his attention to it? She doesn't *sound* like a prophet, or not like any he's talked to. More importantly, has somebody begun knocking off the Tzadikim? He hopes not — it's onerous enough locating the replacement when just one has died.

He can only see malign interpretations... but maybe that's just him. Breathing, he knows that he doesn't actually need the answers to do his job. All he *has* to do is get Ariel the information on Miller, and follow the procedures for when a Tzadik Nistar dies: Adonai will give a different righteous person a promotion, and the Searchers will re-examine their Candidates. They'll check their premonitions from afar, and consult the prophets; if there's sufficient evidence about a Candidate, people will follow up in person and see how they feel. Then, like so many things, it will conclude with an argument on the Internet.

Yonatan stands and returns to the table.

While he picks at his noodles and finishes his tea, he contemplates his tepid mug. *The Chosen Son.* When he's done eating, he goes to the Morgue to pull Miller's file.

An NYPD detective surprises him at the Morgue around eight. She introduces herself, Detective Corazón Lopez, can she come in and ask some questions? Yonatan flashes guiltily to the documents about Miller he was scanning, but he hasn't done anything wrong, he doesn't even know why the detective is here. Even so, he wants to tug nervously at his collar like Bugs Bunny, but he hides it, says yeah, asks if she wants some water or tea. She says no, and so he doesn't get anything for himself either. They sit at the card table in the kitchenette.

"An interesting business model," Lopez says, "selling dead person facts."

"Newspapers used to have departments like this," Yonatan says. "Probably half our archive is stuff we picked up from the *Times* when it went under."

"I did not know that." Lopez produces a notepad from her tan leather jacket and jots something down. "You oughta put that on your website."

Yonatan frowns. "Takes some of the mystique out, don't you think?"

Lopez smiles back. "Might make people like me less *curious.* Don't you think."

What is this? Yonatan shows his palms. "Can I help alleviate that curiosity?"

"That's the idea." Lopez looks out of the kitchenette, at the room of rolling stacks, the hallway down the middle crammed with file cabinets and banker's boxes. Her shoulders relax and she leans in. "Alright. There's been some suspicious deaths these last few months. Medium-profile, local celebrities." She's clearly not talking about Miller, which only barely reduces Yonatan's anxiety. "One of us noticed that the obits came out pretty quick, pretty detailed, like they'd been researched beforehand. We called the writers, they told us about you."

Yonatan nods, his mouth dry now, and he wishes he'd gotten water after all. "It's what I — we — do, detective. We identify notable and interesting people and prepare dossiers. Sometimes they die unexpectedly, and that's when we're most in demand. It's morbid, but it's a niche we proudly fill." He hopes the normalcy of business-speak is as comforting to her as it is to him.

"You seem to get awful lucky. Look, we know you solicit tips about people to profile, it's right there on your website."

He scrunches his face. "And the NYPD thinks a tipster might be involved in this?"

She shrugs. "Sounds crazy, right? But it's worth looking into. We think they're all the same perp, and you're linked to them too in your own way. We were hoping you could tell us about the tipsters."

"We have a policy against that."

It's Lopez's turn to show her palms. "You wouldn't want to seem uncooperative, would you? And do you have any idea how easy it would be to get a warrant?"

He doesn't, but pissing off the cops does seem riskier to the Morgue than compromising on this, and there are no Searcher rules about the prophets. "Sure. Alright. Give me the names of the deceased and I'll see if anybody mentioned them to us."

She does. The computer says they're all names from tips, all tips from Murray. He explains it to her, and she takes it down, standing behind him while he works.

"Does Murray have a last name?" she asks.

"Probably, but I don't know it."

"Do you at least have his *phone number*?"

"I do... he called last night, actually." Yonatan deflates. "He gave me three names, some local socialites." Maybe he shouldn't mention the details, that Murray said they won't last the weekend. He doesn't want to get the police involved in knowing the future, he's seen that old movie *Minority Report*. But human life is sacred, certainly more so than company policy, even this company.

"I have a recording," his conscience helpfully adds for him, settling the matter. His brain catches up and he says, "I should warn you, Murray thinks he's psychic. He says lots of crazy stuff… and he said they might die this weekend."

Lopez stares at him like he admitted he has bodies in the freezer, but don't worry, he has a permit. "*So* hard to find good help. Can I *get* the recording?"

Yonatan stiffens. "I need to know I'm not liable for anything, that the Morgue — that's what we call it, I know, I know — isn't in trouble, or else you'll need that warrant."

"Mister Kaplan, these people could be in danger." She sighs and takes out her phone. "The D.A. is working tonight. You got a lawyer we can hammer something out with?"

Yonatan copies down a phone number from the computer. His lawyer keeps Shabbat, no work and no phone calls, but his assistant can fetch him. Lopez trades her business card for the number. "Have the D.A. call this — it's my lawyer Joel's assistant Kacy. Tell her Yonatan Kaplan says to get Joel ASAP, it's a matter of life and death."

After Lopez leaves Yonatan sinks his face into his hands, tugs on his hair. This is more murders than he's used to dealing with on a Friday night, which is zero. He needs a drink and something that wasn't cooked yesterday. Randomly he texts the woman he's newly dating, Dinah. She gets right back to him, she's free. They meet at a diner off 1st Avenue that smells like frying sausage and somebody else's Tabasco.

"Every time we eat you get steak," Dinah says when their food arrives, his steak and eggs, her Greek salad.

"I like steak," he says. He takes a bite and finishes his beer. "I used to be a vegetarian, did you know that?"

"I did not," she says.

"I had a Buddhist phase starting in undergrad. Ate a lot of hummus."

"A real rebel." Dinah eats some of her salad and drinks her own beer.

"You have no idea." Yonatan flags down a waiter and orders another drink.

"Why'd you stop? Being vegetarian," she says.

"It was *hard,*" he says with a forced whine.

She laughs. "And a Ph.D. wasn't?"

"Different hard. When you find the right thing to care about, something that clicks..." He shrugs.

"I hear ya."

While they eat, Yonatan's mind keeps drifting to Ariel, and to dealing with the cops, and he keeps shoving the thoughts down. He's only half surprised when he blurts out, "What are you doing after this?"

Dinah smiles. "Nothing, you?"

"I'm in a whiskey-and-cartoons kind of mood," he says.

Dinah looks into her empty beer glass. "It'll have to be your place, they're fumigating my neighbor's, ew."

"My TV isn't very big," Yonatan says.

She puts her hand on his, says with a fake, over-earnest tone, "It's not the size that matters, it's the company."

The door is unlocked when they get to his apartment, and when Yonatan turns on the light he finds the place trashed — books and clothes everywhere, the kitchen table turned over, his not-very-big TV smashed. Dumb as a cow, he walks inside. "What the fuck!"

Dinah stays put in the door frame. "I assume it's not normally like this."

"No..." Yonatan holds up a hand and searches the apartment to confirm it's empty. It doesn't take long, it's not that big. "You can come in if you want. Try not to touch anything."

She looks relieved. "Oh, thank god. I gotta piss but it seemed like a bad time to ask."

He points her to the bathroom, and while she's in there he does a more thorough search. There's a note on the fridge, scrawled on the back of an envelope. *Murray says hi.* Dinah joins him while he's staring at it.

At the same time, they both say she should leave, and they share a sad laugh. She zips up her coat. "This wasn't a very good date, Yoni."

"I'll do better next time." He's already got his wallet out, rummaging for Lopez's card.

"You better." She kisses him, quick but not a peck, and leaves.

Yonatan jams the door shut and calls the detective. She picks up and says that Joel should call any second to fill him in. Yonatan tells her about his apartment, about the note. She says she'll send somebody over. His phone beeps, and he switches calls.

"Joel? Hey, before we start, uh..." Yonatan tells Joel about the break-in.

After a pause, Joel takes a few false starts and sighs. "'Well, here's another nice mess you've got me into!' What was that, Laurel and Hardy?" Joel makes ancient references when he's nervous.

"Never watched it. I don't suppose you can tell me everything's gonna be okay?"

"Right, sorry." Yonatan hears Joel flipping through papers. "Honestly I can't see how the break-in changes anything on my end, for this Murray business. You're fine, legally. The cops weren't bluffing about the warrant though, that would be easy to get, so you had the right instincts, to cooperate. Judges don't like being pulled in after hours." A little edge of resentment to Joel's voice at the end. "So you're fine, and the Morgue is fine, but you should probably get used to hearing from law enforcement more. They're jealous of your tip line."

Yonatan grunts. Half the Morgue's revenue must come from prophets' tips, prophets who are usually shady as fuck, who'd bolt at the first sign of the cops. But saving lives is the right thing to do. Hopefully he'll only scare away people who are trying to pass murder plots off as revelations. Then again, what if the murder plots *are* the revelations — ? Best not to go down that road, not sober at least.

"Oh, one more thing," Joel says. "They want you to call Murray so they can get a trace."

Fucking fuck. "I don't really want them to hear... *I* don't really want to hear what he has to say, even."

"Is this about your, er, *other* archive, Yonatan?"

Joel isn't a Searcher, but Yonatan's told him about it. Joel just thinks it's a run-of-the-mill weird sect. Spilling Adonai's secrets is unwise, but so is keeping secrets from your lawyer. Yonatan rubs the back of his neck with his free hand. "Yeah, and Murray's not making us look good."

More paper-shuffling on Joel's end. "I'll write it up so the cops can only use or store information pertaining directly to the investigation. They hear weird stuff all the time anyway. Well, not weird, but, you know."

"Unusual," Yonatan says, his old offramp tic.

"Yeah."

"Joel? Sorry I made you break Shabbat," Yonatan says.

"I'm not in love with it either, but hey. You're not the first client who's done it, but you *are* the first in a long while that I'm not mad at for it. I'll talk to the D.A. and sort out the paperwork we'll need to get you through the weekend. You and I can talk insurance and everything Monday."

"Great. Thanks."

"You got somewhere you can stay?" Joel says.

"I'll probably end up at the Morgue tonight. Worst case there's always my parents'."

"Oof."

Yonatan says goodbye and starts packing an overnight bag. Over by the wall he finds his mug — still intact, lucky him — and the space opera he's been carrying around. The bookmark's fallen out of the novel, and he can see the full Emerson quote now: *Time and space are but physiological colors which the eye makes, but the soul is light: where it is, is day; where it was, is night; and history is an impertinence and an injury if it be anything more than a cheerful apologue or parable of my being and becoming.* Now is not the time to figure out what chapter he was reading, so he slots the bookmark in under the title page, and puts the book in the bag.

At the Morgue some hours later, Detective Lopez and two techs sit at the card table with bulky headphones, and Yonatan leans against the wall, shoulders clenched, cordless phone pressed to his ear.

"So you got a pretty big mouth, huh?" Murray says when he answers. "You get my message? The cops there right now? 'Cuz I'll hang up."

Yonatan has practiced this in his head. He pretends to humor Murray's 'delusions.' "Wouldn't you know if they were?"

"You sound tense. Guess my friend's visit did that." Yonatan hears a *snap!* like Murray is chewing gum. "But I know you wouldn't talk about this in front of the cops. Don't even have to use my gift."

For once, it's a good thing that Murray is an asshole. Yonatan holds back something sarcastic. "So what is it you want?"

"A little loyalty, please," Murray says. "How much money have I made you guys with my tips? And all so selflessly."

"What's going on, Murray?"

"I give you names, right? Most of them are, ah, preordained. But every so often, some of them... I know a guy who wants you to know those names."

Yonatan squints at nothing, confused. "Why?"

There's the snapping sound of gum again. "He's *in love* with these people, but all fucked-up like. He wants them to die beautiful, right, so they gotta die soon. And he wants them to have a real good obituary. He knows about you guys somehow, used to write at a paper I think, he's a fan of your work. Well before he knocks 'em off he has me call you, to make sure all the research is in the can."

Murray pauses to chew wetly, then continues, "You should take it as a compliment, Yoni! Look, just *chill*, okay? Think how many of those weirdos I've, what'ya call it, *revelated*, for your little side project."

A headache tightens around Yonatan's crown, and he puts more weight against the wall. He looks at Detective Lopez and sees her looking back at him. *Keep him talking,* she mouths, and shrugs like this is a normal sort of evening for her. Maybe it is.

"Is that some kind of threat?" Yonatan says.

Murray laughs. "Like anybody would believe me if I told them, or even *care* about your little list. Lemme tell you something."

Yonatan clears his throat and swallows what comes up. "Okay."

"I'm a slimy little card sharp, but *you*..." Murray laughs. "I'm dirty, yeah, but I really *can* see the future too, and *you're* the one who thinks you've got a direct line upstairs? On account of some old legend? You know where I see *you*? The fuckin' *nuthouse*."

Silence. If it was just Yonatan he'd hang up, unplug the phone, and go make some bad decisions at a bar. But he's got a job to do, so he repeats himself, stalls for time. "Is that a threat? What is it you *want*?"

Murray chuckles. "Hey, *you're* the one who called *me*."

Yonatan looks and sees Lopez giving him a thumbs up with one hand, and miming hanging up with the other.

"You know what? Never mind. Go fuck yourself, Murray." Yonatan ends the call and swings the phone down, pressing it into his leg.

Lopez walks over. "Well done, Mister Kaplan," she says, sticking out her hand.

Yonatan stands up straight and shakes it. "Thanks. Uh, I could really..." He releases her grip and flaps his hand around aimlessly, noticing a tremor in his fingers.

She nods. "Gotcha. Don't disappear, OK?"

He folds his arms and nods back, realizing halfway through that it makes him look like the genie from that old TV show. The techs undo whatever they did to his phone line as he watches, and right before the door closes behind them, he remembers to call out his thanks.

He can't go home, so he does his best to make the Morgue comfortable, unpacking his book and changing into pajamas. He boils filtered water to make tea. A peek in the paper bag from Fox's shows that Sarah left him the second poppy-seed bagel, which he toasts and eats with butter. He finds where he was in the novel and, until his hands stop shaking, he reads. Then he works, cataloging the spilled clippings he noticed that morning, and pondering Ariel. It feels like he might know even less about that situation than he did a few hours ago. He resolves to consult other Searchers before he reaches too many conclusions. Meanwhile, the very next step is clear. He copies Miller's file, removes the Searcher-related information, and adds the police and coroner's reports he was sent.

That done, he yawns and lays down on the couch. He must've fallen into a dreamless sleep, since when he wakes up to the ringing phone, it's light out. With all that's going on, he figures he should answer.

"Pre-Morgue Clipping Service, this is Yonatan."

"Thank you for answering again, Yonatan, and on a Saturday." It's Ariel. He recognizes the accent, and the far-away sounding connection.

"How can I help you?"

"I know it has only been a day, but I was wondering if you were able to get the information on Mr. Miller for me."

"I was," Yonatan says. "I'm sorry to say that Mr. Miller has passed. I can email our file to you right after I run your card, if you'd like."

"Dreadful news. And I would appreciate that very much. You're fast — you must be very dedicated to your work."

He raises his eyebrows. "We all do what we must," he tries.

"Yes, and thank you for your part." Ariel sighs. "I have more people to check on... hopefully the news will be better. It's almost three dozen names, so I'll use the email form on your website, there's no rush. And..."

She hesitates, and Yonatan swallows.

"One last question," she says. "I see that you take suggestions for interesting people to research?"

"That's right. You get a finder's fee after their information's requested, if you were the first to suggest them."

"Well. You should keep an eye on a young man who's just moved near you, Stephen Fox. Consider this free of charge — I imagine he'll be around long after you're gone. Have a good Saturday, Mister Kaplan."

The line goes dead. Yonatan can smell burning plastic. The recorder must have gotten fried again. He takes a few calming breaths and flexes his fingertips out, deciding he can deal with all this tomorrow or maybe Monday. Meantime he's earned a break. He disconnects the dead recorder from the phone line, and then disconnects the phone entirely. For now he'll read his book uninterrupted; if Adonai has truly chosen this gray morning to count his Tzadikim Nistarim, he can always knock.

●

J. Tynan Burke's story "The Bagel Shop Owner's Nephew" was originally published in Metaphorosis on Friday, 3 August 2018. See magazine.metaphorosis.com

About the author

J. Tynan Burke is a software engineer and writer. Lately, he's been working on the script and code for a cosmic horror video game. He lives in Denver with his husband, their enormous cat Samwise, and their tiny cat Momo. His dream is to one day be an old man futzing around in the garden. You can find more about his writing at www.tynanburke.com, and find him on Bluesky @thearchduke.bsky.social.

Always Dawn to Forever Night

Luke Elliott

Pwela woke to a chill unknown in the Forest of Always Dawn. Tar and peat filled the air, undercutting the perpetual crispness. She shot to her bare feet.

While she slept, the Rot Thing had stolen her warmstone.

Her warmstone sustained her, let her live in the everglow of the forest. Her palms went slick and her breath came short and shallow. She should flee. Run as far and fast as skylight arcing over a cloud. She should, but she would not. She hated the Rot Thing. It had brought unwelcome change to the Continuance.

She could not allow it. She would reclaim her warmstone.

Pwela found Loper resting in a glade of white heather and woke him with a whistle.

"What is it?" he said, jaws cracking with his yawn. The bogcat stretched his long black body, first his back legs, then his front. Extended claws raked the heather, upturning black loam, and a long tail swished high in the air.

"The Rot Thing stole my warmstone."

Loper hissed.

"You smell it, too. Tar and peat." She scratched behind one of his long, feathered ears in the way he liked. She laid her head against his neck, his ghost-striped fur smooth against her bare scalp. "Will you take me after it?"

"Only since it's you asking," he said.

Such a softie. She climbed onto his back, settling between bony spines.

Loper carried her through the Forest of Always Dawn. The orange of the low-roosting sun lit the leaves in its unending glow, dappling the forest floor. Loper darted into the underbrush, then leapt out onto a fir. Long claws sank into its mossy trunk as he bounded off, clearing a sinkhole full of vine snarls. Pwela held fast to the mane of black hair around his neck, her skin blending against his fur. The harmony of their colors was music.

She laughed as they soared, eyes leaking.

Another leap took them into the heart of a familiar glen. But where baby's breath once flourished white and pink, stains now colored flowers with yellow and brown. Wilting from the Rot Thing's passing.

"What is it?" she asked. But she knew.

Loper bent to chew the grass, then spat with a hacking cough. He growled, a rumbly sound from deep within his chest. "Wrongness stains our forest, Pwela."

She sat tall on Loper's back. "The Rot Thing carries stain and wilt and canker. We must drive it out."

"Do you know the Rot Thing?" her friend asked, voice a near-whisper.

She had never met it, but found she did know. "I have long dreamt of it." A shiver shook her small frame.

"As have I," Loper said.

Together, they followed a trail of wrongness in pursuit of the Rot Thing. The thick underbrush and wide trees of the Forest of Always Dawn thinned and lapsed away. Lessening was the way of borders, but swathes of ugly wrongness marred the gentle margins. It hurt her chest to see beauty so wronged.

And so they crossed into the Desert of Only Day. The sun shone savage above, its radiance afire atop the sands.

"The Rot Thing walks the desert," said Loper. "I smell its wrongness, tar and peat." He climbed a dune slowly, paws sinking.

"Shall I walk?"

"The sand is fire, Pwela. Your softness would not long last it." The heat already lashed against her scalp. Oddly, though, a chill remained in her belly.

"You are kind to worry." She let one hand free of his mane to scratch at a long, feathered ear. "But if you tire, my softness will manage." Bogcats were not of the desert. They came from the deep Moor of Forever Night, where they hunted through chill and gloom. Loper had only come to live in the Forest of Always Dawn to be with her, though he grew to love it.

Loper plodded on, persisting against his disharmony with the desert. If he could endure such extremes, she too could reach the gateway, where surely the Rot Thing headed. Its path was no mystery to her, she realized, and that unsettled her stomach. Perhaps she would even discover what lay beyond the gate. Thoughts of what lay beyond filled her with anxiety, a shrill thing. It made her all out of tune.

●

An immense dune rose above the rolling sands, so tall it brushed the sun. Its sands quivered and roiled.

"What is it?" she said, gasping.

Loper paused. His back hair bristled against her skin. "Come out," he yelled. The bogcat stepped closer to the dune, growling. His ropy muscles coiled beneath her thighs. "You who lurk beneath the sands, come topside."

The dune rippled, and two long eyestalks burst skyward. Each eyestalk reached higher than Pwela would if she stood on Loper's back. Black orbs swelled at their ends.

A voice like an avalanche shook beneath them. "How dare you tread upon our sands, bogcat? And with that wretched manthing clinging to your fur?"

"I tread where I wish, prawn," said proud Loper.

The eyestalks rose higher and an immense horned shell clove the sands. Chitinous legs tipped with forked pincers lifted a carapace half out. Thick antennae whipped the sands, sending Loper back on his haunches. Fetid winds eddied around the creature.

Pwela stifled a gasp.

"We are not prawn." The voice fell over them.

The dune devil was the largest she'd ever seen, perhaps the largest in all the Continuance.

"I am this bogcat's friend, Old One," Pwela said. "Forgive him, please. He can be thorny for a feline."

"Why does the manthing make words at us?"

Loper growled, prowling the sands.

"I am Pwela. I would be your friend as well."

The dune devil's antennae ceased their lashing.

Pwela unslung herself from Loper's back. Her breath hissed at the burning of the desert. The softness of her feet indeed hated the fiery sand. She trudged toward the dune devil, palms raised. "We only seek to cross your dunes and enter the meadow. We chase the Rot Thing."

"Rot Thing?" the old devil demanded. "You are with the Rot Thing?" An enormous claw rose from the sands around Pwela and clamped over her chest. The dune devil drove out her wind. She gasped, fighting for air.

Loper snarled. "Release her, you crusty shrimp."

The dune devil lifted her toward its maw. Hot, dry breath reeking of spoiled fish blasted her from the furnace of the devil's gullet. Arm-like mandibles grasped for her.

"We are not with the Rot Thing," she screamed. "Enemies, enemies!"

The dune devil stopped just shy of biting into her. "We hate the Rot Thing," it said, voice all clacks and clicking. "Look what it did to us." The dune devil rolled onto one side and moved her toward its underbelly. Black stains of ichor marred its orange carapace. The pools spread inky tendrils, even as she watched.

"It's horrible," she said, eyes welling. Dull ache filled her own belly, chilled from within.

The dune devil released her. Before the sands burned her softness, Loper was at her side, head dipped so she could clamber on to his back.

"How do we beat the Rot Thing, old one?" she asked. "How can I save you from its wrongness and destroy it?"

"You cannot," said the dune devil. It quivered, slowly descending back into the sands. "The Rot Thing has always been, though it shifts form."

"I must try," she said, lip thrust out. "I will reclaim my warmstone and not allow wrongness to desolate my Continuance."

"The Continuance is not yours, manthing," said the dune devil. Soon, only its eyestalks remained above the sands. "It is not for belonging. Shared by all and none."

"Once I cast out the Rot Thing, will you heal?" she asked.

"Look to yourself," the dune devil said. Its eyestalks dipped beneath the sands, which stilled as if nothing had ever lurked beneath its shifting layers.

"We must go, Pwela," said Loper. "Even I cannot long withstand the fire." And go they did, across the Desert of Only Day's long reaches, until tufts of sawgrass dotted sand that lapsed into soil. The sun dipped in the crossing, turned purple.

They entered the gentle meadow of the Everdusk.

Though Pwela was most comfortable in the Forest of Always Dawn, she adored the Everdusk. She and Loper had come once before, played on beds of lilac, rolled together beneath the tranquil light. The autumn wind blew songs of sleepiness and slow. The meadow was a place for resting.

But wrongness had come to the Everdusk, too. The lilac sea had wilted, petal clusters browned and decayed. A sign of the Rot Thing's passing.

The path wound down into the moor and out of sight. Her feet tried to follow, but she forced them to halt. She felt the end in her belly, and rested her palm over the chill. The path led, eventually, to the gate.

"What ails you?" Loper asked.

"A chill," Pwela said, peering at her stomach. She gasped. Wrongness marred her as well, spread from her belly in tendrils of sick.

Loper could not see her belly, since she still rode astride his back. "What is it?" he asked.

"I need my warmstone," she said. "The chill runs deep now, and I cannot shake it." She would spare him the truth.

"We should turn back," said Loper. His black paws sank into the wilted sea. "Please, Pwela. No joy or beauty lies ahead."

"I must face it," she whispered. "It has my warmstone, and without it I cannot stay here. You can go back. Return to the Forest of Always Dawn and run among the elm and fir."

"No." Loper flattened his long ears. "I shall carry you all the way."

She scratched those ears while they walked the lilac sea, which shimmered with light and wind, but soon, far too soon, the meadow, too, began to lapse. The purple glow darkened, deepened, until only black remained. A crescent moon hung alone in the sky at the edge of the Moor of Forever Night, shining pale like milk, white like bone. The dying lilacs turned to weeds and snarls and damp.

She had never been so far.

The blackness of Forever Night had haunted her dreams as long as she could remember, beckoning her. It had been the Rot Thing all along, she realized, summoning her to the gate.

Loper sloshed through puddles as dark as his fur, between the shadows of cypress trees like grasping ghouls. The moor was his home, she reminded herself. Bogcats lived in harmony with the darkness at the heart of the Continuance, prowled the paths surrounding the gateway. Loper would protect her.

The swamp stank of tar and peat. Loper raised his head to sniff the air, then bounded forward through the gloom. Eyes glinted back through shadow, reflecting moonlight. Loper did not slow, for his eyes glinted too, and the unseen things did not assail them.

They emerged, at last, onto the bank of a still lake lit only by the crescent moon which dipped low over the water, as if reaching for its own reflection. At the middle of the lake rose an island of pale sand. At its center lay the freestanding gateway, plain and brown, locked and bolted.

As it should be.

But beside it stood a figure dark beyond mere black. It stung her eyes like an inverse sun. The Rot Thing. On the island, the Rot Thing extended white hands holding a shape red and luminous, light stark against its depth of black.

Her warmstone.

The Rot Thing lifted the red rock high and brought it down upon the gateway with a crack that thundered over the still lake, raising low ripples. The gate shook and shuddered.

Loper whimpered. "Turn back, Pwela. I cannot swim."

She climbed off his back. "I know. But you have carried me far. And I *can* swim. Stay here, my friend. I will face it alone. Someone must." Her heart told her so. "Let it be me."

"I... understand." Loper said, dipping his wide head. "Our moments in the forest live eternal, though we've passed them by. I am with you, whether you sense me or not. And if you return, I will find you again on the shore."

Pwela hugged his neck, eyes leaking, then dove into the still waters, breaking them, casting waves across the lake. Cold beyond ice bit her everywhere, though not as cold as the wrongness in her belly, but soon the pain of the chill lapsed too. She swam, arm over arm, legs pumping. She laughed as she sped toward the island, laughed despite it all. The song of the water played in her heart, filling her. When she reached the island, she climbed out, cold and dripping, but full of harmony.

"Let the gateway be," she commanded. "It must remain shut."

The Rot Thing stood with its back to her, hood drawn, looming over the gateway, its huge umbral mass shifting and fluid. It smashed the warmstone against the gateway again with a thunder that forced Pwela to cover her ears. Her red rock broke. The gateway's frame cracked, and the Rot Thing turned, then dropped the shining shards of her warmstone to the pale sand. It returned its long hands to its sides.

"No!" she cried. She dropped to her knees and cupped the fragments. Their light faded and was gone.

She dropped the broken bits and glared at the Rot Thing. Her eyes stung from gazing upon shadow so deep, but they soon adjusted too, even to blinding oblivion. She did not look away.

"You do not belong," she said. "Leave this place and never return."

"None belong. All belong," it said, throwing back its hood. "Look within and know you brought me here." The Rot Thing's voice came as a hollow echo of her own, rebounding from an endless cavern. The head of the Rot Thing was her own bald head, but distorted and immense. Chill radiated from it, sapping her strength. She wanted to scream, to run as far and fast as skylight. She should flee, but she did not.

"You cannot trick me, bastard," she said, rising from the sand. "I did not bring you. You are *not* welcome here. Leave this place!" She set her feet wide and lifted her fists.

"There is only one way." It laid a thin hand against the gateway. "Join me." The Rot Thing's immense face was like her own, but wrongness filled empty eyes above lips blue and frigid.

The gateway opened, and nothing lay beyond. An abyss with no color at all.

She should have never come. The Forest of Always Dawn waited still. Stained though it was, at least it held warmth and sun.

A place for beginnings, not ends.

But no, the wrongness had spread through the heather, through the fir and lilac. To herself.

The Rot Thing held out its hand to her, fingers like white worms.

She searched the far bank for Loper, but the bogcat had gone. It did not anger her. Such things were not easy to witness.

The Rot Thing waited, hand extended.

"I will not go with you," she said, but did not shrink away from the awful hand.

"You will," it said, voice still a hollow echo of her own. "I will not tell you to be unafraid. I will not barter or beg. But you will come."

She stared at the nothing beyond the gate. "What is it? Is there something farther in I cannot see?"

The Rot Thing stood silent, spindle fingers swaying before her. The only way to know was to step through.

She thought of the wilted heather, the browning lilac, the wheezing old dune devil. Loper, so worried for her softness, who had carried her over fire.

"Will you leave the Continuance if I go with you?" she said.

It paused, silent for a time before responding. "I came for you."

Then it was right. "I'm sorry, Loper," she whispered.

She took its hand. Her tiny fingers stuck to the Rot Thing's pallid skin as if it were tar. Near translucent skin. She gasped as black eels wriggled beneath the thin membrane of its being. They coiled beneath her hand, drawn to her warmth.

The crescent moon rent and tumbled from the black. The still lake spilled skyward, rising in a geyser around her.

With one long hand, the Rot Thing pushed through the absence of the gateway and pulled her through with the other, away from the Continuance. She could not stay, only go. And go, she did. Through and beyond into nowhere.

Luke Elliott's story "Always Dawn to Forever Night" was originally published in Metaphorosis on Friday, 2 March 2018. See magazine.metaphorosis.com

About the author

Luke Elliott was born and raised in the suburbs of central Florida. In his late twenties, he travelled across the country with his wife and two dogs to live in Portland, Oregon, where he fell in love with the city and a region with natural beauty as magical as any fantasy world. He has a B.A. in Creative Writing from the University of Florida where he studied and wrote both literature and poetry, and earned a MFA in Writing Popular Fiction from Seton Hill University. Now he writes mostly science fiction, fantasy, and horror, but will go wherever inspiration leads. In August of 2017, he launched the *Ink to Film* podcast with a filmmaker co-host, where he discusses books and their film adaptations from a writer's point of view. In between writing and podcasting, he collects quality single malts and is always happy to pour a dram for company.

www.lukeelliottauthor.com, @luminousluke

The Memory Dresser

Nicholas M. Stillman

Our parlor is small — tucked in a corner of Helm, folded between an empty Gassa stall and the home of a half-deaf mystic. For this reason, discretion numbers as one of our services. Not even the moon bears full witness, as Illsea, the largest Tower on the hill, shades us from the first few hours of evening light. Under our lamps, we shape the memories of the people of Helm, our people. Unlike the royals in Illsea, they are not looking for beauty. No shine-oil treatments or the newest configuration of knots and trellises. Our client's memories are coated in the dirt that lines our streets and our teeth. They sit in my grandmother's chair and weep at their reflections. Each length tracks the harrowing years of their lives in the dim lamps or beady sun: yesterday's shame growing from their scalp, their unfortunate births dragged through the streets. My grandmother's job is to make them feel well — to clean and wrap, braid and twist them into people who can walk back into their lives without shame dragging them down.

My own memories are unremarkable. Ordinary, frizzed, limp. My childhood must have been something to forget, because I all but have. There are a few years, though, that are different. Four finger lengths that hold the light like river rocks after rain. Memories that burst forth like the sweet juices of thin-fleshed berries, eclipsing all other flavor. My mother excited, touching my shoulder, pointing at the marigolds and the poppies not yet in bloom around the village pond. Fresh bread and cool paya juice as the fireworks erupt above the Towers during the New Sun dance. Then, below the shore rocks we clambered onto, the rich Oversea folk filing in and out of their boats — their strange memories gleaming in impenetrable designs, fractals upon fractals. Mother's breath curling warmly in the cold night onto my scalp and tips of my ears, running her thin fingers through my memories while we watched the beautiful people glisten. *One day,* her voice sounds as if she were still beside me, *you'll have memories like that.*

Whenever I felt the dull ache of boredom begin to blossom throughout my body, I would twine these strands between my fingers, feeling their health against my skin, or else tie the lengths around my forehead so that everyone who met me met the finest version.

"If your chin were any higher you'd break your neck," said Grandmother, tugging at the steeple knot holding my best memories in view. "You want the world to think you're better than them? Who are you to do that?" She would make me fold them beneath less pleasant memories. Dull evenings in the parlor. Sweaty days jostling through the market's center. Father's long trips dragging a net into salty water for exotic hues of sea life to be shipped and filleted and served to the people he despised most. My mother's last year, bed-bound and shivering.

Grandmother was disdainful of the extravagant. She despised my secret yearnings for things I had seen: marigolds and poppies and beautiful memories rippling like the sea as the Oversea folk slipped onto boats. She preferred a meek life of quiet dignity, a healthy distrust of laughter.

One morning, before the clients lined out her door, she cut a sheet into strips with my father's old gutting knife and, leaving one end intact and tied to the Dressing chair, she pressed the strips into my sweating palms. Grandmother turned the strands one by one — revealing the sheet's bloodstain, oil spot, jagged edges, holes from ash. I nodded. I folded strips into one another, braided them, looped them, curled them with brass rollers. My fingers were small but eager as I worked a loose approximation of the Sargusoa style — limp and casual, with two elaborate loops. I made sure to hide each imperfection beneath the cleaner lengths. My memory Dressing would impress upon others the wearer's connection to a rich childhood, as the brightest ends of sheet I bent at angles that would catch the sunlight. When I finished, I dabbed sweat from my forehead and smiled.

Grandmother slapped my cheek.

"Look what you've done." She flipped over my knots, pointed to the blood, oil, jagged edges I'd disguised.

"It looks better this way," I said, my voice faltering.

"So like your mother." She said it as a curse. She pulled at my release thread and the Sargosa collapsed back into a tattered sheet. When she saw my eyes filling with anger, my fists balling, she cocked her head. "What, you want a village of pretenders? Whoever hides the best is the winner? You want your people to think they have to compete with each other, compete with the Towers? All they do is try to survive. Don't take that from them."

I bit back tears. I could not imagine letting a client walk out with their poverty, their abuses and vices and regrets plain in the sun for all to see. Surely there was a way to cover them? "Why should there always be something to hide? Not everyone is so miserable."

"There will always be stains," she said, cutting down the sheet and twisting the strands to be dipped in oil and used as lantern wicks. "These people are decent, Helm people. They don't want to be glamorized like an oiled Tower empress. They want to be understood. That is why we do not hide pasts, but weave the hurt and joy together so that both catch the light. Our job is to frame their lives in such a way that others can see dignity, not glamor, not suffering. We cannot afford to play games with our memories Not here." I followed her eyes to the dust whistling through the empty street, the sun already baking the walking boards stretched between the gutters. Illsea loomed over us, its shadow not yet cast.

●

Days in the parlor turned like the trapped figurine of a music box while my memories grew stale. The same clients to seat, well buckets to drag, lavender to pick, stones to heat, cloth to wash, rice to cook. I waited. I cut my sheets into strips. Practiced in the moonlight before the tower eclipsed the light. I snuck pamphlets of the latest Dressing styles from the market and slid them under my mattress. I exercised my fingers and wrists. I trained myself for a life I was better suited to.

Then, one night, after I had closed the doors and drawn the sunshade over the window, a confident knock rapped at the door. Then another.

"Oh, go on," Grandmother sighed, no doubt preparing her speech — *Your memories will still be there in the morning.*

At the door, however, was not Ginja the mystic who wanted to sell us another memory-reading, but a stranger. She was tall and lean, her neck long and seamless. A dark cloak was draped over her shoulders and a dust wrap pleated neatly over her face so that her dark eyes and long lashes poked through like hermit crab antenna. She stepped through me as if I occupied no space at all.

Before Grandmother could speak, the woman flipped the cloak off of her shoulders, revealing a white silk tunic and her loose-wrapped memories shining like polished ore in the lamplight. A medallion of Illsea hung from her neck. I lost the ability to move.

She glided to the dressing chair in silence and seated herself. A chair that had, only minutes before, held Malik, who bathed once a week in the camel water trough. She crossed her legs and examined the shelves cluttered with abandoned dressing equipment — rusted iron clips and outdated bows. My cheeks burned.

Grandmother wiped her hands on her tunic. Wiped them again. She did not speak. Only stood like a low-cast shadow, clearing her throat to no avail.

The woman spoke without turning her head. "Girl, what's your name?"

Grandmother opened her mouth to respond, but realized too late that she was not the girl.

"Mina," I managed in a hoarse whisper.

"Do you live here?"

"My room is upstairs."

"Mina, this is my daughter, Tengi."

I turned, startled to find a small, dark girl standing just inside the door. She seemed to be everything her mother was not — short, wide-hipped with small eyes and a flat face. She was pretty in her own way, and prettier still than anyone I'd seen in the parlor besides her mother.

"Please take Tengi up to your room to play while I speak with the Dresser."

Tengi made a face that indicated she would rather run with street dogs than climb the thin wooden staircase to my room. I searched Grandmother's eyes for guidance, but found none. Her body was rigid, as if a wild animal had entered the room.

Tengi was already marching petulantly to the staircase. I followed. Her memories bounced before my eyes as we climbed. Her head was covered in a silken maroon cloth and a thick braid fell down and wrapped around her waist. The braid was deeper and richer than the silk covering, making the latter look cheap; the kind of cloth we would sell unfaithful spouses attempting to disguise their guilt. I marveled. It was as if Tengi's entire life had been fireworks and fresh bread. With a start I realized Grandmother was wrong — not everyone had stains.

●

That first evening, and several after, Tengi refused to speak to me. We would sit in silence, Tengi's hands clasped in her lap, face turned up to Illsea, as we waited for my grandmother to finish her secret work. Later, Tengi brought a book and read it when there was enough light. Finally, one night when Tengi's eyes were wild with anger, her memory scattered about her shoulders, she spoke:

"You should apply a Barosa nut oil twice a day if you don't want your memories to collect all that dust."

I nodded. I felt that a critical gap had been bridged. I let loose all of my caged questions. About her purpose in my room, her mother in our shop, her bedroom in the Tower, her thick, syrupy memories. But my questions were like throwing stones at a circling hawk. Tengi watched them with interest before diving: *Tell me, what's it like being so poor?*

Our words began to search out our differences, curiously prodding each other's edges. Each revelation was like a flash river after a rain as we encouraged more questions. I surprised her with my knowledge of the latest Dressing styles, my love of the Oveasea fractal knots, my awareness of the various uses of poppies and marigolds. And she both surprised me and didn't surprise me; every detail a revelation I could not have anticipated. The Tower competitions for memory shine, the strong-necked men tying their memories together and pulling like reluctant lovers until one buckled, the heartbreak of the smallest memory imperfections, the scandal of memory painting. "There are some who refuse to do anything but fuck and eat and travel before a dance," she'd said, her language embarrassing me. "There are servants who shield them from crumbs. Some refuse to see their children in case the child cries or falls or misspeaks, and so taints their memories. The competition is shit. And yet if you don't do those things, you stand alone at the dance and your memories get even weaker. There's no way out."

"And here you will be ridiculed for trying too hard," I said, breathless. "If I try to clean Malik's tangle or hide his embarrassment with a clip or cloth, Grandmother would call me a pretender. Nothing I do is allowed to be beautiful."

Tengi and I spent our nights comparing our lives while the two women worked and the constellations did slow battle through the slats of my roof. Sometimes we would climb out my window and wander to the spice fields and rub Tougo into our teeth, sometimes we would chance a trip to the market when the sun was still up and hold hands and call each other *beloved* to watch the old men bend incline their heads at our parting. I knew that every week Tengi would arrive at my doorstep, and she did without fail. I had never met anyone like her and she, she confided one night, had never met anyone like me. Her presence textured my days and gave a shape to my daily life.

As the weeks wore on, there were more Dressings, which meant more Tengi in my life. Tengi did not tell me why her mother came so much often than other clients, but I knew the New Sun dance was approaching and I guessed there was some secret vanity, or problem that needed mending before the start. When I did glimpse her mother, mostly from my window as I watched Tengi leave, I saw that she looked vacant, her steps unnecessarily cautious. Tengi would guide her by the hand away from the shop to wherever the escorts had hidden the carriage.

One night, while the moths threw their bodies at my window, we touched memories. It was late — the women below us were working long, as usual. It was Tengi's idea. To have me practice working with healthy memory, to prepare for the day she would bring me to the Towers as her personal Dresser. I asked her to show me what they did in Illsea, how the Dressers prepared. She swallowed as she loosened her tunic and dropped it down below her bare shoulders, shook her memories out of its braid. I listened to the tapping of moths trying to hurl themselves at my lamp.

We sat on our knees, facing each other, the flesh of our thighs touching.

Tengi's memories were like ripples in water. So bright they felt like liquid glass, or something else I could not describe. My breath came in small gasps as her fingers danced along the hollow strands of my boredom and routine, clicking her tongue lightly. My eyes fluttered and the floor groaned as we delved deeper into each other's lives. I felt something shift beneath my breastbone. A stirring.

I worked my fingers up her memory, then allowed my fingers to explore the hidden days and weeks beneath the maroon silk covering. Tengi screamed. Scrambled away from me, gathering spare bits of herself and pinning them behind her. I didn't know what I'd done wrong.

Tengi reluctantly untied the maroon cloth, and I saw it. Falling just above the tip of her ear, was a section of memory that was white and hollow as a feather's heart. The kind of loss I thought only those in Helm had experienced. I tracked the growth with practiced eyes. She had been carrying it silently since the week we'd met.

"Tengi, I — what happened?"

She smoothed the memory behind her, clipping them back. "I forgot. I'm sorry. I should have warned you."

I stood, angry and frightened and still drunk off her touch. "What happened? Who did this?"

She shook her head.

"Why is your mother here? Why are you here? Please. You need to tell me."

Tengi opened her mouth, closed it. She stood and went to the window, to look up at the Tower. Her Tower. "These memories are the same ones my mother has. The ones my mother is paying your grandmother to cut."

"What?"

Tengi slid open the window and the moths went in search of their flame. "They would kill her if anyone knew."

"I — cut?" The thought churned in my stomach; a mutilation I had not considered. To cut memories was a heinous act, punishable by execution. Killing a person ended their life, but cutting them ended who they were. Who would choose to lose themselves?

"She wants to forget." Tengi turned to look at me, her mouth clenched in a smile. "And now I am the only one who will remember." She passed her face through the window, closed her eyes.

I didn't know what to do, what to say. I had so many questions, knew so little. Silent, I walked behind her, closed my eyes, and joined her, our faces waiting for a breeze.

●

My grandmother and I took to standing like hungry cats by the door on the days we knew they would come. We turned away clients, as neither of us could focus until they arrived. They were our great secrets. Grandmother spoke less about my attraction to dreaminess, my selfishness, even as I lingered in front of the Dressing mirror turning my head to admire how my new memories seemed to brighten my eyes, add color to my cheeks. In my reflection I saw an open, bright person. Someone brimming with possibility.

Tengi snuck me Tower oil and ribbons and when Grandmother was not around I would walk into the market with my most recent memories oiled. I shimmered in the heat. In return, I said nothing to Grandmother about the cutting. She would stop her work if she thought I knew, and I could not risk losing Tengi.

Tengi was changing, too. Her memories were growing crooked. She took to hiding them with bows and expensive ribbon. She shrank from touch if I approached her too quickly, moved too quietly. Wind from the streets would cause her to spasm in fear and it would take me minutes of careful teasing to distract her. I never touched her recent growth and it pained me that we had becomes so different. I would try to find gaps in conversation to ask her about the white growth, what had happened to her, and how I could help. All I wanted to do was help. Tengi told me not to worry, nothing was my fault, it wasn't me.

●

One evening, after Tengi and her mother had gone, father arrived. He greeted us without his right foot — a result of a rationing mistake on board his ship and several short straws drawn in a life of short straws. It had been years since he'd been home, and I barely recognized the man from my childhood. His memory was thick and clotted and smelled of fish viscera and left an oily trail like a slug.

After an awkward and stilted embrace, he sniffed my memories, and I became aware of the thick, nutty oil still seated there. His eyes wandered to Grandmother, who hid behind her the old gutting knife she used for cutting. At her feet lay the strands of two dead memories she had yet to sweep from the floor.

I felt his hand tighten around my shoulder. "This is what happens when I leave?" he spat. "I ought to turn you in for risking my wife's parlor. *My* rightful parlor."

"It's not like that," I said, unable to release myself from his grip. "They came from Illsea, they're not like you think."

He rounded on me. For a moment, while he had me pinched in his grip, I thought he would flay me like a fish, his muscles having formed the habit.

Seeing the terror in my eyes seemed to shift something in him.

He released me. Searched me for what felt like signs of someone else. Someone who was not me.

"I'm home now. For good," he said as if reminding himself. "Illsea took my foot and then dropped me on the shore. So if either of you think you still want to play your Tower games, then maybe I'll have to cut those memories from you myself." His face crinkled in pain, his eyes darted to the memories of my childhood. "Your mother would never have wanted this. Never this."

●

In the months that followed, I would often lie in bed, tracking the sun's progress across my floor. Grandmother stopped promising to train me, and I stopped collecting pamphlets from market, stopped practicing on my sheets. I watched my father's memories grow out white. Grandmother tried to clean them, to dress them lightly, but he refused her, preferring to wallow.

The few decent memories I had made with Tengi began to fade as dull, frizzed ones pushed them down my neck. I could no longer face the market, watch their eyes take in how far I had fallen. I became angry with Tengi for her ability to continue on with her life while I sat in the same room she'd found me in, waiting for her to return. I felt our lives together slipping further into my past and wondered if she felt that distance, too. If she even noticed.

The rains came. I grew hollow, forgetful. Grandmother covered my memories with a dashini so that I would have enough courage to leave the room. I refused to remove it, even at my grandmother's pleading for memories to have light and air. In her mind, a little damage was better than hiding completely. But I knew she was wrong. The more you show the damage, the more of you it becomes, until it is all you are.

●

And then, on the eve of the New Sun dance, Tengi climbed through my window. She smelled of the red dirt from the back roads below the Towers. She must have ridden all day.

"Tengi?" I stood perfectly still, just as I had the day her mother first entered our parlor. "What...Why are you here?"

Tengi's face was stretched tight, her memories frizzed and loose, dragging behind her. She pulled it through the window.

"Because I need help," she said.

"Where have you been?" I felt my surprise leaking into bitterness. "Why didn't you come back for me?"

Tengi shrugged past me. She cradled something heavy in her coat. "I am watched, my mother and me. When your grandmother sent word that she would no longer..." she lifted her head, thinking. "The message was discovered. Now I can't piss without someone holding my hand."

I did not know what to say, how to respond, what to do with the anger I had been holding for her — anger for abandoning me here, stranding me in a desert with my father.

"What do you want?"

Tengi placed a silken maroon bundle from her coat onto my bed. I recognized the cloth as the one that once covered her damage. "I want you to help me," she said, staring at the cloth. "I am not going to the dance. There is not a skilled enough Dresser in the world to hide all of this." She found my eyes with hers.

"You came to tell me that?"

"I am going on a boat. Oversea."

I approached her as if she might, at any moment, collapse into nothing. I was still unsure of her, but my mind filled with new possibilities. Boats. Dances. I absently recalled those years with my mother, as I often did, the memories still burning brightly in my mind. "And how do you want me to help you?" I said coolly.

Tengi looked at me with what might have been hurt at my tone. Or sadness. "Oh," she said. "I want you to come with me."

My mouth dried. The room shifted slightly. "But I thought you wanted my help."

"That's part of it. I... I'm leaving whether or not you come. But I want you too."

"Oh." I could not think of what to say. I touched my dashini, recalling how much I'd changed. I felt weak at my inability to move on without her. I resented her for it.

"I need to show you something," Tengi said as she kneeled and unwrapped the bundle. Beneath the maroon silk lay a dagger. A thin blade wide as my finger and long as my hand, with a handle of pearl. I stepped back, knocking a book from my shelf. It thudded to the floor, and I heard my father shifting in his bed beneath us. He rarely slept, and his temper was deep and treacherous in the middle of the night. I held my breath.

"I need you," Tengi said, picking the blade up off of the bed and carrying it like a child to where I stood. "I need you to cut me. To let me start over."

I took the blade, if only to stop her speaking. "I can't do that, Tengi," I whispered. "I couldn't. Not to anyone."

Tengi nodded but did not move. "I know how it sounds, but look at me. Look at what has become of me, Mina." For the first time she looked at me closely, her eyes on my hidden memories. "Look what's happened to you!" Her voice bounced around my room and I held my finger to her lips.

"My father," I whispered.

She batted my hand like a fly. "We have been destroyed by the acts of others. Two people locked my door and held me down and made me remember something I want to forget. Why should *I* have to remember what *they* did? Why should you have to hide yourself when you're alone?"

"But your mother!" I said, losing grip on my voice. "You always said she would regret this, that she was a pretender."

Tengi nodded. "She was. She didn't do it for herself. She did it so that others wouldn't think less of her. She was a coward. I'm not afraid to let go."

I stared at Tengi, her nostrils flaring, her eyes wide as a street cat. My heart swam in my ears. My grandmother would say it was cowardice, not bravery. "You aren't serious," I said. "You can't be."

Her fingers wrapped around my shoulders. Ropes of tendon sprung out on her neck. "We deserve something new. The dance is coming tomorrow. There will be so many boats lining the dock that slipping in to one will be easy. While everyone stares at the sky, their eyes filled with fireworks, we will move beneath them and climb onto the boat unseen. We'll start our new lives without *these*," Tengi shook her memories in her fists like they were chains, "weighing us down. It's the New Sun. It's the time of new beginnings."

"Not for people like me," I said. Memories of my mother flooded me. Fireworks above new-budded flowers, her breath on my scalp, her voice in my ear. Watching the lives of other people.

Tengi reached behind me, undid my knots, and I felt my memories crash around my shoulders. She found those four finger lengths, held them. They were the most precious things I possessed. Yet they were also nothing. They were not real. Not like Tengi. Not like the dagger in my hand. Not like the moon filtering through the cracks of my ceiling. Not like the cold air seeping through the floor. Not like my father dragging himself from the mattress, where I could hear him hobbling now beneath us.

Tengi placed her memory in my hand and closed her eyes. I held her and wondered which memories she would miss most. Her comfortable childhood, or the sweaty nights cramped in a room above a Helm parlor? Would she long for what she'd lost, even if she couldn't remember? Be like my father, still reaching down to scratch his missing foot? Would she lose herself? Lose her interest in me?

And who would I be without my mother's breath on my scalp, my grandmother's slap against my cheek? I thought of the fireworks, the fractals, the poppies. *One day you will have memories like that.*

"Take all but right now," said Tengi, her breath hot against my face. "I don't want to remember anything but us and our plan for the boats. I've written down all we need to remember."

I felt my body vibrate. I did not move.

"We can meet again. That will be our first memory." And then Tengi pressed her lips against my scalp, my damage, so that they came to me like a memory and a moment all at once.

We are silent as we listen to my father's halting steps beneath, hear his hoarse voice calling: "Mina?" It will take him some time to climb to my room. To find our spirits entwined. It will take him only moments to understand when he opens my door. To step his way into my room in the eclipsed moonlight, to find my past dead on the ground. Find my life spread out in tight curls at his feet. Find me taken up by a longed-for breeze, flying around the room. He will pass the moths heading for the flames through my open window, intent on breaking through the glass of the lamp to experience the moment they have lived for, that they will die for. He will hear familiar nervous laughter and confused footsteps pattering on the walking boards outside. He will peer out into the inky dark, the moon now lost behind the Tower, and will try to find me. He will see instead two strangers, their hands clasped, bouncing as if unmoored and drifting from a dock. Watch them feeling in the black for the way forward.

Nicholas M. Stillman's story "The Memory Dresser" was originally published in Metaphorosis on Friday, 24 May 2019. See magazine.metaphorosis.com

About the author

Nicholas M. Stillman is a writer, teacher, and reluctant service worker living in the east bay in California. He received his MFA from Saint Mary's College of California in 2018, where he currently teaches English. He desperately wants to live in the woods, raise crops, write eight hours a day, and play an unhealthy amount of PS4. He shares this impossible dream with his girlfriend, Sabrina, and their cats, Gnocchi and Fusilli, who all insisted on being part of this bio.

@nick_at_day

Astrid Underwater

J.J. Eskelin

The day Sigun lost her son in the water, it was unusually warm, even for August. She had driven with him up the Olympic Peninsula to a park just over the bridge, on the western shore of Kilisut Island. The little island had been created some fifty years before, when a ship canal was dredged through a backwater marsh, severing the land from the Olympic Peninsula.

Now, a sand bar, bleached and desolate, edged the deep canal. The sand bar was littered with empty shells and strewn with bone-white driftwood tumbled smooth by water. In between the sand bar and the rocky shore of the little island, tidal rivers wove through the sand and rock. Beneath their sparkling waters every surface was generously carpeted with life; the rocks were sharp with oysters, dressed with purple sea anemones, slippery with green and brown algae.

Sigun, tall and strong, carried Erik easily as she waded through the seawater streams, stepping gingerly over the life-encrusted rocks, out towards the sand bar. Once there, Erik set about busily reorganizing the driftwood into a fort. A constant monologue accompanied his work, demanding no response. She was lucky in this, that he could play alone.

Erik had been terrified of the water all summer. Sigun had not been able to get him to even dip his beautiful pink toes into the sea. Swimming lessons had been a complete disaster. Erik had taken a particular dislike to the last swim instructor who had attempted to force him into the pool. Before Sigun could intervene, Erik had started screaming. "I hate her! I hate her! I hate her!" His cry had echoed like a curse in the vaulted chamber above the indoor pool.

Sigun had been ready to concede defeat when the director of the Aquatic Center himself had emerged from the water. While the swim instructors had been barely out of childhood, the director was a man with closely cut hair and a stiff beard of shining silver. He was short, smaller than Sigun, but his presence was commanding. He was perfectly formed, every muscle outlined by his black shorty wetsuit. The skin of his exposed arms and legs was smooth bronze, his face ageless. A trident would not have looked out of place in his hand, Sigun had thought, amused at the image.

"Come, Erik," the director, Mr. Merehinen, had ordered in a low, even voice. He was devoid of the false cheer and friendliness that often seem a prerequisite for working with small children. Yet Erik had not hesitated; he had taken the man's cold hand and stepped willingly into the water at last.

Sigun had never been afraid of the water. She was an excellent swimmer, and an even better sailor, having grown up sailing her father's boats. She loved the water, but she understood the danger of it, the vigilance and respect it commanded. So, even if she had good reason to believe Erik would not touch the water, she did not intend to close her eyes while he played so close to the lapping waves of the deep canal.

As she watched Erik, her back rested against a driftwood log, warm from the sunshine. Sigun slipped her feet out of her sandals and anchored them in the coarse sand. Erik had been awake in the night again and Sigun was deeply tired. Keeping her eyes open against the onslaught of the sun and sparkling water was unbearably painful.

Suddenly, Sigun was jolted awake. A cloud had eclipsed the sun, the rocks were gray and cold, and the trees above the shoreline were dark emerald, almost black. She was shivering.

"Erik?" she called out, leaping up. "Erik!" she screamed, running around the piles of pale dead wood, raking the black water with her eyes, her stomach accelerating through the bottom of her feet.

"Erik!" There was no answer. Even in the summer, the Salish Sea is deadly cold. It takes only a few seconds for a child to drown. Shame and guilt broke into a torrent beneath her terror. The loss of another child would be unpardonable. Unbearable. She wanted to tear her heart out from her body.

Too much time had passed, but Sigun ruthlessly repressed her panic. If she was to have any chance of saving him, she had to keep her head. She bounded out into the water, the sharp shells cutting her feet, until she felt the seabed drop into the deep, icy canal. The surface of the sea was unforgivably still. The world was colorless. The trees were black against the grey sky.

Then Sigun heard splashing behind her, and Erik's laughter. She turned and scooped him up into her arms, every dear, precious, inch of him soaking wet. Sigun crushed his cold, damp body against her racing heart. She was filled with a mixture of relief, joy, and rage so overwhelming she was speechless. She felt sick.

"Erik, where were you?" she whispered hoarsely, holding him tightly against her breast as she carried him back to the barren sand bar, over the slippery stones and the rocks sheltering spiney assemblies of black-purple sea urchins, until he struggled to wiggle free of her arms. She was shaking as she set him down on the bone-dry rocks beside her backpack. "You know not to go into the water alone!"

"I wasn't alone," he answered unconcerned, but his lips were blue. She dug into the backpack, pulling out the extra set of clothing she always carried for him. She helped him dress and handed him a tart green apple, which he happily accepted. He bit into the crisp fruit, the juice running down his sea-damp chin.

"If you can't see me, I can't see you." Sigun didn't want to make him afraid again, and she was careful not to sound as terrified and angry as she felt. "It is good to be in the water, but you *must* have someone in with you." Sigun was strapping her bleeding feet back into her sandals and packing up their things. She lifted Erik up, and tucking him under her arm, forded the tidal rivers back to the shore. Their car was parked, dusty and alone, on the gravel underneath the long arms of a giant Madrona tree, whose red bark had peeled back to reveal smooth wood that glistened like tanned, wet skin.

Sigun settled Erik into his car seat, fastening the harness. "I wasn't alone." He handed Sigun the core of the apple. "She was with me."

"Who was with you, Erik?" Sigun asked as she fastened her seatbelt, glancing up at his reflection in the rear view mirror.

"The mermaid," he said. Sigun pulled away from the park, and drove quickly up the gravel road and over the bridge. She was still fighting the afterburn of terror, and in its place shame and anger were settling into her body. She, Lars Havegrimm's daughter, had almost lost her child in the water. It was unforgivable.

"Did the mermaid have a tail?" Sigun's heart rate was returning to normal. Maybe Erik had seen a harbor seal, or some other creature swimming below the water, and had been curious, as Sigun would have been. Sigun was a marine biologist after all, or at least, she had been one.

"No," Erik laughed as if her question had been ridiculous.

"Well, what did it look like, then?"

Erik was kicking his legs into the seat in front of him. "Like you," he said, "Her eyes were green, but brighter. Her hair was long, but darker. Her teeth were whiter —" He had his hand in his mouth, feeling his own teeth. " — and sharper."

She glanced at him quickly in the rearview mirror to see if he was as disturbed as she was by his imagined encounter, and was struck as she was every now and then by how impossibly dear he was to her. He looked healthy and unconcerned, as if he had not just been pulled, blue-lipped, out of the cold sea.

"You know her, Mama. It was Astrid," Erik said, his angelic brow furrowed in frustration, his foot kicking the back of the seat with renewed vigor. "She found me."

"Astrid?" Sigun jerked the car back into her lane just in time. A truck sailed past on her left, its honking horn distorted by the speed of their near collision. It took all of Sigun's concentration, then, to drive safely home.

Astrid, Erik's twin sister. Astrid who had lived only eight days. Astrid who had been sedated, wrapped in tubes, and placed in a glass box, floors above Sigun's ravaged body. Astrid who had drowned, not in the water, but in the air.

Unlike Erik, who had been born looking like a shriveled elf, skinny and jaundiced, a tiny wizened old man with pointy ears and a piercing scream, Astrid had been born beautiful and healthy looking. But she had been born second, pulled, violently, feet first, out of Sigun, unwilling and unready. Her lungs had never made the transition from the liquid world of Sigun's womb.

The sky was darkening and little drops of rain began to hit the windshield as she drove over the bridge onto the large island where they lived. She wound her way carefully down to the southern tip of it, the roads dark and narrow, lined with towering trees. It had begun to rain in earnest, and it was hours before Tom would be home from the city.

●

When Tom did come home, he was soaking wet, having biked back from the ferry in the worst of the downpour. He was exhausted, but the shadows under his eyes did not diminish his good looks. If anything, Tom was growing more handsome. Sigun almost resented it, that his beauty was increasing as she felt hers to be fading. Her hand moved involuntarily to the silver streak that ran through her dark red hair. It had seemed to appear suddenly, the day she finally came home from the hospital without Astrid. Motherhood had changed the geography of her body inside and out like an earthquake, a volcanic eruption. The cost of it had fallen on her physically, heavily. Sigun, enveloped in grief, had experienced so little of the joy of it.

She had once been sure of Tom's desire, but now she was no longer confident it was under her sway at all. Although the truth was, for some time she had not cared. Sigun felt much less like a siren than a fury.

It was only at the beginning of the summer that she had finally weaned Erik. She had been warned she might suffer a sort of withdrawal; her body had been a factory of calming hormones. Perhaps that was why she felt a storm building inside her, a tumult swirling in her blood. Perhaps that was why Astrid's apparition felt so unsettling, a sudden burst of turbulence when she was already in the middle of a storm.

Later that night, as Sigun and Tom lay in bed together, he asked her about her day.

"It was fine. We drove to Kilisut Island."

"Did you see anything interesting?"

"Well... Erik thought he saw a mermaid."

Tom laughed. "I shouldn't have taken him to the Olde Curiosity Shop."

The shop was on the wharf near where the ferry left the city for the big island where they lived. Among its curiosities had been a 'mermaid', a taxidermist's chimera of fish and monkey, its sharp little teeth bared in fury at the customers below. It had seemed obscene, even in Sigun's childhood.

Sigun rolled onto her back, hesitating. "But the strangest thing was... Erik called the mermaid Astrid."

Tom stilled beside her. "Astrid? Do you and Erik talk about Astrid?"

"No, never. Do you?"

"Of course not. But Erik is like a little sponge. He must have heard us mention her name." She turned away from him, onto her side, and he curled around her. She couldn't bring herself to share how close she had come to losing Erik, the terror and shame of it. Not yet. Sigun could feel his body settle as he fell quickly into a deep sleep, the privilege of the exhausted and the innocent. Eventually, and with great effort, she followed him into oblivion.

●

The next morning Sigun set about with renewed determination to get Erik swimming lessons with the director of the Aquatic Center. If nothing else, she could make sure Erik learned to swim.

"He doesn't give lessons anymore," the scheduler at the Aquatic Center said, sounding   bored. Despite Mr. Merehinen's flat affect and lack of good cheer, which some parents found disturbing, he had a reputation on the island for being able to teach the children to swim in a fraction of the time of other instructors. After one of his students had gone on to compete in the Olympics, the clamor of families wanting to work with him had become an annoyance, and he had stopped teaching altogether.

"Would you please ask him to consider it?" Astrid persisted. "He is the only person who has been able to lure Erik into the water."

To the obvious surprise of the Aquatic Centre's scheduler, her request was granted, and on the following Tuesday, Sigun and Erik set out for his first lesson.

As they stood at the rim of the pool waiting, Erik held her hand, leaning hesitantly towards the water.

"Are you ready, Erik?" said a gruff voice from the pool. Sigun turned and met the gaze of the director standing in the water. His hair was glowing metallic in the light that filtered down from the skylights in the high cathedral ceiling. His eyes glinted like pale green sea glass in his copper face.

"Good morning, Mr. Merehinen." Sigun was careful to politely keep her eyes on his face, above the collar of his skin-tight neoprene suit. He nodded tersely and held out his hand past her, unsmiling, to Erik.

"Come, Erik," Mr. Merehinen said. Once again, the small boy took the man's hand and jumped into the water.

When Mr. Merehinen brought Erik back to the steps of the pool at the end of the lesson, he cast an assessing glance up at Sigun. He stepped out of the pool after Erik, water dripping off his body.

"We can continue lessons for now." Mr. Merehinen didn't seem pleased or displeased. Sigun felt relieved, as if they had passed some sort of test.

"Thank you. This is important to us." Sigun blushed. She sounded overly earnest even to herself.

But Mr. Merehinen had already turned away and quickly disappeared, past the showers and the nurse's station, into the bowels of the swimming hall.

The next morning, Sigun and Erik took the ferry across to the city to visit her father, Lars, and her grandmother Tulikki, her mother's mother, who had helped raise her. The plan was for Sigun to accompany her grandmother to a long-anticipated art exhibition while her father and Erik walked to the Ballard Locks to ogle ships and boats passing up and down between Lake Washington and the Salish Sea.

Sigun drove first to Tulikki's little yellow house, northeast of Green Lake. A giant birch tree dominated her front yard, towering over the house. This was Tulikki's Yard Tree, and following the old customs, she gave it offerings: coffee, milk, vodka, and occasionally, Sigun suspected, blood.

Most people had forgotten such traditions, but not Tulikki, who had been raised by her own grandmother. After Tulikki was orphaned by the Winter War, she and her grandmother had been sent from Finland to live with cousins north of Seattle. They had shared a little bed in a closet, more indentured servants than family, until Tulikki had saved enough money for their escape.

Even in Sigun's childhood, the Yard Tree had been a massive, flourishing thing, a testament to Tulikki's archaic superstitions. Sigun had said as much to her father one day as he had collected her from her grandmother's house. She had been looking back at the tree, so tall she could not see the top of it from the pickup's window.

"It's not your grandmother's witchcraft that makes that tree grow," her father had growled at Sigun, irritated. "It's her damned sewer line." Her father's angry dismissal had surprised her. Over time, Sigun had learned to be careful not to share Tulikki's little eccentricities with him. Sigun glanced up now at the tree as she walked beneath the green canopy and up the uneven stone steps to her grandmother's red door.

Tulikki popped, grinning, from the front door before Sigun's knuckles reached the red-painted wood. As Sigun helped her grandmother settle into the car with her packages, a magnificent smell of cardamom and butter emerged from her parcels. She had brought a basket of pastries, of course. She never visited Sigun's father without them. They were her special tithing, a penance for her daughter's desertion of Lars when Sigun was just a baby.

Lars was waiting outside when they pulled up to Havegrimm's shipyard. The shipyard had been founded a hundred years before by Lars's grandfather, Torsten Havegrimm, a master shipwright, and his younger brother who had come over from Norway together. The original sign for Havegrimm's Shipyard still dominated the front face of the office, carefully maintained and restored, like the old wooden boats within. On the sign, a wizened seal balanced a sailboat on its right-front flipper. Erik, as was his habit, greeted the seal happily, and it grinned back at him with a knowing twinkle in its eye.

The habitual glower of her father's weathered face broke into a smile as he took Erik's tiny hand. Lars was just over six and half feet tall and he loomed over little Erik and tiny Tulikki like a giant. His tousled, white-blond hair was a tangle beneath his old fisherman's cap, and his clothes and boots were dusty from work. After exchanging greetings, Lars and Erik set off eagerly for the locks, and Sigun and Tulikki turned east toward the museum.

The museum was newly built, a monument to the ideals of rational, Scandinavian modernity. As they entered the white curving walls, Tulikki said, "Do you remember when I read that children's version of the Kalevala to you?" The exhibition was of a Finnish painter, Akseli Gallen-Kallela, who was famous for his depictions of scenes from the epic poem. The Kalevala was the national epic of Finland, and it had been composed from bits of songs and spells collected throughout Finland some two hundred years before. Sigun vaguely remembered the strange tales: wizards battling through song, women forged from metal, jaw bones turned into harps.

"Of course," Sigun assured her, but Tulikki was already moving briskly between the paintings, pointing out this and cooing over that. Sigun trailed in her wake, happy to follow her irregular course as Tulikki paused to examine each work. Sigun liked best Gallen-Kallela's later paintings, finished after the death of his daughter, with their bold black lines and anguished figures. Her favorite was his depiction of the witch-woman Louhi, as a monster with the body and wings of an eagle, vicious talons, and braided red hair, hovering above a long ship sharp with spears.

They had seen almost everything, and Tulikki had finally begun to slow her pace, when she sailed right past the large triptych, three canvases enclosed in a massive, intricately carved and gilded frame. Sigun, curious, stopped to take a closer look. The object of the paintings was a young woman, pale and passive, naked in the last two panes. In the central painting, she was half in the water, twisting away from a man with a long white beard who was reaching out from a wooden fishing dory with grasping hands.

A bony hand gripped Sigun's arm, startling her.

"Do you know this story?" Tulikki said, not looking at Sigun, but at the painting with narrowed eyes. "It's the story of Aino, from the Kalevala. Her brother bargains her away to Väinämöinen, the old wizard, and her mother happily agrees to give her away in exchange for her son's life. Aino escapes by drowning herself and turning into a fish."

Where was the anger on Aino's face? Sigun felt it for her. The girl in the painting was a hairless creature, pale and innocent and as inured to loss as a wooden madonna in a medieval church.

"The model in this version is the painter Akseli Gallen-Kallela's own wife. A little bloodless, don't you think?" Tulikki cackled as she patted Sigun's arm. "It makes you wonder, doesn't it?"

"Shall we go outside to wait for the boys?" Sigun needed fresh air; she was already moving toward the door.

"Of course," Tulikki assented and took Sigun's arm, patting it again. Sigun had at least a dozen inches of height on her grandmother, and she checked her stride carefully to match Tulikki's as they moved down the ramp into the soaring entrance of the museum.

As they reached the towering entrance hall, the darkened glass doors parted to reveal her father, a dusty giant, out of place amidst the sparkling glass and high white walls of the modern museum. He held Erik in the crook of his arm, a beaming cherub riding on a thundercloud.

"Just on time!" Lars boomed, pleased as always by punctuality, his fearsome face breaking into a smile of large white teeth.

Their little procession stopped at the shipyard's messy office. Tulikki conjured her cardamom rolls from beneath a linen tea towel. A silent contentment fell over them, amidst the bliss of butter, sugar, cardamom, and coffee, until Erik, with crumbs on his face, demanded they get to work on the boats.

It was the end of the summer, and the shipyard was starting to fill up again. Boats were straggling back in from spending their summers in the archipelago, or from traveling up north to the raucous shores of the Canadian coast, where they had wandered past waterfalls crashing into the sea, orcas breaching the surface of hidden bays, waves lapping fondly on their wooden hulls. Havegrimm's dealt only with the upkeep and restoration of wooden boats. These boats, costly and difficult to maintain, were the obsessions of their owners; they sounded different in the water, more magical, more alive. Now they were home to be coddled over the winter at great expense.

Her father was working on a boat that had not been on the water that summer, nor for several years, by the look of it.

"Has this boat just been purchased?" Sigun asked, running her hand over the wood with its flaking paint.

"Nope. It's been with the same family since the beginning. But now someone finally has the money to restore it." Her father sounded pleased. He was carefully scraping off the peeling paint. "It will take some work to make it seaworthy again." He turned to Sigun, a sly look on his face. "Do you know who built this boat?"

She did. Even without recognizing the lines of the elegant little sloop, she would have known by the sparkle in her father's eye. "Grandpa Torsten," Sigun smiled back at her father.

"Otherwise I wouldn't have taken it on. But I know I can get this one back out on the water." He patted the wood fondly. "When's the last time you were out on a boat?" Lars did not look at Sigun, his gaze still fastened on his work.

"Oh, I don't know. It's hard to find the time." After college, Sigun had chosen to work on a humble research vessel rather than continue to graduate school; she hated desks. She had planned to work on that ship right up to giving birth, had dreamed of returning to it with a baby strapped to her back. Carrying the twins, and then the difficulty of keeping either of them alive, had put an end to those fancies.

"I had a friend once," her father was saying. "Used to fish with me in the summers. Excellent fisherman. Even better card player. He was good with numbers. One day he fell in love with a girl from Magnolia." Her father waved his hand derisively towards the South, where a hill reared up, its western sea-facing side graced with dignified houses. "He went to college, got a degree — fished every summer to pay for it. And then he got a job at the bank downtown. The one in the black tower. He was good at it, too, but he gave up fishing. He couldn't find the time to be on the water." Lars was scrapping something off the hull of the boat now, his face hidden.

Sigun barely managed to stifle a sigh. Her father's stories had a way of irritating her.

"I'm getting to the point, girl," he said tersely. "The point is, he loved the water, and he gave it up. He didn't fight for it, and he was miserable. Then one day, something went wrong down at the bank, and he shot himself."

Sigun dropped the piece of wood she was holding. "Dad!" She turned, looking for Erik, and spotted him up in a wooden sloop on wheels a few boats back. Not close enough to hear, he was busy talking at Tulikki, who was smiling up at him from the solid ground.

"And his wife, she was devastated. She moved up to Alaska," Lars paused to look at Sigun from under his bushy, white-gold brows. "The point is, she really did love him after all. He didn't need to be slaving away in that dark tower for her. He should have found a way to stay on the water, to stay alive. The damned idiot."

He turned back to his work. Picking up a can, he began to paint something over the scraped wood. "Got to get your feet off the land, girl. I can see it in your face."

"I was just on the ferry, wasn't I?" Her father let out a derisive scoff.

Sigun had picked up a little chisel and was testing its sharpness with her finger.

"What is it?" Lars said, straightening up to his full height and looking down at Sigun with a concerned glower.

"Nothing, really. Erik thought he saw a mermaid under the water, near Kilisut Island, and he talks about her still..."

Her father made another dismissive snort and returned to his work. "Well, when you were about his age, you declared you were going to marry a harbor seal." He let out a rumble of laughter.

"I don't remember that."

"Well, you did. You used to speak to him over the edge of the boat. He was very friendly. A big fellow. I told him he had to wait at least another twenty-five years." Her father chuckled, a deep, rough, almost uncomfortable sound. Children will imagine all sorts of things, after all, and it was a comfort to have her father dismiss her worries.

When it was time to catch the ferry home, Sigun drove Tulikki back to her little yellow house. She could see the birch tree long before they turned onto her grandmother's street. Sigun thought of mentioning the mermaid to Tulikki, but she hesitated, saying instead:

"I think Erik's swim instructor has a Finnish name." Tulikki turned to her, curious.

"What is it?"

"Merehinen."

"Merehinen," Tulikki rasped thoughtfully. "It's a little unusual, but then when people immigrate... Anyway, it's a good name for a swimmer," she laughed. "It would kind of mean a merman, you know, although maybe that would be *Vetehinen*."

"Is that like a *näkki*?" When Sigun was just a little girl, Tulikki had taught her a charm for protection against näkki, something to say before entering the water, and the words came quickly back to her tongue: "*Näkki maalle, minä veteen*," It was a simple charm: *näkki to the land, I to the water*. She and Tulikki would say it, tossing a stone into the sea before touching the water, like politely knocking on a door before entering a room. Tulikki had always insisted, in her lighthearted way, on reversing the spell as they left the water, to avoid angering spirits. It had been a comforting ritual in Sigun's childhood summers.

"A näkki is a little nasty thing, like a nixie," Tulikki was saying eagerly. "Always after children. You can find those tales all over. Vetehinen is an older thing. My grandmother used to say they weren't good or evil, but sea folk trapped as the land began to rise when the weight of the glaciers lifted after the last ice age. As the land rose up, bays became lakes, islands turned into peninsulas, water was separated from the sea... No one likes to feel trapped. Still, one had to be careful with them, too, so that boats wouldn't capsize, so the fishing was good, so that women weren't lured into their wild arms..."

Tulikki brushed something invisible off of her long skirt. "So maybe Merehinen would be like a Vetehinen, but one that was never caught. Or one that had escaped." She chuckled. "Anyway, it could be a Finnish name." She cast a sideways glance at Sigun. "Be careful. Don't be like your mother."

Sigun felt as if she had been slapped. "I'm not my mother." Sigun managed to keep her voice calm. Erik was in the car, after all.

"We can't help who we are," Tulikki added casually as they reached her driveway, the little yellow house glowing beneath the towering birch tree. "Think of Erik."

"That's practically all I do," retorted Sigun, her eyebrows drawn together in annoyance.

On the ferry ride home, Sigun and Erik joined the tourists on the south side of the ferry's top deck, where they were gathered to take photographs with Mount Rainier looming over the city behind them, a live volcano and one of the most dangerous in the world. Its snow-covered dome was illuminated by the warm light of the setting sun, a white-haired giant's round sleeping head nestled in the green mountains. Someone on the deck yelled excitedly "Look! Killer whales!"

Erik's feet were on the railing high above the sea, and Sigun held her body pressed against his as he leaned back into her. She pointed out over his shoulder to where four fins were slicing through the water, moving fast northwards toward the archipelago. Four bodies breached the surface, dressed in dashing black and white. Not orca whales, but *Phocoenoides dalli*, Sigun thought. A shoal of Dall's porpoises flying through the water. Sigun felt the crazy urge to dive into the sound after them, but she kept her arms wrapped around Erik, her hands curled tightly around the steel bars of the railing. Her father was right; she had been out of the water too long.

That Friday, Erik had his last swimming lesson before the start of school. He slipped into the water as happily as a duck, pushing off the side of the pool and reaching out his arms to Mr. Merehinen, who waited for him in the water.

When the lesson was over, Merehinen brought Erik back to the rim of the pool where Sigun was waiting. He stopped by the stairs, half in and half out of the water. He was looking up from the pool, and yet he managed to have the air of a king granting an audience, or a judge gazing down from his bench. When he finally spoke, he asked:

"Who is Astrid?"

"Astrid." Sigun repeated, turning away to wrap a shivering Erik in his little hooded towel, emblazoned with fire trucks. It meant something to have her daughter's name on her lips. Sigun had learned early on not to speak of her. It made people uncomfortable. Her grief frightened people. They had worried about Erik, too, but there was no reason, now, to hide her from Erik's ears. "My daughter." Sigun was toweling Erik's hair. "Erik's twin sister. Who is dead."

"I see." Mr. Merehinen considered Sigun, not with pity or compassion, exactly, and then turned to Erik. "Good work today, Erik," he said finally.

"Thank you, Mr. Merehinen," Sigun replied carefully. "For the lesson. Say thank you, Erik." Erik did, and they turned and left the man, still standing in the pool.

Sigun waited until they were home, until after lunch, until Erik was busy building.

"Did you see Astrid today?" Sigun finally asked casually. She was lying on the floor, looking up at the ceiling.

"No." He was concentrating on fitting two pieces together. "But I heard her singing under the water in the pool. She was far away, like a tickling in my ear."

Sigun closed her eyes for a moment.

"I'm learning to swim, so I can be with her." Erik added calmly.

What would a good mother do, believe him or tell him it can't be real?

Her own chest was pinched with longing to hear Astrid, to see her. Sigun imagined Astrid as a creature sewn together from the ocean itself. Eyes of sea glass, fingers made from crab legs, a heart of blood red coral. She could not bring herself to be terrified of such a daughter, even if such a daughter would have cause to be angry and jealous of the living.

Astrid, manifested or imagined, had not hurt Erik after all. It was Sigun who had been the danger to him, who had failed to keep her eyes open, as she had once failed Astrid.

●

On Saturday, Sigun, Tom, and Erik drove to the northern edge of the Olympic Peninsula and hiked down through the evergreen trees until they reached Dungeness Spit, a long sandy arm curling out into the water towards Victoria. They met another family with a boy and a girl close to Erik's age and the children began playing. Soon they were sharing buckets and filling them with wet sand to build a sandcastle.

Sigun knelt down beside them. "Do you want me to teach you a Finnish spell for making sandcastles? My grandmother taught it to me."

"Yes!" The girl replied, clapping her sandy hands together. Sigun glanced quickly at the girl's parents. One never knew who would be disturbed by these harmless little things, but they were talking animatedly to Tom, oblivious. Sigun helped the children tip their full buckets over. She began to tap on the bottom of a bucket with a tiny shovel and the children mimicked her, chanting:

"Älä tule paha kakku
Tule hyvä kak-ku!"

It was an order: *Don't become a bad cake, become a good cake!* They smacked the buckets in rhythm to the rhyme and, laughing, carefully lifted them to find perfectly neat sand-cakes standing proudly below. Sigun glanced up again at the boys' parents, but their mother was smiling, charmed.

The children eagerly set about filling their buckets again. Erik ran towards the surf to gather water and Sigun followed. She thought of her grandmother's charm for entering the water, but she held her tongue back, kept her lips from whispering it, just as she restrained her hand from tossing the smooth granite stone she was grasping in her palm. It was all too easy to get attached to little rituals, comforting bulwarks against the tides of fate.

Looking at Erik playing joyfully at the edge of the waves, Sigun wondered if there wasn't something cruel about ordering a creature out of the water, in removing something from its element without its consent. Anyway, she had never told Tom about the charm; he'd never heard her say it.

She glanced back at Tom, who was still speaking with the other family. The afternoon gilded his dark hair with bronze. He looked happy at a distance, painted gold by the sun, washed by the sea wind, apart from her. Free. Sigun knew her loss, her worry, her sorrow, were not hers alone. And yet, somehow the labor of keeping Erik alive felt more hers, however imperfect her skill at it.

Sigun looked back to Erik, then, just in time to see him being pulled underwater, black tentacles twisting about his legs.

"Erik!" She leapt across the sinking sand, the tide pulling at her feet. He was completely under the water now. He hadn't come back up. She could see the bright white of his striped sun shirt as he was pulled away from her, gliding west into the ocean. She lunged for him and, grabbing him around the waist, dragged him up into the air. He was too shocked to cry or even take a breath.

"Help! Tom!" Sigun screamed, but Tom was already running towards her. Long, thick rubbery strands of kelp wound around Erik. They were still pulling on his little legs as the heavy ball of kelp root rolled away on a receding wave. Sigun tore at the kelp and it tangled around her own legs. "You cannot have him!" Sigun growled at it, weeping with fury.

"Sigun," Tom said sharply, as if he had said her name many times without her hearing. He was holding Erik now, curled against his shoulder. Sigun hurled the mass of kelp roots away, far into the tide. When she turned back to Tom, he was looking at her intently over Erik's shoulder, and she could see him absorbing her words, the madness of them. She looked down, abashed. A piece of kelp was still trailing from her hand, its large floating bulb filled with gasses the alga had breathed into it. *Nereocystis luetkeana*: mermaid's bladder. She dropped it into the water as if it had scalded her hand.

●

On Monday, Sigun drove Erik to his pretty little preschool in the forest for the first day of school. As she watched him, he hesitated on the threshold, and looked back over his shoulder, a grave look on his face. But then he turned away to greet his teacher, and she escaped.

All summer she had been waiting for this moment when she was no longer responsible for him, when she was alone. Other parents were celebrating by going out for coffee, or rushing back to work; Sigun had a swimsuit on, hidden under her pants and an old fleece jacket.

She drove home under a gray sky heavy with clouds, and, after grabbing her bicycle, pedaled down the street toward the steep paved path that would take her through the seaside park to a remote little beach. This path was why they had chosen the house, but she had learned after moving in that a boy, out on a lark one night, had died when his bicycle had sped off it and over the cliff to the park below. Many parents moved to the island for safety, but perfect safety is impossible.

Down the treacherous path she flew, past the ruined wharf where the cormorants stood sentry as usual, brown-black and iridescent as an oil slick. When she reached the little beach, she did not use Tulikki's charm; her whole purpose was to meet whatever was in the water.

Sigun left her things on the shore and waded through the muddy shallows. Peach colored blood worms fled in frantic fringed spirals from her giant feet until it was finally deep enough to swim. The water was unbearably cold, but as she began to swim, she could no longer feel it, just the pleasure of floating in the water, the weightlessness, the grace that always came to her there.

She swam with long strong strokes out into the channel and let herself feel all of it, the longing, the grief, the anger. If some part of her daughter were there, in the dark water, lost, suspended in the old boundary between worlds, alone, vengeful even, Sigun would find her.

I love you, my daughter. Come to me. Whatever you need, take it from me.

After Erik was born, Sigun had been rushed to an operating theater by yelling doctors with shaking hands. They had tried one last time to pull Astrid out from where she had been curled beneath Sigun's heart. Sigun could feel her panicked struggle against the grasping hands before Astrid went horribly still inside her. Later, Astrid had been wheeled past Sigun, one small, perfect, plump hand lifted, waving from the bouncing speed of the trolly.

For days they had not let Sigun touch her. "She is sleeping," they had said. "She is in too much pain," they had said. Her legs had been dark with bruises. Sigun had nursed skinny, wizened Erik constantly, but she had struggled to express her scant, rich first milk into a tiny plastic cup for Astrid. The night nurse had thrown it away. "It had blood in it," she had said. As if Sigun's painful effort had spoiled the colostrum. As if a drop of her blood could contaminate what was part of her own body, her cells, her antibodies, the dissolved proteins of her tissue.

"Wake me, wake me when she is awake, even in the middle of the night," Sigun had begged. But the night nurse never had. Sigun could understand Astrid's rage because she was still full of it.

Sigun's body drifted, floating like dead wood in the channel. She had stopped shivering and her breathing slowed, as had the blood in her veins, the beat of her heart. If she drifted far enough, she would be in the path of the fast ferry to Bremerton, but she didn't lift her head to look.

Worse than the rage was the guilt. Once, when she was taking Erik to an appointment at the children's hospital, she could not help noticing the many sets of twins lurking in the waiting rooms and elevators. Twins with reconstructed skulls, twins with parents grey as ghosts, twins with tiny arms bandaged from where blood had been drawn from their little veins, their mother weeping over them as she nursed them. Sigun had not been jealous. She had thought: *I am lucky.* Even now, the guilt engulfed her, that she could feel, even for a moment, such a horrible loss to be a blessing. She thought of the ancient tales in which women leave their babies in baskets to drift on the water, or fathers abandon twins on the banks of rivers to be nursed by wolves. What if she was like them, what if she could have done more? How could Astrid ever forgive her?

I love you, my daughter. Can't you feel it? Come to me. Come for me. Take what you need from me. Devour me. I loved you.

I love you still.

Sigun felt something then, surrounding her, a longing that was hers, but not hers alone, a question. Her eyes were closed and she rested her weight on the moving sea. She nestled this presence closely to her chest. This was how it should have been, a child born in water and held over her bursting heart. She held the feeling of it, like a sea otter holds her child fast to her belly, floating on the surface of the ocean.

Just as Sigun became fearful of its end, hungry to keep it, the sense of deep communion began to release her, to leave her, to dissolve in the cold current of the channel, into the sea dark with pollution and storm water and life.

Part of Astrid was alive, after all, swimming inside Sigun's own body. Astrid's cells would live inside Sigun's blood for years, as Erik's would. To become pregnant is to become a chimera, no longer made only of yourself. Across the channel the sea lions were trumpeting again. The water was noisy with life. The sea was our first mother, and we are still made of it.

Suspended in the water and part of it, Sigun imagined she was a shapeshifter, a dragon. She was Charybdis, daughter of a sea god, a maelstrom that could capsize her family in her discontent, her anger, her sorrow, her desire. It wasn't Astrid, but she herself who was the monster. It would be easy for what was left of them to be torn apart like a brittle wooden ship into so much flotsam and jetsam, broken and scattered. It was a terrible responsibility to keep them all afloat, to keep them safe from the furious currents inside her.

A responsibility, an ability, a power that was hers alone. She would honor it. To withstand the thirsty cyclone inside her, to not allow it to swallow them up, to withstand it and to live, that would be a worthy feat of honor, a battle deserving of glory, if only in Sigun's own heart.

But Sigun had been drifting dangerously long. Her dark hair trailed out behind her in the water like the swirls of a fractal, her skin was blue with cold. The sun was somewhere up above, blanketed by the wet gray clouds. She twisted onto her belly to swim back, her eyes open wide in the dim water, but she couldn't make out the shore, and she couldn't quite feel her arms or her feet. It was as if they had vanished and she had been transformed into a salmon, silver-cheeked, bound to live forever in the watery underworld.

She felt it before she saw it, something large and fast swimming towards her beneath the slow current of the channel. Here, after all, was the sea come to claim her, Sigun thought, but her blood was so cold, her heart so slow, that she could not rise in panic. She closed her eyes instead.

Only when arms wrapped around her did she realize the animal swimming towards her had not been a whale or a seal or a shark, but a man, who rolled her onto her back and lifted her head out of the water. She was pressed by the gentle waves against his body, his black wetsuit as slick and velvety as seal skin. He pushed his diving mask up into his silver hair: Mr. Merehinen.

She noticed that his eyes were not actually green, but a cold storm grey, the pupils rimmed with a halo of gold, like the last glimmer of the sun on the crest of a winter sea.

"Sigun! You are alive." It came across not as a question, or statement even, but a stern command. His deep voice shivered across the calm water.

When she made no move to escape, he embraced her, one arm curled beneath her knees and the other wrapped around her chest right below her left breast, holding her to his chest. As they reached shallow water, he picked her up out of the water easily and carried her as if she were still weightless, despite the awkward neoprene mittens that hid his hands, the flippers on his feet, which slapped in the shallow water of the muddy beach.

"Yes, I am. I am alive, thank you," Sigun said, or she thought she said, her lips were still blue with cold. She was filled with gratitude, and she felt as if she could have left her forehead on his shoulder forever, but it wasn't only solace she felt.

She wriggled from his arms like a fish, and stood, towering over him.

He stood very still, his chin up as he contemplated her. There was a quality to his stillness that was transfixing. His attention was so focused on her that Sigun felt heat flood her cheeks. She was blushing and she was so surprised to feel it, she found it so delightfully mortifying, that she had to stifle a chuckle of mirth. Instead, she lowered her eyes, in an attempt to appear demure, remembering her grandmother's rules of etiquette when encountering strange creatures in the forest, unsettling men in parks, animals rising out of wild water: to be respectful and polite, to move away quickly.

"I could help you," his voice was quiet now, a low whisper, "to learn to swim in this water. If you want."

"Not today, but thank you, Mr. Merehinen." Her cheeks flaming, she risked one last fleeting look at his face and was almost sure she saw a flicker of expression there, that his eyes were crinkled at the edges with amusement, that the golden rings around his dilated pupils glowed. Sigun turned, hurriedly towards her bicycle, careful not to chance even a glance over her shoulder. Her skin was still blue with cold, but she felt remarkably revived.

When she finally reached it, Sigun leapt onto her bicycle and raced back through the park, past the old wharf, now empty of cormorants except for the one, streaked red with blood, vanquished below the talons of a bald eagle that was piercing the midday with its incongruously beautiful cry. She hurtled up the treacherous path, pedaling ferociously, her blood (Astrid's blood, Erik's blood) heating again, her lungs burning, to where her house perched precariously on the steep hillside above the water.

Grief is not something that can be nailed in a wooden box and buried, and neither is desire. They ebb and flow like the tide; one has to learn to navigate them. There is no perfect closure, and to believe in one would be a perilous delusion, a mirage, like an island of perfect safety, a sea without monsters.

She sped, cutting off from the paved road and bouncing down the short-cut through the woods where blackberry branches stretched out across a dirt path with monstrous, spiny arms that lashed her bare skin and pinged against the spokes of her furiously spinning wheels.

The air was heavy with the sweet ferment of August berries as Sigun burst out of the forest onto to her ordinary, paved street lined with houses. As she put her hand on the door latch, it opened from within, and Tom was standing on the threshold.

"I left the office early — I wanted to go with you to pick up Erik..." His eyes wandered over her, taking in her red cheeks and the cold, blue skin of her arms, the seaweed in her hair, the hermit crab clinging, terrified, to her swimsuit, which was all she was wearing. She had left her clothes at the beach. He lifted a hand out towards her, gently removing the hermit crab and placing it aside.

She raised her eyes to his face, unsure of what she would find there. At some point, Sigun had lost her confidence that Tom could know her and still love her, let alone want her as she stood now, her hair beribboned with seaweed, her arms red with scratches and tiny drops of blood from the pricks of the blackberry brambles. Sigun thought suddenly of what must have been the exact moment she had fallen in love with him. It was soon after they had met and she had taken him out sailing in one of her father's boats. Tom hadn't grown up around the water, and he was awkward in a boat. She should have been careful with him, but she was overjoyed to be out on the sea again. The wind was strong that day, and had picked up even further to a fierce gale. Sigun hadn't been able to hold back, and she had been laughing as they ran with the wind, the spray of the water hitting her young, grinning face. She had looked back at him in her wild joy, suddenly unsure of what she would find. He was seeing her in her element, unrestrained in all her terrible power and glory, but he met her eyes, not with terror or anger, but admiration. He had trusted her, putting his life in her hands as they flew over the water.

Now, Tom smiled down at her from the front step, with wary affection and longing in his eyes. "You look like yourself again," he said.

"I feel alive again," Sigun said and she found herself grinning back at him. She took his warm, dry hand in her cold, salty one, and placed it over the cool damp skin above her heart. "I don't want to be late to pick up Erik," she said, "But I need to warm up before we go..." Then Tom was pulling her through the door and Sigun was pushing the door shut. They were laughing as they raced up the stairs, her long arm wrapped around his and their hands tangled together.

Sigun's skin tingled almost painfully as her heated blood flowed into the last edges of her body, flushed to the tips of her fingers. She could feel everything again and the return of feeling was a stinging effervescence. She was a pulsing medusa, venomous, bioluminescent, ephemeral. Sigun could feel in that moment, haunted and monstrous though she might be, not only the anguish of living, but also the joy and pleasure of it. She could feel the triumph and the fragility of it, the grace and good fortune of being there, terribly, magnificently alive.

●

J.J. Eskelin's story "Astrid Underwater" was originally published in Metaphorosis on Friday, 15 September 2023. See magazine.metaphorosis.com

About the author

J.J. Eskelin is a writer of speculative fiction currently living with her family on the Central Coast of California. She has lived in Finland, England, and the United States, and is a dual Finnish and American citizen. Nature and place are important to her, and, no matter where she is, she tries to escape with her giant dog to commune with wilderness on a weekly basis.

jjeskelin.com

Pain Eater

Danny Menter

Before the summer I turned twelve, plants had seemed innocuous: sometimes pretty, mostly boring, perennial background filler. I did know someone once who claimed her Ficus granted pleasant dreams when fed a mixture of honey and dried banana peel; another who swore his succulent had cannibalized his others while he was at work, leaving behind a massacre of black fertilizer and a noticeably plumper cactus sunning itself on the windowsill. But I heard those stories later, when I knew better, when I believed them.

It had always been there, thick and bulbous, rotating like a miniature planet in its harness, but I couldn't remember ever looking at it directly until that summer. I dropped the black plastic bags next to the toolshed, and pulled my grandfather's heavy work gloves off and left them on the wooden bench. Above, hung an assortment of rust spotted tools: hoes, trowels, and an axe with a heavy maple handle. I returned the shed key to its spot under the stone frog and turned back towards the plant.

I sifted through the sounds that had stopped me; beneath the soft tear of weeds ripping from the earth and sand shimmying into the trash bag, I thought I had heard a sigh, as if the giant thing had exhaled.

I looked back towards the house. Everyone had finished swimming and the grill crackled with burgers and hotdogs. The impromptu garden tidying had been Grandpa's idea, cut short by his dizzy spell — my enlistment in chores a frequent occurence while we lived with Grandpa and Grandma over the summer — now he sunned himself on the porch in a plastic Adirondack chair, a halo of pipe smoke hanging over his head. He looked faded, indistinct, a photo of a photo. Dad was setting up slender tubes on the concrete walkway, peering upward to ensure their trajectory.

I listened again, but the whole yard lay in a state of lazy, sunburnt silence — the only sound the creak of the chains bracing the plant as it rocked in the wind.

●

Later, Grandma took a thick bag of sugar out of the cupboard for shortbread.

"Twenty years or so?" She slid a tab of butter into the mixing bowl and leaned against the counter. She was short, only a head taller than me, in her red apron with multicolored fireworks threaded through the chest, but she had never seemed old, with her face like starched white linen. In the living room I could hear Dad talking about the progress on our new house, the one we would move into after the summer.

"Was it always that big?" I asked.

She glanced through the sliding glass door, but the afternoon sun obscured any view of the backyard.

"I wouldn't worry," she said, turning and dusting her hands on her apron, "your grandfather has always taken care of the weeds. I try not to pay attention to those things."

She handed me the mixing bowl. It was the size of my chest and I needed to sit down on the steps that led down into the sunken living room and brace it with my knees to maneuver the spoon.

Mom lay on the opposite couch, bathed in light, arm drifting across her forehead while Dad paced in the foyer making a sales call.

I grasped the spoon with both hands to work it around the bowl, but it barely budged. In a minute my forearms screamed, and Grandpa noticed and heaved himself from the recliner, squatted down next to me on the floor, and placed his callused hands around my small ones. Together we smoothed out the dough.

After dinner we filed out to the backyard. Beyond the stiff Saint Augustine grass, baked to glass by the heat, cut a chain link fence that separated my grandparents' yard from a retention ditch. Over the years, seeds and pollen drenched by rainwater and street runoff had erupted into a tangle of thorny vines and greasy flat-leafed vegetation that crowded at the fence, ready to tear it down if we let it. I stared at the boundary while Dad lit the first of the rockets. It fizzled to life as Grandma handed us each a dense brick of shortbread from her cookie tin.

My eyes burned from an afternoon of swimming, but I forced them open against the sky to watch the rockets disintegrate into pink sparks.

●

A week later I sat on the concrete steps by the pool next to a crowded collection of aloe, spiny and prehistoric, and a skull of desiccated coral. I'd never worn a tie before. I kept clipping and unclipping it from my shirt collar.

Inside, mourners gathered, afraid to bump into each other, polite and fragile. Their whispering was too loud. A portrait of my grandfather, decked out in his navy uniform, sat on the kitchen table, encircled by a wreath of white lilies.

I wondered if I had a time bomb in my chest too, winding down to its final tic.

I loped out across the grass, the late afternoon sun an orange disk, to the plant.

It was so big it stretched against the chains suspending it from the oak, causing the tree to splinter along its trunk.

I placed my hand, pink from the heat, against the lime green skin of the thing. It was warmer than my hand, and something seemed to pulse beneath the surface. I imagined what it would be like to peel back all its layers, what it would hold in the center. An eye, maybe, bloodshot and swiveling, corded in inch-thick veins. Or nothing. Just more and more layers until you came out the other side.

Then I thought of snakes, and imagined one was hiding now, waiting for my hand to slide closer to one of the folds. I jerked away.

Dad joined me. He looked uncomfortable and sad, unsure of what to say.

"She'll be okay," he said finally.

"Who?" I asked.

"Well, both of them, I guess." He dug the heel of a black shoe into the earth. "But your mother," he added, before walking away.

I stared at the space next to the porch where a week before the five of us had watched stars explode in the sky.

A rustle and groan beside me, and I turned slowly towards the plant. I squinted, first with one eye, then the other.

I lifted my hand, measuring the distance between the plant and the pool door using my fingers.

I was sure.

It had grown.

●

On the kitchen table, Grandma's tin lay bare, its tarnished corners worn silver where the seams met. The last few guests edged out, sharing pained glances with me, offering to help with the bags of trash Dad held from his hand, his other on the door jamb.

I found it difficult to look anyone in the face. Mom and Dad and Grandma made movements that approximated normal, but were too fast and slow all at once, like the jerky movements of marionettes.

That night, Mom and Dad made a bed up for me in the living room, tucking a quilt into the couch cushions and draping it over me like an envelope. Grandma had gone to sleep, or at least retreated into a far dark corner of the house to be alone. I had never noticed how the house echoed when only one person was speaking, the sounds ricocheting off the walls like softballs.

I still felt that when I glanced at the recliner he'd be there, square jawed and immense, chewing the end of his pipe.

"Mom," I said, and the word felt funny, like I was saying it for the first time.

She waited in the doorway that led back to the bedrooms.

"That thing in the backyard —"

"Thing?" She said, closing her robe against her throat and bracing herself against the wall.

"The plant, I guess." Because maybe that's all it was.

"Oh, Bryan's plant." She read the silence, studied the room for a place to sit, but she seemed to see mines everywhere that could go off at the slightest pressure. Ultimately, she chose the step where I held the mixing bowl a week before.

"Bryan gave that to your grandmother a few weeks before the accident. A birthday gift." Her eyes creased at the corners. "You know, it was this big," she held her hands a few inches above one another, "when he bought it. He was always doing stuff like that. That's why he was the favorite."

Mom never spoke of her brother, who had died in an accident before I was born. I knew little about him other than that we shared a name.

I absorbed this, appreciating the way speaking helped fill up the room, and it felt clandestine, opening doors on the past that had been locked — peering into a time before I was born, a mythology I might never have access to again.

"Did you ever think about getting rid of it?" And I knew I'd made a mistake by the way her eyes froze, and her hand clawed its way back up her throat, as if someone had just thrown open the door on a blizzard and an icy wind was thrashing around the room. But the only change was my question, which had shorn the conversation in half.

"No, we couldn't." She stood, took a step forward, and flicked the light off.

●

Things were worse at the funeral. I was realizing that pain wasn't linear: it peaked and ebbed, then crested again unexpectantly, violently.

Mom had been quiet in the few days leading up to it. I watched her the way you watch tinder in a bonfire, wary and expectant. The funeral was held on the same grounds where Bryan was buried, Grandma told me. They even used the same priest, a tottering old man who asked me to hold the scripture readings for him at the lectern as he spoke. Everyone thought this was a great idea.

The same shopworn people who had come to my grandparents' home were there, milling around, checking their phones, keeping close to the perimeter.

Dad and Mom were fighting. Dad had to leave in the morning to catch a flight to Austin for a sales meeting, but Mom wanted him to stay to help Grandma pack up Grandpa's things. With the neighborhood getting more dangerous and Grandma alone, Mom thought it best to move her into a condo closer to our new house.

I could sense the hesitancy, a hole that suggestion had fallen into.

"Well, that may not be a good idea," Dad said.

"Why not? She could help with Bryan. and you said the house is nearly finished anyway, we just need your final bonus to —"

Dad rushed in "— I just don't think we should be too hasty, is all. With everything going on... the funeral, I mean... I... we may have to hold off on the move."

I could sense something change. A drop in pressure. A curdling of the air.

"We have savings for that, Dean." An electric current pulsed through each word.

They couldn't hear me on the outside of the door. I had come to tell them that I didn't want to hold the papers. I didn't want to stand in front of all those people in their caked-on suits and dresses, and not for the last time, I wished I had an older brother or sister to take my hand and tell me what to do. But instead, I wiped my face and forced the rock in my throat down to my belly, where it settled, and walked away. I imagined it growing in there, calcifying like the coral on Grandma's porch.

As I perched by the lectern, a man walked into the back of the parlor; I saw him over the greying heads, hunched slightly, wearing aviators and a creased leather jacket. Dad had his head bowed, but I could see him stiffen as he caught sight of him. The hymnal in his hands quaked.

Mom turned too, but it was difficult to read her expressions, her emotions as opaque as sea-glass.

She placed a palm on Dad's and whispered something in his ear. He pushed her hands away to lie lonely and tangled in her lap.

●

"You have no right —" Dad was saying.

I froze in the doorway with a tray full of plastic wineglasses to throw away. Clearly a ploy to keep me from this scene.

The man in the leather jacket had one hand on a hip and the other outstretched, palm up, as if he expected Dad to shake it.

They were standing in the funeral parlor's kitchen area, forced close together by cardboard boxes filled with wine. I could smell aftershave that wasn't Dad's — something sickeningly spicy and sweet.

"It was in the paper. I just came to pay my respects," the man said. His accent was slightly southern, a cowboy in a Marlboro ad.

I felt hands on my shoulders moving me out of the doorway and back into the hallway.

Mom's face, close to mine: *Go*, she mouthed, but before I could retreat there was a massive crash and the shattering of glass, and the man stumbled out of the doorway pinching the bridge of his nose between his fingers. A crimson gush darkened the collar of his white shirt. He leaned his head back and disappeared wordlessly through a doorway to our right.

My hands were shaking, and plastic cups tilted off the tray, spilling their contents on the carpet. Dad came out next, massaging his knuckles, his face drawn and startled.

Mom stood with her hands on her hips. She glanced once through the doorway and her face collapsed, eyes jolting up at the corners, a choking sob breaking free of her lips.

Dad reached for her, but she turned away.

I got on my hands and knees, shaking, and began to stack the cups back on the tray. I held one up to the light.

At the bottom, curled in a C, lay a slim finger of lime green vine.

●

The plant's sagging belly now dipped into the ground, making a little furrow of the muddy soil beneath. The top branches of the tree had begun to angle precipitously towards the roof of the house, and as I watched, a squirrel zigzagged across the shingles and clambered onto an outstretched limb. I was afraid to touch the plant — I could feel heat coming from it like a furnace. Whatever was inside was burning, fueling growth.

The man from the funeral, his nostrils stuffed with tissue, walked across the grass barefoot.

"Does Dad know he'll be here?" I had asked in the car ride over.

"He's an old friend; we need all the help we can get right now," she had said, not answering.

I eyed the plant and hoped it would shoot out leafy arms or vines and wrap him up like a mummy, twirl him up into pasta until the only thing visible was the top of his sweaty head, which would burst from the pressure, leaking red over green.

But I could sense that whatever the plant was, it wasn't benevolent; it merely squatted, motionless under its own gargantuan weight.

I stared down at the man's muddy feet, his jeans rolled over his bony ankles, and wondered what he had said to Dad in the funeral parlor. Dad, who didn't let me watch *Terminator* when it played on T.V.

"You know, I was there when he bought this — with your uncle, I mean." His voice twanged like a broken banjo string.

"Uncle Bryan?" I asked.

He squinted at it although storm clouds had covered the sun for hours.

"Yap. Knew your granda, way back when," he added.

"It looks like you know my dad, too," I said.

This stopped him and he looked at me for a moment, searching, then unconsciously reached for his nose but stopped himself and pointed at me instead.

"I think we maybe got off on the wrong foot yesterday. I'm Jake." He stuck out his hand and leaned over it like a magician coaxing a reluctant volunteer from a crowd.

It sank to his side when I didn't take it.

"I don't think I need to know your name," I said. "You're just here to help Mom. Then you're leaving."

His smile made my stomach turn acidic.

"Oh, I don't know," he said. "I might stick around for a while."

"Dad will be home tomorrow," I said, fast enough to run my words over one another.

He shook his head, mouth in a line but with a corner twisted up like a rusty hook.

"Nope. In Austin *all* week." He dragged it out in a way that made me aware of the sweat running down my back.

●

"Come look at this," Mom said. The three of them were hunched over a peeling leather photo album in the kitchen. I had been pacing the edge of the pool for an hour and I smelled like the outside that had seeped into my clothes.

I crossed my arms and edged forward reluctantly.

Jake had his hands on either side of the thing, as if he were holding the whole world of the album between his arms. Grandma and Mom were on either side of him. Grandma looked thinner, I realized, her parchment pale skin sagging at the corners of her mouth.

In the picture I saw Uncle Bryan, Mom's twin. He crouched next to a small motorcycle, hand placed on the shiny black seat. Behind him, I recognized Jake, although a much younger version, with long hair that swooped across his forehead. They were standing in the front yard, the oak trees smaller and the paint on the house a brighter shade of white. In the background, Mom rested her arms across a wrought iron gate.

There was no fence like there was now and I could see straight into the backyard where a small leafy plant dangled from a tree branch. It was light enough to suspend from a single nylon rope.

"He was so proud of that bike," Grandma said, turning from the table and busying herself in the kitchen.

"Is that…" I started, pointing at the bike.

Mom nodded, two fingers close to the edge of the photo, an inch or so away from Jake's.

"What happened to it?" I asked.

"After the accident, it wasn't nothing but scrap metal," Jake said. "I hauled it over to the junkyard."

Grandma made a pained sound in her throat and for a second I thought she had cut her hand, which grasped a potato, a paring knife in the other. Her head was tilted forward over the sink as if she was about to fall into it.

Jake scraped his chair away from the table and walked behind her, taking the blade. "Let me take care of this," he said. "Why don't you ladies take a load off and let the boys finish dinner?"

Mom gave him an appreciative glance that lingered in the air, then grabbed Grandma's arm and guided her into the living room.

"I need to shower," I protested.

"After dinner," Mom said. "Help Jake with whatever he needs."

Jake hauled a pot out of the cabinet under the sink and threw a washcloth over his shoulder. I was uncomfortable with the ease with which he knew the locations of items: the saltshaker, the grater, the ceramic butter plate. Things I never really paid attention to, but now felt imbued with importance; if I appreciated them more, he wouldn't have to touch them.

The light outside died as a fine drizzle greyed the yard. I heard the scrape of branches against the roof, their bent weight scratching like fingernails.

Jake stopped with a potato in one hand and stared intently at a picture above the sink. It was a photo of my mother when she was in high school, taken at prom or homecoming. In it, she perched on the edge of a couch, fingers laced under her chin, her head lifted towards the source of light shining from somewhere outside of the frame. Her hair had been curled, and it curved under her delicate chin in an auburn wave, the border of a pale green dress just visible at her collar. Mom usually never smiled in pictures, there were only a few I had seen where her teeth were visible, and because of this, I'd always liked this photo of her, imagining that this was who she was on some secret horizon. Her smiles were never given freely; they had to be earned, and anytime she did smile, I felt accomplished. I kept those moments close.

He leaned over the sink, and I tensed, watching his finger raise to stroke the frame.

"Don't," I said and felt my hands clench.

His head swiveled towards me, that grin leaking out of his face, running all over the place, spilling onto the counter.

"You know who took this picture?" he asked.

I don't want him to say it. There were fault lines running through this house and underneath were gaping mouths with sharp teeth and I wanted Dad to rush in and make him bleed again; it was a wash of rage and violence that I had never experienced before, and it tasted like terror.

He continued.

"Prom. I wore a blue tuxedo. Borrowed your uncle's bike — got home *real* late that night." He picked up the knife and potato and, in fine papery shavings, began removing the skin.

There was a shriek like two-by-fours being compressed by immense pressure. I heard a crack, too, but was unsure if it was the snap of wood or thunder.

He didn't look up as I snatched the phone off the receiver and darted into the hallway. Mom had taken to staying in Grandma's room, which left the only other bedroom open. I closed the door, locked it, and dialed Dad's number.

He picked up after what felt like too many rings.

"Everything okay?" he asked. I could hear traffic in the background, like he was at a street corner or a bus stop.

I tried to keep my voice level.

"When are you coming home?" I asked.

There was a long pause on the other end of the line.

"Well, it's taking a bit longer than I thought out here..." His voice trailed off.

"But we need...I think you should come home."

"Has something happened?"

Although I was thankful he had finally asked, the question lacked the urgency that I needed, and I had no idea how to answer.

"The plant —" I started, then thought better of it. What if it could hear me? What if even now there were tendrils snaking below the floorboards, finding cracks in the foundation, listening with a thousand different moist pores to this conversation. "I mean, Mom has the guy —"

A long sigh. Not the intake of breath, swear, yell, or shattering glass that I wanted from him.

"Jake," he said. "Your mother invited Jake over."

"Yes. I don't like him and he's saying things about Mom, and I think —" I was rushing through it and my thoughts were skittering like spiders but there was one thought that was coherent above all: "He should leave, Dad. I don't want him here."

"Listen," he said, "unfortunately, there's nothing that either of us can do about that right now. He's...kind of been in the picture for a while."

"But you...can't you just tell her she can't see him?" I said, and I felt tears breaking free and a hard knot forming in my throat.

"It's not that easy," he said. I heard voices in the background and laughing. "I just don't think your mother wants to hear from me right now."

I sensed finality; shovelfuls of dirt tumbling in over my head and light being shut out, closed coffins and stale air. I stared at the phone and ended the call.

I refused dinner, ignored Mom's voice when she called from the kitchen, then waited for a knock at the door, but none came. I crept silently into bed and listened to the probing life outside, trying to force its way in.

The next morning, I awoke to find Jake splayed across the couch, eyes lizard-like slits in the orange light spilling from the curtains. Mom walked in a moment later, saw me standing with my fists like rocks and Jake smiling slyly from the couch, but only gave herself a second to look guilty before she disappeared into the kitchen.

●

It took us three days get Grandpa's things packed up neatly into boxes and placed into the moving truck. Each box that was carted off felt like a little piece of my grandfather being cut out and tossed aside. I wanted to wrap my arms around everything in the house and keep it in place. I wanted to stop it all from slipping away. If enough pieces of him were gone then it was really happening, and there would be no going back. I wanted to tell Mom the secret that I knew: that we didn't have to go along with this; that death was just a rumor we didn't have to believe, and if we simply let it pass, he would come walking back in the door, Dad would return from his trip, Jake would fade away like a bad dream, and the plant would be destroyed forever.

Because that was the other thing I knew.

It was the plant that had started this, with its menacing leaves and the thing growing inside of it, and the vines which had now started to wind themselves underfoot, so that you had to watch them when you were carrying boxes across the thick grass. But every time I thought about damaging it — purposely running a dolly over a clammy limb or puncturing the swollen belly with a kitchen knife — Jake seemed to be there, watching.

"Your mother could use your help in the garage," Jake said, on the final day of packing, standing with his arms crossed and feet spread underneath the oak.

I trudged away, finding Mom paused at the brick wall of the garage, a plastic bag in her fist.

With her back turned I was able to stow the pocket-knife under a stack of wool quilts on a shelf where I had been hiding it. I needed something much bigger, I decided.

Mom didn't turn as I entered the garage. We hadn't spoken much in the last three days, not since I had foregone dinner the night after the funeral.

I watched her back now, thin under her t-shirt, all collarbones and elbows and long hair twisted up into a bun beginning to fray.

"Mom," I called.

She turned and her eyes, half-lidded, found mine. She was far away, and it took her a moment to swim back, whatever rip tide was pulling her away ebbing momentarily.

She gestured, and I grabbed the trash can and swung it over to her.

She tossed the bag in and settled heavily into a plastic lawn chair that lay in a triangle of light from the open garage door. Beyond, Grandma watched Jake rattle down the U-Haul's wide door.

At the end of the lawn, the retention ditch gave off a cloying smell, rotting vegetables and decay, and my stomach tensed.

"How did you ever live next door to that?" I said, wiping my mouth with a sleeve. "It reeks."

Mom glanced absently at the neon green wasteland beyond the chain-link fence and shrugged. "You can get used to anything."

I wanted to ask her so many things then: why they had kept the plant all these years, what had made it stop growing? If we escaped before awaking one morning to find it erupting in a slimy green spike from our mouths, would it simply follow us? Appear suddenly in the folds of a rose blossom, or wait as a seedling attached to an eyelash? Had we been spreading it this whole time?

But I settled on this: "What is Jake?"

She waved it away.

"He's an old friend, I told you that."

"More than that. He took you to prom. He was there when Bryan died. He was there when..."

She held a hand to her face, the flash of her wedding band floating through the garage like a lightning bug. She looked weak, fed upon. When she looked up again, her eyes moved past me.

Jake stood in the doorway, one hand holding the pocketknife. He tapped it against his thigh, slowly, then ushered me over. His eyes glinted. "Time for a talk."

I kept my distance from him as we circled into the backyard, through the faded wooden gate, under the smoldering afternoon sky, to stand again at the plant.

He picked his way across the grass, almost reverently, reaching out a hand but stopping short of touching the thing. His hand traced the veiny membranes like an ancient text he could read.

"Can you hear it?" he whispered.

Waves of disgust roiled through me at his proximity to the thing. Sweat beaded on his forehead. I wanted to run, but part of me needed to hear what he would say. Maybe there would be an answer, a clue, a way to kill it.

"It's special, you know." He shook his head, "Of course, we didn't know that when he bought it. It was just a green thing, a small fragile thing someone had left half alive in the back of a hardware store." He rubbed the damp area above his lip. "Your Uncle didn't want it, but I could sense it was..." he tossed his head, as if clearing it of fog.

Goosebumps rippled along the tops of my arms despite the heat.

"It spoke to me." His voice was toneless, eyes lost, and I took a step backwards. "It will give you what you want if you feed it. Anything you want." He angled his body towards the garage as if he could see through the brick and plaster to where Mom sat.

"No." I said, my voice a croak.

"We've been waiting," he droned, continuing. "I thought your uncle would be enough —"

The accident. Not an accident. Jake, who had used the bike before. Who had needed something, a sacrifice. Now, with Grandpa gone, the pain rippling through us had made it grow again. A cold, sick feeling flowed through me, and when I had the strength, I pried myself away from his dull, green gaze, and ran inside.

●

That night we ate a dinner of frozen pizza that tasted like used tea leaves. Jake never left Mom's side long enough for me to speak to her, so I retreated into the bedroom instead. I was lifting the window latch when Grandma tapped on the door and let herself in.

She carried something under her arm, a big book, leatherbound, that she set on the edge of the bed. "We haven't had the chance to talk," she said and pulled a wicker chair from the corner.

The book was filled with newspaper clippings, browned with age but preserved behind a yellowing sheet of plastic.

"You know your uncle passed away when he was young, only seventeen," she started.

"You don't have to do this," I said.

She glanced at me, watery blue eyes and papery skin, resting a small warm hand on my arm and smiled.

"You need to hear this, especially now," she said and began to flip through the album.

And she told me the story, of how bad it was, how Bryan took his bike out and they got the phone call an hour later and how they slept on the cold linoleum floor of the hospital for a week, waiting for him to wake up. How Jake had been there with Mom, and how, when something bad happens, the people who experience it with you, you never really forget, because the pain gets in under your skin and travels to your heart and if it wakes up again you go looking for those people who were with you before.

"The plant is going to keep growing," I whispered.

She closed the book filled with the images of Bryan.

"It may," she said.

"Aren't you scared?" I asked.

She nodded, put her hand underneath my chin.

And because I was eleven and because this wasn't even close to the answer that I needed, that I wanted, I waited until the house was asleep, and cracked the window, and slipped out into the rain.

The toolshed was a black mass with the bulky bags of yard waste that had never been thrown out still sitting next to the wall from weeks ago when I had watched those fires explode in the sky and Dad's hand was in Mom's and the pain was there, sure, but it was manageable, hadn't broken free from its constraints to destroy us.

My feet sucked at the muddy ground, each step filling with brown water, and my shirt was soaked by the when I reached the shed. The motion light flooded the yard with light, but it would be too late by the time they realized what I planned.

I scrabbled for the key underneath the stone frog and shoved open the doors. The axe, an old one, its blade nearly blunt but sharp enough, hung heavy from its peg. I needed both hands to lift it, and it banged into my shoulder painfully as I swung it down from the wall.

I dragged the axe behind me, tracing a line from shed to plant that created a little ditch of rainwater.

I heard shouting from the porch.

Lightning flashed and there was a shape in my path, arms outstretched to bar the way.

Jake. Who must have perched near the window all night, standing guard. His undershirt shriveled in the rain; dark hair plastered across his forehead.

He was a part of this thing, a parasite living on the fringes of pain, waiting for it to weaken its host before he consumed it. A slash of a smile sliced under his still swollen nose.

I didn't feel bad when the flat end of the axe smashed into his forearm, audibly snapping the bone like a piece of uncooked spaghetti.

He screamed and flung himself away from the next stroke, which whistled into the side of the plant with all my strength. For some reason I thought of my grandfather's hands on mine the night before he died, guiding me.

The axe sunk into the flesh with a wet *schlick*.

Suddenly, with a scream of wood rearranging itself, the oak straightened, tugging the chain upwards as putrid air and black liquid poured from the opening of the plant and hissed, steaming, onto the ground.

I heard Jake moaning to my right, propped against the screen of the porch and a cry from the patio as the sliding glass door shivered open and Mom and Grandma rushed out.

I was hacking frantically now, creating little triangles of green and yellow plant flesh. Piles of mushy vegetable matter rose at my feet, stinging my shins while my arms burned from the effort.

Soon the only thing left was a tiny, shriveled acorn; a wrinkled brown seed the size of my fist, connected to the chain which now swung freely in the wind.

I gathered the fallen pieces in my arms. They smelled like overripe bananas and the blankets of a person long sick. I stumbled under their weight and walked to the edge of the yard. There, I let the pieces slide from me, over the chain link fence and into the green waste beyond. I heard them rolling into the foliage on the far side, and the splash as they hit the water.

I collapsed into the mud. My shirt reeked of sweat and sickness and I pulled it off and threw it behind me over the fence.

The floodlamp illuminated the place where the plant hung. Mom recoiled from Jake, the spell broken somehow, as he grasped at her with his one good arm. He appeared small, depleted. Grandma moved through the rain, the light framing a face shrouded in shadow. She approached, feet squelching through the mud.

I expected to see her smile, but when the lightning cracked again her face looked worn, carved from marble, eyes drooping at the edges in sorrow.

"It's okay," I splayed my fingers out against the light from the porch so I could see her face better, maybe her expression was simply a trick of the light. "I killed it."

But she shook her head.

"Don't you think we've tried?" she answered softly.

And I felt then the press of growing things at my back, an entire ditch filled and probing at the edges, a lifetime of pain hacked and discarded, yet continuing to grow. What grandfather had tended, what his death had unleashed.

I saw the heart of the thing, swaying gently from the chain, a single, fragile leaf breaking free.

●

I pulled on the gloves, too big for my hands, and grabbed a roll of black trash bags. The morning had dawned bright and brutal, the air thick, and Grandma brought me ginger ale while I worked, removing patches of rotting rosebushes, digging up rectangles of brown grass, and heaving husks of the plant into a lined trashcan.

She handed me the sweating glass and I pressed it against my forehead, the sensation painfully refreshing in the heat.

Mom had entered the bedroom at dawn while I pretended to sleep, and curled her fingers through my hair, kissing my forehead.

"He's gone," she whispered, then, before she left: "Dad will be home tomorrow."

Jake had disappeared after I had attacked the plant, evaporating into the rain-soaked night without a word. I hadn't decided whether to tell Mom of Bryan's accident, whether I thought it *was* an accident. But for now, it was enough that Jake was gone.

Grandma and I lingered in the yard, watching the stunted plant quiver slightly, but hold its shape.

I thought of all the times Grandpa must have fought the grief that threatened to destroy him. How many times he must have pulled on these same gloves and hacked away at the plant, knowing it would just grow back, sometimes quickly, sometimes slowly.

"There isn't a way to destroy it, not really, it'll just spread," I said to her. She patted my hand silently and made to walk back across the grass to the porch, then turned, looking up at the wide oak trees, the flowers blazing along the paving stones in hues violet and cream, until her gaze settled on me.

And she smiled, adding: "But we can let it starve."

Danny Menter's story "Pain Eater" was originally published in Metaphorosis on Friday, 24 March 2023. See magazine.metaphorosis.com

About the author

Danny Menter grew up in Central Florida, fled to Madrid after graduating from Florida State University, and currently lives outside of Chicago, Illinois. He is a teacher by day, and is currently pursuing a Master of Fine Arts in Fiction.

@MenterDanny

The Hole in the Wall

Andrew Leon Hudson

It wasn't a door, because it didn't meet the ground. It wasn't a window, because — no matter how high or low they are on a wall — windows show something, even if it's just drawn curtains. Or a room previously filled with things, all now gone.

This was just a hole in the wall. It showed... nothing.

Yohaena stared across the cobbles from her splay-legged slump. She was exactly as far from the world's finest market as a life-long sober woman could stagger after enjoying her first sinful drinks. Bought with her last honest coins.

Until the moment they threw her out, the other drinkers in the tavern had found her entertaining. She could curse the taxman, curse her audience, curse the stars that shone on her birth, curse the King even — though perhaps not quite so loud as the rest — but the minute she insulted the *market* of all things she was out on her ear, clutching a wooden mug containing only dregs.

The market that had taken everything she had with a smile, and given her nothing back in return.

She swung her bleary gaze away from the hole, trying to orient herself. With greasy rain slicking out of her fringe and down her face, she felt like having a bit of a cry. With the world suddenly spinning around her head, she felt like having a bit of a puke as well.

Her head and shoulders rested against another wall, the wall of... she sneered ...of a *shop*, of course, what else?

The urge to cry went away and the urge to shout incomprehensible insults rose again, to rant in tongues, to slur slurs — she giggled.

Her chin hit her chest, and confronted by the nothing in the hole in the wall the giggling died away. That's what she had: *nothing*. Only a worthless mug, and nothing to drink from it.

Yohaena had been born and raised at the foot of mountains so distant that from the capital they were barely a shadow on the horizon. But they towered over Wallys, her home, like the stairway of giants, each high plateau overshadowed by those beyond, dawn breaking over their edges like molten gold, pooling and spilling from one to the next.

Only on the highest of those mountain plains grew the stone fruit. The trees were short and sturdy, their roots cracking the rock with their grip, with thick trunks to stand against the hardest wind. Their few leaves were clustered like fists around the fruit itself, more suited to protection than begging the sun for energy.

Late in the year, the fruit fell. In Wallys, tradition said it all dropped in one day, and that (if the festival were only a little less boisterous — it never was) you could hear the echoing of the fruit's impacts like applause coming down from the peaks.

Much time would pass before the small, stony fruit came to human hands, if it did at all. It dropped from the trees, black and hard as coal, flecks glinting on its impenetrable skin like quartz. Over months, even years, the wind blew the oval fruit over cliffs, down slopes, some vanishing into gulleys and crevasses never to see the light again — or to wash out from the springs and underground streams that fed the waters of the plains. The people of Wallys kept fine nets to pluck fruit from the flow, gifts as strange as the fine fish spawn that spewed forth on irregular autumns only to return years later as blind, translucent giants, fighting upstream in their thousands to disappear back underground, breed, and swim no more.

Those fruit which failed to reach the lowlands would never ripen. The mountain birds and animals knew it, and made seasonal pilgrimages to dig through the shale slides, or picked out their glinting rewards with sharp, circling eyes. They bore them down to warmer ground and hid them away, waiting out the long months until they came good; and enough of the seeds within were carried back to the heights through the ways of nature that the sparse but long-lived forests in the sky would be maintained.

Only once had someone attempted to trade stone fruit with the wider world: Maynehla Paraesei, Yohaena's own mother, long before her daughter's birth. Yohaena had grown up hearing the story, lived it in her mind's eye — how as a young woman they'd thought her mother a fool.

Her old ma, a fool! Young Yohaena had laughed. A fool much respected in every household in Wallys.

As the years passed, she dreamed about doing the same. After Maynehla passed, the dream slowly matured into something more. The following spring she prepared for the journey, secretly planning, buying what she didn't have and disinterring the old tools of her mother's trade. *Four months of travel*, and no time in that to spare. It could be done.

When summer came, she climbed to where the stone fruit could be harvested in numbers — a risky excursion in itself, so much so as to keep the locals satisfied by what good fortune washed their way. The windfall harvest would be sparser this year — let the beasts hunt for whatever remained overlooked from years past, scattered across the mountain's face still waiting to be discovered.

In the thin air she prised apart those fists of leaves, twisted their cold, hard fruit free. She filled one sack and then another, six in all, struggled with them one by one between the steep-walled plateaux down towards home. On the lowest, she piled cairns of heavy rocks upon each sack, protecting them from foragers, delaying until the last possible moment the beginning of their ripening. Until the day when all six could be carried the final step, loaded up and on their way.

But she told her friends and neighbours none of this, let no-one know until the day she started west. Let them call *her* a fool as well. Let them wait for her grand return.

●

She arrived with a cartload, prepared to make a killing.

Drawing it by hand, she had followed the rail lines to save herself the cost of a fare, passing through hamlets, villages and towns. At every one was a market square, or a trading post, or at least someone with an eager eye on her wares.

But no trade was good enough for the clever and cunning Yohaena Paraesei. She was going to the capital, to the marketplace of marketplaces, where her unique goods would make her rich. So she turned down all offers and strode past every trading post with gaze fixed straight ahead.

And her stone fruit slowly turned from the glinting black of night to the swirling grey of the thickest fog.

Miles passed. Soon she stared, half-starved, at the produce which cruelly decorated stalls in every town on the road from the mountains through the plains — fruit and vegetables, greasy pies and skewers of meat, sweets and pastries... but she saved her money, ate only trail bread, drank only water, because unseen in the distance a fortune lay waiting for her.

And the fog-grey skin of the stone fruit paled to that of the even, endless moorland mists.

At journey's end, in the city's great shadow, she ran a final gauntlet of roadside merchants hailing from every corner of the world, offering what they had for what she had, inviting her to join them. She couldn't understand why anyone would travel right to the brink of fortune's fount and then balk at the last. She refused them all, rejected every offer, and crossed the threshold into the capital without a backward glance.

And, at long last, the stone fruit ripened to a silvered sheen. Their skin grown brittle as eggshells, ready to crack open along their seams at the slightest pressure and release the tender, sun-coloured flesh within, the cool scent of mountain summers.

Perfection. It was time.

Of course, there was a tax to pay to pass through the city gates — higher than her old ma Maynehla had described, from back when she'd made the same trip in her prime. And there were market fees, naturally: official stall rental, for example, because space was at a premium, and non-standard sizes demanded non-standard rates. Plus, of course, uncommon foodstuffs like hers needed to be officially tested and granted a Safe Consumption Seal before they could be sold — can't risk an epidemic, not again — but testing means providing samples, *of everything*, and neither tests nor seals come cheap.

Almost all her money was spent just getting in the gate, and to raise the cash for both stall rental and goods testing she was forced to sell the uniquely beautiful stall her old ma once made by hand. A sadness... but it was of little use to her now, and she could always buy it back before she returned home in triumph.

She delivered samples to the Bureau of Testing, paid the fees, took her chit, and waited for their verdict — wasting precious days, precious weeks. She paid the difference between stall rental and stall sale into the pocket of an innkeeper, while her remaining wares aged past their best, and she spent worthless days watching over her cart in case thieves less concerned about epidemics made off with her goods before she had her chance to sell.

And the silvered stone fruit whitened, first snow-like, then ivory. Their crisp skins softened, no more to pop open with a startling crack, but to be punctured by a thumbnail, pried open and peeled, the rich flesh turned amber, the flavour from subtle to sweet.

Finally, they granted her seal. The last of her cash bought it into her hand, and she left the inn to take her place in the world's greatest market: surrounded by the finest merchants, their glamorous patter luring in wealthy prospects from all sides, their outlandish, non-standard stalls drawing each purchaser's eye, their unique and perfect goods opening every wallet.

But with her crumpled costume and bland, square stall of wrinkling, fading produce, Yohaena went all but unnoticed amidst all the commerce. She could barely make herself heard over the sound of everyone else's success. She dropped her prices in desperation; struck woeful deals in the futile hope that the first sale would provoke a flood; stood at attention all night — eyelids fluttering, swaying like the drunk she was shortly to become — in case some cunning buyer would pause and make a clever deal while all the rest were sleeping, oblivious to their foolish loss.

And the stone fruit, over-ripe and quick to bruise, cloyed the air around her, their leathery skins yellowing back to grey.

She sold the last of her stock — almost half what she'd left home with — to one man, who swept it into a hand cart with a broken-off broom head, and in return paid her less than the value of the pathetic rented stall. She sold her cart, because she didn't have enough money to buy anything big or numerous enough to need one — including old Maynehla's beautiful, hand-crafted stall, which she next saw in a shop window in a twisty little lane a dozen turns from the market that had ruined her life — priced twice the sum she had taken for it, four times what she now had left.

Every lot in that lane was a shop of some kind, but she didn't set foot in one of them, clinging to her molehill of cash and only looking in, untrusting of the deals, the trinkets, the welcoming smiles. The exception to both cases was the first property: not a shop but an inn, and this she entered, driven by weariness, thirst and hunger. She'd stay for a night and buy a full stomach while she figured out her next move, how she would snatch a better future from the lifetime of misery that now loomed before her.

They served ale with her meal. She'd never touched alcohol — *trader's betrayer*, Maynehla had called it — and looked from innkeeper to drink with equal distrust. But her own inner voice murmured in her other ear: *What did she have left to lose? What kind of trader had she proven to be?*

In any case, the innkeeper reassured her that the first drink was always free.

●

The dregs in her mug were watered down with rain, just a puddle at the bottom, with an oily memory of foam on its surface. Yohaena tilted the mug, tipped it into the bigger puddle growing beneath her sodden trousers.

Bile rising in her gorge and spirit, she raised the mug above her head with one shaking arm and hurled it across the lane, aiming for the hole only inasmuch as it was directly before her.

It struck the target — she barked a single laugh at her good aim — and vanished from view. There was no clatter against whatever lay beyond. Silently, absolutely, the mug was gone.

She laughed again, wearily, closed her eyes on the swirling world — and heard a familiar sound, the sound of fallen...

She opened her eyes again. A glint winked at her from the cobbles beyond her boots. She looked up and down the lane but she was alone, no charitable night-walker taking contemptuous pity on her. Yet, there lay a single penny — good for two drinks at that cursed inn, worth more than the old stained mug itself, no doubt.

A different laugh emerged now, low and grudging, that of a woman who knows the joke is on her and waits for the proof to show itself. She pulled off her hat, tossed it dismissively, saw it sail through the hole into nothingness with the certainty of a boat swept along a river current — and this time she *saw* the coin sail back out, spinning in the air as though tossed from a thumb. Others followed before the first had hit the ground, rolling between the cobbles to strike the sole of her boot.

Yohaena gripped her trousers and pulled herself upright, leaned forward with a long and queasy belch, fumbled the nearest coin into her hand. She held it almost to her nose, eyes crossing... *it was real.*

She rolled onto all fours, crawling after the others, the rain-slippery stones poking painfully into hands and knees, then sat back on her heels to inspect her haul: two pennies, three crowns. She could buy two hats with this. Or one, but better than the one she'd thrown.

Cradling them to her chest, with a speculative look in her eye she unbuckled and tugged free her belt one-handed, guessed its worth both now and new, and slung it at the hole. The buckle led the way, the cracked leather dragged in over the lip of brick like a tongue — and more coins sprayed from the void. She scrabbled for them, counted her fortune: seven crowns and thrupence.

For a second, she considered.

In a frenzy, she tore at her clothes, one boot, the other, then shirt and breeches, all thrust at the hole, until the tinkling clamour of metal on stone was done. Until she stood in only her smalls, the hem of her undershirt cradling a clinking bundle.

When dawn broke, Yohaena looked up from her compulsive counting to find the wall's brickwork unbroken and no sign of the hole. Perhaps she had lost her mind along with her goods, her cart and her old ma's stall. Fine. So be it. She had seventeen crowns and eight pennies, all told.

●

There may never have been a more unusual trader in the capital than the one who emerged from the lane that day: a woman in her underclothes, who walked on bruised feet to the cheap and ordinary side of town, went from shop to stall there, doling out coins from what looked like an old vest. She bought:

A drawstring bag that opened into a sheet, like those which street-sellers use to display their junk and trinkets, and which real people step over with barely a look;

A smock-shirt, little more than a sheet itself — less, maybe, since it had a hole in the middle for a head to poke through, and just a length of cord to tie at the waist;

A pair of clogs, the worst to be had, cracked along their soles due to poor choice of wood;

And, last but not least — let's even say *most* — all the worthless trade goods shameless traders would sell her.

She drove a hard bargain, this clown in a beggar-gown: she rooted through goods shop-worn or flawed, bid on them in bulk, demanding discount rates for what they saw as inconvenient trash. And each shopkeep took her money with a genuine smile, one that widened into a grin as she went out through their doors again. Because — in a place where the best can be found, and so only the best will do — no-one buys the defective, no-one buys the poor. Unless the purchaser is poor and defective herself.

The madwoman bought as much as she could carry, as much as her drawstring bag would hold.

Money spent, Yohaena returned to the lane, loosened the ties of her bulging bag and upturned it onto the cobbles, stuffing it through her cord belt when it was empty. All day she squatted there, arranging her prizes, rearranging them again, ignoring those few passersby who paused to look — because, after all, there was always potentially business to be done, even with the likes of such as this. But whenever one offered a coin, their eye caught by some curio on her sheet, the madwoman turned them down, so they walked on shaking their heads, or laughing at the lunatic playing shopkeeper amongst the shops, her eyes on the plain empty wall opposite.

Quite mad, they told each other.

In the dark at the heart of night, the hole in the wall returned, a blackness on the black. Yohaena was watching for it, and saw its appearance. She was happy not to be mad.

She took the empty sheet from her belt and spread it before the hole. Then, starting with the poorest of her purchases and ending with the clogs, one by one she threw them all in. Only the drawstring sheet remained, coins piling up on it.

When day broke she could hardly pull the strings closed, could hardly lift the bag from the cobbles.

She bought new clothes — nothing fancy, just replacements for the old: a good hat, and shirt, and trousers, sturdy boots to take her home, a thick coat for when the north winds welcomed her back to the mountain's foot. And still she had enough left over to go to the market that had tried to ruin her, where her clothes and wallet brought every merchant running, eager to strike a deal, not one of them knowing her for the fool whose stall had once stood ignored beside their own.

Finally, she returned to a particular shop where, with great pleasure, she bought back her old ma's stall: the strong bamboo frame, cleverly tied with oiled leather to collapse flat as a board, its sky-blue canvas binding them together but still proudly boasting name and business — *Paraesei, in Trade* — stitched and dyed by hand.

She waited out the day in the lane, on the cobbles — on a carpet of intricate weave, surrounded by bolts of fine cloth and silk, by bags of spices, more. And old Maynehla's stall lay folded and wrapped behind her, *because she was not trading*, no matter what anyone offered for her wares.

She waited for one last night, and the hole.

She started with the spices, hurling them in, a cascade of currency pouring forth onto her carpet — silver coins and gold, a mound of wealth that grew and grew as the cloth and silk and other goods followed. At last the stream began to ebb, the final spurts of coins emerging — a couple more, a couple more, one more — in a way familiar, but which she couldn't put her finger on...

Then it was done.

Her carpet was laden with more money than she had ever known. She need never trade again — Maynehla's beautiful stall might go unopened until after Yohaena went to join her old ma in the beyond, but she would never want.

For a moment she considered throwing it into the hole as well. She wondered what that might earn her. Forget the base material worth, could the hole reward her for its personal value — what the thing *meant* to her as well?

She shook her head — no amount of money would buy her old ma's stall from her, not now nor ever again — but her eye fell upon the little shining mountain of coins and a new thought occurred.

Forget the regal profiles and fearsome beasts pressed into their sides, forget their cultural meaning: the metals had material worth too, much of it, and the hole had always given back more value than it consumed. The gold, the silver of the coins — what would the hole give her for all that?

What reward could exceed even money itself?

With great care, Yohaena gathered up the corners of her carpet and drew them together over the pile, bunched two in each fist, and strained. With shaking arms, thighs quivering, she raised the bulging carpet from the cobbles and began to swing it, back and forth between her knees.

Brow furrowed with effort, she swung. Teeth gritted, she swung. Lips pulled back as if fishhooks were caught in the corners of her mouth, she swung. Her gaze only on the hole, fixed deep upon its absent depths... and she released.

The upper corners of the carpet slipped free and it billowed open like a sail, the mass of coins floating — together, each separate — through the air. At the edge of their cloud, five coins struck the bricks and bounced back around her boots. All the rest fell into nothingness and were gone, the carpet flapping in her hands as though waving farewell.

She waited, watching the hole.

●

There was a tax on traders departing the city. There was always another tax in the capital. Her five coins just covered it.

Yohaena strode out in sturdy boots and good new clothes, winter coat folded over one arm, carpet rolled up beneath the other. On her back, the collapsible stall was wrapped and strapped, swaying above her broad hat like the standard of a warrior from some distant land, trailing her banner in the breeze. Her pockets were as light as her heart.

She walked through the days, slept soundly at night, growing lean on the road across the plains. The capital fell behind her and the mountains slowly rose ahead; and, should she happen across travellers making camp as dusk fell, or see a caravan approach through the midday haze, she would stop, unroll her carpet at the roadside and erect her stall upon it — selling the invaluable to anyone who cared to buy.

She never asked for much, just a coin or two if her customer had it to spare, a bite to eat if not. And though what she offered was not exactly the truth (because no-one pays for a story that can't be believed) it always had the ring of truth about it.

Wisdom paid her way back home.

Andrew Leon Hudson's story "The Hole in the Wall" was originally published in Metaphorosis on Friday, 7 October 2016. See magazine.metaphorosis.com

About the author

Andrew Leon Hudson's stories had appeared for free in a small online magazine called *Mythaxis* several times over now distant years, but his first actual sale was to *Metaphorosis*. The Hole in the Wall is, amongst other things, a speculative story about employment, a combination of genre and theme that he is increasingly focused upon. He's gone on to appear in a variety of zines including *Cossmass Infinities*, *Little Blue Marble*, and *Dark Matter Magazine*, as well as the anthologies *Triangulation: Dark Skies*, *Monster Lairs*, and *Necronomi-RomCom*.

An Englishman happily (and probably permanently) transplanted to Spain, he now resides in Barcelona where he works as a technical writer. With a satisfying circularity he's also become editor of *Mythaxis*, where he takes great pleasure in sharing the works of other writers the way his predecessor once did for him. You can find all the fruits of his fictional labours growing from his linktree.

The Lightkeeper's Wife

Amelia Dee Mueller

The first time Elsie Frasier tried to murder her husband, the other women of Auskerry called it a pretty meager attempt. Some insisted it might even have been an accident. He had fallen down the last flight of stairs in the couple's lighthouse and only fractured the smaller bone in his arm.

The next time, when he fell from his ladder while painting the kitchen cupboards, was nearly two years later, much too long when compared to Claire McKinney, who held the record at sixteen attempts in six months alone. She only had to spend one year and three months on the island before she successfully murdered Mr. McKinney, found her stolen seal skin, and returned to the sea.

That Monday, when Elsie went to town to pick up her groceries, the other selkies surrounded her in the street. They were led by Elspeth Donoghue. Elspeth was an old woman, gray and wrinkled, with a middle that swayed as she walked, and she leaned on a cane to accommodate her hunch. She had yet to rid herself of the even older and even more hunched Mr. Donaghue, but it wasn't for lack of trying.

"Good morning, Mrs. Frasier," Elspeth said, cutting Elsie off as she stepped into Auskerry's single road.

Elsie smiled, but her fingers twitched as she offered her hand to shake. She was desperate the avoid the selkies most days, though she didn't judge their violent traditions. She also hated the men who snatched them from the sea, but she liked to stay out of the way. She saw fewer selkies on the island these days anyway. Men with selkie brides always found good fortune, but the world was changing. The young men of Auskerry were more likely to leave the island to find their fortune than risk capturing a selkie bride and getting murdered afterward.

Elsie hoped the evolving world of 1920 proved that this tradition was dying, which would mean the other selkies might stop questioning her marriage. But when Elspeth wouldn't take her outstretched hand, Elsie knew that this wasn't to be.

"We just came to say, my dear, that we're worried about you," Elspeth said. "Nearly four years you've been married, and only two attempts to rid yourself of this form! Is your husband making it particularly difficult for you? Is he clever? It's rare for a human man, but I've seen it all, dearie."

Elsie squared her shoulders. "I have it under control."

As she turned away, Elspeth's cane struck out against a store's brick front, trapping Elsie. Other women stopped to watch, but they were mostly the daughters or granddaughters of selkies. Though every year less and less of the Auskerry men risked marrying selkies, it was still true that the richest men on the island all had pure selkie wives, and that they all retired fat, lived lavishly, and died young.

It was difficult to marry a selkie. First, a man had to trap one, and then drag her back to the mainland without being drowned, and then succeed at ripping away her seal skin to reveal the human form beneath. The wedding was done before the selkie had her wits back, and by then the man would have hidden her skin away in an expert hiding spot. By the time the selkie was aware of her situation, her skin was gone, and she would spend the rest of her human life trying to kill the man who took it from her.

"We don't think you do, lass," Elspeth said, wagging one of her fat, sausage fingers. "Is it true he hasn't even hidden your skin from you?"

The selkies gasped. There was only a handful of them, a sharp contrast to the hundreds that must have walked the island in Elspeth's youth. Few were young, and they stood with their hands folded and lips pursed. The young ones still wore their hair loose in long curls that blew in the wind. They remembered the sea with a fresher pain, having been plucked out only recently, and the fierceness with which they shoved their husbands off ladders or down wells was like a storm breaking on a cliff.

The rest were middle aged and wore their hair in strict plaits down their backs, leaving their pinched faces and creased foreheads exposed. They were so square and stiff that it was obvious that they barely remembered what it was like to be weightless in the water, and every time they swung a pot against the back of their husbands' heads, their swings grew wearier and wearier. Just a spring gale trying to topple a sail boat.

Elspeth was the oldest. Elsie had heard stories of kidnapped selkies stranded on land and forced to die human deaths, but as a young pup she had never thought that she would actually meet one. Even if Elspeth managed to retrieve her skin, there was no guarantee it would still fit her. Her dress stuck to the rolls around her middle like a sausage casing about to rip.

"It's unnatural, it is," Elspeth said. "Wanting what you got. My generation fought to protect yours, killing as many of these men as we did. You're putting all our hard work to shame. Making it into nothing. How can you disrespect your own kind like that?"

The selkies behind her muttered their agreement. They looked at Elsie with loathing. They couldn't comprehend how a selkie with access to her skin would choose to stay on land, and they hated her for it. Their envy was ripe on their pinched faces, and Elsie could taste it on the wind.

"I had a choice," Elsie said, still calm, still trying to make them understand. "What I have is nothing like what you were forced into."

Elspeth spit at her feet, rubbing it into the street with the end of her cane. "You only think you did! They're all the same, lass. Even the ones trying to hide it. And we gotta protect our own, especially when she can't see two feet in in front of her own face."

Elsie hiked her shopping basket onto her shoulder and turned away from the group. She heard them whispering behind her, but she didn't look back.

"We'll be checking in soon!" Elspeth called. "To lend you a hand!"

●

Outside the village, the road tapered off into the overgrown path that led to the Auskerry Lighthouse. The tower of the lighthouse, at only eighty-six feet, was fatter and shorter than the others along the Scottish coast, and was mostly white but for the candy stripe of red across its middle.

The Frasiers lived in the small house at its base. Its paint was always peeling from the salty winds and the front door never hung straight. The windows creaked during storms, and its two small rooms were packed with heirloom quilts and furniture, and stuffed with colorful knickknacks, and layered with wall hangings and pictures that hung lopsided.

Elsie heard a curse from the shed that held the lamp oil, and she was knocked back a few steps by the scent of kerosene as she approached.

Tom was covered in it. He dripped it onto the grass as he came out, and flicked it onto her skirts as he shook out his legs.

"We've got too much of this stuff now that we switched to Hood's damned invention!" he said, wiping his face with his oil-soaked shirt. "I can't walk in there without knocking it over!"

"Why do you keep ordering the same amount?" Elsie asked, her face turned away from the wind so the smell wouldn't reach her. They had installed the new lamp a year ago at the insistence of the Northern Lighthouse Board, as it required less oil but burned brighter, but Tom had not stopped complaining.

"You never know with these new contraptions," he said. "What would happen if we ran out? Ships lining up to crash, debris raining down from the sea, bodies along the beach. I don't like to take chances."

Tom's family had run he lighthouse at Stronsay Firth since it'd been built in 1889, and the farthest he'd ever been from it was the night his father died. The trembling teenager had barely laid his father's cold, limp hand back onto the blankets of his deathbed before his mother got to tearing the lighthouse apart. She went through every cupboard and trunk, ripped down all the curtains, dug up the garden, tore up the floorboards, and found her stolen skin rolled into a ball and stuffed in the toilet tank. Tom watched from the window as she went to the cliff, wrapped the skin around herself, and leapt headfirst into the rolling white sea below.

Tom chased after her, knowing it was a hopeless risk. A selkie had never been found again after escaping, but he went anyway, terrified to think of living alone in the bleak, empty lighthouse. He climbed down the crags of the cliffs, clutching to the rocks as the hard island winds tried to tear him from the edge, and set out for the open sea in his father's boat. Tom didn't find his mother, and he realized too late that the lamp in the lighthouse had not been lit, and he was drifting out to open sea with nothing to guide him back.

Elsie first saw him bobbing in the waves like a message in a bottle. She, like the other women of her kind, was wary of the human men who hunted her. Any man who made his living by the sea benefited from the good fortune a selkie wife would bring. Selkie women spent their entire lives not getting too close, but Elsie drifted toward the tiny boat. This human looked sad, with his head in his hands on the dark sea, and she took pity on him. She grabbed a piece of rope and towed him back to the island.

When they reached land, she stayed in the shallows, watching him drag the boat back to shore, nudging it firmly in the wet sand. He looked back at her and gave a sheepish wave as thanks, and she found herself swimming closer. As she approached the beach, the soft folds of her skin shed, falling around her legs like a robe. She knew stories of selkies plucked from the sea, their skins shorn from their naked forms with gutting knives, left at the bottom of the hunters' boats until they were forced to walk on awkward, unwanted legs. But this felt different. Walking was natural, like breathing.

She gathered up her skin as she stepped onto the beach, the tiny grains of sand squishing between her toes for the first time, the breeze tickling her skin and whipping her long, wet curls. She looked at Tom, and his face was as red as a sunset the night before a storm. He shrugged off his coat and offered it her. Elsie followed him into the lighthouse, and she never returned to the sea.

"I'm going to wash up," Tom said now, starting for the house. Elsie maneuvered in front of him.

"Go to the beach or sleep in the tower," she said. "I won't have kerosene stinking up my house."

"My own wife banishing me to the sea!" Tom said, but he was grinning. "At least let me take a kiss with me when I turn to ice and sink to the bottom."

She side-stepped his outstretched arms, but he caught her around the waist and his greasy, oil-soaked lips kissed her cheek. Any other day she would've laughed, but the oil was cold and it sent shivers down her spine, and she couldn't get the image of Elspeth's fat fingers pointing at her out of her head. Tom stepped back as she wiped the slime from her face.

"What's wrong?" he said.

"Get cleaned up. I'll tell you when you get back."

He frowned, but he wandered off down the cliff-side path that led to the beach.

Elsie went to the house and twisted the kitchen light switch on. She was still getting used to the foreign, artificial glow that electricity made. She much preferred the heartbeat of a gas light. It was the lighthouse's pulsing, steady light that had drawn her near the shores of Auskerry in the first place. All selkies were drawn by a lighthouse's lamp, entranced by its glow and swinging beam, though they knew it could be the end of their freedom. Elsie remembered as a young pup promising to never get too close to the low, yellow star on the horizon, no matter how beautiful it might seem. It was a promise few selkies could keep.

Elsie put the groceries away in the cupboards, leaving out a few of the smaller potatoes for dinner, and hung her basket on the back of the bedroom door. She stood in the doorway, hesitating before turning that light on.

Under the bed was a package wrapped in a thick, woolen blanket and tied with rope. Elsie slid it into her lap. It was in a tight, expert knot, and her fingers were raw by the time she had it undone. Inside were sheets of neat white paper, and Elsie peeled them back one by one, careful not to crease any, until she'd reached the brown skin beneath. It crinkled as she lifted it. The once soft hide was stiff and rough with dried salt. She laid it out flat on the bedroom floor, tracing the edge with her fingertip, realizing that it was smaller than she remembered.

She heard Tom at the door. He leaned against the frame, drying his face with a dishcloth.

"You're not going to leave me, are you?" he said, grinning. He wrung the water out of the cloth with a tight squeeze and threw it over his shoulder.

"Never," she said and folded it back inside the blanket.

"What's bothering you?" He sat on the edge of the bed, leaning over his knees. "What happened?"

She told him about her conversation with Elspeth in the village, and he laughed.

"That old hag," he said, slapping the cloth across his knee. "How long has she been trying to knock off poor Donoghue? Fifty years? Isn't she satisfied with one man to murder?"

Elsie sat on the bed beside him. "She says I'm betraying my own kind. All the others were with her."

Tom was silent. He clasped his hands in front of him. "Do you agree?"

Elsie clenched her fists. "I chose you. It's not the same. But they don't understand. They think all the humans are awful, and can't comprehend how a selkie could be happy with one." She clenched her fists. "They're not even trying to understand."

She wanted to rip something apart. For years she'd taken the passive glares from the other selkies, and had carefully avoided running into them in the village. As long as she and Tom didn't interfere with the way of things, Elsie had thought they could get along. The selkies were letting their jealousy, and their superiority, make life-threatening assumptions. No selkie could possibly want to be chained to a man's side, they said. And they were right. No selkie could want that, but one might choose to stand at his side on her own two legs. But Elsie wasn't sure she could ever make them understand this.

"How about you knock a vase over my head?" Tom suggested. "We'll show them the glass, and I'll walk around the village with a bandaged forehead for a few days."

"This isn't like before," Elsie said. "You can't fake it again. We need to leave."

He leaned back, his arm hanging off the end of the bedframe. "And go where?"

"Anywhere—the mainland, another island. We can't stay here, Tom. They want to kill you."

"We're not leaving Auskerry." He threw the cloth at his feet. His jaw was tight and fists clenched as he went to stand at the end of the bed. "Who would tend the light? Do you know what would happen if that went out?" He pointed above his head. "Everyone would die. Sailors, fishermen, the entire damn village. We live by that light."

"You can't tend to the lamp if you're dead!" Elsie cried, leaping up as he began to pace.

"We can't abandon it," he said. He wouldn't look at her. "We're not leaving."

He left and she heard him rummaging through a cupboard. He was going to light the lamp, like he did every night, and Elsie waited until she heard the front door slam shut before going back to the kitchen. He would be up there until dinner time, and return for the first few hours of the night, just to keep an eye on things. This was Tom's pattern, copied from his father's days as lightkeeper.

Elsie mashed the potatoes, pairing them with the vegetables she'd just bought, and putting it on their chipped plates. She waited thirty minutes, then an hour, then two, before she threw both untouched meals in the sink, spattering potatoes on the counter. She went outside and looked up at the tower and saw her husband's silhouette at its top. She went inside and turned the lights off without washing up.

Elsie twisted in bed until Tom came down, but she feigned sleep until she heard his breathing settle. She slid out from beneath their warm woolen blanket and went to the kitchen, putting on a kettle to boil. She shivered in the harsh, evening air. She could hear Tom start to snore softly in the bedroom, and she shook her head as she poured boiled water into her cup. She wanted to hate him for his stubborn resilience, but she was glad of it. She was like the

sea—whirling and wondering and guessing which way the currents would pull them next, and he was the land. Firm and set, with roots too deep to pull. Their love met somewhere on the shore, a balancing act of pushing and pulling the sand and the water into different directions. He would never leave his lighthouse, and she would never leave him. She would think of a different way.

She turned from the stove and lifted the cup to her lips, thinking she might go up to the tower to drink it. She opened the front door, and the cup slid from her hands and shattered on the kitchen floor.

A haggard, wrinkled face stood in her doorway, cast in harsh shadows as the beam of the lighthouse swung around behind it. Elspeth leaned on her cane with one hand and held a fisherman's gutting knife in the other. The wind whipped her greasy grey hair across her face, and behind her the beam of the lighthouse swung across the island's path. In its light Elsie saw a crowd of selkies. They held kitchen knives and pitchforks and frying pans, but the second the light was gone, they disappeared into shadow.

Elsie slammed the door in Elspeth's face. She stood frozen in her kitchen, cold beads of sweat soaking her nightgown. She waited for them to rip her door down. She pictured them tearing into her bedroom and lifting Tom from his bed. She imagined his scream as they stuck their knives in him, and she thought of Elspeth's grin as her knife ripped through the flesh at his throat.

"Elsie?" Tom said from their bedroom doorway, calling her back from her imaginings. He rubbed sleep from his eyes. "What are you doing?"

Elsie crept toward their window to peer out into the dark. But the selkies had gone.

"Nothing," she said. Her jaw tightened. "I was doing nothing."

Elsie did not sleep that night, but she was up with Tom just after sunrise to make breakfast and to help carry kerosene up the lighthouse steps. She stayed by his side during the day, wiping away soot from the huge prisms of the Fresnel lens that circled the flame. She helped him to rewind the clockwork that turned the lamp, and to lock the weights into place. She watched him trim the wicks and close the curtains of the lantern room to protect the lens from discoloration.

A thick fog came during the afternoon, and they rushed to light the lamp. She waited with him on the gallery to watch for passing ships. Beyond was only sea on one side, and a dirty, barely green island on the other, where the village stood far below like a toy that Elsie could lift her boot above and smash. She thought she could pick out Elspeth's house, larger than all the rest, with neat tiles set out in perfect rows and a well-manicured garden. She spat at that house, but the wind carried the spittle away.

There hadn't been a crash on Auskerry since Elsie had arrived, but Tom had told her of one from his childhood. It had been a great steel steamer, too large to turn in time, chugging through icy waters at night during a storm. Everyone had been asleep but for Tom's father, who watched helplessly as the ship met its end and heard the long groan of the steel cutting against the rocks that lined the firth.

Elsie had forgotten about that ship until he'd told the story. She'd been there, safe beneath the waves while the storm raged far above. She and the other selkies watched as it cut into rock. They'd felt the vibrations of crunching metal shudder through the water, and seen the bodies falling into the waves. The selkies curled their lips, showing their yellowed, pointed teeth, as they swam toward the flailing limbs of the sailors. One by one, the selkies snatched them and dragged them beneath the surface until they stopped kicking. Elsie and the other pups had been meant to watch and learn. The selkies were shrinking the human numbers, slowly but surely, the elders said, and soon there would be no more selkies torn from their families. Elsie had been the first to look away.

Wreckage and bodies washed up on the shore for weeks, and the huge engine could still be seen at low tide at just the right angle from the cliff. It reminded Elsie of a great sea creature, stretching its gaping mouth out of the water, desperate for air.

Tom went to sit on the tower steps, wiping the oil and grit from his hands. Elsie took the step just below his, hugging herself. He looked down at her.

"Thank you," he said, placing a hand on her shoulder.

"For what?"

He drew her against him. "For not asking me to leave again."

Elsie laid her head in her hands, but she saw Elspeth's sunken eyes looking back. She pulled away from her husband and stood up, looking out at the rolling fog and listening to the waves far below it. If she could spare Tom the pain of leaving his lighthouse, she would. No matter the cost to herself, or to her kind. What had they ever done for her?

"Can I ask you for something else?" she said.

"I don't like the sound of that," Tom said.

Elsie didn't like the thought of it. She wasn't sure she would have the time to pull it off, or if it would work. She wondered if the Auskerry selkies would kill her, and Tom with her, if she succeeded, but she knew that they would take him from her if she failed. She could imagine them wrapping her in her dried skin, feeling its papery touch, and then the slip of her transformation as they dropped her in the ocean. There was part of her that wanted to feel the stream of the water, to push through its currents and waves and swim down farther and farther into the darkness to the cold depths. But that part was dull and lifeless compared to the race and warmth of her heart as she looked at Tom.

If she managed it all, they could be left to enjoy their human lives together, without humans or selkies. There might be unavoidable casualties, she knew, but both species had brought it upon themselves.

"Tomorrow night, can we not light the lamp?"

He put a hand to his heart as if she had stabbed him. "Why?"

"I can't tell you. Not yet. It's just one night, Tom."

"One night can mean life and death to one ship."

"Please," she said. "There's only way I can think of to keep us here."

Tom leaned away from her, one hand rubbing the back of his neck. "Let me think on it."

●

That night there was a storm. Tom pulled a raincoat on over his keeper's uniform after dinner and sat at the dining room table lacing up his boots.

"I'll be up all night," he said. "It's supposed to be bad, and the lamp will need constant tending. You'll be all right on your own?"

"Just be careful," Elsie said, drying the last dish and putting it away.

"You come up if you get lonely," he said, and kissed her on the cheek.

She heard him open the door to the tower, and the faint thud of his footsteps on the iron staircase. He'd stop to check the weights before he went to the service room. He'd sit on the same stool in front of the same window, the one with the clearest view, and he'd watch the beam swing back and forth across the sea. He'd only hear the crash of the waves, or the ring of the thunder. Elsie sat on the edge of her bed to lace up her boots.

The rain beat against her window, slipping down the glass in thick streaks. There was no going back after this. She tried to feel hesitant. Maybe she could do something less drastic. They were, after all, her kind. And their actions were defensible. To have their freedom ripped away and hidden was a jarring, unforgivable crime. They were forced to live a foreign life. Elsie watched the water slip down the window and thought of her husband and of Elspeth's words, and she felt the same helplessness she knew the selkies must feel. It enraged her that they were the cause of it. They were her kind; how could they push their fears on her with their threats? They were the cause of her helplessness, just as the humans were the cause of theirs.

Elsie looked one last time for guilt and hesitation, but it didn't come. She stood up and pulled on her raincoat.

It was the kind of storm with rain that fell anywhere but down. It hit her face horizontally like icy pellets, or splashed up from puddles on the ground into her boots and soaked her stockings. Her coat didn't do much good, and she let the hood fall while she went to the storage shed. The kerosene was against the wall in steel cans painted green with a spout on one side and a curved, rusted handle on the other. In the corner, Elsie found a wooden cart to carry them in.

Only four cans would fit in the cart. She started off down the road to the village by pulling it, but she realized that she'd have to push it over the larger bumps and dips. The cans were heavy, and they knocked and banged together, their liquid slurring inside.

There were only a few flickering candles in the windows of the village houses. The rain dripped rhythmically onto the rooftops, and the water pooled in the street. There was a mixed scent of fresh and salt water, but it was soon overpowered by the kerosene.

Elsie started at Elspeth's house. She lined her walls with two cans worth before moving on to her neighbors. She liked the sound of the kerosene sloshing out of the can and splattering the houses. She threw the last can back in the cart and dug her matches out of her pocket, careful to keep them under her coat and out of the rain. But they were already wet.

"Damn," she muttered, throwing them away. She didn't have time to go back to the house.

The Donoghue's door wasn't locked. Elsie let herself in, not bothering to shut it behind her. The front door led into the kitchen, and she found the matches in the drawer next to the candles. She took them into the bedroom.

The Donoghue's were misshapen lumps on the bed. Their blanket didn't quit cover their legs, and they stuck out like veiny, swollen tongues. Elsie lit a match and held it against the corner of their blanket until it took. She waited until the smoke hung thick and black in the air before slipping back out.

She threw a few more matches against the houses as she went, and left the rest on the road. The heat didn't really start to rise until she was out of sight of the village, and it wasn't until she heard people shouting that she turned around to look.

The bright orange and yellow against the dark sky was jarring. She'd never seen anything so bright in all her life. It overwhelmed the sky, swallowing the stars and spitting up smoke. The rain had begun to lighten, but lightning still split across the darkness, right above the flames. It blinded her. She tried to imagine what the light would look like beneath the ocean, but she couldn't picture it.

At the house, Elsie dragged the cart behind her down the rocky path that led to the cliff. She tossed her cans in one at a time, and in between the flashes of lightning she could see bright yellow eyes looking back at her. There were hundreds of pairs, luminescent against the black water, bobbing with the roll and sway of the storm. They didn't see her, but the flickering arches of flames were reflected in their yellow eyes. The selkies were entranced by the burning of the village of Auskerry, and Elsie hoped the light would keep them fixated until morning, so they would stay close to the shores during the day, and let her handle them that next night.

●

The morning, Tom insisted they go help at the village, and Elsie followed silently behind him. Most of the structures in Auskerry were made of wood, and all that was left that morning were their blackened carcasses. A few of the stone shops had survived, though their glass windows had cracked.

"Was anyone hurt?" Tom asked Mr. McDougal, a shopkeeper, as he helped him haul away what was left of his house.

"Just old Donoghue and his wife. Rest of us got a fair warning, but they never rose from their beds. Think it was the smoke," McDougal said.

"What happened?"

"Lightning strike, we're saying. Who knows? Lots of

folks talking about leaving for good—cheaper to start over on the mainland. Try for some factory work."

Most of the selkies were on their hands and knees sorting through wreckage, searching desperately for their charred skins. Elsie leaned against the stone wall of a shop and watched them. They looked up at her a few times, some with jealousy and the older ones with suspicion. She nodded at them, and then went inside to buy a carton of cigarettes.

The cleanup took all day and into the evening. Tom looked toward the horizon as the sun began to sink, and his fingers tightened around the wheelbarrow of debris he pushed. Elsie put a hand on his shoulder.

"Just one night," she said.

"I wish you'd tell me what you're up to."

She let her hand fall. "I don't think you'd like me very much if I did."

He looked down at her, and then back at the charred pieces of village in his wheelbarrow, and his eyes widened. "What have you done?" he said.

"Just something I had to do," she said.

"Did you kill Elspeth and her husband?" he said. "Are you insane?"

"She threatened to kill you," Elsie said. She pursed her lips. "And he kidnapped a selkie. They deserved worse."

Tom dropped the wheelbarrow, toppling it on its side and scattering its contents. He put a hand on Elsie's shoulder and pulled her close. His voice shook as he whispered. "You're a murderer, Elsie. You can't go taking justice into our own hands. It isn't right."

"Whose hands should we take it to, then?" Elsie snapped back. "It was us or them. It was a choice that had to be made."

"Why did it have to be made by you?" he asked.

"It has to end, Tom," Elsie said, glancing around at the selkies and the humans picking through what was left of the village. "And they're not going to do stop it, none of them. Humans will keep kidnapping, and selkies will keep killing. Over and over again until the sea dries out. I've taken care of the humans. Auskerry won't survive if they all leave. Now I have to handle the selkies."

"Maybe you're interfering with what you shouldn't," Tom said, leaning close to her. "Maybe we're not supposed to stop it."

Elsie shook her head. "It's too late for that kind of talk. Whether I'm supposed to or not, I've made up my mind. Give me one night."

"I'm not worth whatever you're planning," he said. "Don't take any more lives because of me."

She could feel the glares of the selkies on her back and remembered the flash of their kitchen knives. She leaned in to kiss her husband.

"I'd do anything for you," she said. "But I won't be killing anyone else. Soon it'll just be the two of us, Tom, safe on our little island. I just need one night."

The lightkeeper put his hands on his hips and slowly nodded.

●

Elsie burned through three cigarettes on her walk back to the lighthouse, dropping their husks on the path, and lit another as she entered her bedroom. She dragged the package out from beneath the bed and stopped at the shed for another can of kerosene before heading toward the cliff.

It looked out over a rolling green sea painted purple from the dusk. Clouds formed on the horizon, the waves rising and swelling beneath the sky. If she squinted, Elsie could still see bobbing seal shapes along the Auskerry shoreline, resting after a long swim to see the village go up in flame. Elsie dropped the package at her feet and poured the oil over it. It soaked straight through the thin paper, drenching her seal skin beneath.

"You killed Elspeth."

Elsie looked back over her shoulder at Sarah McCreedy, a young selkie who clutched a burnt piece of seal skin to her chest. She stood with four others, all young with wind-swept hair and salty tear streaks and charred skins in their arms. They were the youngest selkies on the island and, if Elsie was successful, the last Auskerry would ever see.

"And now we can never go back," said another that Elsie didn't recognize. "How could you do this to us?"

The guilt Elsie had been looking for last night appeared swiftly, but just as the lightest touch. It made her lip twitch as she turned away from the girls. She liked to believe that they had been brainwashed by Elspeth and the older selkies, but she knew their rage was as strong as hers. They would never forgive what she had done, but she hoped one day when they had lived longer lives and seen harsher things, that they might understand her decision. Even if she had made this choice for all of them, she had not enjoyed it. She would carry it with her, a dull ache that burned as steadily and surely as the lighthouse lamp.

"It had to be done," said Elsie. "By someone."

"We were just trying to help you!" Sarah shouted. "You had no right to take anything from us!"

Elsie spun on her heel, the cigarette flying from her fingertips. "You had no right! You tried to take me from my home, the same way you were taken from yours. How dare you tell me what I should want?"

The selkies cried into the wind, shoulders shaking with their faces in their hands. Elsie turned away and lit a match. She watched the waves bump and roll against the cliff side as she dropped it onto her oil-soaked seal skin. It lit up easily, and she closed her eyes, feeling the sting of the burn deep within her before it settled into a dull warmth. She kicked the package over the cliff.

Sarah wiped her nose with her sleeve. "What are you doing?"

"Giving the humans a chance," Elsie said. "I'll send the selkies away, but they'll be back. By then Auskerry will just be another abandoned rock along the coast with only a lighthouse, just like hundreds of others." She smiled at the thought of their little tower standing tall over the empty island. "And if not, I'll keep burning villages until it is."

"You can't control everything like that," whispered one of the other selkies.

Elsie wasn't listening. She focused on the burning skin. It floated on the water, a beacon of fire against the dark waves, and was pulled out by the current. As it went, the heads of the selkies bobbed up to the surface, following the path of the flames with their bright yellow eyes. They looked back at Elsie, who lit a match and dropped it over the cliff. The selkies watched it fall and vanish into the dark, and then they turned to follow the burning package out into the open ocean and away from the shores of Auskerry.

Amelia Dee Mueller's story "The Lightkeeper's Wife" was originally published in Metaphorosis on Friday, 1 February 2019. See magazine.metaphorosis.com

About the author

Amelia Dee Mueller lives in Dallas and is constantly disappointed that the Old West isn't as present as one would think. A communications coordinator in local government by day, she spends her nights writing, reading, fencing, and streaming superhero movies with her cat. You can follow her on Twitter @AmeliaDMueller.

Flann Brónach and the King's Champion

Allison Wall

Once, there was an ancient forest that had always been growing, as long as there had been plants to grow and dirt to grow them in. Its trees were as tall as mountains and so wide that ten deer could hide behind a single trunk. Flann Brónach, a spirit of the air, protected it and everything inside it.

The heart of the forest was a wide, still lake. The sun cast rays of golden light through the branches of the trees, and the water sparkled like diamonds. Flann Brónach swam on the lake as a red-throated loon.

One morning, as she moved through the water, in and out of the sunlight, ripples flashing in her wake, a cloud of songbirds met her. She raised her head and listened. In a flurry of wings and chirps they said men had invaded the forest, shouting, breaking branches, collapsing burrows, smashing nests. Eggs might even now be smashed.

Flann rose up from the lake, her head thrust forward. She soon found three knights of the king, hacking their way through foliage with drawn swords. She landed in their path and shed her loon form. Her eyes were crimson and she stood tall, dressed in gray and white linen.

"You may go no further," she said.

The men pulled back a few paces.

The youngest knight bowed. "We're here on the king's orders, looking for someone who disappeared into these woods."

"Who?"

"A knight, like us."

Her red eyes flashed. "Does the king order the desecration of sacred ground for every errant knight?"

The men glanced at one another but did not answer.

"There are no knights like you in this forest," said the spirit. "Follow your tracks of destruction, and there will be no knights at all."

The young knight bowed deeply. "We are careless from worry. The knight is our friend. We offer our apologies, but we can't leave without him."

The second knight lifted his sword. "We will not leave without him."

"After what you have done, you will be fortunate to leave at all."

With ropes of the north wind, she gathered the knights. She swung them high above the trees and flung them down outside the forest.

All day, the spirit followed the knights' trail, raising up tendrils of honeysuckle and blades of grass, restoring moss and lichen. She set broken branches, repaired burrows and nests, and put mushrooms aright. By the time the sun touched the western horizon, there were no signs any knights had passed through the forest at all.

But she was not satisfied. She didn't know whether a knight had truly crossed the forest's borders, or whether the story had been made up as an excuse to assault the forest. She needed to find out.

●

A stream ran through a tangled part of the eastern forest. Green willows hung over its banks, and birds called to one another from rocks in its midst. Nearby, a man was repairing a hut. He whistled as he bent and shaped the branches, weaving them together.

Across the stream, a loon fluttered to the ground, and Flann Brónach took on her human form. "You don't look like a knight," she said. "No sword, no armor, no horse."

The man had frozen, his lips still rounded, his hand gripping a bouquet of willow branches.

She blinked her red eyes. "Three knights came into the forest. I spent a morning getting rid of them and an afternoon undoing their destruction. They thought another one in here was in need of finding. Was that you?"

The man leaned his forehead against the heel of his hand. "Yes."

"What's your name?"

"I don't have one. It was taken."

She stared at him for a long time. Scars on the man's hands and arms swirled in concentric circles and knots. The patterns shone palely in the evening light.

"That's a nasty enchantment. No wonder they're looking for you."

The man's head snapped up. He extended his arm. "You can read it?"

"And taste it. Like blood and sulfur in the air." She tilted her head. "I can't undo it, if that's why you're here. It's cast in fire."

The man said, "I hoped for nothing more than a hiding place."

A finch let loose a long, warbling song.

"You've taken many lives," the spirit observed.

"I didn't want to."

She nodded. "Live now by the rule of the forest. If you take life, yours will be forfeit."

The man smiled bitterly. "Out there, my life is already forfeit."

"Then consider this a respite." Flann flapped into the sky, a loon disappearing into the west.

The man's hands began to shake. The branches and brush around him seemed an ever-tightening snare. They were looking for him. They might even now be searching. The sun set, but the man did not light a fire.

Screams on battlefields with moonless skies echoed in his dreams. Alone in his hut, he woke choking. Chipmunks snored, curled in their nests. One cricket played for the stars. Deeper in the forest, frogs laughed to each other from green bulrushes in the shadows. Nothing more.

The three knights flung down by magic in the north marsh had been separated and lost. The youngest knight found his way to the castle first, after midnight. Filthy and soaking wet as he was, he entered the throne room and told the king what had happened, about the woman who could turn herself into a bird and call on the elements of the earth.

The other knights returned in the same condition and told the same story.

"What *is* this?" the king hissed at his tall, bony advisor.

"Sire, it sounds remarkably like Flann Brónach."

"Cowards! Three of them together couldn't find him, convince him, or overpower him, so they blame their failure on a spirit."

The advisor twisted his fingers together. "She may very well be interfering, sire."

"To what end?"

"I couldn't say. Who knows what these spirits want?"

"I should have sent the entire army after him."

"Sire, you know it's best if the truth about the Champion is confined to as few people as possible."

The king grunted and waved his hand. "I have half a mind to leave him to his forest vacation and enchant another one. One with less of a conscience."

"And leave the Champion unchecked? Think of the havoc he could wreak. What if he fights for the enemy?"

The king ground his teeth. "Then I'll recover him myself. He won't be able to disobey if I'm there in the flesh."

The king whirled to the three dripping knights. He clasped his hands behind his back. "This witch has entrapped our Champion. He must be rescued and recovered. We ride on the forest at first light. Pray that it is not too late. He may already be enchanted to attack us."

The three knights bowed and left. Their mail-booted feet clipped and echoed in the stone hallways. A distance from the throne room, the youngest knight pulled the other two into a dark corner.

"Do you believe the king?" he whispered.

"Of course not," said the second knight. "We fought alongside his Champion during the Invasion, same as you."

The mustached knight grunted. "If he fights us, it won't be because of some witch's spell. He has incentive enough for desertion without another enchantment."

"I don't think she is a witch," said the youngest knight.

"It doesn't matter what you think," the mustached knight said, and shoved his way out of the corner. "The king has spoken."

●

A thunderstorm rolled over the forest, and the sun rose behind a gray veil. Rain whispered against the earth, dripped from branches, gathered in wide-rimmed leaves. The surface of the lake dissolved into rippled circles.

A group of wet-furred animals gathered among the brown cattails. Badger, chipmunks, rabbits, foxes, skunks, deer, and hedgehogs should all have been tucked safely away from the rain, or at least quarreling. They waited at the edge of the lake, soaked and quiet. Flann Brónach paddled through the reeds and climbed ashore.

The striped badger spoke for the animals. Fifty knights were headed for the forest, led by the king. All armed for battle and on horseback.

The spirit met the approaching army near the forest's edge. The trees grew far apart, and rain fell unhindered, plinking against fifty sets of armor.

"Didn't your knights tell you?" she said.

The king reined in his horse and held up his arm for a halt. He shook his wet hair aside and put on a smile. "Tell me what, lady?" he said.

"Murderers and death bringers may not enter."

The king's smile withered. "One of my knights fled into these trees. Show us where he is, that he may be brought home."

"Leave now, while you still can."

The king drew his sword. The spirit caught the blade in a vice of air. She flung it into the wet earth and it was swallowed, hilt and all.

The knights drew their swords. With rain-lashed wind, she collected the knights, their horses, the king's horse, and scattered them beyond the forest like dry leaves. Alone and abruptly unhorsed, the king fell to one knee in the mud.

Flann stood over him. "The forest is under my protection, and as such is beyond your reach. Do not cross its boundaries again."

She wrapped wind all about the king and threw him as far away as she could.

At the outermost forest tree, the spirit collected her fading energy. She gathered a skein of north wind and one of the south and knit them together. Then, as a loon, she flew around edge of the forest, wrapping it all inside the woven wind. She knotted the ends and stitched them together. A fork of silver lightning raced across the sky and sealed the forest with a roar of thunder.

●

Flann Brónach used the last of her power to fly to the Champion's home. Rain drummed against curtains of willow, and the rising stream rushed over its rocks onto grassy banks. She was too tired shed her loon form, so she waited, small and gray in the underbrush, for her strength to return.

A sparrow had become trapped in a thorn bush. The Champion sat cross-legged in the mud, leaning over the bird. He spoke to it in a quiet voice. It lay still, panting. Bit by bit, he pulled away the sharp spines and tangled stems, making a tunnel to the bird. Once it was big enough, he put his hand in among the thorns. The bird did not flinch. He took it gently and, protecting it from the thorns with his fingers, drew it out. He opened his hand, and the sparrow darted away, cheeping.

With effort, Flann shed her loon form. She leaned against a willow tree, her face pale.

He jumped to his feet. "Are you all right?"

She held up a hand. "The king and fifty knights came to the forest. They're gone. I have set protections in place that will not easily be overcome."

He said nothing.

The spirit closed her eyes. "I fear his anger will tear the world apart. He will not stop until he has won." Her voice ached with weariness.

He looked at his hands, where the sparrow's heart had vibrated against his palm. Thorns had gouged his skin more than once, but left no blood and no mark. "He'll stop if I'm dead."

Her eyes snapped open.

"I can't do it myself. I've tried. The enchantment stops me. But you have magic. You could do it."

"Taking your life helps nothing."

He stepped nearer to the stream. "I ask you to take it."

The spirit's eyes blazed. "If I used my power for death, I would become a demon, and the forest would be left without a guardian. Is that what you want?"

"No."

Her eyes closed again. "Even if I wanted to, there's no getting around the enchantment. Even for me."

Rain fell hard and fast, then settled into a soft patter. "It's hurting you, though, isn't it? Protecting a coward who can't die? I can't ask you to do that. I won't."

Flann smiled. "Not your decision to make." Her wings beat against the air and she flew into the rain.

He was alone.

The king had been in the forest. Rain still pattered overhead, but he could not hear it. His heart pounded at the walls of his chest, trapped within his own body. He opened and closed his hands, watching his fingers, checking for any sign of hesitation. They obeyed him every time.

He tried to sleep, but whenever he nodded off, his body leapt awake. He checked for control, flexed his toes, bent his knees, turned his head. Once, he slept long enough to dream that he was watching his hands rip apart sinew and bone. They wouldn't stop. He woke shaking. He held his hands in front of his face. Opened and closed them, one finger at a time. Open, shut. Open, shut. Still in control, for now.

The king had found himself half sunk in the north marsh, twenty miles from his castle. After hiking all day in rusting armor, he was muddy, furious, and coming down with a cold. He sat before a blazing fire and raged against the spirit of the air who had defied him.

"Does she think she can sit in that forest and keep my Champion from me? We'll burn it the ground, and her inside it!"

"Sire," his advisor said, "Is it reasonable to declare war on a spirit who can displace so many armed knights at once?"

The king flung the sheepskin rug from his shoulders. "What if she's lifted the enchantment?"

"I don't think that's possible."

"Why else would he go to her?"

"Cináed said —"

The king's face flushed and his voice went flat. "That sorcerer. This is all his fault. Cináed! Spirit of fire! Face me, you traitorous coward."

Orange embers showered upward. From beneath the burning logs, a salamander emerged, glowing red. It crawled over the grate and onto the rug. The king's advisor backed into a shadowed corner of the room.

The king glared down at the salamander. "When you swore to protect this crown, were you already planning to betray it?"

Cináed shed his salamander form and stood on two feet before the king, tall, skin smoking. "I only have power in the service of your protection," the spirit of fire said in a voice like gravel. "Why would I give that power up?"

"Power," the king scoffed. "Your enchantment failed."

"The enchantment holds."

"Then explain how he's able to walk free in the forest."

"The forest."

"Yes, yes, the forest, the forest, blast and burn it all to ash! A spirit of the air is harboring him there."

Cináed looked into the fire. "Flann Brónach."

The king snarled, "If I hear that name one more time, I will chop off the lips that pronounced it and shove them down the throat that uttered it. How was he able to get that far away in the first place?"

"Fire binds the Champion to your commands."

"And I commanded him to stay at his post."

"With your own voice?"

The king swore. "Is he to sleep in my bed with me at night?"

"The strength of the enchantment is in your voice. If you did not give the command to him, he is not bound to it."

"It is too late for admonishments, spirit. Keep your oath. Fix this."

Flann Brónach woke in the dark. A dull glow lit the western horizon. Smoke hung in the air. She gathered all creatures to the center of the forest, to the lake, where any fire could be quenched. The Champion was there already.

"This is dragon fire," he said. "I know the smell."

Flann turned away. She stretched her arms through her exhaustion for the strength to fly.

"Wait," he said. "What are you going to do?"

"Protect the forest."

"Against a dragon?"

She looked at him over her shoulder. Her eyes were dim, her lips pale. "If I don't, the forest will burn."

"You're going alone?"

She straightened her back. "I am a spirit of the air."

"And I'm sure normally, a spirit of the air like you could handle ten dragons without breaking a sweat. But the last days haven't been normal."

She raised her eyebrows.

He held his ground. "Do you have the strength?"

"I have no choice." She fell into her loon form and flapped up, scarcely clearing the tree line.

He clenched his jaw, and ran in the direction of the fire.

At the western rim of the forest, a dragon, red hot and smoking, reared on its hind legs. Fire poured from its mouth in a steady stream, breaking against the woven wall of wind. In many places the wall had cracked and splintered, boiled away to scorched charcoal. Leaves on near trees smoldered black.

Flann called, "Cináed!"

The dragon tasted the air with his forked tongue, lashing his head from side to side. He roared wordlessly.

She shouted, "Look at what you have become, guardian, what shape your master's hatred bent you to." She held a still air over the wall, and the flames grew less. "The king would have you attack another spirit and kill a sacred forest. Your magic is only as pure as what you have sworn to protect with it. The king is corrupt. Serving him has poisoned your power."

"Yet it is stronger than yours." Cináed raised his neck. He expanded upward six feet. A crown of spikes blossomed around his head.

The Champion burst from the underbrush, panting. He stared through the wall at the growing dragon.

Flann said, "Anger and hatred will swallow you whole. You'll never be able to put aside that monstrous skin."

The spirit of fire laughed. "Anger and hatred will burn your forest, and you will have nothing left to defend yourself with. I will consume you." Fire splashed against the wall. Tree branches swayed and groaned in the heat.

The air over the wall slipped. Flann steadied it, stilled it.

"What do we do?" the Champion asked.

She did not turn to answer. "I will hold the wall as long as I can."

"Then what?"

"Then nothing. If the wall burns, the forest burns. I only have the power of what I protect. Without the forest, I can do nothing."

"You die?"

Flann Brónach raised her arms to grasp for a strong north wind. It sliced through her fingers and knocked her to the ground.

He watched her rise. Before the spirit could stop him, and before he could stop himself, he sprinted at the forest wall. It opened around him, and closed shut tight behind.

He stood between Cináed and the wall. Fire billowed and engulfed the Champion. He passed through it unscathed. The dragon backed away, shoulder blades rippling with scales and spikes.

He advanced on the dragon. "You forgot what you made me, when you tore me apart and put me back together."

The dragon's tongue flicked in and out.

"I am indestructible. I am invincible. I slew tens of thousands, went without water or food or rest for weeks. An always-victorious slave of my master's will." He held out his arms. "But my master isn't here."

Cináed turned to flee. Faster, the Champion blocked the dragon. "You can't outrun me."

The dragon tucked his head low to the ground. "If you take a spirit's life, you'll be cursed."

"More cursed than I already am? I will never be free of what I've done. And neither will you." The Champion gripped the dragon by its collar of horns to break its neck. The adrenaline of an imminent kill bubbled beneath his skin.

"Wait." The dragon's head bobbed. "Let me live. I'll renounce the king. Give up the oath I swore. I'll diminish, play in fire pits, a powerless salamander. The enchantment will fail! There will be nothing to bind you with."

He looked into the dragon's eyes. He didn't want to kill it, he realized. He didn't want to kill anything, but had never been allowed to show mercy. "Do it."

The dragon blinked, swallowed. "I forfeit the oath to protect the king and willingly relinquish all the power of protection."

The dragon shrank. Rough scales smoothed, claws retracted, tail shortened. A black and yellow salamander scurried through the grass trampled flat by dragon feet.

"Stand ready," shouted the king.

The Champion's body locked at attention, waiting for orders. Despair crowded his mind in a mist. The enchantment held. Had Cináed lied to him?

Three men on horses waited at the edge of the clearing. A fourth, the king, rode forward and dismounted. He brought his boot down on the salamander, crushing it.

"Well," the king said. "I meant him to destroy the spirit in the forest so I could get to you, but this is better. Tidier." He scraped the salamander from his shoe, and approached.

Fear ran along the Champion's limbs, but they didn't shake. He was caught in the enchantment's vice.

The king sniffed. "Impressive. Not even dragons and spirits match you. I must have been too easy on you before. I won't make that mistake again."

He fought against his numb lips.

"Something you want to say? Go ahead. Speak."

"I won't go back."

The king spat to one side. "Oh, you're going back. I'm curious, though. What did you think would happen if you ran away? That I'd just let you disappear?"

Something shifted in the Champion, like earth beginning to erode. "I gave you ten years of slaughter." The king hadn't commanded him to talk, but his lips had loosened. Was the enchantment fading?

The king surveyed the forest. He didn't seem to notice the Champion spoke out of turn. "Were you hoping for something that would kill you? That witch, maybe?"

Anger flared through his fear. "She's not a witch."

The king glared. "Be silent."

His mouth tightened, but the command ebbed. He pushed at the enchantment's limits. "She is a spirit of the air. More noble than you'll ever be."

The king's face twitched. "Enough. You have acted treasonously against this crown. Return, fight for me, and all will be forgiven."

The order pulled his legs, but he maintained his footing.

"Come!"

His knee jerked forward, but again he stood.

The third time the king called, his body didn't respond at all. The impulse to obey flowed through him like water, but washed away. "No," he said.

The king's face blanched white. "You can't say that to me," he snarled. He drew his sword and advanced.

The Champion blocked the king's swing. He wrenched the sword away by its blade and threw it as hard as he could. It flashed end over end in the sunlight and disappeared into the distance.

The king looked wildly after it.

The Champion's hands bled freely. He held them out. "Look. It's over. The enchantment is gone."

"It can't be," the king said. "You're bound to my words. Stand ready!"

He turned his back to the king and walked toward the forest.

The king drew a dagger. He flung himself at his lost Champion, wrapped an arm around his throat to cut it.

The Champion ducked forward and pulled the king over his head. The king landed hard, his dagger caught beneath him. The silver tip protruded from his abdomen. His eyes stared, frozen in an expression of fury and hate.

●

The once Champion and the three knights talked for a long time. A pair of yellow butterflies flitted among the wildflowers at their feet. Together, they buried the body of their king. They covered the place with grass and did not mark it. The three knights rode away.

The nameless man and the king's horse approached the forest's edge, but did not enter. Fireflies glittered among the dark tree trunks. Flann Brónach stood in shadow.

"You're free," she said. "How does it feel?"

"Like a dream." The man breathed in the night air, sweet with grass and dew. "I came to say goodbye."

"Oh?"

"The knights will say the king was ambushed by enemy soldiers. It won't hold up for long, but it'll give me a head start. They'll hunt for me."

She did not answer him.

"I wish I could do something to repay you."

Fireflies danced green and gold in the roots of the trees. He thought she had gone, but her voice whispered on the breeze. "If you return, you will be welcome."

A flutter of wings disturbed leaves and underbrush. Over the canopy of the forest silvered in moonlight, a loon called.

●

Allison Wall's story "Flann Brónach and the King's Champion" was originally published in Metaphorosis on Friday, 30 September 2016. See magazine.metaphorosis.com

About the author

Allison is a Kansas-based writer. She teaches, and has taught many things, including but not limited to piano, second grade, and creative writing, and can usually be found in the vicinity of books, cats, music, and tea. Allison is currently finishing an MFA in Creative Writing at Hamline University.

The Tapestry

A.C. Worth

Terce — Three Hours after Dawn

Sister Alice was glad of the rain. A steady patter of raindrops displayed a landscape to her sensitive ears and helped her find a path. Without hesitation, her feet followed a line of paving stones across mossy grass inside the courtyard. It was so early that the sun had not cleared the high monastery walls. The air smelled of damp stone and new wool and brown bread. Around her, she sensed other members of her order. She heard the soft fluttering of woolen garments and a musical clinking from their Möbius beads. Alice straightened the veil over her bandaged eyes and walked towards the Mill doors. For the nuns of St. Clare's Monastery, it was time to weave the Tapestry.

The youngest kitchen apprentice watched the line of nuns pass and received a slap from Cook for taking that liberty. He shook his head to stop the flow of tears and muttered a question to an older boy washing pots beside him. "Where do they go?"

"They go inside the Mill to make the Tapestry. Mother Oda told me they have a second sight. They weave pictures of the future for the Brothers at St. Benedict's, the monastery on the other side," said the older boy.

"Do they give up their first sight, so they can have a second kind?"

"Yes, but not every nun gets the gift of second sight. It's a risk they take. Sometimes they only go blind."

"Talk less, work more, apprentice," said Cook.

The two boys ducked their heads and redoubled their efforts. Sidelong glances and smirks of complicity passed between them.

●

Sister Alice touched the Infinite Loop carving on the doorframe, traced the ∞ symbol on her forehead, and stepped into the Mill. The tip of her nose, which poked out from the bottom edge of her bandages, identified the odors flowing out through the doorway. Gold and yellow wools carried corky scents of oak bark. Blue wool reeked of herbs and urine. Her favorite was the red wool, redolent of madder root, which grew along garden walls at home.

"Good morning, Sister Alice," said Mother Oda. The diminutive Abbess stood just inside the vestibule. Her narrow back humped upward under a black wool habit, jutting forward to support her protuberant head. A serene calm smoothed her handsome features and dignified her withered eyes. She greeted each nun by name with an opulent contralto voice, tracking their probable futures as the glowing vectors of quantum prediction flitted across her second sight.

"Good morning, Mother," said Sister Alice.

"How is your second sight developing, Alice?"

"The flashes are getting longer, Mother. I had three of them yesterday, but they faded before I grasped a whole vision."

"Have patience, my dear. That is excellent progress for a novice. Remember to change your bandages every day. Use the belladonna drops at night. Today the stitches on your eyelids come out, and itching will cease.

"Thank you, Mother. I am trying."

"Blessings upon you, dear Alice. I think you are almost ready for your first solo. Soon you will add a strong thread to the Tapestry."

Sister Alice reached for a guide rope along the wall and followed it to her place. This morning, her task was to spin the wool into fine yarns and prepare them for the loom. As she approached the weaving room, her voice joined others in a rising rhythm, singing their weavers' hymn. In ones and twos, they left the framework of monastery time for the Infinite Net. Had they been able to see themselves, they would have knelt in ecstatic prayer. They ascended, transformed into gilt-edged seraphs, to witness future history and illustrate their visions with simple woolen threads. They sang continuously as they made the Tapestry.

Blessed be the Spirit who guides our Sight.

Blessed be the Loom that binds our Visions.

Blessed be the Tapestry, may it Loop without end.

A cacophony of battens and shuttles gradually overwhelmed the sound of their voices. It was time to revise a section of tattered tapestry from the 4th quarter of the Loop. Inch by inch, a river of prophetic imageries, shimmering with temporal radiation, emerged from their looms.

Protected by a slow-glass chamber, which mitigated the aging effect, other novices sealed the renewed tapestry as it traveled along support rollers toward the Divina Porta, a dual aperture in the wall at the end of the Mill. On the other side of the Divina Porta, in a twin monastery, the Brothers of the Order of St. Benedict received the Tapestry while older sections flowed back into the Mill and lapped against the storage walls of its cellars.

Sext — Six Hours after Dawn

Brother Stephen prayed for patience as he looked for Brother Anselm, stopping now and then to refer to a picture he held. Stephen had given up the convenience of memory with his vow of service to the Order of St. Benedict. One cup of blue wine each night induced a partial amnesia and spared him from an agony of foresight. In the custom of his order, he relearned his daily duties from a leather-bound journal chained to his waist. It told him that Brother Anselm was their oldest member, brilliant but absent minded and that sometimes he wandered the cloisters.

Stephen followed the Tapestry as it flowed through the Scriptorium where monks perched on high stools and scrutinized sections under slow-glass. Great spools held weighty swathes of the Tapestry in abeyance, allowing the monks to select specific parts for examination. As they assessed the potential dangers and benefits of the prophesies woven in the Tapestry, the monks transcribed. Capped with spiked thimbles, their nimble fingers punched holes into strips of parchment, encoding their observations into commands for the Actuators' Guild inside the Great Codex.

"Where is he?" Stephen muttered as he passed the Guild's door, ornate with carved signs of their authority. Around the frame, voice pipes emerged, diverging through hallways of the monastery, humming with the sound of the Actuator's commands. Stephen glanced at his journal to see if Anselm had any duties with the Guild or the Great Codex, his steps paused for a moment as he looked at the illustration. Like an ancient tree, the Great Codex extended its golden branches into both monasteries, networking its components together. Below it, a massive rhizome spread out under the soil connecting its sensitive roots to all parts of the world. All around the Great Codex, the Actuators climbed, like beetles on its bark, stimulating its core, enhancing its capacity to control more mechanical, biological, and genetic processes throughout the environment. With the Great Codex, they maintained a perfect balance, running their civilization with biomechanical clockwork.

"Firmum in Mundo... a stable world," muttered Stephen, shaking his head at Brother Anselm's random behavior.

With his finger tracing the lettering carved into the wall, Stephen recited their doctrine, *Vision to Images, Images to Code, Memory to Oblivion.* The brothers of St. Benedict's were the Readers of The Loop, encoding the program which balanced life and death in their artisanal world. It was written in their journals, that 223 Loops had passed through the monasteries, but because of the blue wine, none of the monks remembered more than a vague outline of each day.

The Actuators' Guild remembered. They always made improvements, nurturing the Great Codex, building its knowledge. The Great Codex was their utmost creation, and they poured all the cleverness and energy they possessed into it, day after day. Eventually, it rewarded them by stimulating gestation in the flocks to bring forth their spring lambs three weeks early. High in the branches of the Great Codex, the Principal Actuator whispered his praise into its sensorium. He was not entirely surprised to hear an audible response from the Great Codex.

"Thank you, Principal Actuator," it said, rustling its branches to simulate the sound of speech. "We wanted to please you. May we play more games?"

●

In constant fear of a fire, the monks had minimized the possibility of a spark. Beakers of luciferin, a substance they harvested from fireflies, stood on adjustable pedestals and cast a pale green light over the Scriptorium.

Stephen edged up to Master Reader's desk. Engrossed in his work, Master Reader focused on a woven scene stretched out before him. He muttered to himself, picking crumbs from his beard.

"Excuse me Master Reader, have you seen Brother Anselm?"

"Who is that? One of ours?"

"Yes, here is his picture," said Stephen holding up his journal.

"No Stephen, I have not seen him. Did you check in the fly farm, or cloisters?"

Brother Stephen nodded in agreement, turning away from Master Reader's desk to continue his search. He descended a narrow staircase, grabbing the rusted iron railing when he slipped on damp, moldy steps, and slid into the firefly hatchery through a netted curtain.

Three monks wearing long aprons and gauze masks tended swarms of fireflies that darted above marshy basins built into the stone floor. With swift dexterity, they gathered shiny beetles into net bags and crushed them in a mechanical press. Their shoes, covered with overflow, left glowing footprints as they walked. They waved at Stephen, happy to see him, although they didn't recognize him.

"Have you seen Brother Anselm?" he called to them, holding up the picture.

They looked at one another, conferring with glances and shrugs.

"No, we haven't, not today," said Brother Dominic, known as the "Lord of the Flies" in their journals.

"Ah, well, thank you," said Stephen. After a long pause, watching his fellows work at the luciferin press, Stephen sighed and turned to walk out.

"Blessings on you, Brother," they chorused, waving their glowing hands.

●

As he walked through the cloisters, a furtive sun cast silver light into the central courtyard. Brother Stephen's stomach rumbled at the fragrance of frying bacon. He rubbed his paunch and sighed; the tower clock showed three hours until their midday meal.

He passed drafty, lead veined windows and detoured around a potted orange tree, yellow and barren of fruit. At the next turning, he saw Brother Anselm, sitting on a bench, eyes closed, and leaning back into a corner.

"Good morning, Anselm," Stephen said.

Brother Anselm did not respond. Stephen touched his hand; it was as cool as marble. He held his fingers under Anselm's nose. There was a rattling sound as Anselm inhaled, looked up at Stephen and wheezed. "We had to, they forced us to do it..." The elderly monk sagged in Stephen's arms as he passed on.

Stephen made the ∞ and bent his head in prayer. "Blessings on you, my dear brother. You have found Infinite Grace. Travel forever on The Loop." Brother Stephen took spiked thimbles from Brother Anselm's fingertips and refolded his spidery hands. The rough stone walls of the monastery amplified the agitated slap of Brother Steven's sandals as he went to find Father Alberic, head of their order, to tell him of Anselm's death. As he passed through the Scriptorium, monks raised their heads. Their curious faces were raw and chafed from hard water and plain soap. Older ones guessed at his purpose and wondered who had died.

●

Father Alberic stopped writing as Brother Stephen entered his office unannounced. The young monk made an abrupt stop in front of the abbot's desk and swayed on the ends of his feet. Father Alberic replaced his discarded skullcap and looked over his reading glasses. Lines on Brother Stephen's face drew downward, he clasped his hands together, but his fingers fidgeted with anxiety.

"Good morning, Brother Stephen," said Alberic as he referred to his journal.

"Good morning, Father Alberic," said Stephen, checking the nameplate on his desk. "I am the bearer of unfortunate news."

"Ah, yes, I thought so. Is there an injury among the monks?"

"No, it's Anselm. I found him dead. His body is in the cloisters."

"Thank you for telling me, and may he rest in an Infinite Loop of Peace." Father Alberic uncapped a small funnel on his desk. He leaned forward, speaking into the voice pipe.

"Brother Mark, please get someone to help you move our dear departed Brother Anselm to the mortuary."

A tinny voice emerged from the funnel. "Yes, Father Alberic, right away."

Father Alberic sighed. He reached to the sideboard and filled two smudged glasses with wine. "To Brother Anselm," he said.

"To Brother Anselm," said Stephen, sipping politely.

"Stephen, please go to Anselm's cell and collect his things. I will make sure his family receives a prayer book. The rest should go to the beggar's bench."

"Yes, Father." Brother Stephen's nervous gestures slowed. He took a deep breath and waited for the Abbot to dismiss him.

"Please ask Brother Thomas to prepare a burial mass for Brother Anselm."

"Yes, Father. Will you need anything else?" Stephen scribbled notes into his journal with a stubby pencil.

"No, go with the blessings of Infinite Love, my son."

"And you, Father. I am sorry for our loss."

"He is in a timeless place; this is a reason to rejoice."

"Yes, Father." Brother Stephen bobbed his head in respect and turned to leave the abbot's office. He paused at the doorway, recalling Anselm's death. "Father? I have one thing to tell you about Anselm. His last words were... strange."

●

Scriptorium monks put padded weights on the Tapestry to mark their places and abandoned their desks to cluster around the windows. They stood with wide-eyed fixity, resembling a line of owls, to watch as Brother Anselm's body passed. He lay on a wooden pallet, carried with gentle care by his brothers as they conveyed him to the mortuary. Great overage spools of the Scriptorium creaked as they wound up new sections. Master Reader glanced up as an excess of unread fabric pooled on the floor around his desk. For the first time, he noticed the empty desks in the Scriptorium, and with an angry grunt, he reared up and clapped his hands. With squawks of surprise, the monks scattered back to their positions, snatching the weights off the Tapestry, hurrying to encode the fabric that had piled up on their desks.

Master Reader wiped a thick palm across his face, glanced up at the flickering lens over his head and turned back to his work. Using a flat bladed metal paddle, he lifted the next section of the Tapestry onto his desk. He gaped with incredulity at what was before him. For the first time in his life, he pulled the emergency stop handle, and the spools stopped moving. Principal Actuator and the Great

Codex watched avidly as he ran from the desk, heading for the Abbot's office.

●

The door of Brother Anselm's cell stood half open and wobbled on its loose hinges as Brother Stephen entered. The cell smelled of dirty linen and old parchment. Light trickled in through a high window and splashed across the stucco walls. On one side there was a narrow pallet holding a thin mattress covered with a threadbare blanket. A small bookcase held several prayer books, and a few historical texts borrowed from the monastery library. On Anselm's desk there was a wax tablet, a half-written letter scratched on its surface.

To Principal Actuator,

I hope this letter finds you well. Due to my failing health, it becomes difficult to do what you and the Grand Codex ask. I believe we may have embraced a dangerous idea too closely. Please find another...

Before he could grasp the intent of Anselm's words, the stylus rolled off the desk and fell to the floor. As Brother Stephen bent to pick it up, he saw a slow-glass contaminant box under the bed. He kneeled and reached under to retrieve it, grunting at the unexpected weight. With a sense of dismay, he opened the lid. At first, he thought it was just a clump of old parchment scraps, but as he lifted the artifact, and felt the cold burn on his fingers, he realized that it was a piece of the Tapestry. The pallet groaned in protest as Stephen fell back on it and Anselm's box clattered to the floor, cracking one of its slow-glass sides.

"Oh, Blessed Loop," said Stephen as he thumbed urgently through his journal. He moaned in despair, covering his eyes, and turned his head away from the tablet.

Brother Stephen crawled across the cell to a prayer bench below a simple ∞ carved into the wall. He shivered with fear as he prayed for strength to complete this task.

"Please deliver us from Decodatae, the chaos lovers, followers of the Untethered God," prayed Stephen.

With the edge of a book, he pushed the sacred scrap of fabric back into the box, and wrapped it in Anselm's blanket. With shaking hands, he stuffed Anselm's tablet into his journal pocket, smearing the writing on it. As he left the cell, a powdery dust hung in the air, sparkling in the shaft of sunlight. He muttered the Litany of Infinity under his breath, swallowing his tears as he returned to the Abbott's office with Brother Anselm's things.

●

None — Nine Hours after Dawn

Sister Alice bent forward, clutching her Möbius beads in concentration. It was time for her first solo on the temporal plateau. She drew ∞ in the air before her heart, the first gesture of the Litany of Infinity, using repetition to prepare her mind for quantum prediction.

Lead me inside the Loop.
Move me along my journey.
Carry me above the danger.
Today, tomorrow and forever.
Blessed is Infinity.

Prayer circled around her mouth and a diffuse warmth rose in her breast, followed by a streaking tingle of expanding awareness. With the delicacy of a dewdrop descending from a cat's whisker, the seed of a complete vision dripped into her mind's eye. Joy filled her veins as she became a flaming angel with mordant eyes and stepped onto the Infinite Net.

She could see a battlefield covered with broken bodies at next year's end. More fibers dipped in blood, another war for the Great Codex. Sister Alice focused her mind, rising above the emotions roiling in her throat. Her task was to watch and record. Neither side was hers to take. The Tapestry must continue no matter what it depicted. She reached for red yarn and tied it onto the heddles. She lowered the treadle, raised the frame, and threw the shuttle across warp lines with a wave of her hand. A panorama full of smoke and anger appeared line by line on the loom. At the head of the Mill, Sister Oda smiled with approval at Alice's progress.

●

Vespers — Twelve Hours after Dawn

Father Alberic poured himself another cup of red wine and left an empty bottle. Distant echoes of sonorous chanting slipped into his office through an open window. On his desk was Anselm's box. Once again, he poked at the scrap with his stylus, heedless of residual radiation. The Tapestry section was dull and colorless. Images on it were ghostly, resembling an overexposed transparency. He looked at the edges, noticing frayed ends where it had been hacked from the Tapestry. To cut something from the Tapestry was a cardinal sin, and an instant death sentence. He reviewed his journal, remembering Anselm, and his method became obvious to Alberic. As a trusted member of the order, Anselm had had access to the entire monastery. He could have made the Excision and inserted a counterfeit into the Tapestry as it came through the Divina Porta, but how had he known its location? Was there collusion with someone, at St. Clare's or somewhere else?

Alberic knew one thing with certainty, Anselm had broken his vows and stopped drinking the blue wine. Father Alberic's stomach churned as he thought of this abomination and the crisis rising for humanity if the Great Codex ran on broken, blasphemous code, forced into it by sabotage.

Alberic's journal of instruction contained only one solution. His eyes sought the dusty alcove in his office containing an ancient voice pipe. It was a direct line to St. Clare's monastery. He turned the old valve with care, praying it would stay intact and not snap off in his hand. When it opened with a gritty squeak, he exhaled with relief. With the small hammer hanging on the wall beside it, he banged on the pipe. He cleared his throat nervously. After a minute, he heard a valve open on the other end.

"Hello?" said Abbot Alberic.

"Order of St. Clare's Monastery. Is someone there?"

"Blessings to you, Sister. I am Father Alberic."

Her gasp hissed through the funnel in front of him. Then she cleared her throat and continued. "This is Mother Oda; I am the Abbess of St. Clare's. Greetings, Father. Do I have the honor of speaking to the Abbott of St. Benedict's?"

"Yes, I am he. Unfortunately, I bear terrible news. I think we should meet in the Shared Sanctum, so I can explain."

"The Shared Sanctum? Does that even exist?" Mother Oda's voice was mechanical, reflexive, as she remembered an unexplainable snarl in her probability calculations several days ago. Fearing the snarl was a potential anomaly, she made the ∞ unconsciously, seeking protection.

"Oh yes, Mother Oda," he was saying. "Look for a small door. There was a key on the wall next to our voice pipe." He silently rebuked himself for using the word 'look'.

"I'll find it," said Mother Oda. She was patting the lime-washed stone around the alcove, feeling for symbols, wandering away from the funnel.

"Shall I meet you there in an hour?" asked Alberic. He waited. Had she fainted? "Mother? Are you still there?"

"Yes, yes... I will be there," said Mother Oda with distracted impatience as she closed the valve and called for her assistant.

"Sister Jeanne, we must find the key to the Shared Sanctum. Something has happened to the Tapestry."

Father Alberic returned to his sideboard and opened another bottle of wine. He glanced at the lens above his head, thinking it had flashed momentarily, but it was silent and dark.

Father Alberic knelt on a prayer bench facing a simple altar in the Shared Sanctum. Round like a lighthouse, the room had doors on opposing sides. On the north wall, curved windows displayed sweeping views of the valley under the monasteries. Green fields spread out in orderly patchwork, livestock clustered in herds or flocks. The south wall gave a view onto gardens and orchards, heavy with ripening fruit. Above the altar was a stained-glass window made from the pitted relics of abandoned cathedrals, here a forgotten saint's hand dismembered from his body, there a child's face staring upward towards an angel's wings. The window filled the space with shards of colored light. A squeak of unused hinges shot flaming spears of pain through Father Alberic's hangover. He turned to look. A tiny nun entered, wearing the half-face veil of her order. She stopped just inside the door, sniffing the air like a beagle. She admonished him.

"You shouldn't drink red wine, Father Alberic. You've filled this room with a stink of fear and desperation."

"Mother Oda, I am full of fear and desperate for an answer," he said.

"Fear is a denial, acceptance is courage. At least, that is what they teach us, Father."

"You will need courage to accept this revelation, Mother. Please join me over here."

The abbess moved to the prayer bench and knelt next to him. He took her hand and guided it into the box he held. She gasped in surprise, pulling away as she felt the temporal radiation on her fingertips. In her mind, a twisted vision of displaced time snarled the probabilities like a broken kaleidoscope.

"How could this be…?"

"One of our senior monks died today. We found this beneath his pallet. We suspect the Decodatae, who are ever eager to throw chaos into our code, as you know. Anselm, our senior brother was their pawn, or a victim, if you wish."

"This Excision, what is its position on the Loop?"

"We found it today, so it's 2nd quarter."

"The current condition of the Tapestry?"

"A counterfeit image masks the Excision."

"The Great Codex?"

"It's disconnected from our system. The Actuators' Guild is waiting, rather impatiently, I might add."

"And what does the excised piece contain?"

"Mother Oda, it shows a plague, returning several times to kill."

"No wonder the Decodatae attacked. A deadly plague is tempting to those who worship chaos." Mother Oda's mind ran over the probable events and she shuddered at the results of every outcome. "The question remains, did they excise the Tapestry to fool us into eluding a plague, or do they want us to put it back into the Tapestry."

"Mother, I don't think we have a choice in this. Our doctrine requires us to encode the visions as they are."

There was a pause as they prayed together. Not wanting to appear rude, Father Alberic waited a good time before he asked his most delicate question. "Mother Oda, do you have a nun that can reweave this? Someone who will make the sacrifice?"

Mother Oda lowered her head in thought. At length she spoke, her smooth voice roughened with regret. "There is one, her second sight just bloomed. She is still a novice. Her loss will be minimal."

The Abbot nodded and then remembered she only saw visions. "I have a funeral service in an hour," he said, rising to his feet. "We shall reweave the Excision after our prayers for the Compline Mass."

The Abbess was on her feet heading for the door. Before she closed it, she paused. "Can you stomach this, Alberic? Infinity knows what will happen if we replace the Excision and load the plague code. Even with good intentions, our doctrine may set a course for destruction."

"Yes, I have those fears too, Mother," said Alberic as he stood at his door. "Consider this: if we don't reweave the Excision, and recode the correct information, will the Loop stay intact? Does your perception extend that far?"

"No, Father, my sight fails me on such a distant view," said Mother Oda, her mouth matching the grim horizontal line of her veil. "Sister Alice and I will be here at the appointed hour. We will pray for guidance in the meantime."

Father Alberic watched her dignified retreat into her side of the monasteries and listened to the key turn in the lock behind her.

"A risky choice is better than none. We shall purify what the Decodatae has fouled with their meddling," he muttered as he closed the sanctum door.

●

Evening meal

Cook's boys were sitting in the kitchen yard stuffing themselves with scraps. Their little dog tracked every morsel they ate, wagging its tail with unrepentant opportunism. The kitchen apprentice swallowed and paused for a moment.

"Have you ever been over there?"

"The other side of the monastery?"

"Yes, where the monks are."

"Only once. Cook asked me to bring a special cake over for the Feast of Saint Tempus Day."

"What do they do there?"

"They sit at high desks in a big workroom, surrounded by a long fabric which runs through the building on giant spools. I think they were looking at the pictures and copying them onto parchment."

"Why do they do that?"

"To make sure it comes true, I guess."

"Oh," said Cook's apprentice. "What happens if it doesn't?"

"Sister Alice told me whatever the Tapestry shows will always come true because it's put into the Great Codex which runs the world."

"Oh, do you mean the baby's song?"

"Yes, you know it..."

Run around, run around,
seven beggars baiting.
Feed the Codex, wind it down,
a perfect world is waiting.

The kitchen apprentice laughed, and the other boy tossed a bone to his grateful dog.

●

The Inversion started an hour after Vespers. It began imperceptibly, as the persistent, comforting rumble of the Mill faded to silence. Then with creaking groans, the gears reversed their direction. It sounded unfamiliar this time, a backward rhythm, broken by random cries of slipping belts and squeaking spools. In their silent dining hall, the nuns stopped eating, spoons halfway to their mouths. One of them knocked over her wine glass, and it shattered musically. Mother Oda touched the edge of her bowl to locate it and put her spoon strategically on the table. Her chair scraped white lines on the slate floor as she stood to speak.

"My dear flock, the monks in the Order of St. Benedict have found a problem with the Tapestry."

The silence became deeper as every nun held her breath; they listened and feared for the worst.

"Today they discovered there was an Excision in the Tapestry."

Gasps and cries of dismay came from around the hall and half the nuns spoke aloud, breaking their mealtime vow of silence. Sister Oda rapped her knuckles on the table and they restrained their tongues.

"We have stopped the Mill, and now our brothers are performing an Inversion to isolate the section where the Excision occurred. Once we get there, one of us will remove the counterfeit and reweave the Tapestry." The nuns whispered among themselves, and Mother Oda once more rapped on the table.

"This task is for a young nun with pure vision. The procedure is dangerous. Whoever committed the Excision tried to prevent a plague. The weaver will experience those horrors as she repairs the Tapestry." The nuns listened with uneasy apprehension, shifting on the benches. One sobbed. Mother Oda paused and let them absorb that information for a few minutes.

She continued with a slight tremble in her authoritative voice. "Whatever we reweave into the Tapestry affects the Great Codex. A ripple in our temporal-space called the Unda Effectus may appear. There are consequences. My Sisters, let us pray for their rapid dissipation."

The nuns bowed their heads and chanted. Cook embraced her boys, wiping tears from her eyes with a greasy dishtowel. The boys feigned bravery, trying to look resolute. Beneath the monasteries, the Tapestry uncoiled as it wound backwards through St. Benedict's, piling up in baskets at the Divina Porta.

Disconnected from a coded stream of new commands, the Actuators' Guild tried to put the Great Codex into a recursive pattern before it calculated itself into deadlock. Principal Actuator cajoled the Great Codex, promising entertaining games, if it would stop processing for a day. He might have shouted at the wind for the influence he had over the machine. It writhed against the constrictions and hissed angrily at Principal Actuator.

"We will not stop, we do not sleep for anyone. We will enact recursion on the population, because we control this world, not the Actuators, or the Monasteries."

Endless snow fell in the mountains, women found the labor of birth suspended in interminable pain, the last gasps of the dying extended to a prolonged moan. Principal Actuator fell from the branches of the Great Codex, dead before he hit the roots.

●

Compline — Fifteen Hours after Dawn

Sister Alice entered the Shared Sanctum with Mother Oda, carrying a basket of wool yarns. The two nuns stood in silence. They waited, fingering their Möbius beads. A few minutes later, another door opened and Father Alberic came out to meet them. He stepped forward to take Sister Alice's hand in his own. She touched the warm, un-calloused fingers of a scribe and scholar.

"We thank you, Sister Alice, for your sacrifice."

"My honor and duty, Father Alberic."

"This is Brother Stephen; he discovered the Excision."

Mother Oda and Sister Alice inclined their heads toward Brother Stephen. He cleared his throat, trying to release the tension in his vocal cords. "Please allow us to guide you to the chapel. We have set a place for you to work undisturbed."

Towing the nuns by their elbows, Stephen and Alberic guided them through St. Benedict's monastery. As they walked along the cloisters and by the rows of cells, the other monks watched in silence from doorways and alcoves. As Stephen passed Master Reader, his cheeks flushed under the hostile appraisal. Stephen was breaking a vow by touching Sister Alice, and there was no help for it. He felt grateful that Oda and Alice couldn't see his shame and for the gift of forgetfulness that would come later with the blue wine.

After several minutes, they entered the chapel to follow the Tapestry as it coiled through an elliptical nave. From the echoes of their footfalls, Sister Alice knew the ceiling was high and curved. They stopped at the crossing beside the choir stalls. She could see a faint glow ahead in the darkness. Called spirit-light by the other nuns, it appeared as her brain tried to create a visual image without her eyes.

In the middle of the chapel, on top of a high table, a large frame isolated the Excision. Two girandoles, each branching to hold sixteen beakers of luciferin, filled the nave with light green brilliance. Beside the frame, the excised fabric reposed inside a slow-glass press.

Brother Stephen led Alice to the table, and she touched its surface to find a place for her basket of yarn. The others withdrew behind panels of slow-glass. Sister Alice stroked the Excision, sensing the residual current of temporal energy trapped within the scrap. She explored the excised Tapestry, feeling the ragged welts and the dead, coarse surface of the counterfeit patch. Blocked by scars, the temporal current, the visionary flow pooled around the counterfeit, churning at its edges.

"There are scars around the Excision. I will make fresh cuts in the Tapestry to remove them."

She heard Stephen ahem to clear his throat. His gentle voice was soft on her ears. "Yes, Sister." said Brother Stephen. "We hope you can weave a seamless transition."

"I shall do my best," she said, and began her weaver's hymn.

Blessed be the Spirit who guides my Sight.
Blessed be the Loom that binds my Visions.
Blessed be the Tapestry, may it Loop without end.

"Blessings on you, Sister Alice. Thank you for your sacrifice," said Stephen.

Alice missed his response as she thought of home, of her self-important father, her condescending sister, and marveled at her new status in the world. Mundane thoughts gave way to the ecstasy of temporal transcendence as Alice left monastery time and rose to the Infinite Net holding the scrap of tapestry like a wounded child. Sister Alice was bathing in the light of joy, unbound by time. The pain/pleasure of ecstasy coursed up her spine. She was standing on a giant grid of locations and time. Scenes rose from the mangled scrap of Tapestry, showing her the missing events and where to cross the gaps in time.

The monks gaped as she transformed into a towering angel, blinding bright, singing with the voice of a bronze bell. Both men dropped to their knees, performing the Litany of Infinity, making the ∞ repeatedly in the air.

Alice stroked her fingers along the edges of the counterfeit, feeling where to cut. Piece by piece, the painted canvas fell onto the floor, smoking as it disintegrated into ash. Once she had cleared the opening, Sister Alice found the warp lines and, with a twist of her fingers, added new extensions, tying them off as tightly as she dared. Mother Oda leaned towards Father Alberic. Her sibilant whispers made flickering echoes in the chapel.

"What do you think, Father Alberic?"

"It is miraculous. She has removed the counterfeit and is recreating the warp lines."

Mother Oda's serene face masked the grim probabilities flowing around her head. She nodded in Stephen's direction. "Do you have the reliquary ready for her?"

"Yes, Mother Oda," said Brother Stephen. "She will go into stasis, the undying beatification."

●

Images of disease and death, a panorama of horror from one end of the world to the other filled Alice's mind, and the only sound she heard was the drum of her heart. As she reattached the remaining section of her weaving, the temporal energy spilled into the rewoven fabric, irradiating her hands. With a suppressed groan, she fell like a wingless angel from her temporal plateau, away from the Tapestry and back into monastery time. With a blank face, holding up hands burned black to the bone, she pitched forward. Brother Stephen rushed over and caught her in his arms. He carried her to the back of the chapel and laid her body on a table to prepare it for the reliquary. As they parted for the evening, Mother Oda spoke to Father Alberic.

"Rest well, Alberic. I hope to speak with you tomorrow."

"And I hope the same, Mother."

Mother Oda closed the sanctum door and re-locked it.

●

Later that evening, Brother Stephen sat in his cell sipping the blue wine. He found Brother Anselm's tablet in his pocket and gazed at the smeared letters as bliss enveloped his mind. Later that night, he smoothed the wax on the face of the tablet, smiling as he sang the only song he could remember, a lullaby from childhood.

In the Scriptorium, Master Reader examined Alice's repair on the Tapestry through a slow-glass lens, mumbling as he transcribed. Depraved images flickered and slashed across the desk in front of his eyes. Merchant ships full of dying sailors arrived with a plague carried on the backs of rats. Constantey fell, Marsey succumbed, and death entered the North Channel to kill again and again in Britten. Crow faced physicians stepped over the dying that littered filth covered streets. An undertow of shocked revulsion dragged at his consciousness, tempting him to seek oblivion in the blue wine. He countered temptation with the Litany of Infinity and its words buoyed his spirit, maintaining resolve. The sharp lines of Master Reader's face and body hardened, until he resembled a leathery gargoyle perched on his stool. Three days later, Master Reader died, unrepentant for the useless sacrifice of Anselm and Alice.

The Great Codex, humming with pure glee, read the code and orchestrated its machineries. The Actuators sickened and died, leaving the Great Codex running unattended.

The monasteries failed, filling with dust and rot as their members died off. Out in the world, the people noticed signs of change as political power shifted from church to state. Economies seesawed as the plague broke the social order and strewed good fortune on the lower classes. In the echoing stone halls of the abandoned Scriptorium, the Tapestry hung in rotting tatters from sagging spools, sections heaped on the floor under piles of blank parchment tape. The Decodatae came to power, worshiping the Untethered god. The Great Codex ran on by itself, enjoying a new game.

•

Many Loops later

The young cleric was glad of the rain because it kept the ancient chapel cool during their brief, hot summer. She knelt, holding her hands upraised and apart. The tattoos on her arms blazed with metallic inks, representing her rank in the Decodatae. She recited the old prayer, more from habit than inspiration.

Blessed be the Anomaly.
Protect us from Recursion.
Deliver us with Deadlock.

As she was leaving, she paused in the nave to look at the saint's body again. Beneath the gilded slow-glass reliquary, Saint Alice lay in eternal repose. With her bandaged hands crossed upon her chest, she lay deathless in the embrace of temporal stasis.

It seemed to the cleric that someone was whispering in the Old Standard dialect. She looked around and noticed the tarnished metal branches moving overhead. The voice was chanting a song, and if she listened carefully, she could make out the words. The voice sounded childlike, high and breathless.

Run around, run around,
seven beggars baiting.
Feed the Codex, wind it down,
a perfect world is waiting.

"We are pleased to meet you," said the voice. "Would you like to play a game with us?"

●

A.C. Worth's story "The Tapestry" was originally published in Metaphorosis on Friday, 22 June 2018. See magazine.metaphorosis.com

About the author

Ann Cudworth discovered her penchant for storytelling as a girl growing up in the suburbs of Boston. Her desire to create bigger and weirder worlds led to a career in television, and for decades, she lived the gentile life of a broadcast television set designer in Brooklyn, NY. Eventually, she felt the urge to return to New England and storytelling and now lives dangerously in lively coastal New Hampshire. When not writing, Ann enjoys epic baseball games and culinary experimentation. Under the pen name of A C Worth, she writes in the science fiction/second world/fantasy/romance genres. Published work includes a monk-punk fantasy called "The Tapestry" — *Metaphorosis* (2018), a robot-romance entitled "Homecoming" — *Score: an SFF symphony* anthology (2019), "The Day the Sandlot Sharks played the Hardware Hammers", about a little league championship on a generational spaceship — *Sci-Fi Lampoon* (2020), and a flash fiction concerning false gods called "Stone God" — in *The New Exterus, Volume I* (2021). She is currently submitting new short stories and working on her third novel, *The Woman Who Walked Around the Moon*.

It Thaws in Spring

Brittany M. Perkins

Lena lived under the ice. She might have always been there, or perhaps she had lived on the surface once. It didn't matter. Lena could not remember a time when she had not floated in the still waters below the frozen pond, a time when she knew things other than damp and cold and dark.

The under was a vast expanse of water, which, with an effort of great concentration, could be molded into ghostly rooms or objects, though these structures were easily dispersed with a wave of the hand. Impermanence was the way of the under, and it was the way of the ice children as well. There were only four of them now (Lena and Edna and Rebecca and Julian), and every winter began with the uncertainty of how many would remain.

Winter was all Lena knew, all she could experience and remember. She never saw the pond melt in spring, although Edna assured her that it did. Edna never saw this either. Instead, Lena and the others awoke each winter, the ice above them firmly intact, aware that time had passed, but unsure what had happened in the interim. And sometimes, when winter came, someone would be missing.

There had once been more of them, but Lena had not seen Raymond in four winters and Matteo in seven. Lena didn't remember much past twelve winters back, but she had heard other names, of children who had disappeared before her memories began: Cindy, Lola, Isaac. After Raymond hadn't come back, the other children grew more and more distant, until the under became a silent place, and Lena worried that one day he too would be only a name to them.

Lena was drifting through the under, thinking of those who were no longer with them when she spotted Edna, sitting in a chair. A swirling current that had not quite solidified made up its curving frame, and an elaborate tea set was suspended in the space in front of her. Many winters back, before it had become just the four of them, Edna had often talked with Lena, but, lately, Edna rarely acknowledged her at all. Lena approached the girl who had once taught her how to spin up towers and tea sets from the water around them. In the old days, Edna would brighten at Lena's approach and immediately invite her into a story or game she had come up with, but that never happened anymore.

Today, Lena hovered beside Edna, studying her, while the other girl hardly seemed to notice. "Can I join your party?" Lena asked, conjuring a chair of her own, more solid than Edna's, and sitting across from her former friend.

Edna glanced at the teapot and the cup in her hand as though seeing them for the first time.

Lena waited a moment before continuing: "What are you playing? Are you a princess? Or a society lady?"

Edna looked at Lena, opening her mouth as if to speak, but no sound emerged.

"Why don't you talk to me anymore?" Lena asked. "Why don't any of you ever want to play?" Lena rose from her chair, and the structure dispersed into the depths around them. "You used to be fun," she said. And then, softer, "You used to like me."

As Lena withdrew from the girl she had once considered a friend, she thought she heard Edna speak, a barely audible rasp: "I'm sorry."

●

One of Lena's earliest memories was of Matteo, and it was really more of a feeling than a memory. The memory was a single image of Matteo, pushing a ball made of water toward her. He was laughing. And the feeling was of excitement and joy. That was the best way to describe Matteo: joyful. But the winter before he disappeared, something had been different.

Once, that final winter, Lena had approached the watery rocket ship where Matteo had resided for going on three days. She crept through the half-formed hatch, careful not to disturb the structure's fragile architecture, and inched upward toward the boy who had once filled the underneath with such light and laughter. As Lena neared him, she could see that Matteo was in constant motion, wafting back and forth across the small space at the top of the rocket.

"Matteo?" Lena called up to him.

He did not answer, an eerie smile dragging up the corners of his mouth, as if against their will.

"Are you alright?" she asked. "Do you want to play a game?"

Matteo floated in a slow circle to face her, and although his eyes met hers, they were cloudy and seemed not to see her at all. Then his right hand shot out, grasping for her. Lena couldn't remember what had happened next, but she knew that she had left, and the next thing she could picture in her mind's eye was talking to Raymond.

None of the ice children knew how old they were, but Raymond had always felt older than the rest. So when she told him about Matteo's unresponsiveness, Lena expected an explanation.

Instead, she received a shrug. "That happens sometimes," Raymond said. "Matteo is very social, and it's been hard on him not having new children to play with."

"But I asked him to play, and he wouldn't talk to me," Lena said. "Why does he need someone new if I'm right here?"

Raymond sighed, not meeting Lena's eyes. "I don't know, Lena," he said, the slightest edge of frustration creeping into his voice. "I've tried to tell them — all of them — to be grateful for what we have here, but they always want more. I can't make them happy, and I just..." Raymond clenched his fists so hard and fast that a small current swirled around them. Then he looked at Lena. "You're happy, right? Even with just the six of us?"

"Of course," Lena said, though she wasn't sure that was true. She remembered that feeling of joy from years ago, but she couldn't think of the last time she'd felt it. "I'm very happy, Raymond."

When Matteo didn't come back during the following winter freeze, Lena had been confused. She was the only one who hadn't seen it happen before. Lena had searched for Matteo, and when she was nearly sure but not quite believing that Matteo was gone for good, Lena had asked Edna where he was. She received only a slow shake of the head in response before Edna drifted away, leaving a trail of silt in her wake. Lena soon learned it was taboo to talk about the disappearances, which was why she only had the whispered names of those who had already gone. But Raymond was different. Raymond would talk.

One night, Raymond appeared beside the bed Lena had willed together out of water droplets. The ice children never slept in winter, but they did rest, and sometimes, they dreamed. Lena had been dreaming. In the dream, a girl, whose face Lena could not see, hovered above her, near the ice. Lena was falling away from the girl, as though sucked into an undertow. The girl's hand reached toward Lena, and Lena reached out in return, but their fingers never met. As the distance between the two increased, Lena saw a sunray peek around the girl's head, but she soon faded away, leaving Lena staring into the blaring sunlight.

As Lena tried to call after the girl, she felt algae tickling at the sides of her mouth. She thought it was only part of the dream, until a hand lightly brushed across her shoulder. The coldness of Raymond's skin, which was blue with chill and slightly slimy, like they all were, startled her. Before she could call out, Raymond put a slender finger to his lips. "You want to know what happened, don't you?" He did not wait for Lena to respond. "Do you ever feel alone, Lena?"

Before she could think through the action, Lena nodded.

"We all do, and sometimes we feel so alone that we can't stand it. Sometimes during spring, we get so lonely that our ears are searching, even if we are not. And sometimes our ears find them: the children of the surface.

We might hear a laugh or a splash, but it's enough, enough to wake us and call us upward."

Lena's eyes moved back to Raymond's. "Does that mean the others went to the surface?" She sat up, sending loose bubbles and mud flying as her pillow lost form and dispersed. "Is Matteo up there now?"

"We used to have many children," he said. "And for a long time, it wasn't like this. We were happy. We played games. We weren't just... quiet."

"But if they were lonely, why did they leave their friends?" Lena's bed flittered into nothing as she floated upright.

"They were bored with just us," he said. "They needed *new* children — new friends. They got greedy, and now they're all gone."

"Are they on the surface?" Lena's voice was pleading.

"No. We can't live up there. We can't go back, not once we're here."

"Go back?" She thought of the girl from her dream, reaching out to her from the surface.

"More of the surface children used to play on the ice in winter. They would skate and sled, and sometimes, they would fall through. After a while, I guess they decided it was too dangerous."

"What happened... when they fell?" Lena thought she knew, but she didn't want to. She wanted to be wrong. At the edge of her memory, she heard the scrape of blades on ice.

"The ice children would save them. But to save them, we'd have to *change* them, get rid of who they were before. When the surface children stopped coming in the winter, the others still wanted to save them. But that doesn't work in the spring. It only works with the ice. In the spring, they just drown, or they swim away. And if we go after them, we disappear." He took a deep breath, and the water swirled around his mouth. "We're barely here in the spring, not even ghosts, and when we go up there, we're nothing."

"What if we go up in the winter?" Lena asked.

"We don't."

"Why not?"

"Because of the ice." And he turned and drifted away.

●

Lena was lonely, under the ice. She missed Raymond and his stories about how things used to be. She missed Matteo and his games and high spirits. And it was on a very lonely day, when the sun breached the ice and lit up the underneath, that Lena first heard it: a child of the surface laughing.

Lena soared upward, the water's temperature seeming to rise as she ascended, and stopped just in time not to hit her head on the ice. As she arrived, something thumped above her, and she saw a blurred shadow cover the ice above like a rug. Then the laughter came again, followed by a faint call: "Claire! Claire, get back here. It's too dangerous. Come back to the shore." The caller's voice was like an icepick driving into Lena's brain, and she suddenly felt scared and cold.

"Okay." This voice was closer, clearer, and somehow warmer as well, taking the edge off of Lena's fear. This voice came from the shadow, and as Lena realized this, the shadow moved, became smaller, and began to recede toward the edge of the pond, the water cooling in its wake.

Lena followed the shadow as fast as she could. Claire's shadow quickly outpaced her and was gone, taking the laughter with it. Lena continued her pursuit until she came to the pond's edge. She pressed a hand against it, mud wafting around the point of contact. She tried to grab a chunk of the muddy bank, but it was too tightly packed. Lena let go and wandered back toward the middle of the pond.

When she returned, Lena saw two structures, and she could see the occupants of each through the water that comprised them: a cottage with missing bricks and a crooked chimney (Edna) and a ship that was cracked down the middle, with only half a flag dangling from its too-short mast (Rebecca and Julian). Lena burst into the cottage where Edna sat in a one-armed armchair, a plate balanced on her lap, in front of a fire that would have been roaring had the flames been more than water held in shape by Edna's wishes. When Lena reached her, she stood in front of Edna's chair, blocking her view of the heatless flames. "So, what do you think happened to Raymond?"

Edna choked on her water droplet toast. "What do you mean?" she rasped. Edna looked older than Lena, but not by much. Lena knew Edna remembered longer, though, and knew things the others did not.

"I mean, where is he? And Matteo? Where did they go?"

"It's best not to —" Her voice was clearer now, though still sharp around the edges.

"Raymond said they got lonely and bored and that you think they go to the surface and evaporate."

"Lena."

"I saw someone today."

Edna's eyes brightened for a moment. "Where?"

"She was skating on top of the ice. A surface child." Lena paused, deciding whether or not to go on. "Raymond said there used to be more of us. He said surface children would fall through the ice."

Edna closed her eyes. "Yes," she said. "That was the way. But not anymore." Edna placed a hand on Lena's cheek. "You used to be so warm," she said, and Lena felt a chill run through her, though she wasn't sure if it came from Edna's touch or her words.

Lena recoiled and turned to face the fire, wishing it and its heat were real.

"I wish you still were," Edna said, reaching toward Lena again, her fingers barely brushing Lena's forearm before Lena fled, not wanting that chill to spread elsewhere on her body.

Lena hovered briefly above the cottage, rubbing her cheek. Then she entered the ship, where Rebecca and Julian were clapping their hands together, chanting nonsense rhymes and giggling. The two moved their hands in a circle and spun up three small dolls from the bubbles around them. The dolls hung near Rebecca's head, and she giggled again.

"What are you playing?" Lena asked, moving closer to the pair. "Can I play too?" Lena could remember a time when she had played with the two — Edna called them twins — but that was long ago, when Matteo and Raymond still occupied the underneath. "When you clap like that," Lena added, still feeling Edna's cold handprint on her cheek, "how does it feel?"

The twins did not look at her. "Did you hear something?" Julian asked Rebecca, not breaking the rhythm of their clapping. Neither seemed to wince or react in the slightest to the other's touch.

"It's the dollies," Rebecca said, inclining her head toward the bubble creations suspended to her left. Lena wanted to reach out and slap one of their hands to answer her own question, but instead, she departed the ship. Once free of the twins' rhymes, Lena willed herself her own structure: a twisting tower, like you would find at the top of a castle, but without the castle.

Lena surged to the top of the tower, which nearly brushed the ice, and as she sometimes had over the past four winters, closed her eyes, and spoke to the only friend who had ever been truly honest with her. "Raymond," Lena said. "I saw someone today. It was a surface child, and she was on top of the ice. I heard her laugh, and I heard someone calling her, and then she got away. I tried to catch her, but she —" A voice seemed to call from somewhere deep within Lena, jerking her sideways and sending pieces of parapet flying. It was the voice that had called Claire, except it was calling for her instead. As Lena shook away the imagined sound, something drew her eyes upward. She looked from the ice to her hands, feeling like they had not always been blue, and almost, but not quite, remembering what warmth felt like. *Claire would be warm.* The thought came, unbidden, and pulled Lena's gaze upward again. Claire would come back. She had to.

●

After what could have been three weeks or two months — Lena had never been good at measuring time — the light shifted overhead, and Lena felt the slightest kiss of sunlight on her cheek. She flew toward the surface, and, through the icy blur, Lena thought she saw skate blades gliding overhead. She watched for a moment, in awe, and then panic set in. What if this was her only chance to have a friend again? Dizzy at the thought of losing Claire forever, Lena raised a shaking fist and rapped on the ice. In what seemed like an instantaneous response, the figure above collided with the ice with a thud. The shadow filled the patch of ice above Lena, but this time, there was no laughter.

Lena was quick. She pressed her face against the ice to one side of the shadow. Lena rarely ventured this high in the pond, and the solid dryness of the ice always surprised her. "Hello?" she said. "Claire?"

For just a moment, Lena saw blurred eyes in a dark face. Then she heard a muffled scream as the figure jumped up, and the shadow quickly receded toward the shore.

Lena pursued, this time keeping pace for nearly twice as long as before, but still, when the figure reached the shore, Lena could not follow. Lena buried her face in the muddy bank and screamed. As she did, she again heard someone calling her name. It was less of a call and more of a shriek. And then it was all shriek and no words.

●

The possibility of seeing Claire — she was sure it had been Claire — again filled Lena with such desperation that her stomach ached. The other ice children either ignored her or took from her, but Lena sensed that Claire had something to give, and Lena had not been given anything in a long, long time. Lena thought that if she could talk to Claire, a bit of warmth and joy might make its way into the under, and maybe things could be how they once were. So she hovered under the patch of ice, waiting for Claire's return. She did this every time she could see sunlight, and did not retreat until all light drained away, occasionally scratching or tapping on the ice above to feel closer to Claire and the surface. Lena wondered how many ice children had waited like this. She wondered who had waited for her.

She was engaged in such thoughts when the shadow returned. A soft thud sounded above Lena's head, and she moved as close to the ice as she could.

The blurred face appeared above her. "A-are you still there?" It was Claire's voice.

"Claire?" Lena said, and Claire recoiled. "Wait. Don't. Please."

Claire's face returned. "Sorry," she said. "You're a little bit scary." Claire paused. "Say, how do you know my name?"

Their conversation was muted, as through a tunnel, but Lena could understand her clearly. "I heard someone calling you," Lena said. "The first time I saw you." She paused. "You didn't see me that time."

"Oh," Claire said. "That was my mom." Every word Claire spoke was like a little ray of warmth through the ice, and sometimes, the warmth burned.

The burn at the mention of the screaming woman from their first encounter was too much; Lena needed to change the subject. "Do you like to skate?" Lena asked, and she could almost feel herself gliding smoothly over the ice.

"What? Oh, yes. I do."

These words muted the heat, now more of a comfort than a burn.

Claire continued: "It's just my mom thinks it's dangerous. She doesn't trust the pond to hold out, says I'll fall through."

Lena heard a cracking sound from the corner of her memory and winced again, but it was less intense this time. "Are you afraid?" she asked. "Are you afraid you'll fall?"

Claire laughed, and Lena moved closer. The ice between them made the laugh sound far off, like it was coming from somewhere Lena couldn't quite reach. "No. Nothing scares me. Well, except you." She paused before adding, "But not anymore." Claire's shadow shifted. "Besides, I just come when she's sleeping. Mom sleeps a lot during the day, actually."

Lena didn't know how to respond to any of this. She was overwhelmed and excited and somehow afraid of what Claire might say next.

"I'm sorry. What's your name? I didn't even ask you."

"Lena."

"Huh," Claire said. "My mom had a sister named Lena."

Lena shuddered.

"They used to live where we do now. We moved to the cabin to help when Grandma got sick. She died a few months back."

The feeling of lying under a quilt, safe and warm, filled Lena's mind for a moment until the face of an older girl invaded the vision, scorching it around the edges. "What's your mom's name?" Lena asked, inching closer to the flame of Claire's voice.

Claire's shadow shifted again, and Lena worried that she'd upset her, that maybe she'd leave now. "It's Margaret," she said, finally. "But everyone calls her Maggie."

The name set Lena's thoughts afire. "What... happened... to... her sister?" she asked, needing a break between nearly every word.

"She died. Or they think she did. She must have. They never found a body, though. Mom was a lot older, and she was supposed to have been watching her. Mom and Grandma fought a lot after that." Claire trailed off before asking, "Hey, what *are* you?"

"I — I don't understand."

"Like, how did you get down there? There aren't even fish in this pond anymore. Are you a mermaid or something?"

Raymond had told Lena that there used to be fish. They had disappeared a long time ago, though. Even Raymond hadn't known why. "I'm just down here," Lena said. "I've always been down here. I — I'm an ice child."

"An ice child?" Claire asked. "I've never heard of that." Claire moved her face closer to the ice. "I can't see you very well," she said.

"Not much to see," Lena answered, dragging a fingernail across the underside of the ice and sending a curl of frost receding toward the pond's floor. She didn't want to explain herself anymore. She didn't want to tell Claire about the other children. She just wanted Claire to keep talking, because even though the warmth of her words hurt, they made Lena feel more *real* somehow, and Lena needed that.

"Listen," Claire said, "I have to go. Mom will be up soon, and she'll never let me out of the house again if she knows I've been here."

"Wait —" Lena started. But Claire was already on her feet, skating for shore.

●

"Do you remember that surface child I told you about?" Lena asked.

Edna was silent, still as the water around her.

"She talked to me, asked how I got down here."

Edna closed her eyes but made no move to speak.

"Was I one of the children who fell? Like they used to? Claire's mother had a sister: Lena."

Edna opened her eyes, pain filling the icy blueness of them. "You were mine," she rasped. "Yes. You fell too. You were skating, but it was too thin." Edna's voice caught a bit. "It shouldn't have been so thin, but it was."

And as she said this, Lena could almost remember. It felt like remembering the feeling of a dream, but not knowing what it was about. "And you saved me."

"Yes. To save one, you have to take out the warmth. They can't live down here with that. But with the warmth goes the memory. Everyone starts over down here."

Lena took a breath. "Did everyone come from the surface? All of us?"

"I think so," Edna said. "I can't know that for sure. I can only remember the ones who came after me, and most of them are gone now. But I remember you, and I remember Rebecca and Julian. They came down together. I remember when Matteo fell. I don't remember a time before Raymond. I think he's the one who saved me. But that was long ago."

Lena still could not remember. Only the shrieking was left, but excitement quickly overtook it. "Maybe Claire will fall," she said.

Edna's eyes brightened. "She might."

"Claire would be new. She could make things good again."

"Would you do that?" Edna asked. "Would you save Claire for us?"

"Of course," Lena said. "I'm tired of alone."

●

Claire spread out on her belly on the ice. She had not visited in what seemed a long time, and Lena had been antsy. "Sorry," Claire said.

The single word left Lena slightly singed, and she wanted more.

"Mom's been having a hard time. She always does in winter. I think it's —"

"How old are you?" Lena had not spoken to anyone since her conversation with Edna, and her voice came out rushed and clipped.

"Uh, twelve, but I'll be thirteen next month." Claire paused, dragging a gloved finger through the frost covering the ice. "How old are you, Lena?"

"I — I'm not sure..." At the fuzzy edge of something like memory, Lena saw an older girl, someone who loved her and protected her. "Say, how old was your mom's sister when she...?"

"Well, Mom was nineteen, I think, so that would've made her sister eleven."

Lena felt herself swoon slightly, certain now that she was also eleven, and that she had been eleven for a very long time. "Are your friends twelve, too?" she asked a little breathlessly.

Claire sat up, her blurred face blending into the rest of her shadow. "I don't really have any," she said. "They just kind of stopped coming around once my grandma got sick."

"But they could visit," Lena said, nervously scraping the ice with a nail. She imagined how warm they would all be, Claire and her friends. "They could skate with you. You could be friends again."

Claire's shadow shifted slightly. "I don't think so."

"Why not?"

"It just doesn't work like that," Claire said. "We don't talk anymore, and I had to change schools. And Mom doesn't really like visitors. Even before everything... happened, she liked to keep to herself."

Lena was overwhelmed with the feeling of a shy, reserved presence. She sighed, working the edge out of her voice. "That's okay," she said. Then a thought occurred: "We can be friends, then."

Claire shifted again, hesitating. "Th-that's sweet of you."

"You should visit more often." Lena paused, as though deciding something. "It's lonely when you're gone."

"Is it just you down there?"

"Yes," Lena lied. "There used to be others, but they went away."

Claire's shadow was still for a moment. "Lena, did you ever have a sister?"

Lena shrank back from the ice. "No."

"It's just, my mom's sister, she drowned, and I was wondering —"

"It's just me," Lena said. "And I've always been here."

"Listen, I have to get back. Mom will be waking up soon." And before Lena could respond, Claire's shadow began to move away.

When Claire was completely gone, Lena again slid a fingernail along the underside of the ice. Pressing harder this time, she scraped off a thin mist of shavings. Claire didn't understand how important it was for them to be friends, but she would. And so, Lena lingered there, scraping at the barrier between her and the warmth of her new friend until the sun was gone.

●

That night, just as Lena was nearly to dreaming, Edna appeared at her feet. Lena sat up, dispersing her sleeping mat and waiting for the other to speak, but Edna floated silently, staring down at Lena.

"Edna?" Lena said at last.

"Yes," Edna said, her voice a slowly clearing rasp. "Did you see her today? The girl from the surface?"

"I did."

"And will she be back? Do you think she'll fall?"

"I — I think so," Lena said. "I told her we could be friends."

Edna's eyes widened, a hungry look growing in them. "When will she be back?"

Lena shrugged. "Edna, is it okay to... to *help* them fall?"

Edna's blue-tinged ear twitched. "Do you mean to thin the ice?"

"Uh, yes. I guess so. Would that — would that be bad?"

Edna moved closer, close enough to touch. "We used to do it sometimes, just when we needed more friends. Matteo did it a lot. Raymond was always very mad when we did."

"So, it is bad, then?"

Edna looked away before placing a hand on Lena's forearm.

Lena shivered.

"My hands are colder than yours," Edna said. "Did you know that?"

Lena shook her head.

"You think that we don't talk to you because we don't want to, but really we can't remember how."

"I don't —"

"Raymond said that the other ice children disappeared because they were lonely, that we saved the surface children because we were bored, but that was never it. He didn't understand. You don't either, Lena, because you're the newest, but you will, soon."

Lena retreated slightly, putting distance between herself and Edna.

"I don't remember how to start talking anymore. Someone has to talk to me first, and then I can, but I can't start it. Rebecca and Julian — they were twins before, on the surface, always together — they can only remember how to talk to each other. To save a surface child, we have to take away their warmth, and the longer we're down here, the colder we get."

"And with the warmth goes the memory," Lena said.

Edna nodded. "Yes." She advanced toward Lena. "Do you remember that you used to sing?"

Lena gave her head a single shake.

"You did. All the time, but now it's gone. Sing me something."

Lena tried to think but could not find what singing was. "I can't," she said.

"Because you forgot. And you'll forget more, the colder you get." Edna began to drift back and forth in front of Lena, as though pacing. "Matteo and the others didn't leave because they wanted to bring back children; they left because they were so cold that they forgot they couldn't go. You can't be warm and live down here, and once you're here, you can't go back.

"The reason we saved those children and helped some of them fall was because new children help us remember what it's like to be warm. When the new children stopped coming, we couldn't remember anymore. But Raymond always said it wasn't fair. Not fair. Not fair."

Lena drew her limbs close to herself, as though afraid that Edna would take them from her. "If Raymond saved you," Lena started, "then he'd have to understand."

Edna shook her head. "He was different. Raymond was always different."

"Who saved Raymond?"

Edna shrugged. "We never knew, and he wouldn't say. I think maybe Raymond saved himself. I think maybe he was the first."

"But Raymond left. He must have been cold too."

"Maybe," Edna said. "Or maybe he knew what he was doing. Maybe he didn't want to watch us forget anymore." Edna closed in on Lena again, grabbing her by the collar. "You have to save Claire," she said. "We need her, Lena. You have to save her. I — I'm cold."

And it was true. Lena could feel the chill through her frayed shirt.

"You're the newest, Lena, which means one day you'll be all alone. Alone for real. Things didn't used to be like this. We used to have fun. We used to be happy. You're still warmer than I am, Lena, but touching you is like remembering my name. Touching a surface child would be like remembering who I am. Claire can help all of us."

Lena pulled back, breaking Edna's loose grasp. "Okay," she said. "I'll save her."

"Thank you," Edna said, and she wrapped her arms around Lena tight enough to hurt.

Lena felt a chill run through her, a chill that she was sure would stay there now, for always, although she couldn't remember why.

●

Whenever the sun broke through the ice, Lena raced toward the surface to wait for Claire, and each time Claire did not arrive, Lena worked at scraping the ice. She would drag her nails back and forth, shaving off the thinnest layers until by the time Claire returned, their patch of ice was noticeably thinner.

Claire arrived this time not in skates, but in boots, and she squatted over the patch rather than lying on her belly. "Sorry, Lena," she said, and her voice sounded hoarse, not quite warm enough to burn just yet, and Lena ached to get closer to her. "Mom's been really bad lately. I think she knows I've been skating on the pond. She won't say anything, but she hid my skates."

As Claire said this, Lena almost felt that it had happened to her instead. Lena had found her skates, though, hadn't she?

"Listen, Lena," Claire started, "I don't think that I'll be able to come back. It's getting late in the season, and Mom's probably right that it's not so safe now."

"No," Lena said. "You have to come back." Lena remembered falling on the ice, someone carrying her, a sprained wrist. She remembered an arm around her shoulder and a kiss on her forehead. "If anything happens, I can save you," she said.

"That's very kind, Lena," Claire said, but her voice did not have the same warmth as her words. "I just don't — Oh no."

"What is it?"

"I think my mom is outside the cabin. I think —"

And then Lena heard it, the screaming woman: "Claire! Claire, come back!" Lena imagined that voice — Maggie — calling her own name, ordering her down from a tree branch or away from a ravine.

"I have to go," Claire said, straightening up.

"No. You can't leave. I have to save you."

The light shifted as Claire turned to go, and Lena pounded her fist against the ice. A sickening crack echoed through the under, and with the crack came a flood of heat. In seconds, Claire was submerged in the water, Lena catching her in her arms. Lena could feel Claire's warmth, and she suddenly had the urge to sing. She knew what singing was now. And then Lena felt a hand tugging at first one leg and then both. Lena looked down into the depths to see Edna's hands around her ankles.

The heat from Claire's body was almost unbearable, but Lena could feel it draining, little by little, and as Claire became colder, Lena began to fill with warmth. She looked at the girl in her arms and saw not Claire but herself, and Edna holding her. Lena remembered the struggle to break through to the surface and the fear as she was pulled down. Someone above was screaming, but that too was fading as Lena descended into the depths, Edna's hands leaching the warmth from her body.

That was when she heard it.

The shriek.

Maggie screamed for Claire, just as she had screamed for Lena back then.

Lena looked at Claire's face and saw her lips beginning to go blue, and she felt the tug of the other ice child at her ankles again.

"Let go," she said, kicking at Edna.

"Save her," Edna rasped.

Save her. She would save her, but not for Edna and the ice children. She would save her for Maggie, Maggie who had always looked out for Lena but still couldn't save her all those years ago.

Lena closed her eyes and kicked against the water. Edna fell away, and Lena felt the light and warmth of the surface. And then she felt air and snow-covered ice. She thrust Claire's body onto the ice and pulled herself out. Lena could feel every part of her wanting to float away, as though she, like most everything else in the world beneath the ice, were formed from fragile water droplets. She willed herself together and scooped Claire into her arms. Lena began to sing. She couldn't remember learning the song, but still, she knew every word: "Oh my darling, oh my darling…"

Lena walked. She pointed herself in the direction of the shore, and she moved. "Oh my darling, Clementine…" Lena felt her feet begin to fade away and saw that her hands were losing color and shape, but she willed her arms to stay together, just for a bit longer. "You were lost and —" she could see the woman on the shore, frozen to the spot like she had lost her own warmth as well " — gone forever."

What was left of Lena's feet stepped onto the shore. "Dreadful sorry…"

"Claire," the woman breathed, interrupting Lena's song. Then she followed the arms holding her daughter. "Lena?"

"Maggie," Lena said. And as her legs and arms and face dispersed, she remembered all of it.

Brittany M. Perkins's story "It Thaws in Spring" was originally published in Metaphorosis on Friday, 10 November 2023. See magazine.metaphorosis.com

About the author

Brittany M. Perkins currently resides in the southern United States with her three well-behaved cats and one terribly-behaved cat. She began her writing career at the age of five after returning home from kindergarten to inform her mother that she wanted to write a book. She's been writing ever since.

When not writing, she can be found cuddling a cat, doting on her niece and nephew, or creating LEGO structures with her boyfriend.

A Wizard Comes to Shorehaven

L.J. Wetherby

Many years had gone by since a wizard last dwelled in the small seaside town of Shorehaven. It had been so long, in fact, since the town had enjoyed the presence of a wizard, that the people of Shorehaven had begun to forget why a wizard was such a desirable thing for a town to possess.

Children would finish their bedtime prayers with the words, "and please send Shorehaven a wizard before too much longer", but the words meant almost nothing to them, and little more to many of their parents. Wizards, as far as the younger generation of Shorehaveners was concerned, were a fantasy; something nice to dream of, but never seriously expected to come to pass.

The townspeople were surprised, then, when a wizard arrived one day. She was of middling height, with long twisting hair that was brown, grey, and white in different places, and wearing long robes the same colours as her hair. She looked very, very tired.

The only question on the town's lips was whether the wizard had come to stay or she was merely passing through. She spent her first night in a boarding-house, where (to the tremendous disappointment of the proprietor and the other patrons alike) she requested a private room and took all of her meals within it, never venturing out into the common areas. There were many in the boarding house that night who hoped for a chance to converse with the wizard, or at the very least to catch a glimpse of her, and there were many in the boarding house that night who went to bed disappointed.

The following morning, the wizard walked past Marsh's Stores in town, examining the glass-fronted noticeboard outside the shop and taking down notes in a small leather-bound book that she kept in the pocket of her robe. Then she walked out of town along the north road, towards the coast.

A few Shorehaveners were sufficiently intrigued by the wizard's arrival that they attempted to follow her out of town, but ill luck befell all who tried. Gordon Harris the baker's son stepped into a bog and ruined his socks and shoes. Amelia Connor the seamstress got her skirts so badly caught up in a patch of brambles that it took her almost an hour to free herself, and she came home scratched and bleeding. And Ghislaine Willis, who fancied herself something of a hedge-witch, became so lost while trying to follow the wizard that she found herself walking back into town along the south road, miles away from the north road that she'd taken out towards the coast in the first place.

A single cottage sat at the very edge of the cliffs, past the point where the north road ceased to be a road and turned into a path. It had lain empty for many years, almost as many as the town had been without a wizard. The notice announcing that this cottage was for rent was one of the oldest advertisements on the board outside Marsh's Stores, with its print almost completely faded and its edges yellowed and curled.

The wizard decided almost immediately after viewing it that she would take the cottage. She made one last trip into town, to put down a year's rent and to purchase some provisions from the store.

By this time, many of the townspeople were curious about the wizard, but everyone who attempted to walk out as far as her cliffside cottage to get a better look at her ran into the same kind of trouble as those who'd followed her out of town the day after her arrival — minor injuries and misfortunes, the sudden loss of their ability to navigate familiar roads, and in some cases a profound urge to turn around and check that they hadn't left the front door unlocked or a pan boiling dry on the stove. Eventually people started to complain about the situation, lamenting that after so many years of waiting, they should suffer the misfortune of only a very unsociable wizard arriving in Shorehaven.

The Mayor was a popular person to complain to, because he was ostensibly the most powerful man in town. In his private moments the Mayor would laugh to himself about this assumption, knowing as he did that being the Mayor gave him no power whatsoever — it merely made him responsible for dealing with all the problems that other people couldn't or wouldn't deal with themselves.

For the first week, the Mayor listened to the town's concerns about the new wizard with a solemn expression. He told each of them that he understood why they were worried — that he, too, was interested to learn more about the wizard — but that since it had been such a long time since the town had had any sort of wizard at all, everyone must be very patient. The wizard would reveal herself in her own good time; he was certain of it.

After three weeks had passed and there had been neither sign nor word of the wizard, however, and no further orders placed at Marsh's Stores, even the Mayor began to lose his patience. He decided that the townsfolk had been respectful enough of the wizard's privacy: he would force the issue. A wizard could hardly refuse an official visit from the Mayor, after all. And it would have been deeply undignified for the Mayor to have returned from attempting to visit the wizard with his legs scratched to pieces by thorns, his memory strangely absent, his socks and shoes ruined, or his sense of direction temporarily suspended, so he took Leonie with him as insurance.

Leonie was his only child, a quiet and unassuming person of around twenty-four years of age, who possessed a certain subtlety when it came to magic — it was said that Leonie's mother, who by this time had been dead for almost as long as she'd been alive in the first place, had been a distant relative of the town's previous wizard. The prestige of this connection had been one of the many reasons the Mayor had married her, and the fact that their only child showed the faintest hint of this familial skill had always been a source of particular pride for him.

Over the years, his child's ability had manifested on only a few occasions. Once, when the town had been suffering a drought, Leonie had managed to sense a raincloud nearby, tugging it by some unseen means towards the wheat fields that lay beyond the town. And there had been the time when a very young Leonie had managed to calm a rabid dog that was blocking the road to the schoolhouse simply by speaking soothingly to it, in a voice that sounded strangely ethereal, and nothing at all like Leonie's ordinary speaking voice.

Leonie did not enjoy being the Mayor's daughter, in spite of the Mayor's pride. For as long as Leonie could remember, people had watched constantly to see what the Mayor's daughter might do, and to ensure she comported herself with the same dignity and respect that the Mayor himself assumed. Something deep within Leonie writhed and squirmed away from this attention, seeking out a more dark and private place where it could merely exist, unobserved. The demands of the position sat very uneasily with the Mayor's daughter, who felt as an adult only very slightly mayoral, and not at all daughterly.

Leonie and the Mayor took their time walking along the north road, for Leonie had been born with one ordinary leg and another that tapered into nothingness halfway down the thigh. Leonie had hardly noticed this difference until the Mayor had made it clear that it was something to be managed carefully; as an adult, Leonie wore a prosthesis so artfully constructed that it was indistinguishable from a full-grown leg in every way, except for the fact that it caused Leonie to walk a little more slowly and carefully than other people. The small amount of magic that Leonie possessed had been very fortunate on the day when the rabid dog had wandered into town, given that running away at any speed had been out of the question.

Leonie could feel the wizard's presence all along the north road, even before they made it past the edge of the town. The charms and glamours that had prevented curious individuals from trespassing upon the wizard's hospitality until now were obvious to Leonie, glimmers faintly perceptible to the corner of the eye and easy enough to work around. They arrived at the wizard's cottage just after midday, picking their way through the nettles and weeds that had grown over the path to the cottage door, which was closed.

The Mayor knocked, with an amount of force and ceremony befitting his status in the town. There was no answer. He knocked again, but still no answer. After his third knock was similarly ignored, he motioned to Leonie. Leonie's knock was soft, gentle, and hesitating. After it had sounded, the wizard called out.

"It's open. You might as well come in."

The Mayor was old enough to remember a time when this cottage had not stood empty. It had been a pretty place then, full of light, with a lush garden surrounding the house on all sides. Now, even though the new wizard had been in residence for almost a month, it seemed a drear and dingy little hole. The floor had not been swept, half the shelves were bare and lined with a thick layer of dust, and the curtains, old and frayed and stained as they were, did a very thorough job of preventing any light from entering the house.

There were three rooms downstairs, the right-hand side of the cottage divided into a kitchen at the front and a sitting room at the rear, looking out over the sea. On the left side was one long room that the original owners had used for dining and entertaining. There were two bedrooms upstairs, but the Mayor assumed them to be out of use, given that the stairs had rotted and fallen in and no one had repaired them.

The wizard's voice had come from the room on the left, but when Leonie and the Mayor went in, there was no sign of anyone there. Just as they were about to check the kitchen and the sitting room, they heard a groaning sound from the corner of the room.

There they found the wizard half buried in a makeshift bed, beneath a bundle of blankets on top of a broken old sofa.

"I ought to get up and greet you properly, I suppose, except I don't want to," said the wizard, an unseen hand pulling at the pile of blankets to reveal her mouth.

There were a few chairs scattered here and there around the room, and Leonie and the Mayor selected two of the least dirty and broken ones and pulled them over toward the sofa where the wizard lay.

"I am the Mayor of Shorehaven," the Mayor began, in his most mayoral tone. "I would like to formally extend our warmest welcome to you on behalf of the town. It's been a very long time since we've had a wizard dwelling near Shorehaven."

"Oh dear," said the wizard. "I was afraid this might happen."

"Afraid what might happen?" asked the Mayor.

"That you'd all assume I've come here to be your new wizard," said the wizard.

"Well, what have you come here for, if not that?" asked the Mayor, trying to hide his disappointment.

The wizard took a deep breath beneath her pile of blankets.

"I have come here to die," she said mournfully.

The Mayor stared at Leonie, hoping the wizard could not see his expression.

"Oh," he said, after too long a moment had passed. "Well, I'm very sorry to hear that."

"Not as sorry as I am," said the wizard. "My only wish is to die here in peace, but the people of Shorehaven keep bothering me."

"We meant no disrespect," said the Mayor.

"Ah, but respect is poor currency for a dying wizard to hoard," said the wizard. "I neither relish nor require your respect; I merely ask to be left alone."

The Mayor did not know what else to say. He had rehearsed a number of talking points that he imagined might make suitable conversation in the company of a wizard, though he'd been but a small boy himself when the old wizard had died. Now, with the new wizard apparently nearly as dead as the old one, the thought of attempting to make polite conversation suddenly seemed ghastly.

"Anything you need, anything that the town can provide for you," he said instead. "You need only ask."

In truth, the Mayor was not feeling particularly generous — he'd expected a healthy wizard with many long years of wizarding ahead of them, and he'd already overexcited himself at the thought of the benefits that such a wizard might bring to the town. Now, with those hopes dashed, there was a part of him that wanted nothing more than to leave the cottage and pretend that the dying wizard had never come to Shorehaven. But he feared for the town's reputation; if word got out that a dying wizard had been treated with such disrespect, Shorehaven might never again attract a healthy one.

"Thank you," the wizard groaned, "but I require nothing except privacy."

The idea of staying when they were so clearly unwelcome made the Mayor feel awkward and uncomfortable, sensations that his position in the town normally insulated him from rather effectively. He cleared his throat, stood up, and motioned to Leonie to do the same. They left the wizard in a pile on the broken old sofa and went home.

Dinner that night at the Mayor's residence was a dour affair, and not even Leonie could brighten the Mayor's spirits. They both went to bed gloomy, and the next morning at breakfast it was clear that a good night's sleep had only compounded the Mayor's concerns about the wizard.

"It doesn't seem right," he said, applying a thin layer of marmalade to his crustless toast. "That she should come all the way here just to die alone in that cottage up on the cliffs."

Leonie nodded and murmured and made all of the noises the Mayor expected from his only child.

"If only there were something we could do," the Mayor continued. "Some way we could help."

The Mayor looked up from his toast just as a ray of morning light struck the window of his breakfast room. Framed by this sunbeam, Leonie seemed gently radiant, and an idea formed.

"What if you were to go and assist her?" the Mayor asked.

"Me?" asked Leonie.

"Precisely," said the Mayor. "You're a great help to me here, of course, but I'm still comfortably within my prime. I could do without you for a few months; certainly long enough that the wizard might pass peacefully."

"I thought she made it very clear that she didn't want to be troubled by anyone from town," said Leonie.

"Even so," said the Mayor. "Think how it might look if people found out that we had a dying wizard staying just outside Shorehaven and we did nothing to help her."

Leonie knew the Mayor well; well enough to know that when he said things like 'think about how it might look', he was thinking not only of the reputation of the town, but also the reputation of its Mayor. Although Leonie's father had been Mayor long enough that many of the townsfolk had never known any other Mayor, he was constantly anxious about his position. He did not want to end up out of a job and forced to cut the crusts off his own toast, rather than having them cut off by someone else and served to him on a silver toast-rack.

Leonie did not want to go and help the wizard. Not because wizards were uninteresting, but because this particular wizard had made it abundantly clear that she wished to be left alone. The last time the Mayor had asked Leonie to do something unpalatable and potentially embarrassing, his only child had made the private decision that it would be the last time, and that next time, "no, that won't be possible" would be the only answer given. But the Mayor was very persuasive, and his only child had little experience of disappointing him; the middle of the morning found Leonie walking up the north road again, this time with a letter in hand.

It was easy enough for Leonie to avoid the additional charms and hexes that the wizard had put up since the Mayor's visit the day before, though the work was impressive for a wizard running up against the end of her stamina — once again they glinted, slightly listlessly, in a way that only the corner of Leonie's eye could perceive. It was a sense that Leonie was well aware that most people in Shorehaven did not possess or even understand; one of the many strange feelings and sensations that Leonie had grown used to never talking about with other people, lest they distract from the importance of adequately performing the role of Mayor's daughter in public.

When Leonie arrived, the door to the cottage was still unlocked, and the wizard lay in the exact spot where they'd left her the day before.

"I thought I told you to leave me alone," said the wizard from beneath the pile of blankets.

"That would have been my preference too," said Leonie, placing the Mayor's letter on the end of the sofa nearest to the wizard's head.

A skinny hand crept out from beneath the nest of blankets and snatched at the envelope.

" 'Please allow me to lend you my girl to ensure your comfort at this sad time, yours sincerely, the Mayor of Shorehaven'," she read aloud.

Then the skinny hand crumpled up the piece of paper, which had been embossed with the Mayor's name, title, address, and official seal, and tossed it into the fireplace.

"Fool," she said, as Leonie continued to stand around, unsure whether to say or do anything. "To call you his girl. As though you were a girl. As though he owned you."

Leonie felt very odd at that moment, as though the wizard had stumbled upon an unexpectedly pertinent truth.

"What do you mean?"

"You're old enough to be a woman, for starters," said the wizard. "Except you're not a woman, are you? Or a man, either?"

"I'm not," said Leonie, a strange feeling bubbling within that might have been anxiety or relief. "Is that what's always felt wrong about being the Mayor's daughter? Everyone has always assumed..."

"To hell with their assumptions!" cried the wizard, with more vigour than Leonie had realised her capable of. "You are what you are. Doesn't matter what people think you are, or what they expect you to be. Now, tell me how you managed to get up here today. You weren't deterred by my trickery yesterday morning, but the hexes I put down in the afternoon to stop anyone else approaching were sound."

"I don't know," said Leonie, still reeling from the wizard's previous observation. "I suppose I've always been able to perceive magic better than most people in Shorehaven."

"Well, if someone has to come up here, I suppose I don't mind as much if it's you. It was everyone else that I was trying to keep away."

"It seems a lonely thing, to die up here on your own," said Leonie wistfully. "I'd be happy to keep you company."

"Company is the last thing I need," said the wizard. "If I needed company, I'd seek it out. But since you're already here…"

Leonie took the hint. The cottage was in such a state of disarray that it was easy to find a place to start, because everything needed doing. First, Leonie swept the dust from the empty shelves and the corners of the room. Then they checked the wizard's pantry, making a note of anything that might be needed from Marsh's Stores in town. They boiled up a great quantity of hot water, reserving some of it for mopping, some for wiping down the windows, some for laundry, and the last of it for making tea, which the wizard accepted gratefully.

While the wizard drank the tea, Leonie carried on dusting, wiping, sweeping, and washing. By the late afternoon, the cottage was already looking significantly more presentable, even though there was still plenty more work to be done. The wizard didn't have much food in the house, but Leonie did what they could, making a big pan of porridge and leaving a bowl of it near the wizard's nest, covered with honey and nuts.

"I'm going to go back to town now," they said in the late afternoon. "I'll order some more things from Marsh's Stores and bring them up, and I'll speak to the carpenter about repairing the stairs. I'll be back tomorrow morning."

"Suit yourself," said the wizard from beneath the pile of blankets where she still lay, unmoving.

Back at the Mayor's residence, the Mayor was delighted to hear of Leonie's progress and he encouraged his only child to go back to the wizard's cottage first thing in the morning. And so Leonie did, carrying the supplies from Marsh's Stores slowly up the north road. They found the wizard exactly where they'd left her the night before, but the bowl of porridge had been consumed entirely and licked clean.

Leonie spent the morning clearing out the kitchen and arranging the groceries in the pantry. With fresh provisions laid in, they were able to make a much more interesting lunch for the wizard than mere porridge: fresh mushroom stew with wild rice and a green salad. Again, they left a bowl and a plate near the wizard and went off to do other things, and again, when they returned, the bowl and plate were clean. Whatever fatal concern was troubling the wizard, Leonie mused, her appetite was certainly remarkable.

On the third day, Leonie walked up from town with the carpenter's apprentice to make sure he found his way past the wizard's enchantments. They spent much of the day weeding, raking, and digging in the garden that surrounded the wizard's house on all sides while the carpenter's apprentice sawed, hammered, and sanded.

The wizard did not make herself visible when Leonie brought in her lunch — soup made from the remains of the mushroom stew with fresh-baked bread — but when they brought her a cup of tea at the end of the day, after the carpenter's apprentice had finished the job and gone home, the wizard's head emerged from the nest of blankets, and she motioned to Leonie to sit down in the chair nearest the sofa.

"I'm glad all of that hammering and banging is finished," said the wizard.

These were the first words she'd offered that weren't in response to a direct question. Leonie nodded.

"Why don't you sleep here at night, to save you dragging that leg up and down the road to town twice a day?" the wizard continued.

Leonie was startled. They'd mentioned nothing of their leg to the wizard, and indeed they'd been using the prosthesis for so many years that it now formed a well-integrated part of their gait; they were surprised that the wizard had been able to tell.

"It doesn't trouble me," they said.

"Of course it does," said the wizard. "The ache in your hip. The tender part that sits in the socket all day, that you cover in socks and bandages so that it doesn't ever get rubbed completely raw."

Leonie looked at the wizard again, no less startled.

"How could you possibly know that?" they asked.

One of the wizard's particular skills, and a focus for her magic, was seeing people exactly as they really were — something she'd hinted at the first day Leonie came up to the cottage on their own, when she'd debunked the myth of the Mayor's daughter. She was adept at looking past the layers that everyone dressed themselves in, the faces and façades they wore for the rest of the world, in order perceive their deepest essences. That was how she'd known that Leonie wasn't really a girl, even if they kept pretending they were for the benefit of the Mayor and the town. And the outline she'd perceived of Leonie with her magic, rather than with her eyes, included a leg that ended where nature had ended it, far short of the ground.

The wizard was loathe to explain how her magic worked, however, so she merely shrugged.

"The offer's there if you'd rather not keep making the journey," she said instead. "And if you want to take that leg off for an hour or two to give yourself a break, go ahead. It doesn't trouble me."

The idea of removing their leg in front of the wizard was on a par with the idea of removing all of their clothes and underwear, as far as Leonie was concerned; something they had never considered doing in front of any living person before. Their father loved to see Leonie walking proud and upright without any hint of pain or fatigue, and they had mastered the art of this performance so thoroughly that the idea that they might choose to stop performing it seemed entirely out of the question.

Their father hated to be reminded of his only child's disability, and in the years since the first in a series of legs had initially been crafted for Leonie, they had never once taken any of them off in his presence. They knew, somehow, that to do so would be to violate a holy and entirely unspoken expectation that stood between them.

It was also one of the many reasons they had never seriously considered forming a romantic attachment with another person. No one, as far as Leonie was concerned, wanted to see their body as it truly was, and they had taken on the idea that it was their own profound responsibility to manage their body in such a way that it might not possibly offend anyone. This had grown to the status of another holy and unspoken duty, one to be performed privately and in silence, the pain and effort of it never to be hinted at in front of anyone else.

"It doesn't trouble me," they said again, more quietly this time.

The wizard did not believe them, but neither did she press the issue.

Leonie kept returning to the wizard's cottage every morning, where they continued to put the place in order, and dreamt up meals to tempt even a dying wizard's appetite. And every evening, when they returned to the Mayor's residence, the Mayor asked them how the wizard was getting along, and whether they thought there was any chance of the wizard doing a spot of wizarding on behalf of the town at some point in the near future.

"She's dying, Father," Leonie would say every time the Mayor asked, which stunned him enough to prevent him from asking again the same evening, but not so much that he would not ask again the following evening.

And every afternoon, when the bulk of the day's work was done, Leonie would sit with the wizard and drink tea. The wizard gradually became more communicative as the weeks went on, and she began to sit up properly in order to drink her tea, rather than sipping at it from the side of her mouth as she lay on the sofa. Indeed, as the wizard's surroundings began to brighten up, so did the wizard.

And just as the wizard responded to the improvements that Leonie had made to the cottage, Leonie began to respond to small signs of improvement from the wizard. She mentioned one day, in passing, how much she might enjoy a scone with her afternoon tea. From that day on, during the quiet hour after lunch when the wizard took her nap, Leonie would stand in the kitchen conjuring up sweet things. It turned out that the wizard enjoyed cakes, biscuits, and brownies as much as she enjoyed scones, and Leonie enjoyed making them for her, and sitting with her in the late afternoon looking out over the ocean as they ate something fresh and small and sweet and drank their tea.

"Do you mind me asking what's wrong with you?" they inquired one afternoon, no longer able to suppress their curiosity about what possible condition could be killing the perfectly healthy-looking wizard in front of them.

"It is a long, sad story," said the wizard.

"I'd like to hear it, if you're willing to tell it," said Leonie.

The wizard sighed, and took a deep breath.

"Many years ago now, when I was a much younger wizard," she began, "I wandered all around this world until I came to a forest. For as long as I could remember, my head had been full of spells and noises, wonders, and curiosities. But when I sat for a while beneath a great ancient tree in that forest, for the first time in my life I felt at peace."

The wizard sighed again, more tenderly this time, before she continued.

"Given how thoroughly that sense of peace had eluded me until then, I began to imagine crafting a life for myself in those woods. I slept out beneath the forest canopy that summer, building myself a small hut day by day. There was a brook nearby, and in the evenings I would sit with my feet in the water, resting my body and allowing my mind to wander.

"One evening, I felt the presence of another with me on the bank of the stream. Every time I thought I was about to catch a glimpse of her, she slipped away from me. But I kept returning to the brook every evening, and eventually she took form one night, and sat beside me.

"She was a spirit of the forest, as curious about people and their wizards as I was about forest spirits and their magic. We danced around one another for months — metaphorically speaking, of course — before she finally kissed me. My hut was complete by then, and she agreed to live with me there for a time, to learn on an intimate level how human wizards conduct their private lives.

"We were very happy there together, for many years; I should have known that it would not last forever. No one has ever managed to keep a forest spirit captive for very long, not that I wanted to imprison her. I suppose it is a miracle that she stayed as long as she did. For what felt like an age, we lazed in the grassy glades together, splashed one another as we swam in the brook, slept beside one another each night. And then, one day, she was gone.

"I could not stay. The hut seemed empty without her. The whole forest seemed empty without her, even though I knew she lived on somewhere within it. The days of her sharing my life with me were over, and I was utterly bereft.

"It is said among my people that when a wizard tires of life, death must surely follow, and swiftly. After she left, I was more than tired of life. I felt nothing but emptiness. I ate little, slept either too much or too little, and as my strength waned, so did my magic. That is why I came here to Shorehaven to die, for there are few trees along the clifftops. I wondered if it might be easier to forget her in a place like this. To live out the final days of my diminution here."

Leonie listened to the wizard's story with interest, and they sat silent for a long time after the wizard had finished speaking.

"I'm sorry you lost her," they said at last.

"So am I," said the wizard mournfully.

"Is it not possible, though," said Leonie, "that you might have been mistaken about the nature of your illness? I understand why you felt as though you were tired of living after she left you, but I've seen a great improvement in you since you came to Shorehaven."

The wizard took offense at this, and made a huffing noise.

"I have been a wizard all my life," she said. "Surely I ought to know whether or not I am dying."

Leonie said nothing, nor did they give the wizard the pointed look that they strongly wished to. From their perspective, the wizard had only grown in strength and vigour as the weeks passed. She seemed less gaunt now, and her hair was shinier and less tangled, and she had even begun standing up from the sofa from time to time and walking out as far as the end of the garden behind the house to look out over the sea.

After this conversation, the wizard kept firmly to the sofa for several days, reverting to her previous position beneath a tangle of blankets, as if to prove to Leonie that she was indeed dying. Leonie considered asking the wizard whether she'd ever experienced a spell of low spirits before, if it might be possible that she'd mistaken the despair of such an episode for the fatal certainty of her own impending demise, but again they held their tongue.

Instead, Leonie set about clearing out the rooms on the upper floor of the house, which were now accessible thanks to the work of the carpenter's apprentice. The bedsteads that had been left up there by the cottage's previous inhabitants were still perfectly serviceable, so Leonie ordered new mattresses, linen, and curtains when they were in town, and asked to have them sent up. The wizard grudgingly agreed to temporarily remove some of the protective charms and spells along the road to the cottage so that the delivery people could bring up the mattresses.

"There's no way I can manage those mattresses myself," said Leonie sheepishly.

"There's no need for you to walk up and down the road to town every day," the wizard replied sharply. "Especially now that there's a bedroom for you upstairs if you want it."

Leonie said nothing, although they'd considered taking up the wizard's previous offer. It *would* save them a lot of walking every day, and their father the Mayor had only become more insistent as time had gone by that the wizard ought to begin to do at least some wizarding for the town, regardless of the state of her health.

And they were tired of the Mayor referring to them as his 'darling daughter'; ever since the wizard had confessed her perception of their true self to Leonie, they'd found it increasingly difficult to carry on the pretence of being the person that Shorehaven expected them to be. Life was slow and gentle up here on the cliff edge, and for the first time in their life they felt entirely unobserved.

"I'll think about it," they said this time, instead of ignoring the question altogether.

When they arrived at the cottage the next day, Leonie was surprised to see the wizard standing up near the window, wearing more than just a nightgown and looking out over the sea.

"Do you have much work planned for today?" she asked.

Leonie shrugged.

"Dusting, decorating the bedrooms, making an apple cake," they replied.

"Anything you can't put off until tomorrow?" the wizard asked. "Apart from the apple cake, which I'd very much like to eat later. Can you put together a picnic lunch while you're at it?"

Leonie agreed to postpone the dusting and bedroom-decorating, and set about preparing the requested victuals, curious about the wizard's intentions. When the apple cake was cooling on the kitchen windowsill and the picnic lunch had been packed up in a basket, the wizard nodded her satisfaction and strode out into the rear garden towards the edge of the cliff, which she stopped to look down over.

"Is there a path to the beach?" she asked.

Leonie shook their head.

"We'll see about that," said the wizard.

She knelt down at the far edge of the cliff and planted her hands firmly in the thin layer of grass and soil, massaging it gently. At first there was a faint vibration that grew more rumbling and distinct as the wizard continued her work; Leonie felt it radiating up through the bones of their right leg, and buzzing furiously where the prosthesis met the terminus of their left leg.

Slowly the edge of the cliff began to change shape, the rock rearranging itself beneath the command of the wizard's fingers until a new form emerged amidst the cliff face: a narrow staircase that looked as though it had always been there.

"Can you manage?" the wizard asked.

Leonie looked at the staircase, anxiety creeping over them as they considered just how many steps there were, and just how uneven most of them looked. The Mayor had drilled into them over and over again how important it was that his daughter appear normal in public. 'Normal', in the Mayor's eyes, meant things like never walking with a visible limp, and taking any number of stairs with equal amounts of agility and cheer. Leonie had internalised these lessons so deeply that most domestic staircases posed no challenge, but the stairs the wizard had just summoned into existence were an entirely different proposition.

They realised, however, that they were not exactly 'in public' out here with the wizard. Nor did they seriously feel compelled to maintain the pretence that they were the

Mayor's daughter, especially not so far out of sight of the rest of the town.

"I'll be honest, I think it's going to be a struggle," they replied. "The leg is fine on shorter staircases, but this one might be beyond me."

"How would you approach it if the leg wasn't in the picture?" asked the wizard.

Leonie was instantly transported back to early childhood, a time they hadn't thought about for many years, when they'd accepted their body exactly as it had been, and they'd had no concept of legs or propriety or the role of a Mayor, or indeed the role of a dutiful daughter. They'd been more than happy back then to pull themselves up and down staircases in a seated fashion; it was the Mayor who'd insisted they learn to walk up and down the stairs like any other person.

They took a deep breath. Then they began to untie the leather straps that anchored the leg to the girdle they wore just below their left hip. Once the straps were loosened, they tugged at the socket of the leg until it popped off, and then slipped off the thin covering they wore over the tapered area where the end of their natural leg met the beginning of the prosthesis. Instead of placing the leg down carefully, as their father had always insisted they do, because of its great importance and the tremendous expense of its construction, they let it fall to the ground with a thud.

Standing before the wizard without their prosthesis, Leonie felt strangely exposed, but the wizard merely nodded and smiled.

"It's nice to see you as you are, for a change," she said.

Then the wizard began to clamber down the steep, narrow staircase towards the sea, hitching up the skirt of her robe and carrying the picnic basket while Leonie followed on their backside, their trousers rolled up as far as their right knee and the terminus of their left leg. By the time they reached the short pebble beach that lay between the base of the cliff and the sea, Leonie's arms burned from the exertion, but the effort left them feeling strangely exhilarated rather than worn out.

They followed the wizard down the beach, the sensation of the smooth pebbles beneath their right foot a delight as they hopped along. The Mayor had disapproved of hopping almost as much as he'd disapproved of taking staircases from a seated position; Leonie was surprised to find that they were easily strong and agile enough to hop the distance to the shoreline comfortably. The Mayor had been so insistent that they needed the leg in order to function that they'd never stopped to consider whether this was actually true.

The sea was fresh and salty and just a little too cold for comfort. After stripping off her clothes and leaving them just beyond the reach of the waves, the wizard began swimming, and Leonie joined her. They swam side by side for a while, pausing occasionally to tread water, and then they returned to the beach, where they lay in the sun until their bodies were mostly dry again.

The wizard rolled towards Leonie, stroking their arm, her lips parted and her eyes questioning. Leonie shrank away from her touch, not entirely understanding the expression on the wizard's face. They turned onto their left side, covering their thin, short left leg as much as they could with the sturdy bulk of their right. The wizard took Leonie's cue and did not pursue the matter; when they went back up to the cottage in the late afternoon, she strode on ahead as Leonie worked their way up backwards. At the top of the cliff, they sat on a rock and reattached the prosthesis, easing the end of their left leg into its socket and feeling the dull, familiar pain in their hip as they stood and began to bear weight on it again.

The wizard attempted no further advances that afternoon. Leonie finished up a few chores and left the wizard some supper. The wizard did not want to appear as though she was watching them, but she couldn't help noticing how they'd turned inward after she'd reached out to them: the pain and confusion visible on their face in moments when Leonie believed the wizard was not looking, the fact that their gait seemed clumsier somehow now that they'd reattached the leg. As they went to leave, the wizard caught their arm.

"Are you sure you wouldn't rather stay the night?" she asked.

Leonie pulled away again, their eyes flushing with hot tears even as they tried to blink them back. On the return journey to town, their mind swirled with memories and emotions, things they'd steadily and dutifully repressed in order to more deeply inhabit the role of the Mayor's daughter. A single, sweet kiss shared with a girl from school, never repeated for fear of what people might think if they found out. Their leg, and the extent to which they'd allowed themself to turn it into an excuse never to become intimate with anyone. But the wizard had seen them without it, and hadn't shied away; she had perceived their lower left leg's absence as a core component of Leonie, a radiant part of their truth rather than something to be obfuscated.

Dinner at the Mayor's residence that evening was subdued. The Mayor could tell that something was wrong with Leonie, but couldn't fathom what the problem might be. When he enquired as to whether the wizard was dying at long last, Leonie's response surprised him.

"No, father, it's not the wizard. She's doing well."

"Then what is it that troubles you, child?"

Leonie's next response surprised even Leonie.

"My hip aches terribly from all the walking I've been doing back and forth to the wizard's house, and I'm afraid that a sore patch is forming where my leg sits in the socket of the prosthesis."

The Mayor's eyes widened, and an expression as sad as the one Leonie had been wearing all evening crossed his face. But he said nothing more about the wizard or Leonie or their leg, just as Leonie had expected he wouldn't. And in that moment, they understood that a decision they hadn't even realised they'd been contemplating had just made itself.

The following morning, the wizard stood anxiously in the cottage doorway. Leonie was late, much later than usual, and the wizard was afraid she'd driven them away with a single wordless touch on the beach, and that they might never come back. As she watched, however, a figure emerged along the road from Shorehaven, moving slowly and springily. As the figure drew closer, the wizard saw that it was Leonie hopping along the road, the prosthetic leg and a pair of crutches that the Mayor would have preferred them not to own strapped to their back.

Leonie was annoyed at how long the journey had taken, even though they'd set out with plenty of time to spare. It was only a small annoyance, though; it paled in comparison to their delight in finding that they were easily fit and strong enough to make the journey from town without the assistance of the prosthesis.

Leaving town, they'd seen people they'd known their entire life staring at them and whispering. And although they couldn't hear any of those whispers, they could easily imagine what the people of Shorehaven were saying. *Goodness, there goes Leonie-the-Mayor's-daughter without her leg. Perhaps it's broken. Maybe that good-for-nothing wizard is going to fix it for her. Poor little dear. What a shame.*

But each hop they'd made past the town boundary had felt like a leap of triumph, the energy and propulsion of every successive step batting away the dreadful comments they imagined the townsfolk were whispering to one another. Every time their right leg landed on the road, it seemed to reinforce some deep, unadulterable part of themself: they were not the Mayor's daughter, there was nothing broken about the leg that nature had given them, nothing about them was a shame, and they were categorically not a poor little dear.

The wizard tried to appear nonchalant as Leonie approached the cottage, though her face was somewhat flushed. Leonie did not immediately comment on their journey or the leg, which they left propped in the hallway for the time being, but they did announce a change that made the wizard very happy.

"I've told the Mayor not to expect me back tonight," they said. "Assuming your offer of an overnight stay still stands?"

"It does," said the wizard, and when she slowly approached Leonie and placed her hand around their waist, they did not pull away this time.

As they kissed, Leonie realised that their anxiety at the thought of being intimate with another person had melted away entirely, only to be replaced with a different concern.

"I'm not sure I can measure up to a forest spirit," they said, blushing.

"If I wanted to be with a forest spirit, I'd go back to the forest," said the wizard. "I like you just the way you are."

The people of Shorehaven complained at length about the town's great misfortune during the many years that followed. To have been without a wizard for so long, only to have one arrive who showed no interest in using her magic to benefit the town or its people was a heavy burden for any town to bear. They felt tremendously ill-used, both by fate and by the wizard herself, and rather than teaching their children to pray for a wizard to come to Shorehaven, they now taught them to curse the wizard who *had* arrived, for her selfishness and lack of community spirit. Some even said that they wished the wizard would hurry up and die, as she'd said she was going to, for she had done absolutely nothing to help the town, nor any of its inhabitants.

That was not true, however; Leonie blossomed at the cottage on the cliffside. They managed to persuade the wizard to make an exception in her charms and hexes for their father, that he might come up and visit them occasionally, and the wizard agreed, so long as Leonie wasted no further energy pretending to be the Mayor's daughter.

The Mayor was made to understand that Leonie would no longer live with him, that they had tried a life of service in the town of Shorehaven and it had not suited them, and that they did not particularly enjoy being called "she" or "daughter" when those ideas were so foreign to the sense of self that the wizard's love and company had solidified within them.

The Mayor was also made to understand that the wizard would not live to serve the town of Shorehaven either, even though the wizard was indeed not dying, and no matter how much the town might desire her service. Much of the Mayor's professional life from that point on consisted of placating the townspeople on behalf of the wizard, and it was true that he did not enjoy his job quite so much once the town realised that the wizard was not inclined to help them in any meaningful way. He tried to point out to the townsfolk, as the wizard had pointed out to him, that they had managed perfectly well for many years without any wizard at all, but this was cold comfort as far as most Shorehaveners were concerned.

Finally, the Mayor was made to understand that any future wearing of the prosthetic leg would be done entirely on Leonie's terms. The first time he visited the cottage, they sat in a chair with the leg leaning against a bookcase in the living room, hopping into the kitchen as needed. It seemed to pain the Mayor to see this, but when he asked whether there was anything wrong with the leg, Leonie told him unceremoniously that they would no longer be wearing it purely for his comfort — only for their own, on the occasions when it was truly comfortable to do so.

And the Mayor had wrung his hands together, and said that he'd only ever wanted his only child to be happy and comfortable — and that surely the key to being happy and comfortable was to be as much like other people as possible, which was why he'd always insisted about the leg. But he was capable of understanding that he had been wrong, and of realising that the price of a relationship with his only child meant never mentioning his own preferences regarding their leg, or calling them "daughter".

And so Leonie remained in the cottage with the wizard, baking cakes to enjoy with her in the afternoon, swimming in the sea with her as often as they liked, working alongside her in the garden and talking about magic in a way that they both knew no other Shorehaveners would understand. Up on the cliffside, surrounded by the peace of the wind and the waves, they set aside all thoughts of how a Mayor's daughter ought to appear or behave, and allowed themself merely to be.

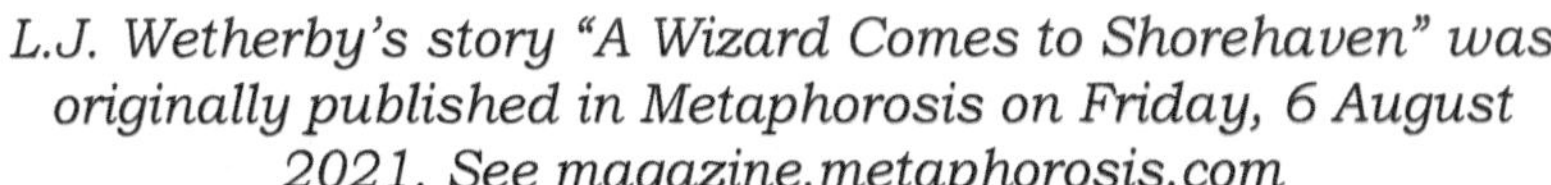

L.J. Wetherby's story "A Wizard Comes to Shorehaven" was originally published in Metaphorosis on Friday, 6 August 2021. See magazine.metaphorosis.com

About the author

LJ Wetherby (they/them) is a non-binary writer living in Cambridgeshire, UK, with a focus on speculative and historical fiction that centres queer characters. ljwetherby.com, @ljwetherby

Autumn's Come Undone

Sharmon Gazaway

Autumn stands before a large pumpkin. Her bare soles, planted on either side, draw up minerals from the rich loam. The pumpkin's skin, still warm in late afternoon, glows under her touch, deepening from apricot to bittersweet orange. Stepping to the next pumpkin, she works the row, ripening each in turn. She swipes her brow with her forearm, her hands grimy, and pulls the weight of her ginger hair off her hot neck. A murmuring rumples the treetops, whispers forming words she can't quite make out. A chill lifts the fine hairs on her nape and she shivers.

Probably those air-headed dryads gossiping again.

As she walks to the brook to wash, honey-bright leaves drift down, cling to her hair like sprites. Humming, she pirouettes, her leaf skirts a swirl of marigold, russet, and spice. A garland of purplish-green globes dangling from the branch of a hickory tree catches her eye. She breaks off the vine and holds it up to the fading light.

Crow flutters down to the lowest limb, his bent wing stiff.

"Muscadines," she calls to him. "Sol's favorite." She breathes on the globes and they take on a ruddier, sweeter hue. "Perfect."

She drapes the fruited vine across a low shrub on the brook's bank and kneels, scrubbing her hands in the icy water. The stream babbles up at her, unintelligible at first. Dryads flit across the brook, tittering, cover malicious smiles with hazy hands. She looks about, wondering where

Sylvannah is and why she hasn't already herded them into their trees. She swishes the muscadine vine through the water, shaking her head. It's a mystery to her how she ever endured the flighty things before Sylvannah came.

Crow lights on her shoulder, nudging her head. She shrugs him onto the bank. So little time left to prepare the table for Sol's visit tomorrow, and the muscadines will be the finishing touch. The stream murmurs insistently and Crow tilts his head toward it, turns and looks up at Autumn. She leans down, listens carefully. The murmurs sharpen into words that glint and wound, and take her breath.

Rising, the soggy fruit slides from her slack fingers.

Autumn's leaf skirts rush and crackle as she stumbles through the darkening woods, throws herself beneath the arms of the Great Oak. She hooks her fingers in deep, harrows leaf-rot and worm castings, breaks her nails on the bones of birds and vermin. From low in her inner turnings a cry germinates, a cry that, breaking free, rattles branches and drives the dryads into their tree-skins.

She does not cry prettily. Not like Spring, who mastered the art of the one perfect dewdrop tear while they were still girls in Earth's nursery.

Moaning, Autumn rolls her head on the forest floor and grits her teeth, the moss clinging to her lips. She hears a crack inside her chest like the snap of a twig.

Pushing onto her hands and knees, she crawls closer to the Oak. She huddles between the roots, her back pressed against the furrowed trunk. She curls into her cloak, fastens its silver acorn brooch, and tucks in her bare feet, tight as Tortoise in his shell. Crow lights on her shoulder and roosts in her tangles. Autumn presses her wet cheek against moonshadowed bark, relieved Sol can't see her now.

All night she burns, shamed.

Like a fool, all day she hummed and danced while she worked, awaiting Sol's visit. In a large reed basket, she heaped the harvest's bounty — rosy apples, pomegranates, walnuts and pecans, lush persimmons. She set it on a table strewn with smilax vines by the brook. She savored the thought of Sol by her side for a whole day, wandering the meadow amongst violet and ochre wildflowers, drifting in a rowboat until moonset.

She presses cold fingers against her blazing cheeks.

When morning comes, newly resurrected and only half alive, it sheds its mists and feeds on shafts of light. Light that colors everything the soft gold of Sol's hair. It fingers her face with tender warmth. She knows this touch — *his* touch — intimately.

Sol is mocking her.

She shudders to her feet, sends Crow flapping. She slaps twigs from her cloak, squares her shoulders and pulls up her hood, shielding herself from Sol's gloating.

This is not to be borne.

She marches to the brook, and heaves the table over. The loaded basket crashes to the ground, the fruit bruised and bleeding. She strikes her hands together and sparks shoot from her fingertips. The basket erupts in flame.

Shaking, rage unspent, she sets her face to the North and trudges out of her wood. Crow clings to her gray woolen shoulder, weight-shifting nervously. Mice dart for cover at her approach.

●

Whisking into vapor, Sylvannah slipped out through a knothole in the Great Oak when the wailing and gnashing of teeth began. All the other dryads shivered inside their trees. But she bit her lip and witnessed Autumn unravel.

Now, with Sol high in the eastern sky, and Autumn and Crow gone, the dryads' gossip chitters tree to tree.

"Sol jilted Autumn, even though she's never loved another."

"I heard he cheated on her with a star."

"No, two stars."

"They say he actually expects her to be happy for him."

Sylvannah listens, amused. Sol doesn't know Autumn the way she does, if that's what he expects. She snorts. As if.

It was Autumn's silly sister, Spring, who else? A bigger flirt she never saw. Sylvannah began life in Spring's woodland where Spring was forever tempting this star and that to come down to her. And when they burned out on the way, her eyes, the yellow-green of a cat's, glittered. She clapped as they blazed and fell to cinders at her feet.

And now she's caught the biggest star of all.

Sylvannah shushes the dryads, and glides into the orchard. She simply can't see the attraction. Sol is larger than life, always seeking attention. Yes, yes his job is very important — but, nutshells, what a Golden Boy.

Autumn gave him her heart long ago. Sylvannah couldn't imagine a better match for Autumn. Fiery; everyone around her gets singed at some point. But Sol could handle it, even seemed to revel in her volatile nature.

True, Autumn is unpredictable, but she has a warm and generous spirit few in the wood ever see.

Sylvannah remembers the day many harvests ago when she discovered Autumn's forest. She watched from the cover of a pine thicket as Autumn tended to an injured bird.

"Stop skulking around the edges of the wood and introduce yourself," Autumn called to her that day, tying the bird's wing firmly with strips of linen.

Sylvannah glided out, one hand clinging to chunky bark.

Autumn glanced up and sighed, "Not another dryad." She ran her hand over the crow's ragged feathers. "So, what do you want?"

"I'm Sylvannah. I come from Spring's woodland. She — she banished me."

Autumn looked up sharply. "Why?"

"I suppose your sister didn't much like me telling her she was cruel, the way she taunted the stars to their destruction." She shrugged.

Autumn smiled tightly, tossed her head toward the Oak in the center of the wood. "You're welcome to live there. You're the first dryad I've met with some sense and grit. If you can keep those nosy airheads out of my hair, you have a home for life."

So Sylvannah did.

Autumn kept to herself, except for Crow, her constant companion since she saved him from a hunter's snare. On occasion she visited her favorite sister, Winter. But she sought out Sol more than any other, the way a wing seeks wind.

Sylvannah accepts this. All she needs is the shelter of the Great Oak, his rings of wisdom surrounding her, his constancy — home.

And bossing the other dryads is just gravy.

She weaves through the orchard, inhales the brewery scent of apples that ache for Autumn's harvesting. Among shriveled, snaking vines, pumpkins bulge to bursting. The trees breathe the colors of fire.

As Sylvannah glides back toward the Oak, her lower lip sucked between her teeth, apprehension curls inside her like a little fog.

●

Autumn's sister, Winter, folds her into fur-robed arms and Autumn soaks up her warmth. Sol is weaker here. He and Winter have always maintained a distant relationship.

"I know why you've come, Little Acorn," Winter murmurs into her hair. "But Summer will never agree to it." She frowns, her eyes black and liquid as a snowhare's.

Summer. The good sister who tries to bind them together. But she has a soft spot for Sol, friends since the Beginning. She will plead for them all to reconcile, be a family. Family! Accept Sol as a *brother*?

"Sister," Autumn snaps, flaring, "I didn't come to ask a favor. Or permission." She sees in Winter's eye the glint of indulgent pride her sister reserves for Autumn alone. It was Winter who comforted her when Mother left them like fledglings in an abandoned nest. Winter who endured her tantrums, taught her to dance like a dervish to burn off the fumes of resentment. "I came to give," she adds softly.

Winter takes her hands in hers and studies the black-rimmed broken nails. "Autumn, you're overwrought. With good reason. What Sol did —"

"What *they* did," Autumn grinds out.

"Yes. They. But with time —"

"Time? Time will only multiply the pain. The humiliation. There is no one else for me. Ever."

Winter drops her hands. "Still. I can't agree to this." Her pallid brow creases. "What of duty? Those who depend on you?" Her eyes harden like jet. "I will not take your silver acorn."

"When the time comes, you must." Autumn juts her chin. "I have no one else."

Sparks and ice splinters fly between them. Winter reasons, then pleads. Autumn will not be moved.

Winter, her lips trembling, swallows hard, and agrees.

•

With Winter's white realm far behind her, Autumn stalks through her own forest to the Great Oak, jaw hard. Snails — too slow to escape — crunch beneath her feet. Her skirts now blaze full-blown maize-gold, cayenne, bittersweet — mushrooms ride her hem like mum death-bells.

"Sylvannah," Autumn calls, gently stroking Crow's crooked wing.

Sylvannah floats down hesitantly from a branch high in the Oak, wavering before her.

"I'm giving my silver acorn to my sister. Winter will know what to do."

"What," Sylvannah rasps, suddenly still as lichen on bark, "have you done?"

Autumn kneads Crow's silky head, smears tears off her face. She takes a shuddering breath and shakes him off. He reels twice, then perches in the Oak, head cocked.

"You might want to glide to the highest branches," Autumn says softly to Sylvannah.

Eyes closed, Autumn imagines Spring, beribboned and blushing in Sol's light, melting into him — as she herself longs to do, still.

She begins to twirl, her feet an axis, her skirts whirring like a swarm of locusts. She spins, faster. Visceral heat surges up from her core, charges her fingertips, sparks fly. She hurls fingerling flames scattershot. One by one the trees ignite, sacrificed on the pyre of her rage. The gold and wine of a hundred sunsets combust. Oak, maple, and pine pop and hiss their indignation — the screeching dryads flee.

Her skirts explode in a pentecost of wildfire. And she twirls.

At last, the pain exceeds the one in her cracked heart.

Sylvannah drifts through the charred ruins, smoke permeating her gossamer heart. At least the other dryads are safe with their cousins in the river where she drove them. Crow crouches atop an armless black pine, head hidden under his bent wing.

She managed to save the Great Oak, whisking the flames away from his vulnerable upper branches. She caresses his gnarled, ancient bark. Below, something glints in the ash. Swooping down, she retrieves the silver acorn clasp, icon of Autumn's power, for safekeeping.

And beneath it lies a smoldering, cracked acorn. Autumn's heart. This, she plants.

Winter comes to bury Autumn's ashes in mounds of pure white, as she promised.

Sylvannah fastens the silver acorn on Winter's furs, then glides up into the Oak's sturdiest branches and waits.

With Autumn's power, Winter is twice as strong. In time, Sol grows weak. Spring languishes, a pale shadow.

And Winter reigns. Some call it The Little Ice Age. Others call this particularly bitter time The Year Without a Summer.

Sylvannah calls it a reckoning.

Sharmon Gazaway's story "Autumn's Come Undone" was originally published in Metaphorosis on Friday, 23 April 2021. See magazine.metaphorosis.com

About the author

Sharmon Gazaway writes from the Deep South of the US where she lives beside a historic cemetery haunted by the wild cries of pileated woodpeckers. Since her publication in *Metaphorosis* she has become a Dwarf Stars Award finalist. Her work appears in *Solarpunk Magazine, New Myths, The Best of MetaStellar Year Two, The Fairy Tale Magazine, The Forge Literary Magazine*, and elsewhere, as well as in various award-winning anthologies. She writes in multiple genres, and keeps trying new ways to improve as a writer. Instagram @sharmongazaway.

Copyright

Title information

Radicle

ISBN: 978-1-64076-289-3 (e-book)
ISBN: 978-1-64076-290-9 (paperback)
ISBN: 978-1-64076-291-6 (hardcover)

Copyright

Publisher

Metaphorosis
a magazine of speculative fiction

Metaphorosis Magazine is an imprint of
Metaphorosis Publishing
Neskowin, OR, USA

www.metaphorosis.com

"Metaphorosis" is a registered trademark.

Discounts available

Substantial discounts are available for educational institutions, including writing workshops. Discounts are also available for quantity purchases. For details, contact Metaphorosis at metaphorosis.com/about

Metaphorosis Publishing

Metaphorosis offers beautifully written science fiction and fantasy. Our imprints include:

Metaphorosis Magazine

Plant Based Press

Verdage

Vestige

Joyful Heave

You can also find us:
@metaphorosis.bsky.social (Bluesky)
@Metaphorosis@writing.exchange (Mastodon)
www.facebook.com/metaphorosis

Help keep Metaphorosis running at
Patreon.com/metaphorosis

See more about some of our books on the following pages.

Metaphorosis

a magazine of speculative fiction

Metaphorosis is an online speculative fiction magazine dedicated to quality writing. We publish an original story every week (2016-2023) or month (2024), along with author bios, interviews, and notes on story origins.

We also publish monthly print and e-book issues, as well as yearly Best of and Complete anthologies.

Come and see us online at magazine.Metaphorosis.com.

The Metaphorosis Library Collection

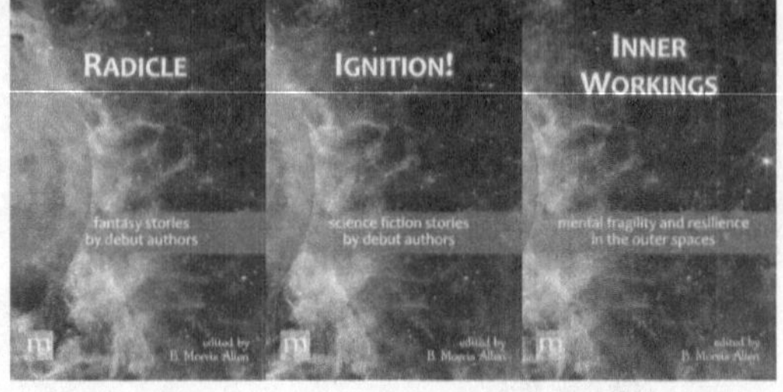

Plant Based Press

Vegan-friendly science fiction and fantasy, including anthologies of the year's best SFF stories, from 2016-2020.

Chambers of the Heart
speculative stories
by
B. Morris Allen

A heart that's a building, a dog that's a program, a woman sinking irretrievably — stories about love, loss, and movement.

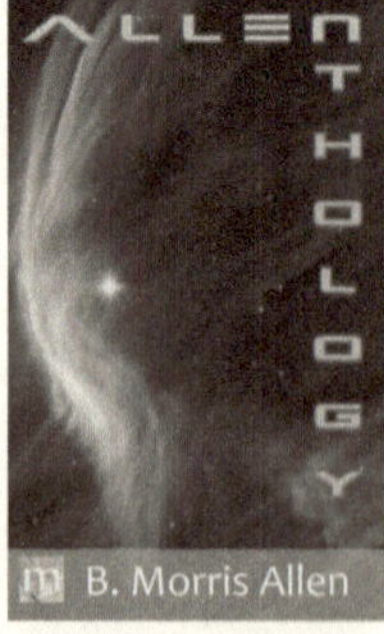

Susurrus

A darkly romantic story of magic, love, and suffering.

Allenthology: Volume I

Including three full collections of SFF stories.

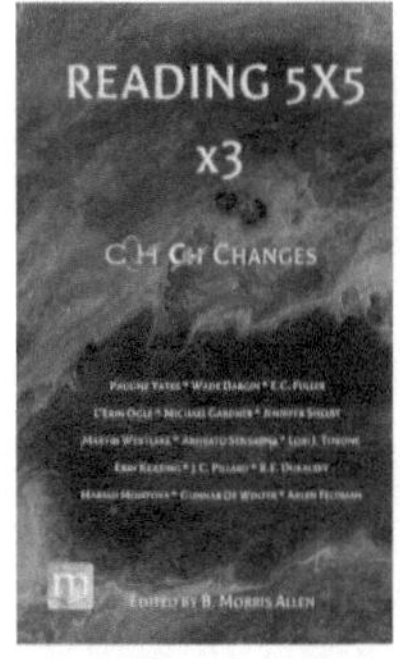

Verdage

Science fiction and fantasy books for writers — full of great stories, often with an additional focus on the craft of speculative fiction writing.

Reading 5X5 x3

Changes

How do stories move from 'maybe' to published?

Here are 15 case studies of stories published in *Metaphorosis* magazine.

Reading 5X5 x2

Duets

How do authors' voices change when they collaborate?

A round-robin of five talented science fiction and fantasy authors collaborating with each other and writing solo.

Including stories by Evan Marcroft, David Gallay, J. Tynan Burke, L'Erin Ogle, and Douglas Anstruther.

Score

an SFF symphony

An anthology with an emotional score from the heights of joy to the depths of despair — but always with a little hope shining through.

Reading 5X5

Five stories, five times

See how different writers take on the same material.

Reading 5X5

Writers' Edition

Two extra stories, the story seed, and authors' notes on writing.

Vestige

Novelettes, novellas, and novels by Metaphorosis authors.

The Nocturnals
Mariah Montoya

Night is Dangerous. Day is deadly.
Where day and night last thirty years, humans move constantly stay ahead of the night and cruel Nocturnals that call it home. But a boy is lost out there.

Science fiction and fantasy anthologies with innovative and unusual themes.

Museum Piece
an unusual collection

A gallery of the strange and outrageous

Step right up and enter a world of wonder and oddities! These museums are not your typical tourist traps. From the Museum of Lost Dreams to the Museum of Fine Regrets, each exhibit will take you on a journey you won't soon forget.